I0831846

Parnell Hall
Presents

MALICE DOMESTIC 14: MYSTERY MOST EDIBLE

MALICE DOMESTIC ANTHOLOGY SERIES

Elizabeth Peters Presents *Malice Domestic 1*

Mary Higgins Clark Presents *Malice Domestic 2*

Nancy Pickard Presents *Malice Domestic 3*

Carolyn G. Hart Presents *Malice Domestic 4*

Phyllis A. Whitney Presents *Malice Domestic 5*

Anne Perry Presents *Malice Domestic 6*

Sharyn McCrumb Presents *Malice Domestic 7*

Margaret Maron Presents *Malice Domestic 8*

Joan Hess Presents *Malice Domestic 9*

Nevada Barr Presents *Malice Domestic 10*

Katherine Hall Page Presents *Malice Domestic 11: Murder Most Conventional*

Charlaine Harris Presents *Malice Domestic 12: Mystery Most Historical*

Nancy Pickard Presents *Malice Domestic 13: Mystery Most Geographical*

Parnell Hall Presents *Malice Domestic 14: Mystery Most Edible*

Parnell Hall Presents

MALICE DOMESTIC 14: MYSTERY MOST EDIBLE

An Anthology

Edited by
Verena Rose, Shawn Reilly Simmons
and Rita Owen

Published by Wildside Press LLC
www.wildsidepress.com

ACKNOWLEDGEMENTS

The editors would like to thank John Betancourt and Carla Coupe at Wildside Press for their constant and unwavering support to Malice Domestic and these editors.

The editors would also like to express their special thanks to the selection committee—P. J. Coldren, Christine Trent, and Victoria Thompson. As a result of their hard work and dedication to excellence, we present for your reading enjoyment *Malice Domestic 14: Mystery Most Edible.*

TABLE OF CONTENTS

All stories are original to this Anthology

continued

PREFACE

PARNELL HALL PRESENTS
A BRIEF, BIASED HISTORY
OF THE CULINARY MYSTERY

I remember nearly thirty years ago at the Midwest Mystery Convention in Omaha, Nebraska I moderated a panel of first-time novelists, and one of them, a cute young girl (I use the sexist words advisedly) had baked cookies, and handed them out to the audience to celebrate the publication of her first novel. We all thought that was adorable.

Diane Mott Davidson went on to have a very nice career, and the culinary mystery became a major subgenre of the cozy mystery. More and more books began including recipes. Titles with plays on food became commonplace. More and more books featured scrumptious delicacies on the covers. No one saw these series as derivative. Readers ate them up. (I'm sorry, I couldn't help myself.)

The culinary field continues to grow, and there is no indication of the trend reversing. Even I have fallen under the spell. My private eye novel, *Cozy*, satirizing the genre, is full of recipes. (The cat also solves the crime, but that is the subject of another anthology.)

Anthologies of culinary short stories are also popular. I myself have been asked to contribute to two of them. Since I am an unlikely choice, one can only imagine how many there must actually be.

It is my pleasure to introduce the Malice Domestic 14 anthology, *Murder Most Edible*. The stories have been chosen from blind submissions by some of the finest writers in the genre. (Full disclosure: my story wasn't. I was asked to write it, so you're stuck with what you get.) All of the stories involve food or drink, in one way or another.

Some of the stories include recipes. My story doesn't. The Puzzle Lady can barely boil water. I could have included a crossword puzzle, but she can't do those either.

I included a crime.

That she can do.

Parnell Hall

MYSTERY MOST EDIBLE

ILLUSTRATION: DEANNE NETTLES

A CUP OF TEA
A Puzzle Lady Story
By Parnell Hall

Cora finds the latest mystery to come her way an annoyance, that is, until she sees the opportunity for a paycheck.

"It's always annoying when the hostess drops dead," Cora Felton said as she and her niece drove home from Miss Merryweather's tea party.

Sherry Carter rolled her eyes. "Could you *be* any less sensitive?"

"I doubt it," Cora said. "I was going for the record."

"Please, this is not funny. Miss Merryweather was a nice lady."

"Accent on the word *was*," Cora said. "She's not nearly as nice now, and I see no reason to tiptoe around the situation."

"How about sparing the feelings of a close friend or relation?"

"She has none. The woman was a loner. I'm surprised she had the gumption to serve tea. To what end? Well, hers, actually. But aside from that, what earthly purpose did her teas serve, except to force me to dress up and be civil to a bunch of people I can barely tolerate?"

"You like Iris Cooper. And you have nothing against Chief Harper's wife."

"True. And she has nothing against me, since I never slept with her husband. Which puts him in the minority, if Melvin's book is to be believed."

Cora's least favorite ex-husband had written a tell-all about his life with the Puzzle Lady. In order to justify his rather large advance, Melvin had exaggerated, embellished, and out-and-out lied. At least half of the book, Cora figured, was utter fiction. But since there were large portions of the '80s and '90s she didn't remember, Cora was hard pressed to say exactly what.

Cora didn't mind, as long as Melvin didn't mention her *real* secret, that the much-vaunted Puzzle Lady was a total fraud who couldn't solve a crossword puzzle with a gun to her head. Cora was the Milli Vanilli of the crossword community. Her niece Sherry actually constructed the crosswords and wrote the Puzzle Lady column. Cora just supplied the pretty face.

"You love murders," Sherry said. "Here's one happening right in front of your eyes, and you couldn't care less."

"There's nothing to do. The woman simply died. Mrs. Harper called her husband, so the chief of police is on the scene. He has to act as if it were a crime, though it probably isn't. But I don't. I want to go home. On the other hand, if you want to go back and gossip with the girls, feel free."

"That isn't what I meant at all," Sherry protested, but as usual in arguing with the Puzzle Lady, logic did not necessarily prevail.

***

Sherry's daughter Jennifer came pelting out the front door as they pulled up the driveway. The young girl's eyes were bright. "Are you going to solve the murder, Auntie Cora?"

Cora slammed the car door and favored Jennifer with a reassuring smile. "There was no murder. The woman just died."

"No one killed her?"

"No."

"Then why did she die?"

"She was just old."

"Older than you, Auntie Cora?"

Cora opened her mouth and closed it again. She exhaled in exasperation. "Oh, hell."

Jennifer pointed. "Auntie Cora said *hell.*"

"That was cute when you were three," Cora said. "It isn't now that you're eight."

"I'm nine."

"Oh, don't be nine," Cora said. "If you're nine, I must be . . . nearly sixty."

Sherry opened her mouth and raised her eyebrows.

"Shut up," Cora said, "or Jennifer is going to hear Auntie Cora say a lot worse words than *hell.*"

"Bet it's a murder," Jennifer said, and skipped across the lawn.

***

Chief Harper called the next day. "It's poison."

Cora and Sherry were in the kitchen making cappuccinos. "What's poison?" Cora said.

"Sorry. I've been around you too long. I'm starting to sound like you. The Merryweather case is a homicide. She was poisoned. Arsenic. The arsenic was in her tea. So it wasn't heart failure. Someone did the old woman in."

"*Did the old woman in* doesn't sound that professional either, Chief. Are you serious about this, or are you just kidding with me?"

"I don't kid about murder. Barney Nathan just called with the autopsy report."

"Barney Nathan," Cora snorted. "Will that man never stop being annoying?"

Cora and the doctor had had a brief affair. Ever since, she was convinced he was paying her back with each autopsy. In this judgment, she wasn't necessarily wrong.

"Anyway," Harper said, "it's now officially a murder."

"Is there a crossword puzzle involved?" Cora said suspiciously.

"Absolutely not."

"And yet you called me anyway. Shall I take that as a vote of confidence?"

"You can take it any way you like. It's a murder. You're good with murders. I thought you should know. Anyway, I'm about to inspect the scene of the crime. Would you like to go?"

"Hell, no."

Chief Harper was surprised. "You wouldn't?"

"I was just there. It was boring the first time."

"You're not coming?"

"No, I'm not, Chief, but would you mind telling me what you're looking for? The woman was poisoned. The poison was arsenic. The arsenic was in her tea. What do you expect to learn from the crime scene? How it got in her tea? As far as that goes, you'll either find a bottle of poison or you won't. If you do, it'll either have fingerprints on it or it won't. If it doesn't, it really tells you nothing, unless there's a way to trace the bottle. I'd like to help you out, Chief, but my niece has a jujitsu tournament, and I wouldn't miss it for the world."

Cora hung up the phone to find Sherry Carter staring at her. "I do *not* have a jujitsu tournament."

"Not you. Jennifer. It's just annoying to say great-niece all the time. Not that Jennifer's not great, but you know what I mean. Niece is shorthand."

"Jennifer doesn't have a jujitsu tournament either. Wanna tell me why you're so keen to miss this particular murder?"

Cora shrugged.

***

Chief Harper called back later. "Miss Merryweather has a sister."

"Oh?" Cora said cautiously.

"Her name's Ethel. She lives in Montana."

"Why are you telling me this?"

"I gave her your name."

"Why would you do that?"

"She asked for it."

"Chief, you make no sense when you feel guilty. Obviously, you think you've done something wrong. What is it this time? Giving the sister my name?"

"Sort of."

"Spit it out, Chief."

"She wants someone to investigate."

"Oh, for God's sakes."

"Well, you're an investigator."

"I am not."

"You investigate for Becky Baldwin."

Becky Baldwin was a young Bakerhaven attorney. Cora often assisted her with her cases.

"I've investigated for the defense. Is the sister accused of anything?"

"No, she'd like you to examine the crime scene."

"Do *you* want me to examine the crime scene?"

"Well, I wish *someone* would. I can't find anything useful. That leaves me with questioning the witnesses, and one of them's my wife. I'd do practically anything to get out of that."

"Sorry, Chief. I can't help you."

***

Cora no sooner got off the phone when it rang again. She scooped it up. "Forget it, Chief, I'm not doing it."

There was a pause, then a woman's voice said, "Cora Felton?"

Cora's eyes widened. She recovered quickly. "I'm sorry, Miss Felton isn't in right now. May I take a message?"

"This is Ethel Merryweather. Phyllis's sister. Chief Harper gave me her name."

"Yes," Cora said, offering no help whatsoever.

"My sister died yesterday at tea. It now appears that she's been murdered. I called Chief Harper, but he was most unhelpful. He doesn't seem to know that much about it. Odd, for a chief of police."

"Just because he doesn't tell you something doesn't mean he doesn't know it. The police are discrete about their inquiries. They don't give out much information."

"But I'm her sister."

"Well, then, I suggest you come down to the police station and talk to the chief directly. It's harder to put someone off in person."

"I'm in Montana."

Good, Cora thought. *Now, if I could just get off the phone*. "That, of course, makes it more difficult. But if the chief finds anything of importance, I'm sure you'll be the first to know."

"Frankly, I'm not. That's why I need Cora Felton. She's the

Puzzle Lady, isn't she?"

Cora was reluctant to admit it, even in the guise of a third person. "I fail to see what that has to do with the situation. You don't have a crossword puzzle for her, do you?"

"No, but she has a reputation for assisting the police in solving crimes."

"Her reputation extends to Montana?" Cora said. She couldn't help a flush of pride.

"Oh, yes. There was a piece in the *National Enquirer*."

Cora grimaced. She knew exactly what piece the woman was referring to. It was a report on some of the more salacious details from Melvin's book. Going by the *National Enquirer* article, the Puzzle Lady's expertise at solving crime derived from the fact that she was practically a criminal herself.

"Well, I'll be sure to tell her you called."

"Wait! You don't have my number."

"Oh."

"And I didn't tell you what I want. I have no confidence in what the police are doing. The chief inspected the crime scene and found nothing. I can't believe there's nothing to find. I'm sure the Puzzle Lady could find something."

"Well, I'll pass along your vote of confidence. But I'm afraid there's nothing much she can do."

"Well, will you at least take down my number? I want to hire the Puzzle Lady and I'm prepared to pay her well."

There was a pause.

"Just a moment," Cora said. "I think I hear Miss Felton now."

***

Cora stood in the middle of the living room where just the day before she'd been sipping tea. The crime scene was virtually undisturbed. There was an outline for the body, and a marker where the teacup had fallen, and that was about it.

Cora sized up the room and remembered where everyone was sitting. On the couch was First Selectman Iris Cooper, who couldn't have done it; Chief Harper's wife, who couldn't have done it; Judy Douglas Knauer, long-time real estate agent from whom Cora had actually purchased her house, yet another woman who could not have possibly done it.

In the chair next to them was Dierdre Benedict, ninety-two if she was a day, deaf as a post, and nearsighted to boot. Had she been able to clunk her walker over to Miss Merryweather's teacup, she would hardly have had a spare hand to wield the arsenic.

Next to her was Mrs. Cushman, of Cushman's Bake Shop. If Mrs. Cushman were guilty, Cora intended to let her get away with it. The proprietor of Cushman's Bake Shop couldn't bake a lick, and trucked in all her scones and muffins from the Silver Moon Bakery in Manhattan. Cora was not about to deprive herself of those sumptuous treats just to solve some silly murder.

Next to Mrs. Cushman was a woman Cora didn't know, which put her way at the top of the suspects list, despite the fact she turned out to be the wife of the local minister.

Rounding out the party were Sherry and Cora.

Cora put her hands on her hips and cocked her head at Chief Harper. "So, what did you do, Chief?"

Harper looked at her. "Do?"

"Yes, do. I'd hate to duplicate your actions.

Chief Harper was suddenly very uncomfortable. On being asked to describe how he'd processed the crime scene, he was hard pressed to come up with very much that he had actually done.

Cora came to his rescue. "All right, Chief, let's see what we've got." She pointed to the marker on the floor. "That's where you found her teacup?"

"That's right."

"You had it analyzed?"

"I did."

"And found arsenic?"

"That's right."

"Did you analyze the other teacups?"

"Of course."

"Was there arsenic in them?"

"There was not."

"So, she had arsenic in her teacup. Where did it come from?"

"If I knew that, I'd know who killed her."

"Did you analyze the teabags?"

"Teabags?"

"She didn't use tea leaves, she used individual teabags."

"There were no teabags in the cups."

"There were. She took them out before she served the tea in order to maintain an illusion of gentility."

"Did you really say *an illusion of gentility*?"

"What's wrong with that?"

"It doesn't sound like you, somehow."

"What do I sound like?"

"You'd say, like she was trying to be a lady."

"I don't sound like that."

"You always sound like that. The lowbrow speech. You know a lot of words, but you want to sound like one of the guys."

"Never mind. What about the teabags? Did you inspect them?"

"No."

"Are they still here?"

"Well, we didn't take them. And this is a crime scene. The house has been sealed."

"All right, where is the kitchen garbage?"

Cora found it under the sink. A plastic basket that slid out on rollers.

"Here we go, Chief. They're still wet. You want to lay some paper towels out on the counter?"

Cora fished the teabags out of the trash and lined them up on the paper towel. "All right, I bet I can tell you which one was hers."

"How?"

"Look at the tabs on the end of the string. They have the brand name printed on them, see? *SHROPSDALE*, in big letters. And underneath, in smaller type, *A Hint of England*. That's a blue one. Most of them are blue ones. But one of them is silver. Instead of *A Hint of England*, it says, *Whispering Well*. That one will be hers."

"How do you know that?"

"Actually, Judy Douglas Knauer told me. She heard it from Iris Cooper."

"And where did Iris Cooper hear it?"

"From your wife."

"What?"

"Not to worry, Chief. Everyone gossips. And this is pretty innocuous. Phyllis had high blood pressure. Hard to believe, but that's the story. She drank decaffeinated tea, but she liked to serve regular so as not to seem an old fuddy-duddy. I'll bet you a nickel her teabag is decaffeinated. It's probably also full of arsenic."

Cora glanced at the kitchen cupboards. "Let's see where the teabags came from. They weren't lying around loose. There must be a SHROPSHIRE box somewhere."

There was. Cora took it out and opened the lid. The box was half full of little teabags in little square packets. Most of the packets were blue. A few were silver.

"There you are, Chief. The source of the poison."

"You think I should have it analyzed too?"

"You can if you want to. I doubt you'll find anything."

"Why?"

"Because the woman's dead. No point in poisoning her if she's dead."

Chief Harper whipped out his cell phone and called Dan Finley, one of his officers. "Dan, take a run out to the Merryweather house. I've got some evidence for you to process."

***

"Now," Cora said, as Chief Harper hung up the phone, "if you don't mind, I'd like to search the crime scene."

"What do you mean?" Harper said. "You searched the crime scene. You found the murder weapon."

"I don't get paid for finding the murder weapon. I get paid for finding the will."

"The woman hopes to inherit?"

"Just the opposite. The woman is *afraid* she'll inherit. She wants nothing to do with the place. She thinks it will be a nuisance. She and her sister weren't close. She expects the will to name some other friend or relative as the beneficiary and she'll be off the hook."

"That's absurd."

"Not really. She doesn't want to own the property and have to pay the taxes on it, or go through the hassle of selling it. After all, she's in Montana. Dealing with the property would be very inconvenient."

"That sounds fishy to me."

"That's because she's not paying you," Cora said brightly. "Anyway, she'd like me to inspect the crime scene and find her sister's will. You weren't looking for a will when you inspected the crime scene, were you?"

"No," Chief Harper admitted.

"So let's have a look."

***

Fifteen minutes later Cora turned from the mantelpiece triumphantly. "Congratulations, Chief. You just found the key to a safe deposit box."

"I did?"

"Yes, you did, and fine work, too."

"Where did I find this safe deposit key?"

"In one of the tchotchkes on the mantelpiece."

"Any reason I'm finding this instead of you? I thought the sister was paying you to investigate."

"Yes, but she's paying me to find the will, not the key."

Harper grimaced. "Why do you have to be irritating?"

"This is obviously the key to her safe deposit box. The bank is never going to allow me, a private citizen, to open it. But the chief of police, making an official investigation, would surely have no trouble. I doubt if you'd even have to get a warrant."

"So, you want the safe deposit box opened, in return for which you'll let me take credit for finding the key?"

Cora shrugged. "I don't want credit, Chief. I want cash."

***

Cora waited upstairs while the banker and Chief Harper went down and opened the safe deposit box.

Harper was back minutes later with a large manila envelope.

"Is that it, Chief?"

Harper tapped the envelope into his open hand. "Your arrangement with the sister is that you get paid for finding the will, regardless of what it says?"

"That's my understanding, why?"

"She was wrong. I'm afraid she inherits everything, including the house."

"Anything else in the box?"

"Just some stock certificates."

Cora's eyebrows raised. "Oh? What are they?"

"Nothing I've ever heard of. The Goldstar Corporation, for goodness sake. If she's lucky, they'll pay the taxes on the house."

"Well, that doesn't help much. But the good news is, I can get paid."

***

"I have client for you."

Becky Baldwin looked up with suspicion from her desk. Cora was always drumming up clients for the attractive young attorney, and not all of them were desirable. "Oh?"

"Nice old lady. You'd like her."

"What does she want?"

"She doesn't want anything. She's dead."

"And yet she wants to hire me. And what does she want me to do?"

"Probate her will."

"Well, that's something I can do. How many heirs?"

"One."

"Sounds like a fairly easy job."

"Well, it would be. Except . . ."

"Except for what?"

"You're a slow, meticulous stick in the mud."

"That doesn't sound like me."

"You have all these papers that have to be signed and notarized in your presence."

"Nonsense. We can notarize 'em and FedEx 'em."

"No, it has to be in person. And it's going to be difficult, because the heir is in Montana."

"What about the air in Montana?"

Cora looked at Becky suspiciously. "You did that deliberately, didn't you?"

Becky smiled. "Not as much fun when it's the other person doing it, is it?"

"Becky, you're a lawyer. You can argue anything, and you can find a reason for anything. Find a reason the woman has to be here to inherit."

"There is no legal reason she has to be here."

"You think she knows that?"

"No."

Cora shrugged. "So make one up."

***

Ethel Merryweather arrived the next day. She was clearly the victim's sister. She was a mousy little woman, just like Phyllis, but while Phyllis was mousy and pleasant, Ethel was mousy and unpleasant.

"Well," she complained. "I've never been so inconvenienced in my life. Come all this way just to sign a paper. Whoever heard of such a thing?"

The fact the woman was absolutely right did not make her seem any less obnoxious. She was in a bad mood to begin with, and the sight of Becky Baldwin did nothing to improve it. "You're a lawyer? Are you even out of college?"

"Think of her as a lawyer in training," Cora said. "But when she draws up papers, they're ironclad. The minute you sign them, the inheritance is yours. And the five-hundred-dollar cash bonus is mine. Miss Baldwin has drawn the papers so there can be no mistake."

"You don't trust me?"

"I trust you, but you live in Montana. It's hard to take you to small claims court."

"I assure you, I pay my bills."

"And this paper assures me you do too. So, since you've come all this way, we've provided you one-stop shopping." Cora indicated the people present in Becky's office. "Judy Douglas Knauer is here to handle the sale of your house. Chief Harper is here to hand over the contents of the safe deposit box. I'm here to get paid—you won't even have to waste a stamp. Iris Cooper is here as a notary public to notarize your signature. And this young couple," Cora said, indicating Sherry Carter and Aaron Grant, "are here to witness your signature so you won't have to get anyone to do it."

"Well, let's get on with it," Ethel said. "I have no desire to stay here any longer than I have to. Such a small town. Transportation here is virtually nonexistent. I had to get a car service."

"Sounds inconvenient," Cora said. "Well, if you want to get on with it." She stepped aside and gave the stage to Becky Baldwin.

"Here you are," Becky said. "You'll want to read that over before you sign."

Ethel did not want to read that over. She grabbed the paper and dashed off her signature.

"And now the witnesses."

Sherry and Aaron stepped up and signed.

"And now the notary."

Iris Cooper stepped up with her notary stamp. She stamped, dated, and signed the document.

Becky took the paper and looked it over. "Everything appears to be in order."

"Excellent," Cora said. "Now, would you like to get the house disposed of?"

"No, I'd like to take possession of my property."

"Good idea," Cora said. "And then you can write me a check. In fact, why don't you write it now, since I delivered on my obligation by finding the will."

"I won't be ordered around," Ethel said testily. "Is there any law that says I have to write the check in order to receive my inheritance?"

"There is not," Becky said. "Sorry, Cora, I'm afraid there is no way to compel her to give you the check. Chief, would you care to deliver to my client the contents of the safe deposit box?"

"Certainly," Chief Harper said. "My deputy, Dan Finley, has it. Dan, give her the envelope."

Officer Dan Finley had an aw-shucks quality which made him seem boyish. "I'm sorry, Chief, I can't seem to find the envelope."

"What?"

"Yeah, I know you told me to bring it, but I can't put my hands on it."

"I'm sorry, ma'am, but we don't seem to have the envelope."

"You know," Cora said, "if you drop by the police station tomorrow morning, I'm sure Dan will have located it by then."

Ethel glared at Cora. She reached in her purse, pulled out her checkbook, and scrawled off a check.

Cora inspected it. "This seems to be in order. Chief, as a personal favor, do you think you could expedite the delivery of the envelope?"

"I'll see what I can do," Harper said. "Dan, you want to go out and check your car?"

Dan smiled. "I don't have to, Chief. It turns out it's right here in my inside pocket."

"Excellent. Give it to Miss Merryweather."

Dan extended the envelope.

Ethel gave him a look as she snatched it out of his hand. She smiled in satisfaction, though, when she had the envelope in her possession. She ripped it open and pulled out the stock certificates. She unfolded them and looked.

Her face fell. "What is this?"

"What is what?" Chief Harper said.

"These are shares of Phillip Morris."

"Yes, they are. That surprised me somewhat. That she would go with such a company. They've diversified, certainly, but their roots are still in tobacco."

"This isn't Phyllis's stock," Ethel protested.

"What are you talking about?"

"These aren't her shares of stock."

"Oh? How do you know that?"

"How do I know anything? Phyllis never had shares of Phillip Morris. She bought shares of small, speculative companies."

"Obviously in her later years she decided she needed something more stable."

"She did no such thing. Phyllis had Goldstar stock. She always had Goldstar stock. She bought it years ago, and she always hung on to it, even when they almost went under. She even bought more."

"I don't see what the problem is," Chief Harper said. "Obviously your sister realized she was holding on to worthless stock so she sold it for whatever she could get and bought something of value. I should think you would be happy you were inheriting a stock that's actually worth something."

"Oh, you do, do you? What kind of a fast one are you trying to pull? Where are my sister's stocks? What did you do with them? Don't think you're going to get away with this."

"Get away with what? Really, Miss Merryweather, I don't know what you're talking about."

"I'm talking about the Goldstar stock that was in her safe deposit box until someone stole it. I'm not saying it was you, but it was someone, and I'd like to know who had access to that box."

"I can get the banker in here to testify, if you want, but he'll tell you the box was never opened except by your sister herself."

Ethel leveled a finger at Cora Felton. "Was *she* in the bank when the box was opened?"

Chief Harper hesitated. "Yes, but she wasn't in the room."

"It doesn't matter. Did you *show* her the contents? Did you give her any chance to make the substitution?"

"Why would I want to steal the stock?" Cora said. "Was it valuable?"

"Of course it was valuable. That's why it was stolen."

"So you knew the stock was valuable," Chief Harper said. "Your sister told you. When Goldstar finally struck pay dirt after years of failure. She called you all excited. And that's when you decided to kill her."

Ethel sucked in her breath. "Ridiculous!"

"That's when you sent her that box of tea. You knew she always drank decaffeinated and served the regular to her guests. You poisoned one of the decaffeinated teabags. There weren't that many. She'd get to it soon enough.

"You also knew her habit of throwing away the teabags before serving the tea, so there was a good chance the poisoned bag wouldn't be discovered. Even if it was, no one would know you sent her the box. After all, she wouldn't be poisoned until months after she got it."

"Nonsense," Ethel said.

"But you made one big mistake," Harper said. "You wrapped it too well. Your sister was frugal. She saved anything she could recycle. Your package was wrapped in stiff brown paper. She unwrapped it carefully, folded it up, and stashed it away in a drawer of reusable papers. I found it there with your return address on it, and that's why we brought you here to collect your inheritance. As you so correctly pointed out, it is not those shares of Phillip Morris, it is those Goldstar shares you killed your sister for. Unfortunately, you won't get them, because a killer cannot inherit from her victim. Too bad. Otherwise it was the perfect scheme. Dan, would you do the honors?"

"My pleasure," Dan Finley said. He clapped handcuffs on Ethel Merryweather's wrists, and recited the Miranda warning.

***

"Well," Sherry said, "I hope you're proud of yourself."

"I am, rather."

"Good. Would you mind letting me in on it?"

"In on what?"

"Chief Harper's performance in Becky Baldwin's office."

"What about it?"

"I've never heard him sound so much like you. It was almost as if you fed him the lines and let him take the credit."

"Now why would I do that?"

"I'm sure you had your reasons."

"It's very simple. I wanted my five-hundred-dollar bonus. I told Chief Harper he could have the credit if I could have the cash."

"Yeah. I don't buy it for a moment. You were going to get the cash regardless. And the poor man looked so uncomfortable, parroting those ideas as if they were his own."

"Oh, hell."

Sherry smiled. "Auntie Cora said *hell*. Come on, Cora, what is it?"

"I don't want to be some spinster who solves dainty drawing room murders. I'm not that person. I'm a private detective. I work for an attorney. I carry a gun," Cora snorted. "A little old lady is poisoned at her tea party. That's a stereotypical cliché cozy crime."

"You're not a spinster. You've been married more times than the Gabor sisters."

"You're too young to reference the Gabor sisters."

"Well, you're too young to be a spinster."

"That's not the point," Cora said irritably. "It's a matter of perception. I know I'm not Mike Hammer. I just don't want to be Miss Marple."

"Are you kidding me?" Sherry grinned. "You're Miss Marple on *steroids*."

BROWN RECLUSE

By Marcia Adair

Agoraphobia is a crippling disease, especially when combined with accusations of murder. Harriet Brown needs a friend who also loves baking and isn't afraid to learn how to fight back against lies.

Harriet Brown beat the butter, sugar, and eggs with a practiced hand, then stirred in the mashed bananas. Next came the dry ingredients, which she deftly combined thoroughly into the rest. The trick was not to over mix it.

"Now for the secret ingredient," she said to her eleven-year-old companion.

"I get to pick it," Emily Stanford piped.

Harriet pushed a lock of silver hair off her forehead and smiled at the girl's enthusiasm. She had no doubt Emily loved baking with her. Or that the girl loved the sweet magic of flour, butter, and sugar. Or that she loved the way Harriet let her select anything she wanted for a surprise taste—even if it was terrible. Harriet grinned, remembering the time an impish Emily slipped chili powder in the cherry pie. Silly girl. Above all, she knew with certainty that Emily loved having her as a secret friend she'd been forbidden to see. Harriet loved it, too.

"Close your eyes," Emily whispered.

Harriet complied while Emily stirred fragrant Vietnamese cinnamon into the batter. "Cumin? Butterscotch? Oregano?" she teased.

"You'll never guess." The girl giggled as Harriet opened her eyes. They filled a greased loaf pan with batter and popped it in the oven.

They settled on the couch for a visit while the Banana Bread Surprise baked.

"Why do they call you the Brown Recluse?" Emily asked.

The innocence of children, Harriet thought. A sad light crept into her eyes. "Well, my name is Brown. And I live up in this big old house all alone and don't see many people. That's what a recluse is, you know."

How else could she explain the town's cruel moniker to this wide-eyed pixie?

"But isn't a brown recluse a killer spider?"

"Well, yes and no," Harriet replied, carefully measuring the right amount of truth into her answer. "If a brown recluse feels attacked, it can give a very nasty bite. People don't die from it, though. Not usually," she added under her breath. "Ignorance sure makes people think foolish things, doesn't it?"

Emily pondered Harriet's words. "Yeah. And do foolish things. Like calling you a murdering evil witch."

Harriet drew a deep, sorrowful breath. "Yes. Like that. Why do you suppose they do it? "

"Because you act weird sometimes."

It was true. If she had to go out—to get groceries, for example—panic always seized her. She'd be choosing peaches or some such at the market, only to be engulfed with an awful sense of dread. She was sure she was dying right there in the produce aisle. Panicked, she'd flee the market, shoving her half-filled cart madly into any hapless customer or display in her way. Agoraphobia, the doctors called it.

"And because of Mr. Brown," Emily whispered confidentially.

Harriet felt gut punched. Her abusive husband had died mysteriously a year earlier. Just keeled right over at the kitchen table one evening after dinner. Though investigators had found no evidence of a crime, neither had they determined a cause of death. That absence of clarity left a lingering cloud of suspicion that fed the town gossips like a hot dish at a church social. She was convinced they took her panic attacks as guilty proof she killed the man to end his cruelty.

She'd heard Amy Mullen suggest she'd poisoned him with a secret herb she grew in her garden—fine behavior for a church secretary, for heaven's sake. But what could you expect? The Reverend Boxter was no kinder. Rumors spread. Hope sank. Whispers grew. She'd even overheard Emily's parents and others forbid their children from so much as talking to her.

Truth be told, she grew a little angrier every day at how people condemned her. At the boys who threw tomatoes at her porch and called her names as they ran away. At Amy. At the reverend. At the small town and its small-minded residents.

Everyone judged her harshly except Emily. Defiant and adventurous, she actually knocked on the door one day last year and asked Harriet point blank if she ate children like people said in town. After Harriet had stopped laughing, she invited Emily into the old Victorian house with the peeling blue paint to find out for herself. Emily took the dare. Instead of meeting her predicted demise, she discovered a new, secret friend.

"Well, I don't think you're evil. Or a murderer. Or a witch. I think you're nice."

"And of course, thanks to you, I'm not entirely a recluse," Harriet said. She gave a grandmotherly smile, appreciating her young lifeline to the world.

"I want to be a recluse, just like you," Emily said softly.

"What on earth for?"

"Then I'd be safe from my brother."

"Paul? He's one of the tomato throwers, isn't he? About fourteen? Kind of a ringleader?"

Emily nodded and looked down. "He's mean to me. One night he snuck into my room and took the head off my favorite doll." Her eyes welled up.

"And if I don't do everything he says, he . . .he . . .," she stammered. "He says he'll hurt my new kitten." Tears flowed down her cheeks. "You know how he calls you a witch?" Emily asked with a quavering sniffle. "I wish you were, so you could make him disappear. Like Mr. Brown."

Harriet looked hard at the girl. "Mr. Brown died unexpectedly, dear. It happens." Her voice took on a stern edge.

Emily shrugged. "Okay. Paul could die unexpectedly, too, then. If you wanted him to."

The oven timer dinged. Harriet and Emily went to the kitchen and pulled out the loaf to test its doneness. Emily stabbed a toothpick into the heart of the bread.

"Just. Like. That," she muttered.

"Consider it done," Harriet whispered.

Then the doorbell rang. Harriet peeked out from kitchen. Through the leaded glass sidelights, she saw Reverend Boxter peering in. She cringed at yet another of his unwanted, unscheduled pastoral calls.

***

A week later, Emily took her usual secret route to Harriet's house. She rode her bike on side roads and alleys around to the back of the house. After stashing her blue Schwinn behind the hydrangeas, she clattered up the service porch steps and burst into the kitchen, slamming the screen door behind her.

"This," she shouted, waving a piece of paper. "We have to do this."

Harriet looked at the flyer announcing a church bake sale in two weeks. "This? Why?" She felt palpitations at the mere specter of a social event.

"Becauuuse," Emily said with an exasperated eye roll. "We bake amazing things. And it's for the church. And it would be fun. And all the parents let their kids buy anything they want. And if you don't like it, you can leave. And . . . And . . . maybe it's heaven's way of helping you not be a recluse anymore."

Not be a recluse anymore. The words woke a sleeping hope in Harriet's heart. For a brief moment, she almost believed it could happen. Almost believed she could go to town without having a panic attack or being pointed at. Maybe even have friends. A tiny smile dared to play on her lips.

Heaven's way. Emily's words elbowed to the front of her mind and ripped her from her reverie. The last time she'd hoped to heaven, her world went to hell.

It was right after her husband's untimely demise. Struggling with both genuine grief and guilty relief, she'd bared her soul to Reverend Boxter, hoping he could guide her out of her torment. He'd promised to help her. She'd dared to hope then, too.

A few weeks later, however, she'd arrived early for a counseling session. She pushed open the carved oak door to the reverend's study. There was Amy, splayed across the massive desk, rumpled and unbuttoned. A Bible and hymnal clattered to the floor as Reverend Boxter pressed against her with greedy, hungry hands.

Harriet gasped. They jumped up. After the secretary's rapid exit from the room, the reverend composed himself. For a long moment he looked at Harriet, apparently deciding what to say. Then he took a deep breath, like he did before each sermon, and whispered, "If you tell anyone, you'll regret it. Everything you've confided to me during our counseling sessions? It won't be confidential anymore." Then he smiled like a crocodile.

Right after that, the first tiny rumors started, an insurance policy to remind her of what he could do. She was certain he was the source. That was when people began to turn against her. It was when his unscheduled pastoral calls began, each one designed to remind her that silence was golden. It was when her agoraphobia took hold. It was when she became the Brown Recluse.

Emily looked expectantly at Harriet, still waiting for an answer.

"Hmpf," Harriet replied tersely, the smile gone from her face. "Not likely heaven's looking out for me."

Emily sighed and searched for a new tack. "Well, then, you could do it because I want to and you're my friend and you want me to be happy."

Harriet smiled at the winning argument. "You are a force of nature, Emily Stanford. Okay, I can try. I'll for sure help you bake something. But will I be there? No promises."

"I know exactly what I want to make," Emily squealed. "The best-est thing ever. Brownies."

Harriet's face blanched. That's what her husband had been

eating when he died so suddenly.

"Is something wrong?" Emily asked. "You look like you've seen a ghost."

More like the devil. "No, dear," Harriet replied, composing herself. "I'm fine. I know exactly the recipe we should use."

***

At Emily's urging, they practiced so many recipes before the big bake sale that Harriet's house smelled like it was made of chocolate bars. Cream cheese brownies. Avocado brownies. Almond milk brownies.

Emily developed a rating system, from one to a gazillion. In the end, it was Harriet's original recipe that scored a gazillion.

"I'm going to add a secret ingredient," Emily confided the day before the event. "To make it extra good."

"Me, too," Harriet said with a sly smile.

***

The Saturday of the bake sale dawned sweet and bright. Emily arrived at Harriet's at eight a.m.

"Everything's all set out so we can get started right away," Harriet said. "Food's due by noon." They walked to the kitchen and donned their aprons. "Ready? Set . . .?"

"Go!" Emily shouted.

Harriet turned on the radio. "Satisfaction" was playing. She cranked it up, changing the lyrics as she started mixing the ingredients. "I *can* get some satisfaction."

When the pans were prepared and the batter ready, Emily did a little dance. "Okay, now close your eyes so I can add my secret ingredient."

"Any hints?"

"It wouldn't be a secret if I told you. Now keep your eyes closed."

Harriet heard some rustling of a plastic bag being pulled from the pocket of Emily's pink seersucker shorts. The sound of sprinkling. Stirring. More rustling.

"You can open your eyes now," Emily said.

"Well, you look like the cat that ate the canary. Still not going to tell me what's in there?"

"Nope." Emily's eyes sparkled.

Harriet didn't see or smell anything new. She dipped a finger into the batter and took a taste. Still nothing she could identify. She shrugged.

As the brownies baked and then cooled, she pondered the impending bake sale. The mere thought of leaving her safe home made her break out in red, itchy hives.

Emily gave her a concerned look. "Are you okay?"

"Feeling a little lightheaded is all. Maybe I need some fresh air. Be right back," she said and walked unsteadily to the garden.

She returned with some raspberries and mint leaves to garnish the top.

"Time for *my* secret ingredient." She smiled wanly.

"I heard Paul bragging to his stupid friends that he was going to buy all the brownies. They're his favorite. He's such a pig. Isn't gluttony a sin? Shouldn't it be punished?"

Harriet thought about Paul's cruelty to her and Emily. She thought about the town's hurtful gossip and shunning. About the reverend and Amy. "Yes, dear. Sins should definitely be punished."

She and Emily exchanged a long, understanding look. They glanced at the brownies and smiled.

"So, are you coming to the sale?" Emily finally asked. "Say yes, pretty please with sugar on top? Today will change everything. I know it."

"I don't know, Emily. We couldn't go together, and you know how I feel about leaving the house."

"But I'd be right there if you needed anything. No one would mind if I helped someone in need at the church, right? This is your chance to show everyone you're not a Brown Recluse. It's what you said you wanted."

Going out, being with people—it *was* what she wanted, more than anything. She scratched her worsening hives and sighed. "All right, Emily. I'll try."

The girl ran up to Harriet and gave her a hug. "You can bring the brownies and say you made them. I can't carry them on my bike."

Shortly before noon, Emily left the house, riding her two-wheeler the six blocks to the steepled sandstone church on the town square. A playing card clothes-pinned to the spokes whapped out a happy tune. A few minutes later, Harriet picked up her plate of brownies and marched down the hill toward all she feared and desired.

She went straight to the sales table, with its array of sweet treats.

Amy was overseeing the event. She nervously took Harriet's offering and set it down quickly, as if the plate itself might be caustic. "Well, um, thank you, Harriet," she choked out, glancing away. "Did you make these yourself?"

"Complete with my special ingredient from the garden," she deadpanned, forcing eye contact and enjoying the discomfort she was causing.

"Harriet. I'm so glad you're here." The reverend's voice boomed across the church lawn, loud enough to wake Mr. Brown in the adjacent cemetery. Harriet cringed, and her mouth went dry.

Others stared, but Amy averted her gaze as the reverend arrived and busied herself with arranging the baked goods.

Emily sidled up to the table.

"Well, hello, young lady," he said. "Emily, have you met Mrs. Brown?"

"How do you do," the girl replied.

Harriet smiled at the feint.

"Ah, brownies. These look good enough to eat," the reverend blathered, delivering his corny line used whenever food was near. "That's what I'll be buying."

"No," Emily burst out. "We'll bake you another batch. I mean, Mrs. Brown will. My brother is gonna buy all the brownies today. It's like a bet with his friends or something."

"Oh. Well, good things come to those who wait, eh?" The reverend sighed and wandered off to another group of parishioners.

"What was that all about?" Harriet asked as they stepped away from the table.

Emily gave her an innocent look. "What was what all about? Hey, I really shouldn't be seen hanging out with you. You know, parents. But there's a nice shady spot over by that maple tree. You can watch everything from there, okay? I'll see you later." Emily skipped away.

Harriet's hives had become fiery welts. Walking to the shady spot, she wanted to break into a full run and keep going. *No. This is my chance to have a normal life again. I can do this. Breathe, Harriet, breathe. Slow and calm. You're not going to die.*

As Harriet reached the maple, Amy announced the beginning of the sale. Paul rushed to the head of the line.

Emily snuck back around behind the tree. "There's my stupid brother," she whispered to Harriet, watching him carefully. "He really is going to buy all the brownies. Whatta pig."

Paul walked off with a dozen plates of brownies, including Harriet's.

"I told him to look for the paper plate with pretty tulips on it if he wanted to buy ours—um, yours," Emily said. "He told his friends he was going to tempt fate—you know, eat something the Brown Recluse made."

Harriet was crestfallen. Her special brownies, sold on a cruel dare?

Emily seemed not to notice. "I hafta go to the bathroom. I'll be back in a minute."

Harriet sat alone under the tree, alone in the town, alone in the world. Alone except for the rising panic that battled with her resolve to stay. Even outdoors, she felt the walls closing in around her. Her head started swimming. Her breath was coming harder now.

She watched as Paul and a group of his tomato-throwing friends gathered in a snickering circle. They pushed and jostled, daring each other to take the first bite of Harriet's dessert. "Ya big wuss. You're all talk." It took a double-dog dare before Paul snatched one of Harriet's biggest brownies and downed it in two chomps. For full effect, he danced a cocky swagger.

Then suddenly he stopped. His eyes grew wide. His hands flew to his throat. He gasped, then collapsed to the ground.

The other boys jumped back and stared. Finally, one of them yelled for someone to call 9-1-1.

Harriet froze. This couldn't be happening. She hadn't put anything bad in those brownies. She'd swear to it.

Paul's parents looked up at the commotion across the yard. When Mrs. Stanford realized it was her son on the ground, she screamed, and Mr. Stanford ran to him.

"It was that witch's brownies!" shouted one of the boys. "She killed him!"

All eyes turned toward the Brown Recluse. Then she saw the pointing and heard the cries.

"I knew it!"

"She can't be trusted!"

"She *is* a witch!"

"Call the cops!"

"Just like her husband died!"

"Murderer!"

Police and ambulance sirens drew nearer.

Emily returned from the bathroom and ran to her mother.

"That evil woman over there," Mrs. Stanford told a cop loudly, pointing at Harriet. "She poisoned the brownies, and my poor Pauly ate them. Arrest her."

"She did?" Emily looked at her mother with innocent eyes. Her mother drew her in closer and nodded.

A tear crept down Harriet's face as she witnessed the betrayal.

The cop headed over to Harriet. "Ma'am, did you bake the brownies on the tulip plate?" The officer towered over Harriet as she sat on the ground.

"I . . . I . . ." Harriet stammered. Her mouth was itchy and she felt sick to her stomach.

"Ma'am? Are you all right?" The officer leaned in closer, just in time to catch Harriet as she stopped breathing and collapsed.

***

Emily stood crying on the church lawn. She watched the ambulance peel away with her brother and secret friend, her parents following in their car. Her tears turned to sobs when she thought about poor Harriet, with no one to visit her or care whether she lived or died.

"There, there, dear." Reverend Boxter had sidled up and slipped an arm around her. "I'm sure they'll be fine. Have some faith." The words relaxed her. Then he pounced.

"By the way, what did you put in those brownies?"

Emily froze, then pulled away. "What? I dunno. Mrs. Brown made them."

"Now, Emily, it's a sin to lie—especially to a minister. I think we both know you helped make them. And we both know you must have put ground nuts in as your secret ingredient."

Emily stared in disbelief.

"I've seen you at Harriet's more than once when I've come for my pastoral calls, Emily. I know you visit her regularly. I know what you do there. I know about your baking and your secret additions."

He'd spied on them? She remembered him peering in the sidelights that one time she was there baking.

"No. I don't . . . I didn't . . . I never . . ." she protested.

"Now, now, let's not add more lies to your sins. Everyone knows your brother is allergic to nuts, and you made sure he bought your brownies."

"Maybe Harriet added them," she deflected.

"You know your brother is allergic to nuts," he repeated, "but you didn't know Harriet is. She must have tasted the batter, unaware the brownies were tainted. With her allergies, she never would have sampled them if she'd known about the nuts. It had to be you."

Emily felt like a rabbit in a snare. She wanted to run, but it was no use. Reverend Boxter knew everything.

"Don't tell my parents. About any of it. Please," she begged, stepping farther away from him.

The reverend stood with his arms crossed over his large belly and smiled like a fisherman reeling in a catch. "Well, my dear, there's only one way I can agree to that—and that's if you never see Harriet Brown again. Honor your parents and stay away from that murdering evil witch."

Emily's eyes filled with hot tears. Abandon Harriet? The only one who understood how abused she was by her brother? The only one who made her feel safe?

Then something about the reverend's words caught her ear. Murdering. Evil. Witch. She'd heard them before, from her parents and others in town. Now from the reverend? Suddenly it dawned on her. . . .

She looked at him for a long, calculating minute. "Yes, Reverend Boxter," she said demurely. "You're right. Maybe I could come talk with you about my sins sometime."

"Of course, dear girl. I'm glad we understand each other."

He gave a reptilian smile, then waved Amy over. "Do you think you could take Emily home with you until her parents get back from the hospital? I think she could use a friend."

Amy reached out her hand. Emily slipped her own small fingers into the woman's tight grip.

***

A week after Harriet returned home, Emily knocked softly on her back door.

"Come in," Harriet said coolly. "I didn't hear your bike coming up the hill."

"I walked today." The girl entered the kitchen sheepishly. She held out a wilting bouquet of daisies and black-eyed Susans she'd pinched from the church garden.

Harriet put the blooms in water, then sat at the kitchen table.

"How's your brother?"

"Fine."

"Care to explain what happened at the bake sale?"

"I didn't know you were allergic to nuts," Emily murmured, staring at her scuffed sneakers.

"But you knew your brother was."

Emily nodded, abashed. "I didn't think it was that serious. He used to just get itchy. It was supposed to be funny, because he was so mean to me."

Harriet understood. Revenge had crossed her mind more than once as payback for all those who kept her isolated and captive with their judgments and gossip. That included Reverend Boxter and his unwanted pastoral calls, subtle reminders of what he'd do if she told his secret.

"I brought you something else, too," Emily said. "Another friend."

She stepped onto the back porch and returned with Amy.

Anger flashed across Harriet's face, and she jumped up from the table. "What are you doing here?" she demanded. "It's not enough you gossip about me and call me a Brown Recluse? You have to invade my home, my sanctuary? Get out. Both of you."

They stood their ground. Emily walked up to Harriet and hugged her hard around the waist. "You need to hear something first."

Amy nodded. "Emily and I had a long talk after the bake sale. We discovered the three of us have something in common." Her eyes welled with tears. "Emily, could you step out to the back porch for a few minutes, dear? This is for grown-up ears."

Emily complied reluctantly.

"Harriet, there's something you don't know about that day you walked in on . . . well, you know." Amy's cheeks flushed hot. "It wasn't an affair. Reverend Boxter was attacking me. You actually saved me when you arrived unexpectedly."

"Oh, Amy."

"He's been doing it for over a year," she confessed softly.

"And he blackmailed you into silence, I bet," Harriet replied, gently laying a hand on Amy's arm.

Amy nodded as a lone tear trickled down her cheek. "One day, I foolishly confessed to him that I'd cheated on my husband when we were engaged. He was going to expose my secret and ruin my family. I love my husband and kids, Harriet. They're my world. I couldn't risk it."

"So you suffered his abuse in silence to protect your family."

"It gets worse. He said we had to keep you quiet about what you saw. He's the one who started saying that you were a Brown Recluse and a murdering evil witch. He made me spread rumors, too. He wanted to make sure you wouldn't have any friends to tell."

Harriet let the enormity of it all sink in. Sadness and rage flooded through her. She shook her head and sighed. "I believe you. He threatened me, too. He said he'd tell everyone about confidential things from our counseling sessions if I told anyone about him and you," Harriet said softly. "That's when my agoraphobia got worse."

Amy nodded sympathetically. "And Emily told me he threatened her, too."

Brooms suddenly clattered across the back porch, and the young eavesdropper tumbled through the door. She splatted on the kitchen floor. "Did someone call my name?" she asked with a grin.

Harriet brought out a plate of fresh oatmeal cookies. She made coffee for the adults and poured a glass of milk for Emily.

"We have a problem," she said. "The question is, what are we going to do about it?"

They munched and sipped and mulled. They considered all the

ways Reverend Boxter lied and abused and manipulated them and the town to cover his crime. All the pain he'd caused. And him a man of the cloth. Somehow, merely reporting him to the church and police didn't seem sufficient for his sins.

"Justice is a dish best served cold," Amy mused.

"Revenge," Harriet corrected. "Revenge is a dish best served cold."

Amy shrugged. "Justice. Revenge. Po-tay-to, po-tah-to." A gleam came into her eye. "Maybe the phrase should be 'revenge is a dish best served warm . . .'"

"'. . . from the oven,'" Harriet said, finishing the thought. Emily looked at the two women with wide eyes.

"I know exactly the dish," Harriet said. "In one of my counseling sessions, I mentioned my nut allergy when he offered me some almonds. Reverend Boxter said he was deathly allergic to pineapple."

Without another word, they each grabbed a cookbook and started thumbing through for ideas. Pineapple upside-down cake was too obvious. The same with Pineapple Surprise Cookies, with their dollop of pineapple jam in the middle.

In the end, they selected Cranberry Orange Cookies.

"All we have to do is substitute pineapple juice for the two tablespoons of orange juice. Maybe a splash more for good measure," Harriet said.

"One tablespoon for each of us," Amy suggested.

"But isn't that . . . evil and murderous? Like he said you were?" Emily asked somberly.

The women paused and thought.

"Yes, it is," Harriet finally said. "Tell you what. If that bothers you, use the orange juice. And if it doesn't bother you, use pineapple. We'll take turns and close our eyes when the others are adding the juice. We'll call them Cranberry Orange Surprise cookies."

They got out the baking supplies and each took turns mixing the ingredients.

When Emily popped the pan of cookies into the oven, Harriet went to the phone and rang the church.

"Why, hello, Reverend Boxter. I'm surprised to hear you answer the phone yourself." She winked at Amy.

"Amy didn't show up for work today," he replied with annoyance. "She's gotten so unreliable lately. But that's my problem, not yours. What can I do for you?"

"I could really use a pastoral visit today, if you have the time."

"Why, of course. I suppose having a close brush with death has stirred up lots of questions about life and the hereafter. I'm about to head out for lunch, but why don't I swing by in an hour?"

"Perfect," Harriet said. "We'll definitely be talking about what it's like to nearly die. You simply can't imagine."

An hour later, the doorbell rang. "Reverend Boxter. How good of you to come. Let's have a seat in the living room. How was your lunch?"

"Thank you, Harriet," he said, heaving his girth on the settee. "Lunch was . . . well, disappointing, to be perfectly honest. Nothing but a salad. The wife has me on a diet."

"You? Nonsense. What you should have is a little something sweet on the side. Know what I mean?"

He chuckled. "Well, it wouldn't be a real sin now, would it? But promise not to tell the little woman."

"Oh, you know I'm good at secrets." Harriet smiled broadly. "You relax. I'll be right back."

Harriet disappeared into the kitchen and returned with the treats. "They're my Cranberry Orange Surprise cookies."

"Why, they look good enough to eat." He beamed, popping one into his mouth and picking up another. "Mmm. Might you have some coffee to go with them?"

At that, Amy emerged from the kitchen with a freshly brewed pot and poured him a cup.

His jaw dropped. "Amy? Why weren't you at work . . .?"

Then Emily emerged and laid some napkins by the plate. "You'll need these," she interrupted sweetly.

"And *you*, missy," he sputtered.

His eyes widened as he looked at the trio he'd tried so hard to separate, silence, and control. He tasted the cookie in his mouth and went pale. "I think I'd better go." His voice quavered.

"Don't be silly, Reverend," Amy said, pushing him back onto the settee with one finger as he tried to rise.

"You're here on a pastoral call," Harriet reminded. "You mustn't shirk your duty."

"Indeed," Amy added. "Have another cookie. We insist."

Emily nodded.

The reverend looked aghast at the plate of cookies and started to sweat.

"What's the matter, Reverend?" the Brown Recluse said. "They're just desserts."

A SLICE OF HEAVEN

By Laura Brennan

A middle-of-the-night callout brings a mental health worker face-to-face with temptation.

It was three a.m. when my beeper went off. I smacked at it and nearly knocked the lamp off the bedside table. What a night. I wasn't even supposed to be on call, but Estelle was on maternity leave, Gail had managed to get herself into Intensive Care with food poisoning, and the new girl, what's-her-name, had up and quit after two weeks. Score one for me. I knew the minute she'd flounced in with her iced chai latte and perky smile that she'd fold the first time she was faced with a crazy.

Not that I'm supposed to call our people "crazies." The Department of Mental Health frowns upon the term. They'd rather that we case managers call them "clients." *Tomato-tomahto.*

So now it was three in the morning and I was the only one available to answer the Bat-Signal. I'd been up until midnight, sitting on the floor in the hallway of a drafty row house, talking a pot-smoking teenager out of cutting herself. Her mom had bugged out the week before and moved in with her dealer boyfriend. In addition to the teen, there were five-year-old twins and a dad who'd been spooning on the couch with his Johnnie Walker. It all added up to a chat with social services, the smug bastards. They'd probably take over the file and I'd never see the kid again.

Yet another reason to not remember names.

I dragged myself out of bed and wriggled into a pair of jeans. Normally, I dress up for my client visits—I want them to think of me as the professional in their sorry lives—but at three in the morning, anything above jammies would do. The jeans were a little tight. I pulled on a sweatshirt to cover my muffin top and speed-dialed the machine. The clients know the drill: name, number, whatever the hell's the matter. Well, my clients do, but this wasn't one of my regulars. No name, plenty of sobs, and a number on the log that I didn't recognize. I sighed and fired up my laptop. With luck, I could plug the phone number into the system and it would spit out a name. The drenching rain had finally let up, but there was still a miserable chill and a biting wind. Maybe I could get away with just calling her back . . .

Then one sentence broke through, perfectly clear. "I think I killed him!" she said.

Dial tone.

I felt a shiver, not of fear but of anticipation. This was the real deal. This was the shit that made the other shit worth doing. A name and address popped up on my screen. Deloris Fischer. I grabbed my briefcase and dialed 9-1-1 as I ran for the car. Let them pull me over for driving with a cell phone glued to my ear. It was all in the line of duty. I'd caught a murder.

Roz was on dispatch. I repeated the message from Deloris, requested an ambulance and asked if they could send a uniform to meet me there. I thought I did a damn good job of keeping the excitement out of my voice.

"Hang on a sec," Roz said and put me on hold.

Mount Granite was a small town. I'm sure some people moved here with visions of Mayberry, but the only thing the two villages had in common was that everyone knew everyone else's business. How could we not? We all lived on top of each other, grey macadam streets sandwiched between strips of row houses, all sharing thin walls and leaky roofs. No hunky sheriff or doting Aunt Bee had lured me to this pit. I was roped in with cold hard cash, the promise of a job despite the downward spiraling economy.

Roz, on the other hand, had been born in this dump. She marked her days in vodka shots and put-downs but she was always on top of things at dispatch. Putting me on hold was inexplicable. It was a full two minutes before she came back on the line.

"Y'all *en route* to the scene of the crime?" she asked.

"The woman's only a mile out of town, Roz. I'm not *en route*, I'm pulling up to the curb. Where the hell is the ambulance?"

"We heard from Ms. Fischer just before you called in," she said. "Deceased's name is Hector. We're a little busy here just now. Sheriff thinks you can handle this one solo."

I couldn't have heard her right. "You want to repeat that?"

"Call in if you need backup."

"There's a dead body, or at least a dying one. I need paramedics—"

She hung up, but not before I heard laughter burst out in the background. Somehow, I was being punked.

Respond, I told myself. *Don't react*. I took a deep breath and managed not to punch the steering wheel.

I thought about driving home, going back to bed, quitting my job and moving somewhere civilized, but I knew I wouldn't really do any of those things. What I didn't know was whether or not I'd pull out my emergency candy bar, which I kept stowed in my glove compartment. Soothing myself with food was how I'd survived the same chaotic childhood that had propelled me into the mental health profession. Heal thyself, that was always the goal. Helping others along the way was only a paycheck.

I could do this without chocolate and caramel. I could handle this.

Leaving the glove compartment closed, I hauled my briefcase and myself out of the car. I had parked across the street from the Fischer house. A mile out of town meant single family dwellings. No shared walls, perhaps, but still that shared small-town taste for fake deer and tawdry pink flamingoes. As I slammed my door shut, a gnome glared up at me, malevolent ceramic eyes reflecting the yellow street lights. I glared right back. If the police wouldn't come out for a dead body, they sure as hell weren't going to haul ass for a little noise disturbance.

I picked my way around the puddles and crossed the street to the Fischer house. No resin-and-plastic dotted this lawn. A white picket fence bordered the small grass yard. I opened the gate and walked up the path. Here, all was orderly. Tidy. I rang the bell.

The door flew open. Deloris Fischer might have been frantic, but she kept a tight lid on it. Her grey hair was pinned, her Hello Kitty robe belted, her mouth in a thin line.

"Took you long enough." She disappeared back inside. "Well, come on then. Close the door. You don't want to let the others out."

Others? As I shut the door behind me, something rubbed against my legs. I jumped. Deloris poked her head through from the living room door.

"Not allergic to cats, are you?"

"No," I said.

"Good." She motioned for me to follow her in. "Mind the Balinese. He doesn't like strangers."

That made two of us. The Balinese stalked off. Clearly, I wasn't worth his time. By now the penny had dropped. Hector was neither husband nor lover offed in a moment of passion. I had been dragged out of bed for *catricide*.

Deloris perched on the edge of the couch and plucked at a linen handkerchief. I looked around for a place to sit. Most of the obvious choices—the rest of the couch, an easy chair, an ottoman—were already occupied. A dozen or more cats lounged, slept, or meandered around the room. I went to move one of them from a side chair only to be stopped by Deloris.

"Beatrice doesn't care to be touched," she informed me. Deloris nodded toward a folding chair tucked against the wall. "That's for guests."

I popped the chair open across from her and sat. The plastic creaked under my weight. I tried not to picture it collapsing and me landing in a big, fat heap on the floor. I pulled my clipboard out of my case and got to work.

Deloris dabbed at her eyes and answered mechanically as I went through the details I needed for the paperwork. Unless someone was bleeding out, I always started with the boring stuff. I wanted my crazies to get in the habit of answering my questions before I asked anything important.

"Your usual case worker is Gail Dundee?" I asked.

"Yes," she answered. "Although I have officially requested someone else."

I was surprised. Unlike me, Gail was generally appreciated by her clients. Deloris, however, pursed her lips.

"Dog person," she said shortly.

I nodded and moved on, but she persisted. "Do you like dogs?" she asked.

I kept my face impassive. "They're the cat's meow," I answered. We stared at each other for a moment, neither one breaking eye contact. Suddenly, she laughed. It was a harsh—dare I say, barking?—laugh, and the tension in the room ebbed.

"I knew you were my kind of gal," she said. "The moment I saw you." She leaned forward conspiratorially. "I could tell from your teeth."

I froze. She stood. "You don't want any tea or coffee staining those beauties," she said. "I'll get you some lemonade."

"Just water," I managed. That was always safest for me. There was no temptation with water, no calories to regret. She tut-tutted, but after a moment she returned with what I'd asked for.

I wanted to forget her remark about my teeth. I went on to the next question, and the one after that, trying to calm myself with the familiar routine. But I couldn't let it go. Getting a new dentist had been one of the perks of moving to Mount Granite, someone who would know I'd had extensive work done—there was no way to hide that—but wouldn't know why. I could pretend it had been an accident, or genetics, or even vanity, and not that years of purging had eroded my entire mouth. I could leave the shame behind me.

Or I thought I could.

"What did you mean?" I blurted out. I couldn't help myself. It was as much of a compulsion as reaching for the tub of Häagen-Dazs. "What did you mean about my teeth?"

"They're perfect," she said. "Caps, of course, and expensive,

I'll wager. But you didn't let money stop you. I'm the same way." She sipped her lemonade and looked around thoughtfully. "It's not easy keeping this house clean. So much dust in the summer, and now with the rain. Do you know, yesterday my sister actually shook her wet umbrella all over Cleopatra? She said it was an accident, but I saw her laughing. And the dirt! That handyman, tromping in to use the bathroom with his muddy size-twelve boots. Thoughtless!"

She glanced at my shoes. I tucked my feet under the chair to hide the soles, just in case. Her behavior bordered on obsessive, but that wasn't why I was there. "Would you like to talk about Hector?" I asked.

Immediately, her eyes welled up. "He was such a wonderful friend," she said. "Always by my side. And so clever! The cleverest of all my cats."

I made sympathetic noises and shifted into autopilot. Death was so tedious. There was nothing to do, no advice to give, you just had to let them talk it out and pretend to care.

I wished now that I had stopped long enough to eat some fruit, or at least grab one of those god-awful nutrition bars before I flew out on my errand of mercy. I don't do well when I'm hungry. As Deloris droned on, I thought about my call to dispatch. Roz's nonchalance seemed more studied, more mocking, in memory. The laughter—there had been a male voice in the background, maybe two. I pictured the whole station hovering by the phone, taking pleasure in my humiliation. I was tolerated in Mount Granite, but I would always be an outsider. I would never be welcomed. I would never be loved.

"Am I boring you?" Deloris' voice jerked me back to the present. I looked up at her, truly grateful to be wrenched from my own thoughts.

"Of course not," I lied. "I'm just a little tired. It's been a long night."

On cue, my stomach rumbled. I gave her my most pathetic smile and hoped that she'd put her grief to bed and let me leave. Instead, she narrowed her eyes and got to her feet.

"I have just the thing," she said, and took off for the kitchen. "Follow me."

"No!" I called after her. "Nothing for me. Thank you!" She ignored me. I rose to me feet, panicky. I was tired, I was hungry, I was lonely and demoralized and food was my kryptonite.

Ruthless honesty did not endear me to my clients, but it was the only thing I could count on. I saw things the way they were, not the way I wanted them to be, and when I had pulled myself together and followed her into the kitchen, I saw a lemon poppy seed cake under a heavy glass dome and I knew instantly that I was doomed.

"Have a slice," she said.

She pulled out a bar stool and sat at the kitchen island. There was no way to escape—and I wasn't sure I wanted to. In the absence of love, sugar wasn't the worst substitute I could have found.

"Everyone loves my poppy seed cake," Deloris said, rather smugly. "The handyman had three slices this morning. Even my sister took home a piece, and she's always going around saying that she's the better baker. Hah!"

I barely listened. She lifted the glass dome and the smell of freshly-baked goodness overwhelmed me. My shoulders relaxed. I heard myself saying, "Thank you. I'd love some."

As I sat across from her, there was a screeching meow. The Balinese had followed us into the kitchen. Deloris moved like lightning, scooping him up and carrying him back to the living room, cooing all the while. Apparently, the kitchen was a cat-free zone and I was glad for the sudden solitude. I glanced quickly at the back door: locked with a simple bolt, no chain to fiddle with. I could be gone in a flash. If I could get up. If I could leave the cake behind. Before I could make up my mind, Deloris had returned.

She cut a generous slice of the poppy seed cake and smiled as she handed me the plate. I looked into her eyes as I took it, and my hand trembled. She knew, I was sure of it now; she knew my secret. That smile had been superior, triumphant even. I picked up my fork and cut off the tiniest bite.

"Thank you," I told her. And I put it in my mouth.

It was magnificent. The flavors were perfect, the texture light. I took another, a bigger, bite. I licked my lips. Deloris was pouring herself more lemonade, prattling on about her cats, watching me all the while. I couldn't even pretend to listen. The cake on my plate was heaven; my hell was that it would never be enough. I blinked back tears of frustration. Even if I ate the whole cake, I could never have enough. I took another bite.

"Are you crying?" Deloris asked suddenly. She had the oddest look on her face. In an instant, I remembered that I was supposed to be the adult in the room. It was my job to provide comfort, not to take it, not even from lemon poppy seed cake. My years of training kicked in and gave me a breath of space.

Just enough for me to lay down my fork.

"Hector," I managed. At his name, Deloris, too, blinked back tears. All I could think of now was getting out of this kitchen, getting away from temptation. I pushed myself back from the island.

"Perhaps," I said, "you would allow me to pay my respects?"

She nodded quickly, as surprised as I was by the sudden turn in the conversation. A door I had assumed was to a pantry turned out to open instead onto a flight of stairs leading to the basement. She flipped a switch and a single, naked bulb lit the way.

"Mind the top step," she said. "It's higher than the rest. That useless handyman was supposed to fix it, but of course he never did."

I followed her, managing not to trip on the surprisingly steep staircase, grateful only to be leaving half a slice of cake on my plate. I had done it. I had walked away. The effort had exhausted me, but soon I would be able to go home and sleep and leave Deloris to her feline friends. I just had to get through Hector's wake.

The basement took me by surprise. As neat as the rest of her house had been, this room was a disaster. Crates were scattered around, old clothes and rags piled high, chairs scratched beyond salvation, even a single size-twelve boot, just visible behind a mound of junk. A muddy boot. Quickly, I looked away.

Hector was near the furnace. Perhaps he had sought out its warmth in his final moments. Glassy blue eyes stared up, unseeing. We stood over him, Deloris and I, without speaking. She was silent in grief, and I was desperately searching for the exact right thing to say.

"Perhaps," I ventured, "we could cover him?" Deloris started to make a negative gesture, but I continued, unheeding. "Not a sheet, of course, but a hand towel perhaps? A dish towel? You had a lovely blue one in the kitchen, I noticed. It would match his eyes."

I shut my mouth then, afraid of rambling. There was a long moment where Deloris didn't answer and I didn't move. I didn't even breathe. Finally, she nodded.

"Yes," she said. "Yes. How perceptive you are. It would be the exact right shade."

"I'll go fetch it," I murmured and moved away slowly. The last thing I wanted to do was spook her. I had just taken the first step when I felt her hand grab my arm.

I tensed, but all she did was pat me awkwardly. I didn't think she was used to touching people.

"Thank you," Deloris said. "I was wrong about you. You do understand."

She released my arm. "I'm so glad you didn't finish your cake," she added, and turned back to Hector.

I thought of Gail as I walked up the stairs, going on her third day in Intensive Care. Gail was hard-working and she cared about her clients, but her one fault was that she was greedy, always sneaking seconds whenever there was an office birthday or celebration. I thought of the poppy seed cake, carefully protected from the cats with the heavy glass dome. Hector, of all her cats, had been the cleverest. I wondered what he'd finally been able to get into.

I walked into the kitchen, picked up the platter with the poppy seed cake, glass dome still in place, and carried it straight out the back door. I had been right; the door opened quickly and I was gone in seconds. I walked to my car and locked the cake in the trunk. Then I stuck my hand down the back of my throat, my fingers grazing my teeth in a way that was familiar and comforting and terrifying at the same time. I heaved all over the glaring gnome. Then I did it again, and again. When there was nothing left in me, I took out my phone and dialed 9-1-1.

Roz didn't hang up on me this time.

There had been a foot inside that size-twelve boot.

THE EXTRA INGREDIENT

By Joan Long

Welcome to a southern diner where the food is home-style, the welcome is warm, and generosity is the order of the day. However, young hostess Lexi has a problem . . .

Eighteen-year-old Lexi Neff could read people. When she looked into their eyes, she saw beyond any façades. She knew if they were wounded, angry, sad, or hiding secrets.

Introductions were brief on Lexi's first day of work at Three Egg Kitchen, little more than hurried smiles and "hey"s from the waitresses. No time to dawdle. The southern diner's front door would swing open in minutes. At six a.m., hungry customers would stream inside and expect to be seated promptly. That was Lexi's job—greet 'em and seat 'em. She was the new hostess at Three Egg, where booths were made of varnished pine, photos of vintage pickups and orange blossoms hung on the walls, and the aroma of fresh coffee said G'morning.

A sunburned waitress, who called everyone Sweetie, gave Lexi fifteen minutes of training. "Being a hostess isn't hard, Sweetie. But if anyone gives you grief, go to Darlene."

"Who's Darlene?"

"Our chief cook. She's not the owner, but she sure as heck runs the place. At Three Egg, Darlene is god. Remember that, and you'll be just fine."

"When do I meet her?"

"Well, right after you take these folks to table eight. C'mon in," she called to a man and woman entering the diner. The woman carried a sockless, squirming baby on her hip.

Lexi recognized the couple from high school, even though they didn't seem to remember her. They'd been seniors back when she was a freshman, the same year her mother had been diagnosed with cancer.

As Lexi seated the family, she caught the young mom's eye. The woman was exhausted, and she was irritated with the man. Lexi turned away. Not her problem.

"It's time you meet Darlene," the waitress said, motioning

toward the kitchen.

Together, they walked past a baker's rack where bags of new-crop pecans and jars of local honey were displayed for sale. On the far end of a countertop sat the diner's cash register. A few feet behind it, an open doorway led into the kitchen.

"Hey, Sweetie," the waitress called to the cook. "This is our new hostess, Lexi Neff."

Darlene tipped her head at them. She was busy, placing a stack of pancakes into a take-out box. A stretchy net covered her graying hair. She wore a crimson-colored apron and stood nearly six feet tall. She closed the top on the box and handed it to the waitress. "Give this to the man hanging around the dumpster, okay? He looks hungry."

The waitress rolled her eyes. "Another homeless guy? You're such a softie." To Lexi she said, "Darlene thinks she can solve people's problems with food."

The cook tsk-tsked. "Someday you might need a little help, too. 'Do unto others,' you know."

The waitress nodded and took the box outside, leaving Darlene with the diner's new hostess.

Lexi immediately looked into the cook's deep brown eyes. The woman's soul lay bare. She believed in right and wrong, good and bad. Darlene was judge and jury.

Darlene saw only a short, cute girl who could stand to gain a few pounds. "Welcome to my kitchen. Did you eat breakfast before coming to work?"

"No, I don't usually eat this early."

"Well, when you get your break later, come see me. I'll fix you up with a snack." The cook peered over Lexi's head at the hostess station. "Looks like you've got customers to seat."

Lexi went back to work but returned to the kitchen five minutes later.

"Break time already?" Darlene asked.

"No. My dad's here. I just sat him at table four." She shuddered. "Can I hide in here? Please?"

"Is something wrong?" Darlene wiped her fingertips on her apron while she peered at the thin, balding man seated at table four.

"My dad's stalking me. I'm not talking to him, so he shows up here on my first day of work."

"Why aren't you two talking?"

"Because he beat my mom again. She's covered with bruises."

Darlene stood taller, her left eyebrow arching toward her scalp. "That's terrible. Did you call the cops?"

"No, Mom won't let me. She's too afraid of him."

Darlene's eyes narrowed as the man ordered from the menu. "Has he ever hit you?"

"Oh, yeah. Lots of times. He's a monster." Lexi sniffled. "I thought I might be safe at work. But every time I walk anywhere near him, he says stuff to me. He won't let me alone."

The cook scowled and placed her fists on her hips. "Stay here in the kitchen with me, and don't you worry. I'll make sure he doesn't come to this diner again."

"How?"

Darlene didn't answer. But when the man's order reached her kitchen, she turned her back to Lexi while she fixed his breakfast. Two eggs, bacon, and wheat toast on the plate. Grits scooped into a bowl. She reached up for a purple canister that sat alone on a high shelf. Then she sprinkled a white powder from the canister into his bowl of grits, added a pat of butter, and stirred well. Food fit for a monster.

The man ate everything and left a generous tip. The next morning, he returned to Three Egg.

Lexi rushed into the kitchen, her arms crossed over her chest. "I thought you said my dad wouldn't come back here."

Darlene's jaw dropped when she saw the man in her diner again. He had returned, looking sad and almost sick. "Your dad must have a strong stomach."

Lexi's eye twitched. "He hit my mom again last night."

"Tell me she called the cops this time."

"No. I told you, she won't *ever* do that."

"Okay. Then I'll take care of him." The cook squeezed Lexi's shoulder. "I'll tell one of the waitresses to cover your hostess duties for a while. You can fold napkins beside the register till your dad is gone."

Lexi nodded but didn't immediately leave the kitchen. Instead, she pointed to several pies sitting on the counter. "Wow. Did you make those?"

"Yes, they're for a charity fundraiser tonight. My daughter will be coming by to pick them up. Are you hungry, Lexi? I have a blackberry cobbler that will be out of the oven soon."

"I can't say no to cobbler."

"Then I'll put a piece aside for you. Now, get moving. I have some cookin' to do."

Darlene pulled the purple canister from the shelf and whipped up a special batch of pancakes for Lexi's abusive father. From inside the kitchen, Darlene watched him eat. After one pancake, the man's forehead began to sweat. He drained a glass of water and burped. She would have continued to watch him if the kitchen's back door hadn't squeaked open.

"Hey, Mama. I'm here for the pies."

Darlene crossed the room to give her grown daughter a hug. "Just one more pie to box up. Then they're yours."

As they talked, the sunburned waitress stuck her head into the kitchen. "Sweetie, a guy puked up his breakfast in the bathroom. Want me to comp his meal?"

"No. What's he doing now?"

"Just sitting at his table, looking sickly."

"Don't comp his meal."

"Okay. Whatever you say."

From inside the kitchen, Darlene and her daughter peered out at Lexi's father. "He gets no sympathy from me. He beats his wife," Darlene told her daughter.

"That guy? No, that's Ted Neff. He's a friend of mine from work. His wife died of cancer two years ago."

"That can't be right. His daughter, Lexi, is our new hostess. She told me he beat her mother just last night."

"Lexi—Lexi Neff works here? Oh, Mama, that girl lied to you."

"Why would she do that?"

"Maybe because she moved in with her lowlife druggie boyfriend a few weeks ago. Ted says he's been trying to talk Lexi into coming home, but she won't listen to him. He doesn't want her to get into any more trouble."

"*More* trouble?"

"Yeah. She was caught shoplifting twice, but Ted got the charges dropped. And worse, she stole money from that blind beggar's cup on Fifth Street."

"No. From the old man who plays his guitar on the sidewalk?"

"That's the one."

"You're sure she did that?"

"Positive, Mama. She's probably stealing tips from your waitresses, too."

Darlene sucked in an angry breath. Then she motioned for Ted's waitress to join her in the kitchen. "Listen, I changed my mind. Comp that guy's meal and tell him the next three are on me, okay?"

"Are you sure?"

"Yes. Do it. And after he leaves, tell Lexi to come see me, please."

Five minutes later, the hostess popped her smiling face into the kitchen. "You want to see me?"

Darlene didn't look into Lexi's eyes. Instead, she closed the purple canister and returned it to the shelf. “Grab a spoon, Lexi. I fixed some cobbler just for you.”

A DEATH IN YELAPA

By Leslie Budewitz

The coast of Mexico offers wonderful adventures and fantastic food. Unfortunately, it can also be a dangerous place for the unwary.

The waves broke over the bow of the water taxi and the cold salt spray misted my face. I smiled up at my husband. The sea breeze whipped his dark curls, his sunglasses reflecting the diamond glint of a January day off the western coast of Mexico.

My husband. Adam and I had been married all of twenty-three days, but our Christmas Eve wedding on a dude ranch in Jewel Bay, Montana, might well have happened on another planet.

"Bahía de Banderas is the seventh largest bay in the world," said the blond man seated in front of me, his voice rising above the roar of the outboard motor. "The name means the Bay of Flags."

His wife, her highlighted hair tied back with a black chiffon ribbon, turned her gaze in the other direction.

"Erin, look." Adam pointed at a school of fish leaping through the water, not thirty feet off starboard.

"Dolphins?" I asked.

"Dorado," he said. Adam had spent a few months in Mexico after college, hiking and kayaking. He'd planned our slightly-belated honeymoon himself, telling me to make sure my passport was current and that I had a good bathing suit. Then, three days ago, he'd said we'd be vacationing in our own private casita on the most unspoiled beach in western Mexico.

Is there any wonder I'm head over heels for the man?

"Mahi-mahi. Dolphinfish." The blond man rested his arm on the back of his wife's seat and spoke over his shoulder. "Not to be confused with Flipper." He cackled.

"Oh, shut up, Max," his wife said. "No one wants to hear your stupid jokes." In profile, I could see her prominent cheekbones and strong jaw, makeup so expertly done you almost couldn't tell it was makeup. Full lips in a trendy red-orange, though I suspected the pout came naturally. Chic tortoiseshell sunglasses. I was sure I'd seen her browsing in an art gallery off the Malecon, when we were in Puerto Vallarta.

The two women sitting next to us raised their eyebrows, and one winked.

Max faced forward with another chuckle, and Adam and I exchanged a quick smile before turning our attention back to the jumping fish.

Twenty minutes and a hundred fish later, we landed in Yelapa. My mouth fell open, literally, at the sight of the picture-perfect village wrapped around the calm, blue inlet. A row of three-story haciendas, each a different color, faced the water. Some were private homes, others small hotels. Then came the charming casitas with their deep porches and a cluster of open-air bars and restaurants. Bright umbrellas dotted the beach.

Adam and I scrambled onto the pier—new since his last visit—and grabbed our backpacks. Max stood in the boat, surveying the surroundings, while his wife tried to disembark. Her white skirt was too narrow for her to get both feet on the pier easily and she stumbled, hands flailing as she shrieked, one cork-soled sandal flying.

Adam caught her. I rescued the errant sandal.

"Thank you, thank you," Max said. He stepped on to the pier, hand out. "We're Max and Parisa Porter, from Calgary."

"Oh, for Pete's sake, Max," she said. "You were willing to let me fall in the water. They don't care who you are."

"Teresa? Nice to meet you. I'm Erin Murphy, and this is my husband, Adam Zimmerman. From Northwestern Montana."

"PUH-reesa," she said. "Like Paris with an A on the end."

"You been here before?" Max had the manner I associated with a college football player-turned-stockbroker but not the size—halfway between my five-five and Adam's six-one, neither fat nor slender, he had thick lips and parted his blond hair in the middle.

"I have, she hasn't," Adam said. "It's our honeymoon."

"I knew it," Max said. "Didn't I tell you, sweetheart? On the boat. They gawk at each other like newlyweds."

We said a quick goodbye, though not before agreeing to meet them some evening for a margarita. "Or that *raicilla*," Max said. "Bootleg booze. Puts hair on your chest and ideas in your head. You know—*loco*." He pointed a finger at his ear and twirled it.

A few minutes later on the beach, I paused to kick off my flip-flops, eager to feel the golden sand between my pale, Northern toes. On the pier, Parisa stood beside a huge pile of luggage, arms folded, while Max waved his hands at the boatman.

"Negotiating for delivery?" I speculated. "To one of the big houses?"

"This ain't the Grand Hyatt," Adam replied and gestured to a turquoise casita with a palm-thatched roof.

The perfect honeymoon hotel.

***

"Well, if it isn't our American newlyweds," Max Porter called when he spotted us the next afternoon from the beachfront *palapa*. The palm-thatch canopy covered a few white plastic tables surrounded by white plastic chairs. "Looks like you've been out making waves. Not what we did on our honeymoon, eh, Parisa?"

What was your first clue? I wanted to ask. The bathing suits? The snorkels, the paddleboards?

A dark-haired young woman delivered a basket of chips, a bowl of salsa, and two frosty margaritas. Max beckoned. "Join us for a drink."

Chips and salsa and a cold Pacifico or two had been our plan but not with the Porters.

"Uh, thanks," Adam said, then turned to me. "I could do with a quick shower. What about you?"

Saved. "Good idea. Maybe if you two are here later—"

"Ohmygod, this is awful!" Parisa Porter flung her tortilla chip on to the table, bits of salsa splattering across the white plastic. "They can't even wash dishes right. It tastes like soap." She shoved her chair back—not easy to do in the sand—and flounced off, also not easy to do in the sand, especially in platform sandals.

Max's jaw tightened and his nostrils flared, then the jolly look returned. "My wife knows what she likes. We'll catch up with you two lovebirds later. When you're not out adventuring." He cackled and followed her.

Adam picked up the chair Parisa had knocked over, and by unspoken agreement, we sat, trying not to laugh.

I dipped a chip in the salsa and took a tentative nibble. "Oh, it's fine. It's got cilantro in it, that's all."

Adam cocked his head.

"About fifteen percent of the population thinks cilantro tastes like soap. Maybe less down here." We gave the waitress our order, and she picked up the Porters' untouched drinks. "I read about it recently. It has to do with your ability to detect certain bitter compounds. So some people taste soap while the rest of us—"

"Get to eat all the chips and salsa," Adam said, sporting the crooked grin I love. The waitress set a tin bucket of beer on the table and popped two caps. Adam raised his bottle toward me and we clinked.

"I'll drink to that."

***

On our third morning in Yelapa, our luck ran out. We'd taken a guided sunrise kayak trip and were now relaxing under the palapa, sipping fresh juice and waiting for our *huevos rancheros*.

"Look who the tide washed in," Max said. He sat, not waiting for an invitation. I glanced in the direction he'd come from and spotted Parisa. She'd given up on her shoes, the sandals dangling from her well-manicured fingertips as she slipped on the loose sand.

Adam popped up. "Max, Parisa, hello. Join us?" He pulled out the fourth chair and Parisa sank into it gratefully. At least, I thought she looked grateful, the way her shoulders dropped and she heaved out a ragged breath. I couldn't tell for sure—she'd kept her sunglasses on, despite the shade.

Our plates came. I didn't hear Max's order—I was too busy salivating over the glorious fried eggs dressed with *pico de gallo* and perfectly placed on a crisp tortilla, a sliced avocado and a spoonful of refried beans and rice on the side.

But I did hear Parisa ask for a Bloody Mary, and I didn't blame her.

"Fascinating place, you know," Max said, and started in on the history of the indigenous people—he called them the Yelapanese, though whether that was a real word or one he'd made up, I had no idea. We heard about First Contact, supposedly with a military man who was a cousin to Cortez, the early missionaries, and the treaties with the King of Spain. Since we were eating, we were a captive audience, and the history was interesting, if too detailed.

"Whatever their intentions, those old Spaniards recognized paradise when they found it," Max continued. "The Mexican dry forest—monsoons half the year, tolerable in winter and spring."

Parisa sipped while he recited average temperatures for late January—sixty-two point one degrees for the low and eighty-three point eight for the high.

"For you, that is," he said with another cackle. "Much cooler for us. Sixteen point seven and twenty-eight point eight."

The old Fahrenheit-Celsius bait and switch.

"You must sleep with the guidebook under your pillow," I said, and a smile flitted across Parisa's face. "I love how it's all so local. No chain restaurants or hotels. The people who live here run the businesses. Everything we're eating is grown or caught right here."

"Except the beer," Adam said.

"What do you two do back home?" Max asked.

"I run a local foods market," I said.

"She's the heart and soul of the place," my beloved added. "And the brains. I run a wilderness camp for kids. What about you?"

“Financial planner,” Max said, confirming my guess. When I glanced at Parisa, he answered for her. “My wife’s job is to make me look good.”

Turned out the Porters had signed up for the same afternoon tour as we had, along with the two women we’d seen on the boat and a handful of other tourists. At the edge of town, away from the bay, we boarded a small bus painted in vivid shades of green. To blend in, I supposed, as if any wild bird or animal would be fooled.

The Porters sat across the aisle from us. To my surprise, Max did not continue his recite-the-guidebook routine as we wound through the forested hills, deferring to the actual guide who sat behind the driver on a tall stool and told us all about the region’s flora and fauna.

The bus stopped for lunch in a hillside village. Somehow, we managed to get separated from the Porters and sat with the two women, Jackie and Jill, who turned out to be mystery-writing buddies from Washington State.

“We flew in to Puerto Vallarta from L.A. with them,” Jackie said. “I don’t know who’s worse, him or her.”

“Oh, him, for sure,” I said. “Though maybe only because she doesn’t talk as much. Are you scouting for victims for your next book? And how do you write together?”

Over chips, salsa, and cold beer, the two women chatted about their books and writing process. Turned out one lived in Seattle, the other in Spokane, but distance didn’t slow them down, thanks to email.

“It’s good that we live three hundred miles apart,” Jill said. “Keeps us from killing each other.”

After chips came gazpacho, the thick tomato-cucumber soup garnished with fresh cilantro. I could hear Parisa’s exclamation of disgust from twenty feet away, and revised my opinion on which Porter the mystery writers should dispatch.

Back on the bus, our guide announced a side trip upriver to the Cocodrilo Sanctuary.

“Crocodiles,” Max said loudly, in case anyone couldn’t figure it out themselves.

I had honestly never considered the breeding habits of crocodiles before, nor even seen one live, but they were fascinating. As long as they stayed inside their fenced, jungle-like swamps. The guide explained how this facility helped preserve the biodiversity of the species through a selective breeding program.

“Crocodile Nazis,” I heard Max say. “Good place to get your crocodile boots.”

“In our next book,” Jackie joked in a low voice.

Another function, the guide said as he cradled a baby croc in his arms, was education. Did we know how powerful a *cocodrilo*'s jaws were? "Thirty-seven hundred pounds per square inch. Greater than any other living animal." He let that sink in, then lunged forward, holding out the baby, who snapped its jaws and we all screamed. "But, they prefer chicken."

On the boat ride back down the cool green river, I sat next to Parisa, between Jackie and Jill.

"You like all this outdoor stuff?" Parisa asked, and I nodded. She shuddered. "Don't go out on your own. It isn't safe. Don't you live near grizzly bears?"

"Yes, and I do hike on my own, even though my mother and sister tell me not to." Somehow, that led to me pulling out my phone and pulling up wedding pictures.

"You and your sister could be twins," Jill said.

"I have a cousin who looks so much like me," Parisa said, "that people are always confusing us, even though Calgary is a big city and we don't spend much time together. I hate it."

I thought it quite wonderful to look so much like one of the people I loved most, but I kept my mouth shut.

Back in Yelapa, we all collapsed into beach chairs. The beach sellers must have been waiting, because the moment we were settled with drinks and snacks, they swarmed us. The colorful pottery was stunning, and I bought a set of serving bowls, though carrying them home would be tricky. The silver jewelry didn't tempt me. But the pie. Oh, the famous Yelapa pie. I chose coconut cream, Adam banana cream, and we traded bites.

I was about to wave "no" to the little man carrying a bundle of sundresses when a fringed knee-length number in shades of blue caught my eye. Alas, it caught Parisa's, too, and before I knew it, Max had paid the man full price for it and two more, not even pretending to bargain.

"There's another one in the same fabric," Adam pointed out, but it didn't have the fringe so I shook my head. The man picked up his load, considerably lighter now, and trundled down the beach.

A moment later, Max stood. "Gotta stretch after all that sitting," he said, and wandered off.

We swam, napped, and devoured fish tacos. When the sun finally set, the tourists cheered, and the locals laughed and shook their heads as if we were crazy. *Loco*.

***

The next morning, Adam and I caught an early bus and headed inland to a village where he'd lived briefly. The road was winding and narrow, like the mountain roads back home. I loved every bumpy minute, peering into the jungle for the birds we'd seen yesterday, grabbing Adam's hand when a tree-climbing snake stared back at me.

We strolled the cobbled streets Adam remembered fondly, and found the house he'd shared with three other crazy *Americanos*. We toured the church with its shrine to a saint I'd never heard of. On the main street, in search of lunch, we spotted a sidewalk café next to a hole-in-the-wall clothing shop.

"Grab a table," I said. "I'll just be a minute."

I ducked inside and let my eyes adjust after the bright sunlight. A rack of beach dresses stood in the middle of the room. I was reaching for an orange-and-yellow print when the hanger moved and I spotted a woman on the other side of the rack, flipping through the dresses.

"Hey," I said, but she turned away. Her hair was held with a silver clip today, not the usual ribbon. She'd already bought three dresses on the beach—why did she need more? But then, a woman like Parisa always wanted more dresses, didn't she?

I felt hot and wiggly, embarrassed. Like I should have known she wouldn't want to talk to me when she had the choice. I didn't want a dress anymore. I just wanted to leave.

"I'm sure it was her," I told Adam five minutes later, after a long draw on my beer. We were sitting in the ubiquitous white plastic chairs at one of the ubiquitous white plastic tables, dipping the freshly-fried chips into salsa redolent with peppers and herbs. Tinny music from an old boom box filled the air. "Why would she ignore me like that?"

"Strange. I thought they were going fishing. Granted, shopping does seem more her style."

"Yeah, but after what she said about going out alone? And she would never take that bus if she didn't have to."

"No other way to get up here," Adam said. "Unless she hopped a cargo truck."

Which is how we got home, after we downed too many tacos, walked too far up a dry river bed, got lost, and missed the bus. We didn't see Parisa or Max, or anyone we knew, and that was just fine.

***

"Did you hear?" Jill said. She was standing on the front porch of the lemon-yellow casita next to ours. I'd taken a quick shower after our delightful misadventure, and kinda wished I hadn't been so hasty in the clothing shop—a cool cotton cover-up would be perfect right now.

"They found a woman's body near the river mouth," she continued. "She was partially eaten by a *cocodrilo*. Her body is so badly damaged they can't identify her."

My stomach felt like a *cocodrilo* had bitten it. According to Jill, who spoke fluent Spanish and heard the story from the girl at the beachfront café who'd been interviewed by the *policia estatal*, no one remotely matching the victim's description had been reported missing.

We didn't see Max or Parisa that evening. The mood among the tourists was subdued and I imagined that the Porters, like many others, had stayed in for the night. After dinner, we returned to our front porch, and the sun set with only a handful of silent witnesses.

We didn't see them the next day, either. In truth, we didn't see much of anyone except each other. When we left the casita, it was to grab a quick bite, then hike up the stone trails carved into the hillside to the swimming hole, where we swam and splashed in the waterfall. Though the death of the unidentified woman highlighted the dangers of foreign travel, there was nothing we could do and no point letting it interfere with our plans.

***

Early one morning, we went fishing with a local crew, returning to shore just as other vacationers were ordering their *jugo de naranja* and *huevos rancheros*. That night, we ate dorado we'd caught ourselves, and pronounced it the most delicious dinner ever. We went kayaking again, and Adam talked me into parasailing. We visited with the mystery writers and other tourists, lounged in the sun, and enjoyed not-so-restful siestas in our casita.

One afternoon, Adam decided to actually nap during siesta time, but I was feeling restless. Instead of staying on the beach, I took the trail behind the haciendas up the hillside and over, down toward the river. The trail was well-used and I wasn't worried, even though I had it to myself. Jungle flowers dotted the dense greenery with color. I heard birds I couldn't see, and my skin drank in the cool, damp air.

I hadn't taken a vacation, or even more than three days off in a row, since coming back to Jewel Bay a year and a half ago to take over the Merc, the business my family had run in some form or another since 1910. No reason to let such foolishness continue—I had a great assistant manager and a stellar sales clerk, and a high school student came in every afternoon to pack up our online orders. I might be the heart and soul of the operation, but I wasn't indispensable.

I strolled along the river, eyes and ears alert for snakes and *cocodrilos*. The river began to widen and I saw an opening in the thick growth where it met the ocean.

This must be where it happened. Where the unknown woman died. I shivered. There was no crime scene tape, no *cocodrilo* bones, no signs of death or mayhem. The sense of gloom was all in my head.

I turned to leave and slipped on a pocket of mud. I reached out to catch myself on the nearest tree and as my hand hit a branch, my fingers snared something else.

A black chiffon ribbon.

***

Calling the police in a foreign country isn't as easy as you might think if you've never done it before. Adam's leftover Spanish wasn't up to the job, and when we told the waitress what we wanted and why, she grabbed her throat and her eyes rolled back in her head. While Adam tended to her—you don't run a wilderness camp without some serious medical training—I scanned the beach for other help.

Jackie and Jill were sitting under an umbrella with books in hand. Jill made the call with ease, while Jackie went in search of the young waitress's mother.

The *policia* arrived by boat and interviewed me at a table under the palapa. We spoke in English, thank goodness, since my Spanish hadn't progressed much beyond *cerveza* and dorado. And you don't usually need to talk about beer and dolphinfish when you're being interviewed by the police.

"*Gracias, señora*," the uniformed detective said and rose, signaling the end of our conversation. I noticed how easily he managed the plastic chairs in the sand. "We'll notify the embassy, and if we need more *informacion*, we'll—what's your phrase? Be in touch."

"What's going on?" Max's voice interrupted. "You two lovebirds get caught doing something you shouldn't have?"

The detective faced him. "Your name, *señor*?"

"Max Porter. My wife and I are visiting from Calgary. That's in Canada. What's this about?"

A flicker of recognition that needed no translation crossed the detective's face. "We are just asking questions, *señor*, about the body found by the river. No need to be alarmed." He gestured toward us. "We missed this observant American couple when we did our initial interviews. We missed you and *Señora* Porter as well, did we not?"

He drew out the first syllable of "Porter," gesturing with one hand in a manner so cordial that he might have owned the place. For all I knew, he did.

"We don't know anything worth saying," Max replied. The day was hot and a thin bead of sweat had formed behind his ear.

"Nonetheless, I should like to speak with you."

"Ah, sweetheart, here you are," Max said. "These men would like to chat about the poor woman found in the jaws of the crocodile. Such a tragedy."

Parisa crossed the sandy beach easily, wearing a pair of black leather flip-flops instead of her usual cork-soled platform sandals. As she tilted her head to listen to her husband, I noticed that her hair was held back in a silver clip. I'd seen one like it, I knew. Maybe in one of the beach sellers' trays.

We ordered beer and snacks and sat under an umbrella out of earshot as the officers spoke with the Porters. What Parisa might have known about the *cocodrilo*'s victim, I had no idea. But I knew she'd been in the jungle near the river. I only hoped she'd seen something that would help the police solve the mystery.

The Porters didn't come down to the beach that evening. We saw them the next morning when we came in from snorkeling, sitting at their usual table talking intently. To my surprise, they didn't call out. We waved but didn't stop. It was our last full day in Yelapa, and we wanted to catch another glimpse of the reedy-voiced Mexican parrotlet and take another swim beneath the waterfall.

The late afternoon sun had turned the inlet into a sea of diamonds when we met the mystery writers for margaritas before dinner. They were bubbly and full of chit-chat, and I knew I would enjoy reading their books when we got home.

Max and Parisa joined the crowd on the beach in time for dinner. She was wearing the blue dress I had wanted. I had to admit, it looked great on her. Everything did.

"It would have looked even better on you," Adam whispered into my ear. How did he always know what to say?

For our last night, the tables were covered with bright cloths, a candle and a jar of hibiscus flowers in the center. I tucked a red blossom into my dark hair. A creaky sound system cranked out a motley mix of Mexican songs, reggae tunes, and classic rock.

The Porters were seated a few tables away. I kept sneaking glances at them. Something puzzled me, but I couldn't say what.

No chips and salsa tonight. We started with *ceviche*, the snapper so fresh it was practically still swimming, seasoned with lime and chiles, garnished with cilantro leaves. After that, we had our choice of *cochinita pibil*, the classic slow-roasted pork shoulder with onions pickled in citrus juices, or cilantro salmon with a tomato-*habañero* salsa. We chose one of each to share.

“The only problem with vacation is that it ends,” Adam said. “Look. Even Parisa’s enjoying herself.”

I laughed. That’s what was different. She was actually talking to Max, her features expressive, instead of studying her nails or staring off into space. A bottle of tequila sat on their table, and Max was clearly indulging.

Our dinner came and we dove in, savoring every fresh, spicy bite. I glanced at the Porters. Max had a hand on Parisa’s leg where her dress had ridden up and I knew what had confused me earlier.

No fringe.

And Parisa was eating.

She was eating cilantro.

I pushed back my chair and found Jill. Bless the woman, she asked no questions but made the call, translating my words for the police dispatcher. The American witness had new information that could identify the victim in the Yelapa death, she said, information that would also prove it had been a crime, and identify the killer. They should come immediately.

They did, in two marked boats that drove right up on the shore. Half a dozen officers jumped out, armed, uniformed, and stony-faced. The detective we’d met earlier took Adam and me aside and quizzed me. Then he fired instructions at his men. Two officers spoke to the waitress, who pointed and gestured, giving directions, and the men marched down the beach to where the locals’ tiny houses clung to the hillside. Several barefoot children—where had they come from?—ran ahead, laughing and shouting.

It seemed the officers were well-known and not unwelcome—friends and relatives.

Around us, the other visitors ate and drank, though I could feel curious glances sweep over us. No one left. Something about armed officers standing on the perimeter of a space tends to keep people put.

A few minutes later, the two officers returned with the little man who sold dresses to tourists.

“*Si, Señor* Detective.” He confirmed that Max had followed him off the beach and bought the second blue dress, the one without the fringe. No, he hadn’t asked why. Why would he?

Why indeed?

Señor Detective gestured and his men took Max by the arms. “I am arresting you, *Señor* Porter from Calgary, for the murder of your wife.”

“What? What are you talking about? This is my wife.” Max tried to wave a hand toward the woman in the blue dress without fringe, the woman in flat sandals with a clip in her hair instead of a ribbon. The woman who could eat cilantro without making a face. The woman I'd seen shopping in Puerto Vallarta the day before Max and Parisa arrived on the same flight as Jackie and Jill. The woman who hadn't recognized me in the shop because she had never seen me before.

"She's your wife's cousin," I said. "The one who looks so much like her that even your friends back home can't tell them apart. The one your wife can't—or couldn't—stand."

Max, the man who knew the guidebook backward and forward, had picked this village because it was remote enough that he could take Parisa out into the jungle and be assured of finding harm for her to fall into, yet easy enough for her cousin to reach on her own and take her place.

The detective sent for the bus driver, who confirmed that he'd brought an extra passenger back to Yelapa earlier in the week. We hadn't seen her on the return trip because we'd gone exploring, missed the bus, and hitchhiked back in the bed of a rusty pickup driven by a man we didn't know but who surely lived nearby and would vouch for our story.

"She's *loco*," Max said. "She's been drinking that *raicilla*. She's seeing things."

But I had never been more sober, or more sure.

***

We had time for breakfast the next morning before the water taxi came. Jackie and Jill sat with us—they were leaving, too—and the waitress brought our usual orders.

The eggs were fried to perfection, the corn tortillas bursting with flavor, the tomatoes and avocados the fruit of the gods. Fingers pinched together, I plucked off the cilantro leaves and set them aside.

Vacation may be good for the soul, but it can be murder on the appetite.

THE PIE SISTERS

By Richard Cass

If too many cooks can spoil the broth, can the same be true of bakers and pies?

"Dummy makes a darn good pie, don't she?" Dabney Urquhart said.

"Daddy, I've told you calling Doreen 'dummy' isn't nice. She isn't deaf, you know. She can't help how she is."

"Doesn't know the difference, does she, honey?" he said to Doreen.

He was short, skinny, and bald, pipe arms coming out of the short sleeves of his plaid shirt, liver spots on his scalp. Susanna thought the jug ears and the wattle under his chin made him look more like a rube farmer than a man who owned half the county.

The two of them sat across from Doreen at the big mahogany table, passed down from the first generation of Urquharts, who'd settled this land.

Doreen's moon-faced innocence made her look inert. She didn't talk very much and Susanna was pretty sure there wasn't much going on behind those wide, watery eyes.

"Damn," Dabney said, rising from his chair, as if inside of him a camel was passing through the eye of a needle.

"What is it, Daddy?" Susanna said.

"Those gosh-darn stones." He winced and pressed a hand against his side.

"Was it that third piece of pie?" Susanna watched without pity, her hands folded on the table. Doreen hummed in the back of her throat.

"Get me some bicarb, darling, will you?"

"You know we need to get you into Dr. Townsend's office."

The old man paled further.

"No gosh-darn doctors. All they ever want to do is cut you up and feed you pills. Steal your money."

***

"He's going to be all right, Susanna. But it's good you called. I wish I could convince him to come into the office. I've got a laser that would break those stones right up. He wouldn't have to put up with the pain."

Townsend appreciated Susanna's looks in this town where the females either married at nineteen or left altogether. She wore her black hair short and mussed, a lavender linen shirt with tight stretch jeans, and a city girl's amount of makeup. He had a sudden nostalgia for his residency years in Boston.

Doreen poured him coffee, her tongue peeking out the corner of her mouth. Susanna had gotten her to do some things, as long as they were small and careful. She'd cut him a nice neat piece of rhubarb pie to go with his coffee.

Susanna sighed.

"He is a cuss," she said.

"You must have known that before you came home."

"I only came back to make sure Doreen was being cared for. His health, as you know, isn't what it used to be."

"Yes." Townsend played with his fork. The wedge of pie had a golden-brown crust, the sugar sprinkled on top catching the light like glass. "The kidney stones worry me less than his heart. But he says he won't take any pills."

She made a soft sound of resignation. "He's as stubborn as a child," she said.

She glanced at Doreen.

"Why don't you try that pie, Dr. Townsend? Doreen has become a very good baker. It makes me so happy she's found something she's good at."

Townsend carved the pointed end of the slice away with his fork and ate it. He closed his eyes.

"My, that is good," he said. "What's her secret?"

Susanna smiled, teasing. "Well, that wouldn't be a secret, then. Would it?"

He cut away another bite, dragging a limp piece of leaf from the inside.

"What's this?"

"Oh," Susanna said. "She likes to put the leaves in, too. She says it gives the flavor body."

Townsend frowned.

"All right." He pushed the leaf to one side of his plate. "It is delicious."

***

Dr. Townsend also acted as the medical examiner for the county, so when Dabney Urquhart died two weeks later, the emergency services people called him right after they responded to Susanna's 9-1-1 call.

Townsend stood in the doorway of the downstairs bathroom,

staring at Urquhart's body slumped on the toilet. The state police investigator, Ted Nigel, he knew only slightly, mostly for not talking too much and his habit of sucking caramels all day long.

"Looks innocent enough," Nigel said. "Not sure there's any reason for me to be concerned. What do you think?"

"If I were guessing?" Townsend said. "He had a problem with kidney stones. And wouldn't do a thing about them. Looks like the strain of passing one blew out his heart."

"Dicky ticker," Nigel said.

Townsend remembered one more thing about the investigator, that he liked to play with words.

"I wonder who inherits," Townsend said under his breath.

Nigel perked up. "He doesn't look like a rich man. Or live like one."

"Land rich. He owns three hundred acres fronted on the main road. Developers have been after it forever."

"This time around." Nigel unwrapped a caramel and tucked it in his cheek, giving him the look of an oversized chipmunk. "Boom to bust to boom again."

Townsend looked at the deflated body of Dabney Urquhart and sighed.

"You'll let me know if anything turns up?" Nigel said.

"Of course. But I have to say it looks pretty cut and dried."

***

"Biggest kidney stones I've ever seen," Townsend said over the phone. "I was his primary care guy. I should have pushed him harder to do something. But it was the heart. Abdominal aortic aneurysm. Not at all unusual."

"Then whence the fencing?" Nigel said. "Just scratching a mental itch?"

"Stones like that? Ten, twelve millimeters? Bigger than marbles. Very unusual."

"You know, my father was a GP in Britain during World War II."

So now he knew Nigel was an Anglophile, too. They were the ones who insisted on calling England Britain, even at this late date.

"Really?"

"He treated any number of people from the countryside with terrible kidney stones—because of what they were eating."

Townsend felt a ping.

"Such as?"

"There weren't many vegetables available. They ate beet tops, carrot shoots. Rhubarb leaves."

"Rhubarb," Townsend said.

"Oxalic acid." Nigel pronounced it cheerily. "Highest concentration in the leaves. Baking soda can make it worse. Killed any number of souls in weakened conditions. The sick, pregnant."

Or someone with a damaged heart. Townsend's stomach lurched. He'd eaten a piece of Doreen's rhubarb pie and it hadn't bothered him a bit.

"Interesting," he said. "Thanks for the history lesson."

He set down the phone and shook his head. How could he explain an accident like this to Susanna? She'd be devastated. And could Doreen even understand what she'd done?

***

I like making the crust. Susanna always gets to make the insides but I don't mind. I like to mix the flour and the shortening and the salt, a little bit of ice water. She lets me use the mixer but you can't turn it on too long or else the crust gets tough. The same with rolling out the dough too much. It's okay to use the mixer, as long as Susanna's there.

When I'm all through with the crust, she lays the bottom in the pan. I cut the rest into strips so she can make the crisscross top. I'm all done then, so she sends me in the other room so I can let her work.

***

"Well, I certainly never heard of that," Susanna said. "They're poisonous?"

Townsend researched Nigel's father's story and found it suspect. There had been a death in England attributed to rhubarb leaves but the story's provenance was questionable. All the other legends around the death-dealing qualities of rhubarb seemed to trace back to that one old tale.

"In large enough quantities," he said. "More than anyone could ingest in a single piece of pie."

"Obviously, if I'd known, I wouldn't have let Doreen include them. She said she liked that extra bite of flavor."

"Regardless," he said. "Probably better to have her quit doing that. Wouldn't want anyone to get sick."

Susanna touched her lips with a fingertip.

"Daddy was a glutton for pie," she said. "He'd eat two or three slices a night."

"Not sure that made a difference," Townsend reassured her. "Still."

"Thank you, Doctor. I'll make sure Doreen doesn't do it anymore."

***

Talking's slow but thinking isn't. Susanna doesn't call me Dummy the same way Daddy did, but I can tell she thinks it. It's a lot quieter without him yelling all the time, plus Susanna doesn't have me making pie crust every day, rolling it out, cutting it into strips with the big knife.

She thinks I don't understand the phone calls, either, to the real estate lady with the tight dress, the lawyer, the boss of that place Daddy wanted to send me. When she came home from Boston, she said I could live in the house forever, but she doesn't mean it now.

"This will be our last pie," she says, bright as a bird. "For Dr. Townsend. You can do the filling this time."

She hands me a cup of white powder.

"Mix this in with the fruit," she says.

"Sugar?"

She looks at me sharp, like I said something smart.

"Just a little baking soda, honey. That rhubarb's a little acidy."

She calls me Honey when she wants something else. But she's nervous and smells that way, too, like hot metal.

"Here," she says as the doorbell rings, and hands me a spoon. "The fruit's all done. You can put the crust on top yourself, can't you?"

The voices in the parlor now are Dr. Townsend and that policeman with the candy, from the night Daddy died. Susanna doesn't know how voices carry in this old house, how I heard her talk about sending me away.

I slide the big knife out of the drawer and cut the dough into strips. I don't want to go anywhere and I feel like I want to cry. The filling is full of chopped-up leaves and a white slurry mess. I weave the strips of crust across the top and listen to the conversation in the other room. I hear the word "tomorrow."

Susanna steps back into the kitchen, brushing her hands together like she's dusting the flour off of them.

"Well, that's all taken care of," she says. "What a nice job you're doing."

I turn around from the pastry board and look at her snaky smile. I raise the knife to my shoulder and wonder how it would feel to slide it into her chest. Talking is slow and thinking is faster but doing is the fastest of all.

I look into Susanna's blue eyes and I wonder if we really are sisters at all.

TOO MANY COOKS ALMOST SPOIL THE MURDER

By Lynne Ewing

Baking competitions can be cut-throat, especially when the winner has clearly stolen your *recipes. But how is she doing it? And what can you do to regain your rightful place as champion?*

All three judges smiled as they savored my caramel-chocolate lava cake. The oldest, a thin man with kind eyes, took a second bite. I watched his tongue swirl over his thin lips. “Perfection,” he said.

“Thank you.” I’d caramelized my own sugar, and for an instant, the tick of a clock, I was back in my kitchen whisking in the butter and cream, perfecting my recipe.

I held my breath as Cecily Evers, the celebrity chef, bit into one of my little round cakes.

“Heavenly,” she declared as she wiped a dribble of chocolate from her chin.

Everyone in the auditorium was watching me, everyone except Lindee Wheader who was pressing a dishtowel against her eyes to catch her tears. Her red velvet cake didn’t measure up. I could taste the desperation in her baking—too much vanilla and not enough chocolate. She hadn’t won a competition in three years.

I glanced sideways at Angela Jensen, my bake-off nemesis, who looked nervous behind her huge, batter-spotted glasses. Even she thought I’d won.

The judges walked back to the front of the auditorium and gathered on stage. I waited for them to call my name, Jacqueline Oree.

The microphone screeched as the judge announced, “This year’s winner is . . .”

I was ready to step forward, a gracious but humble smile on my face.

“. . . Angela Jensen for her *moelleux au chocolat au caramel au beurre*. Well, a lot of French words to say her caramel-chocolate lava cake, which is the best of the bake. Come up here, Angela.”

I gulped. She’d stolen my recipe. Again.

My best friend Melanie grabbed my elbow as Angela waddled

up to the stage to rapturous applause that rightfully belonged to me.

"Smile," Melanie whispered. "Don't let her see your distress. You know how she loves to make people feel worse when they're down."

Through a stiff smile that hurt my cheeks, I said, "But it's my recipe."

"You can't know that for sure," Melanie said.

"I'll find out for sure. Taste buds never lie."

While everyone applauded Angela, I snuck over to her station, picked up one of her little disc cakes that looked exactly like mine and stole a bite. Warm delicious chocolate trickled over my lips and down my chin as the salted caramel delighted my tongue.

"Mine!" I shouted, spraying chocolate crumbs over her stove and onto the next workbench.

"What are you doing?" Melanie pulled me back to my own pile of mixing bowls.

"I don't care how many French words she used," I grumbled. "That is my recipe."

"Next time, don't tell her what you're planning to bake."

"I didn't this time. I never spoke a word to her about it."

"Then it was only a coincidence. No one can match your cheesecake. Enter it next time. I'll feature it in my cookbook."

I couldn't think about cheesecake at the moment because Angela was headed toward me, pushing her way through the crowd of bakers who flocked around her, fawning and wanting her secrets. A few even asked her to autograph their aprons.

"All that adoration rightfully belongs to me," I said. "I can't congratulate her."

"You don't have to. I'll congratulate her for both of us." Melanie headed for Angela who swept around her and continued toward me.

"Good contest." She extended her chubby hand, the fingers still greasy with butter. "Too bad they don't give prizes for second place. You would have won a red ribbon."

I hated her victorious grin.

Luckily for me, the local news reporter shoved me aside so I didn't have to shake Angela's slippery hand.

"What are you planning to cook at the next bake-off?" the reporter asked.

"*Tourteau Fromager*."

"And for those of us who don't know French, could you translate?" she asked.

Angela smiled at me. "Cheesecake."

"I'm going to kill her," I whispered to Melanie. "I'll stuff a crouton down her throat. Everyone will think she swallowed wrong. Her table manners are atrocious."

"You need to calm down before you have a heart attack," Melanie whispered. "Your face is flushed and people are starting to stare."

"I'm going to have a few words with the recipe thief."

"That wouldn't be wise." Gently, Melanie led me outside to the parking lot and opened the passenger-side door of her car. "Please don't go back inside. You'll only end up doing something you'll regret later."

"She needs to be exposed," I said as I slid into the car.

"You don't have proof that she stole the recipe, and if you accuse her, you'll only look foolish."

"I don't care what others think. Right is right."

"If you don't care about your own reputation, then worry about mine," Melanie said. "I want to be remembered for my cookbooks, not for being the best friend of the bake-off lunatic Jacqueline who accused the winner of thievery."

"I'm sorry." I wasn't sorry. I thought of a way I could go back inside. "I need to get my equipment."

Melanie patted my shoulder. "I'll collect it for you, and while I'm doing that I want you to concentrate on the next competition and stop agonizing over this one."

I let out a sigh. Melanie was right. I needed to stop grousing and focus on tomorrow. The PTA was hosting its annual competition for after-school snacks. Most likely Angela wouldn't even bother with a little competition like that.

A knock on the car window startled me. Lindee peered inside, her face streaked with flour and frustration.

She started to speak as I rolled down the window. "Angela's stealing your recipes the same way she stole mine. She won't be satisfied until everyone is calling you a has-been baker like me."

"No one calls you a has-been, Lindee." Absolutely everyone did, including the food editor of our local newspaper, who'd compared Lindee's last cake to a stale loaf of brioche. "Did you ever figure out how Angela was stealing your recipes?"

"Family Sharing," Lindee said. "When we were friends starting out, our recipes went up to the Cloud and came down on our shared devices. Somehow she's still using that to get into our computers."

"But I no longer store my recipes on my computer. I write them in my journal."

"Even so you must place your orders for special ingredients online, right? You can't buy Saigon cinnamon or Dutch chocolate locally. And what about Madagascar vanilla and *fleur de sel*?"

I gasped. "Good ingredients make all the difference." I felt ashamed that I hadn't been more careful. I could see that this was partially my fault.

"Are you entering the PTA snack contest?" Lindee asked, changing the subject.

"I am. And you?"

"I won't be there. I'll be home working on my red velvet."

Poor dear. I watched her cross the parking lot, defeat on her shoulders, and wondered if I looked that miserable.

Mentally I gave myself a shake and pushed those thoughts away. In their place, I imagined myself standing in front of the PTA parents and showing them how to make stir-fried oatmeal on the days they were too tired to bake cookies. I'd only shared the recipe with Melanie, who planned to put it in her cookbook under easy recipes.

"Are you feeling better?" Melanie asked as she set a plastic tub filled with my dirty utensils on the back seat.

"I'm feeling as good as a loser can feel." I sniffed.

She climbed into the driver's seat and patted my hand. "Tomorrow you'll win the PTA competition and then you'll feel better."

"I hope so." I needed the win to boost my self-confidence, which was at a deflated-soufflé low.

***

Late Monday afternoon, the PTA met in the Home Economics department at the local high school. I had my ingredients and skillet tucked in my canvas tote.

Angela was already standing at her stove. Butter sizzled in her skillet. She poured a cup of steel-cut oatmeal into the pan.

No! I felt my insides slide. She couldn't.

She added sugar and vanilla, and kept stirring.

Impossible.

I stepped closer and watched the sugar and butter give a crispy coating to the oats that began to cling together.

When she tossed in raisins, my scream ripped through the room. "That's my recipe!"

Everyone stared at me, even Angela who dumped the crispy sweet oatmeal and raisin snack onto a paper towel with a *thump* that turned the attention back to her.

"This is my stir-fried oatmeal," she announced as she sprinkled a pinch of *fleur de sel* over the treat to enhance its flavor. "It's a quick easy snack for the days when you feel too tired to bake oatmeal cookies."

The president of the PTA, a tall woman in a red suit, bit into a cluster of sweet crunchy oats. “Delicious. Kids will love this.”

“Mine.” My voice came out so feeble and thin that no one even glanced at me.

Defeated before I’d even put skillet to flame, I left.

Melanie caught up to me when I was halfway down the block. “The judges are calling your name. Aren’t you going to compete?”

“What for? Angela’s already used my recipe. I wish I knew how she’s stealing my work.”

“Maybe she crawls through that back window that you leave open a smidge in case you’re ever locked out.”

I paused. A definite possibility. She’d only have to remove the screen and then climb inside, an easy reach, even for someone of her short rotund size. I imagined her reading my cooking journal, sampling my butters and tasting the spices I’d ordered from France. This had to stop and I knew how to do it. I said good-bye to Melanie, already plotting my trap.

***

That night, I turned off my phone and worked on my cheesecake recipe. I added three more eggs, cut the sugar in half, and for fun, tagged on a teaspoon of pineapple flavoring and one of cinnamon.

“Here’s something for you to steal, Angela.” I set my bogus recipe on the counter where it would be easy to find.

A key turned in my lock. The back door opened and Melanie stomped into my kitchen. “Why aren’t you answering your phone? You worried me to death.”

“Sorry, I was concentrating on my cheesecake recipe.” I was eager to tell Melanie about my trap. “Will you join me for a cup of Darjeeling tea?”

I set the kettle on the stove, assuming that she would, then went into the dining room to collect my finest porcelain cups from the china cabinet. When I came back, the teakettle was whistling and Melanie was staring at her phone.

“I’ll have to skip the tea,” she said. “My sister’s having car trouble and needs a lift. I’ll see you tomorrow.”

I drank the tea alone. I didn’t even need sugar. My plan was that sweet.

After following my nighttime routine, I turned off the lights, but I didn’t go to bed. Instead I sat at the top of the stairs, in the dark, and waited for Angela to climb through the window.

***

I awakened at an unfortunate angle, my neck sore from leaning against the banister, sunlight already streaking through the windows.

My cell phone chirped.

"Angela's not baking cheesecake," Melanie said when I answered.

"How do you know?" I glanced at the time, unhappy to discover that I'd slept through most of the morning when I should have been baking croutons to fill my mail orders.

"Angela was in the supermarket, buying ingredients for red velvet cake and telling everyone who would listen that she'd decided against her *Tourteau Fromager* because the pineapple and cinnamon that she'd thought would give it a certain *je ne sais quoi* gave it a *je ne sais* not. She said it tasted wretched."

I felt suddenly dizzy. My bogus recipe still sat on the counter where I'd left it, but somehow Angela had not only stolen it, she'd already tested it.

"This can't go on," I said. "We have to break into her house and find out how she's doing this."

"Isn't that against the law?" Melanie sounded worried.

"Of course it is, but so is stealing my recipes." Actually, I wasn't sure about the last fact, but Melanie seemed to accept it as true. "Angela teaches a cooking class tonight. We'll do it then."

That night, I hurried through the shadows to meet Melanie. The scent of Madagascar vanilla saturated the air near her. Normally I loved the pleasant fragrance, but this much was cloying. I could barely breathe and took an unintended step back.

"Sorry about the smell," Melanie said. "I was comparing vanillas for my cookbook and spilled a few drops."

The aroma was unquestionably stronger than a few drops. She must have overturned a bottle. But why lie about something so trivial?

"The lights went off in Angela's house a few minutes ago," Melanie said, turning my mind back to our planned break-in.

"Let's do it." Though I sounded brave, I felt sick to my stomach with anxiety.

We entered the backyard through a side gate and followed the rock path around her spice garden to the porch, a milky glow of moonlight guiding our way.

"That's strange," I said. "Why would she leave her back door open?"

"She's probably airing the kitchen." Melanie didn't sound concerned.

I hesitated. "An open door is an invitation to come in and she's not the welcoming type. Maybe she's set a trap."

"Why would you think that?" Melanie stood in the doorway, her hand on the light switch.

"Because," I explained, "if Angela can steal a recipe so mysteriously, then maybe she's able to listen in on our conversations as well and knows about our plan to break into her house."

"There's only one way to find out." Melanie switched on the light and left me standing on the porch steps.

After a long moment I followed her into the kitchen. Any available wall space was covered with framed pictures of Angela receiving her cooking awards. Pans hung from the ceiling, gently clunking together from the breeze that drifted through the back door.

I took another step and my foot crunched down on broken glass. The smell of Madagascar vanilla that flooded the air wasn't coming from Melanie. A shattered bottle of the expensive flavoring lay on the floor.

"Where do you think a person would hide stolen recipes?" Melanie opened a cupboard filled with spices.

"I'm not sure." I stepped around the huge kitchen island and almost slipped in the cake batter puddled on the floor. "It looks like Angela spilled a bowl of batter and didn't bother to clean it up."

Melanie came over and stood beside me. "Maybe she was running late and had to leave the mess in order to get to her class on time."

I pointed to the whisk that lay on the floor below more splatters on the wall. "I think she threw the whisk in anger. Does she always get so upset with her cooking?"

"Maybe she became frustrated with Lindee's recipe," Melanie suggested.

"A possibility, but why make a mess that you only have to clean up?"

I heard a car door open and glanced at Melanie who stared back at me with terror in her eyes.

"We have to hide." Melanie grabbed my hand and pulled me toward the pantry.

I wrenched back. "We can't hide in there. If she's returning because she forgot an ingredient, the pantry is the first place she'll look. We need to leave."

The knob on the back door was turning.

"She'll see us if we dart across the kitchen now." Melanie slid the pantry door open and yanked me into the dark.

"We left the kitchen light on," Melanie whispered, shivering violently against me. Her stone-cold hands gave me goose bumps.

Whoever it was stepped around the kitchen island, the batter acting as an adhesive that gave a slurpy kissing sound to each step.

A moment of silence followed and then the pantry door slid open.

Melanie screamed, her fingernails piercing my skin.

I stared at Lindee Wheader who screamed in return and looked ready to pass out. When she started to fall, I caught her before she collapsed in a faint.

Melanie and I helped her into the living room, all three of us tracking pink cake batter across the blue carpet.

"Lindee, are you all right?" Melanie asked as we propped her on the couch. "Do we need to call the paramedics?"

"You scared me to death," Lindee said. "What were you doing in Angela's pantry?"

"The same as you." I sat beside her and rubbed her back. "We're trying to find out how Angela has been stealing our recipes."

Lindee started to cry. "I'm desperate. I added a cream cheese filling to my red velvet cake and somehow she got my recipe and plans to use it at the next bake-off."

"How do you know?" Melanie asked.

"My cousin works as a cashier in the supermarket. Angela told her that she'd perfected her red velvet cake by adding a cream cheese filling. My recipe! But this time she's not getting away with it." Lindee pulled a small bottle of garlic juice from her pocket and held it up as if it were a flask of poison. "I'm going to sabotage her ingredients."

Before I could stop her, she raced into the kitchen, entered the pantry, flicked on the light and froze. The bottle fell from her hand and shattered, the smell of garlic stinging my nose as Lindee suddenly pressed back against me, stepping on my toes.

"Move back!" she yelled.

"Lindee, what's wrong?" I asked.

"Call the police," she said in a shaky voice.

Melanie and I peered over her shoulder.

Almost hidden behind dozens of fallen baking pans, cake flours, and bags of sugar, Angela sat on the floor, her head propped against a broken shelf, blood and pink cake batter drying on her gray-blue face. Her cell phone was on the floor as if she'd tried to call for help.

"Is she . . . dead?" Lindee asked.

"She certainly looks it," Melanie replied.

"She's dead," I whispered. "Let's make the call."

We backed out of the pantry and used Angela's landline to call the police.

***

Less than an hour later, we sat on the couch, breathing the odd mix of vanilla and garlic, as the detective, a large, bald man with a deep scar on his neck, paced back and forth, reading his notes.

The coroner was in the pantry with a police officer, examining the recently deceased Angela.

We'd already explained to the detective how we'd found Angela's body and why we'd entered her home. He kept looking at us and shaking his head, which made me feel like a criminal.

I was wondering what it would be like to cook for hundreds of inmates in prison when the detective asked, "Can you think of anyone who might have wanted to kill her?"

Did his question mean he didn't think we were guilty?

"Anyone who knew her had reason enough." Lindee's words broke through her sobs.

While she recounted all the foul things Angela had done, I reviewed the evening again and something occurred to me. I nudged Melanie. "Let me borrow your phone, dear."

Without questioning my motive, she handed it to me. I looked at the first picture in her camera roll and sighed. "Detective, you don't need to collect fingerprints or DNA. I know who killed Angela."

"It was Lindee," Melanie said before I could speak. "I figured it out, too."

"I did not." Lindee sat up taller and wiped her eyes.

"When you learned that Angela was making your red velvet cake, you came here and confronted her. The argument got heated, words turned into fists, and while you were fighting, the cake batter spilled. You hit her with one final blow and when you realized she was dead, you hid her in the pantry and left. But then you came back because you realized you'd forgotten your recipe. That's why you were so terrified when you opened the pantry door and saw us. You thought Angela had come back from the dead."

"That's not what happened," Lindee said.

"Then tell us what did happen." The detective looked at Lindee, pulled a pen from his pocket, and opened his notebook again.

"I came in through the back door and startled Angela, and that caused her to knock over the bowl of batter. I grabbed my recipe off the counter and started to leave, but she was screaming that it was her recipe. She rushed after me, slipped in the batter, fell and hit her forehead on the counter edge. She stood up on her own, blood and cake batter dripping down her face, and continued to yell that the recipe was hers. When she threw the wire whisk at me, I ran."

"Then why did you return?" the detective asked.

"After I got home, I realized that Angela could still bake my cake and win with my recipe unless I did something drastic. She teaches a cooking class on Tuesday nights so I came back with a bottle of garlic juice, determined to sabotage her ingredients."

"You knew she was dead," Melanie said. "The real reason you came back was to wipe away your fingerprints and make sure you hadn't left more clues than your recipe."

"That's not true." Poor Lindee was trembling.

I couldn't let her take the blame for something she hadn't done, though that meant betraying my best friend. "Detective, Lindee isn't the killer."

"Then who is?" he asked.

"The same person who's been stealing our recipes." I looked at Melanie, my heart breaking. "I should have figured it out sooner because I'd only told Melanie about my recipe for stir-fried oatmeal—"

"Stir-fried oatmeal?" He gave me a quizzical look.

"It's quite tasty, really. Melanie was the only one who knew about my snack idea and yet Angela used it at the PTA snack competition."

"I never gave her your recipe," Melanie insisted. "She stole your notes."

"But I never made notes for such a simple recipe. And last night while I was collecting the cups for our tea, you took a picture of my bogus cheesecake recipe that I'd left on the counter."

"I did not."

"But you did. The picture is still on your phone. You deleted your text to Angela, but you forgot to delete the original picture." I turned the phone so the detective could see the screen. "And, Melanie, your sister never called. That was the lie you told me so you could leave and talk to Angela."

"All right, I stole the recipes," Melanie confessed.

"You stole my red velvet!" Lindee looked ready to pounce, seeming to miss the fact that I'd accused Melanie of murder. Or perhaps the theft of the recipes was the greater crime in her mind.

"Angela came up with the idea," Melanie said. "Because she'd won so many bake-offs, the sales of my cookbooks would skyrocket if she gave me a front cover endorsement, which she offered to do, but in exchange she needed a little help to ensure her continued success."

"Our recipes!"

Melanie bent her head in shame, her tears dripping onto her hands. "It was easy to do because you both trusted me."

"Not anymore," Lindee mumbled.

Melanie looked at the detective. "I stole the recipes, but I didn't kill Angela."

"The evidence is against you," I said. "When I met you tonight, the scent of vanilla clung to you, and later, when we got to Angela's house, there was a broken bottle of vanilla on the floor. Obviously, you'd visited her earlier."

"I did, but only to tell her I wasn't going to steal any more recipes," Melanie explained. "She went into a rage and threw the bottle of vanilla at me. The flavoring splashed on me when the bottle shattered on the floor. I left and went looking for you. That's why I know Lindee killed her. Angela was alive when I left."

"But I didn't kill her!" Lindee yelled.

"No one killed her." The coroner stepped into the living room holding an evidence bag with a crouton inside. "Her death was an accident. She simply swallowed wrong. A crouton obstructed her airway. She died of asphyxiation."

***

That night, no one even questioned me about the spicy Caesar salad that I'd left on Angela's kitchen table. Everyone assumed she'd tossed it herself. After all, she was always stealing my recipes.

I had been the last one to visit Angela, who still had cake batter and blood smeared on her face. I flattered her out of her foul mood and asked her to sample a crouton from my new recipe.

I had cut the crouton down to the precise size needed—it's amazing what you can find on the internet these days.

The moment she popped the crouton into her mouth, I pinched her nostrils, clapped my hand over her mouth and waited until her eyes widened and her struggle weakened, then I released my hold on her mouth.

She gasped, sucking in air, and the crouton, crisply baked, flew down her throat on her last breath. She wheezed and choked but didn't have enough air to curse me. I stayed long enough to watch her stagger into the pantry and grab her cell phone from the shelf where she'd left it. But by that time she was already dying.

Melanie is the only one who doubts the coroner's report. I've noticed lately that she's reluctant to try my new recipes. I can't say that I blame her.

PIG LICKIN' GOOD

By Debra H. Goldstein

Pig Lickin' cake is a traditional Southern treat. Mama's were always a huge hit at the annual fundraiser, even if the making of them brought back memories of a tragedy . . .

My mama knew how to make a cake. You could guarantee if there was a church bazaar or potluck where desserts were going to be auctioned off, Father Horst would stop by our house a few weeks ahead of time to ask Mama to donate two of her cakes. Normally, he didn't care what kind of cakes Mama made, but for the annual Ladies Auxiliary Fourth of July Potluck fundraiser, he'd come, hat in hand, sweet talking her to bake two of her Pig Lickin' cakes. He'd tell her there wasn't anyone else in the whole county who made a cake as light and moist as her Mandarin orange specialty.

Even though she hated the ladies of the auxiliary, she'd do anything for him—even breaking the promise she made every year to never make another Pig Lickin' cake. According to Mama, she owed him. Father Horst was the only one who spoke up and said Daddy shouldn't be on death row.

Not that it had made a difference. Everyone from around here, 'cept Mama and Father Horst, knew it was an open and shut case. After all, they had a dead man, a suspect standing over the body, and a bloody knife pried from Daddy's left hand. The jury wasn't even out for an hour before it came back with its guilty verdict. It was clear to the jurors that Daddy had killed Judd Brown.

The first few times we went to church after the trial, we sat in the same center pew we always had. Mama stared straight ahead, but I saw the ladies of the auxiliary point at us and I heard their whispers. They thought an eight-year-old was too young to understand what they were saying, but I wasn't. That's how I learned the details of Daddy's trial, and that while nobody was particularly sorry Judd Brown was dead, they sure pitied Mama and me.

On the Sunday right after the hearing, instead of listening to Father Horst's sermon, Ms. Ida and Ms. Mae, the president and vice-president of the auxiliary, whispered in hushed tones to anyone who hadn't crowded into the courtroom about how they testified, hand on the Bible. They wanted everyone to know that the last day Judd Brown took a breath on this earth, they walked into the church's kitchen and saw Judd lying on the ground with Daddy bent over him. Daddy's left hand was curled around the handle of the knife stuck in Judd's chest. He used his right hand to wave them back.

Even though Ms. Ida kept her voice low, I heard every word she said. "I screamed! He turned and stared at me with the coldest eyes I've ever seen. Even now, if I shut my eyes, I can still see those—hard and cold pieces of coal twinkling with the brilliance of a diamond."

I squeezed my eyes as tightly closed as I could, but the only eyes that came into my mind were soft brown ones that matched my cocker spaniel's.

The year after Daddy went away, after Father Horst came by the house before the Fourth of July Potluck, Mama started letting me help her make her Pig Lickin' cakes. My job, like Daddy's used to be when he helped her, was gathering up the ingredients to make the second cake. I got a yellow cake mix, can of mandarin oranges, vanilla pudding mix, powdered sugar, vanilla extract, and a can of crushed pineapple out of the pantry. The margarine, four eggs, and Cool Whip came from our refrigerator.

Once I placed the ingredients on the table, I kept quiet so instead of sending me out to play, she'd let me watch her add the cake mix, stick of softened margarine, teaspoon of vanilla extract, and half cup of the orange syrup drained from the canned oranges into the bowl of her electric mixer. After she mixed everything on medium-high for four minutes, she declared the mix to be well-blended. I didn't know about that, but it sure looked real light and fluffy before she dumped the drained oranges into the bowl. She mixed those up, too, until they broke into itty bitty pieces.

Satisfied, she tipped the mixer back and poured the batter from the bowl into a nine-by-thirteen pan and put it into the oven at 350 degrees. After she set a timer for thirty minutes, she returned to where I waited near the mixer.

When she said "Go," we each reached for a beater to lick clean. It felt a little funny. For the first time since I'd ever played the beater game, Daddy wasn't there jostling me before he let me grab the right beater.

As the years went by, Mama and I fell into a pattern of making the cakes together and then I'd deliver them to the church. I think Ms. Mae, still a fixture of the Ladies Auxiliary, must have forgotten who I was because whenever she told the story of her day in court, she stopped whispering around me.

I heard her tale so many times I got so I could predict when she was going to pause and pull out her hanky, monogrammed with its big *M*, to dab her eyes. After her silent moment, she'd look at whoever was listening and tell them how she cried on the stand as she explained to the jury how she screamed when Daddy yanked the cake knife out of Judd's chest. "He held it in his hand. We weren't going to wait and see what he did with it. Ida and I ran from that kitchen. We were plumb afraid he was going to use that knife on us. It's a miracle he didn't follow us."

He didn't. He simply stood there according to our police chief's testimony that I read in a copy of the trial transcript Mama left on the kitchen counter one night. I guess she'd been trying to write something to convince the governor not to electrocute Daddy. Usually she worked on things to save Daddy only when I went to bed or wasn't home, but I guess something had distracted her and she forgot to put the transcript up. What with the date set for Daddy's electrocution and me getting ready to graduate high school and move on to Mississippi State, she might have forgotten to make the Pig Lickin' cakes if Father Horst hadn't reminded her about them when he made a special trip to our house to pick up the letter to the governor.

She couldn't say no to the good father, but for the first time that day, after the cake cooled and I washed the mixing bowl and beaters, Mama let me make the icing. Under her watchful eye, I carefully drained the can of pineapple, putting its liquid aside. I put the vanilla pudding mix in my clean mixing bowl, poured the pineapple juice onto it, and added half a cup of powdered sugar. I ran the mixer until all my ingredients were combined. Then, I whipped in about half a carton of the Cool Whip that had softened in the refrigerator. Once everything looked fluffy, I stirred in the drained crushed pineapple.

Mama ran her index finger over her beater. When she plopped her finger into her mouth, the shine of the wedding ring she still wore caught my eye.

"Perfect. I think the cake is cool, so you can turn it over onto the white platter and then spread the icing onto it."

I kept silent. Mama wasn't done talking.

"Don't forget to cover the sides. You wouldn't believe how many people forget to cover an entire cake."

I nodded. I'd seen plenty of cakes at the church bazaars that were heavy on icing on the top but barely touched on the sides.

"Once you spread that icing evenly, put the cakes in the refrigerator until you take them to the church tomorrow. I'm going to bed. I'm tired." She kissed my head and left me with the two cakes to ice and the transcript sitting on the counter to read.

The police chief's testimony was straightforward. "I pulled my gun before I walked into the kitchen in case he went crazy on us like Ida and Mae seemed to think he would, but he simply stood between the kitchen counter and where Judd lay. He still was holding that big cake knife in his left hand. I told him to drop it. He stared at me for a second before he let the knife fall from his fingers and held his hands out toward me. I guess he thought I'd handcuff him immediately. Instead, I kept my gun pointed at him while my deputy bagged the knife. Once my deputy was beyond his reach, I holstered my gun and cuffed him. He came peacefully with me."

After Daddy was sent to meet his maker, Mama hid the transcript in a drawer with a lock of his hair, a picture of the two of them and a very young Father Horst cutting up when the three might have been in high school, and a picture someone snapped of a more serious Father Horst marrying Mama and Daddy. Because nothing in that drawer ever moved between the times I looked through it, I decided Mama never opened the drawer. That's why, the year I went to law school, I took the Pig Lickin' cake recipe she'd written out and the transcript from the drawer with me. I don't know what I hoped to do with the transcript, but I thought having it might help me find answers to the many questions running around inside my head.

In law school, I was taught never to ask a question in a courtroom if I didn't already know the answer to it. My instructor used the example of a man accused of biting off the nose of the man he was fighting with. A witness had identified the lawyer's client. The lawyer asked, "Did you see my client bite off the plaintiff's nose?"

"No, sir," the witness answered.

Triumphantly, the lawyer postured for the entire courtroom. "Then, how can you say my client is the guilty party?"

"Because I saw him spit it out."

I guess Daddy's court-appointed lawyer missed that lesson because he asked the police chief, "How can you say my client is guilty?"

The police chief's answer was short and sweet. "The icing on his fingers."

"Icing?"

"Yes. There was a Pig Lickin' cake sitting on the counter. I guess he tried to cut himself a piece with the knife before he ended up using it on Judd."

"What makes you so sure he'd used the knife?"

"There was an indentation in the icing of the cake and icing on both the defendant's hand and the knife. There wasn't icing anywhere else in the kitchen except on the cake itself."

The transcript reported a laugh, but I don't know if it was the police chief reacting to his joke or from the courtroom audience chuckling. It didn't matter; the jury agreed the icing on his fingers and knife was enough evidence for Daddy's conviction. Still, something gnawed at me whenever I made and brought one of those easy-to-make Pig Lickin' cakes to a potluck or a party.

I'd take my finished cake from the refrigerator, cut it in squares, and at the last minute carefully place a mandarin orange on top of each square exactly like I'd done before I took Mama's cakes to the church. I had to be careful not to graze the top of the cake as I placed the oranges on each piece to avoid messing up the icing.

That's when it probably hit me, but I didn't put it all together until I came home for Mama's funeral after Father Horst called me at my New York law office to tell me she'd died unexpectedly. Crazed by the empty house, I made two Pig Lickin' cakes for the coffee and cake reception that was going to be held after her memorial service.

Father Horst came by the house to pay his respects the night before the funeral. He followed me into the kitchen after I offered to make him a cup of coffee. When I reached into the refrigerator for milk, he saw the iced cakes.

"They're for the reception. I had to make something."

"Those are perfect. I'm going back to the church when I leave here. Would you like me to put them in the fellowship hall refrigerator for you?"

"That would be most kind, but do you have the time to wait while I top each square with a mandarin orange?"

"No problem." He took the milk container from me, poured some into his coffee, and handed the container back to me. While it was still hot, he picked up the mug and turned its handle away from where I stood to his left. My eyes rested on his hands while he continued talking until I had to concentrate on putting the mandarin slices on each piece of cake without getting icing on my hand.

"I'm going to miss your mother. You know, your daddy and she were my friends long before they ever got married. Why, if she hadn't had eyes only for him, I might not have taken my vows and could have ended up being your daddy."

I kept my lips pressed together.

Father Horst smiled as he leaned forward, giving his lips a little lick. “Know what I’m going to miss the most?”

“No, sir. I don’t.”

He pointed toward where I was placing mandarin orange slices on the last few cake squares. “Her Pig Lickin’ cakes.”

“But she only made those once a year.” I glanced at my hand. As much as I’d tried to be careful, I’d still gotten a little icing on it.

“Not until . . .” his voice trailed off. When he spoke again, he’d moved on to a slight variation of his topic. “Of all her cakes, these were always my favorite. I used to run the bidding up on them during the church’s silent auction until I could guarantee winning one of them. I’d pay for it and while everyone was busy eating, I’d slip away from the social hall to take my cake to the rectory. I wasn’t going to share it with anyone.”

He laughed. “I confess and hope you’ll absolve me of my guilt about loving your mother’s Pig Lickin’ cakes.”

“And should I absolve you of loving her so much you let an innocent man be put to death?”

Father Horst moved away from me. “I don’t understand.”

“But I do.” I held up my right hand which still had traces of icing on it. I got up and walked toward the sink. Deliberately, I washed my hands and dried them with a dishtowel. Turning back, I met his gaze.

“Daddy was right-handed like me, but the police chief mentioned Daddy’s left hand when he testified about the icing and the knife. If Daddy tasted the icing or put an orange on the cake, he would have instinctively used his right hand, so the icing would have been on his right hand like it was on mine. That means he intentionally got icing on his left hand.”

Father Horst narrowed his eyes, so I could barely see his pupils. “You’re not making sense. We all unconsciously use different hands to do different things depending upon how we’re standing.”

“When you pointed, took the milk container from me, or poured milk into your coffee, you used your dominant right hand. You even turned the coffee mug so you could hold its handle with your right hand. That’s what we do unconsciously. Mama was a lefty. That’s why she always grabbed the left mixing bowl beater while Daddy and I fought over the right one. She would have gotten icing on her left hand while putting the last touches on the cake. From the things I’ve heard about Judd Brown’s lewd behavior, you probably know why she stabbed him, but that doesn’t matter anymore. I gather when she came to you to confess, she told you something like Daddy came in, sized up the situation, sent her from the room, and grabbed the knife with his left hand to make it look like he was the one who'd killed Judd."

Father Horst stood silently in front of me, his mouth clenched tightly.

"Did you love her so much you wouldn't turn her in?"

"No, I loved God and my vows more than her. I took a vow of confidentiality, respecting matters heard in confession. I couldn't convince her to go against the agreement to be silent she'd made with your father, but I spoke out on his behalf and against capital punishment."

Now it was my turn to be confused. "But you tormented her by coming around every Fourth of July for those blasted Pig Lickin' cakes. That's a strange way to show you love someone."

"You misunderstand. That was my way of showing God's love for your mother. Her penance was having to make two Pig Lickin' cakes on each anniversary of the murder. I simply helped give her an avenue through which to make her act of penance."

He reached for my hand, but I shook him away. I got through the service and returned to New York that night. The first thing I did was tear up the Pig Lickin' cake recipe Mama had written out for me. It didn't matter how Pig Lickin' good or easy that cake was, I knew I'd never make one again.

QUICHE ALAIN

By Marni Graff

Wanda Jackson, filming her autobiographical television movie, insists on authenticity in the bistro scene—and that includes her former lover's famous quiche.

The raspy drawl of Louis Armstrong singing "La Vie en Rose" filled the French bistro decorated with rattan and wood chairs.

Three couples sat at round marble-topped tables, having coffee as a waiter carried a steaming cup of hot chocolate to an elegantly made-up woman in her late seventies, seated alone. Her red hair and floral dress were accented by an armful of gold bangle bracelets. She angled her head in thanks as the large cup was set in front of her.

The waiter bowed and glided away. The woman took a delicate sip, then looked up in confusion that quickly turned to joy as a white-haired man appeared before her. He placed a croissant next to her cup, and took the opposite chair.

"Alain! It's really you," she whispered.

"*Oui*, my dear," he said with a trace of French accent. "Now eat to keep your strength up. We have a lot to talk about." His hand covered hers in an intimate gesture.

She smiled and bit into the croissant, her bracelets tinkling, then chewed and frowned. She spit out the morsel and yelled, "What kind of crap is this?"

"Cut!" The director's voice boomed from the control room.

I gave my best friend, production assistant Meg Pittman, a look of sympathy as she hurried to Wanda Jackson, the actress starring in this television movie. My charge was up to her usual hijinks.

"Wanda, what's wrong?" Meg's brow furrowed over brown doe eyes.

The control booth door slammed as the director, Ron Dowling, rushed in. "Yes, Wanda darling, whatever is the matter?"

Ron Dowling wasn't my favorite director. The short, intense man had a cocky attitude and liked to keep women in their place—beneath his tiny, Birkenstock-clad feet—unless they were the money draw for a project, like Wanda Jackson.

My name is Trudy Genova, RN, and I work as a medical consultant for the Passion Broadcasting Junction studio in Manhattan. I check medical scenes in scripts, work on set with actors and directors, but can also be the medic for a particular star.

This was my job for Wanda Jackson, the Oscar-and-Tony-award winner, who had been teaching acting at NYU's Tisch Film School until her health declined and she decided to publish a memoir. PBJ convinced her to film her story and play herself in the final scenes.

It was difficult. Severe arthritis and osteoporosis made her daily life painful, and Wanda had a major heart condition few people knew about. She planned to retire from public life once this movie was in the can.

That brought us to today, filming the last scene of the movie to be released the same day her book will be published. *Wanda Jackson: The Untold Story* would be sold all over the world, in Kindle and hardcover, from Audible to the DVD of this movie. That the untold story only matched the reality of Wanda's life at times didn't seem to bother anyone working on the project.

Like in this final scene, in which Wanda supposedly reunites with the love of her life, celebrated New York chef Alain Duchamp.

In reality, Wanda and Alain never fully reconciled after she'd refused to have his children in favor of her career, or so studio gossip went. They reconnected for torrid spells, yet broke up repeatedly. As the years advanced, she finally avoided him and his restaurants completely—well, perhaps until now. I'd heard Alain recently refused her entry to his restaurant, named after his famous dish, Quiche Alain. But who knew if that was true? Gossip was rampant on a movie set.

I watched from my perch out of camera range in case Wanda needed me. The actress fixed Dowling with a scathing look.

"You want to know what's the matter? Where should I start?" Wanda's Texas drawl became more pronounced when she was annoyed. She held up one gnarled hand, graced with sapphire and ruby rings, and counted off. "First, that croissant tasted like cardboard. I have no idea where you found that travesty, but the baker has obviously never been to France. Get me something that tastes like Paris to put me in the proper mood."

Dowling scowled. Meg blushed. She'd run up to the Au Bon Pain on the corner that morning.

"Second." Wanda ticked off another finger. "That waiter should wear a crisp white apron, top folded inside, tied around his waist. And third, you *cannot* have American Louis Armstrong singing an iconic French song. Find a recording of the original Edith Piaf version—in French, mind you." She smiled sweetly.

I anticipated the sarcasm Dowling had trouble controlling. "You still have two fingers on that hand."

Wanda tilted her head to one side and pretended to think. She could best him any day. I liked her for it. "No, that will do."

Dowling drew himself up to his brief height and called out to the prop master. "Barney, take care of the apron." He raised his voice. "Sound? Get me Piaf, in French." He sneered at Wanda. "Not sure the food needs to be changed. Can't you just *pretend* to eat the damn thing—it's called acting."

I saw the twist of scorn on Wanda's mouth and knew Dowling had overplayed his hand.

Wanda crooked her finger. "Trudy, my wheelchair. Get me away from this Neanderthal. We're done here."

I rushed forward with her chair and helped Wanda stand to pivot into it. She could shuffle a few steps, but normal walking was beyond her. Wanda stifled a moan as she sat down. With her most recent fractured vertebrae still healing—aging must really be a bitch—how she turned up at the studio every day was a miracle.

As I adjusted her legs on the footrest, I watched Meg pull out her cell to call Inchul Jones, Wanda's driver and houseman, to bring her car around earlier than planned. The part-Asian man was wiry, strong, and surprisingly tall. He always gently carried Wanda into and out of her car.

Dowling rushed to limit the damage. "Now, Wanda, we can get any food you like. Brioche? Maybe a nice baguette?" He rose to the tips of his elfin toes in anticipation of her answer.

Wanda looked him up and down, which didn't take long. "I want something I can take small bites of, something incredibly French—I want Quiche Alain!"

Silence fell over the soundstage at this unlikely declaration. Meg hurried from the studio, cell phone again at her ear, to try to put this fire out.

With that pronouncement, Wanda waved me on. I dutifully pushed her around thick cables that lined the floor, deftly weaving between the cameras, to the heavy soundstage door. Dowling hurried after us.

"Wanda, be reasonable. There's a six-month waiting list just to get into Quiche Alain."

And they don't do take out.

Wanda raised her chin and glared at Dowling. "You want me here tomorrow? Find me a piece of Quiche Alain. Trudy, let's go."

Dowling hurried to open the hefty door but let it slam behind us, his frustration overcoming his good sense.

I had a feeling this would not end well.

***

Wanda and I waited outside the studio. The red brick armory building looked like a castle, complete with turret. It was used for the popular soap *Thornfield Place*, filming on location this week while we finished these final scenes for our movie. Situated down the block from Lincoln Center, the studio stood in the precinct of my boyfriend, NYPD Detective Ned O'Malley, and his junior partner, Tony Borelli. Tony and Meg had been dating longer than us, but the four of us made a good team.

Wanda sighed, bringing me back to the present.

"Do you need pain medication, Wanda?" I'd originally called her Ms. Jackson, only to be told she was Wanda to everyone. When I worked with her, I dispensed Wanda's pills; when she left the studio, I gave her medication over to her caretaker, Lettie Thompson, a sturdy woman who'd been Wanda's best friend back in Texas.

Wanda patted my hand. "No, thanks, dear. I'll wait for home, or it's much harder for Inchul to get me inside. Once I'm settled the pain relief will be grand—not much else to look forward to these days. Except a crisp martini."

I kept silent as we watched the traffic roar past the studio on this bright fall day, the cacophony of taxis and heavy trucks mixed with limos and cars that complemented the city.

She patted my hand. "Don't get old, Trudy. It's hellish."

I leaned down to whisper in her ear. "But you do it with such grace and panache." I caught a strong whiff of Estēe Lauder's Youth-Dew, liberally applied each morning. The woody, earthy scent from the 1950s was Wanda's signature scent. I lightly kissed her soft, powdery cheek. In just a few months, I'd become fond of her.

She smiled. "You're a good girl, Trudy. Tell Meg if she reaches Alain to say, 'Tootsie says please.'"

A black Lincoln Town Car slid in front of the curb and Inchul Jones jumped out. The older gent wore a bolo tie with his cowboy boots and jeans in deference to Wanda's roots. He raised an eyebrow, concern evident on his face, as he checked Wanda's condition. "You're early, Wanda. I was winning that last poker hand, too." He opened the rear door.

Inchul liked to pretend he spent his downtime playing cards and slinging whiskey in a local saloon. Manhattan was hardly the Old West. Wanda told me he'd been devoted to her for years, and while she worked, he parked at a friend's garage, then sat in a diner doing crossword puzzles and drinking coffee.

"Wanda's decided she's done for the day," I explained, rolling her closer to the curb even as I rolled my eyes at Inchul. "I'm not sure Dowling agreed."

Together we helped Wanda stand and slide onto the seat. Her moan was pitiful, and Inchul frowned even as he kissed the top of her head.

"Wanda needs meds as soon as she's settled at home, Inchul." I handed over the pill vial and clipped Wanda's seatbelt.

The actress leaned back, seemingly exhausted by that slight exertion. I wondered how much was physical and how much emotional. With her heart condition, it was difficult to tell.

Inchul patted her hand, then stowed her chair in the trunk. I redid my ponytail as the car pulled away from the curb, then went inside to tell Meg about Tootsie.

***

That evening Meg told me she'd left two messages for Alain Duchamp, one with the request for a piece of his namesake quiche to use in filming, and the second, "Tell him Tootsie says please." The maître d' had assured Meg the chef had received her messages.

This morning I found Meg in the PBJ lobby, tucking her cell away when I arrived. "Any luck?"

She beamed. "Lettie texted. Alain dropped off an entire quiche!" We high-fived each other. "Look at us, excited over an egg-and-cheese tart."

Wanda's Town Car pulled up and I hurried outside to help. Today would be the end of filming, with a luncheon planned for afterward, Inchul and Lettie included. The tall woman exited the far side of the car holding a pink bakery box aloft in triumph. Inchul opened the curbside back door with a flourish for Wanda, unclipped her seat belt and kissed her hand, then popped the trunk.

He opened her wheelchair, scooped her up, and helped me settle Wanda. She wore the flowing dress she'd worn yesterday for continuity, a personal favorite from her own closet. But she looked drawn, with dark circles under both eyes. Pain creased her face.

"Bad night," Lettie whispered. Wanda groaned as she adjusted herself. Lettie's eyes misted over. "Stubborn cow would only take half a pill before we left." She handed me the vial.

"Do you want the other half, Wanda?" I jiggled the pills. "Maybe with a cup of tea?"

"No, Trudy, I just want this damn scene finished. Then I'll take a whole one, promise."

It was a quiet trio who accompanied Wanda. Inchul pushed the wheelchair inside, and Lettie carried the pink box, while I led the way to hair and makeup. The two would stay for the filming of this last scene before the congratulatory luncheon.

Things move slowly in filming, and this morning was no exception. Dowling pranced around as if he'd baked the quiche himself. The box was passed to the prop master for safe keeping. A gaffer instructed his best boy to adjust several klieg lights, moving the carbon arc lamps with a long pole. Once Wanda was wheeled onto the set an hour later, the actor playing Alain told her she looked lovely.

In reality, Wanda looked like hell. The makeup gal had done her best to hide the circles under Wanda's eyes, but the rings of pale concealer made her look like a ghost. It was clear she was suffering, and I wondered about a fresh fracture. I told Lettie I might need her help to persuade Wanda to have an X-ray taken once we were done.

Lettie shook her head. "After the luncheon, maybe. This is her swan song. She won't hear of missing it."

I nodded but felt unhappy. Wanda had refused the other half of her pain pill again. She had to be in agony.

Finally filming started. Edith Piaf sang "La Vie en Rose." Her bird-like voice singing in her native French added a huge impact to the bistro feel. Extras pretended to chat and drink at the little tables.

After two false starts for microphone adjustments, the assistant director snapped the clapperboard and yelled, "Action!"

The waiter, this time appropriately aproned, placed a steaming cup of hot chocolate in front of Wanda. She sniffed appreciatively, closed her eyes and raised her chin, and for a moment, I could believe she was reliving special Paris days, waiting for her lover.

The actor playing Alain Duchamp appeared, holding a thick wedge of Quiche Alain aloft. Wanda's face lit up; her eyes glowed.

"Alain . . . it's really you."

He put the dish down and took a seat. "Yes, dear. Now eat to keep your strength up. We have a lot to catch up on."

Over the next twenty minutes they reshot the scene three times. Each time they uttered their lines, Wanda ate a piece of quiche as if it were the first time.

On take four, Wanda swallowed a forkful of quiche, made an appreciative noise, and took another bite. She sipped her chocolate, and "Alain" took her hand in his as their eyes met.

"And cut! That's it, folks, in the can!" Dowling's voice boomed from the control booth. The klieg lights shut off with a loud thunk, leaving low lights on. The actor playing Alain thanked Wanda and left to take off his makeup. Wanda dropped her fork, her hand trembling. She frowned at her shaking hand. She tried to talk, but her lips juddered and her tongue seemed thick in her mouth. Was she having a stroke?

“Meg, call an ambulance.” I swung into action and rushed Wanda’s wheelchair over and Inchul helped her transfer. She grabbed her stomach, her eyes beseeching me. *Oh, Lord, what’s happening?* I ran the chair to the next set, her bedroom. “Inchul, help me get her on the bed.”

He had tears in his eyes as he carefully lifted Wanda onto the bed and kissed her cheek. Lettie piled blankets on her while Meg brought my bag. I fought to check Wanda’s blood pressure as she began thrashing about, drooling copiously, her lips turning blue.

“Palp 60, she’s crashing!”

Dowling joined the bedside group and had sense enough to keep his mouth shut. Meg charged over with the studio’s defibrillator as Wanda started a full convulsion. Lettie helped me turn Wanda onto her side so she wouldn’t choke on the saliva flowing from her mouth.

Wanda was dying right in front of me. I felt powerless, even as I heard sirens approaching the studio. Lettie started to sob loudly; Inchul put an arm around her shoulders, tears falling freely down his face.

In desperation, I grabbed an EpiPen from my kit and jabbed it into Wanda’s thigh, hoping the adrenaline would jolt her dying systems into action.

The dose had no effect, and with a huge sigh, Wanda shuddered and was still. Absolute silence emanated from the people ringed around the bed.

Meg reached to turn on the defibrillator until Lettie stopped her while I listened to Wanda’s heart.

“No.” Lettie sniffed through her tears. “Wanda added a DNR to her living will after her heart diagnosis—no resuscitation.”

I took the stethoscope out of my ears and shook my head.

The studio door crashed open and two paramedics ran inside with a gurney. They stopped at the foot of the bed, gaping at the dead woman.

“DNR,” I explained, and one nodded and came to my side.

“May I?” He held up his own stethoscope and listened, then consulted his watch. “Time of death, 11:33 a.m.”

***

I blew out a breath and took charge. Wanda had been my patient, and I owed her this. No way was I leaving it to Dowling. Besides, after hearing so many stories from my detective boyfriend, I knew the steps to take until the police arrived. “Inchul, guard the studio door. No one in or out but police.” He hurried off.

"Police?" Dowling objected.

I held up a hand. "Meg, throw a clean towel over Wanda's food and drink and guard it." She left to do my bidding. "Lettie, stay with Wanda, please."

I turned to the paramedic, who by now surely knew where I was headed. "Wanda exhibited poisoning symptoms. Can you guard the soundstage until forensics seal it as a crime scene?"

The two nodded and left for the soundstage door.

"Poison?" Dowling's eyes bulged. "I know you're upset you lost a patient, Trudy, but this is overreacting."

"I didn't lose her. She's right here, dead on this bed, and unless I'm mistaken, not from natural causes. Now do you want to be seen as helping the NYPD or hindering them? Because you could help enormously by gathering the crew in one place for questioning."

Even as he rushed away, I was dialing Ned.

***

Two hours later, after the forensic team's arrival, and after consultation with the medical examiner, Wanda's body was taken to the morgue for autopsy. I'd spoken to Ned's ME friend, and explained my hypothesis, based on Wanda's symptoms.

The quiche and hot chocolate had been taken for analysis, but at first glance, the ME agreed with me that the sequence I'd described pointed to a quick-acting poison. We posited several types, including belladonna, but were waiting on the rapid testing of the quiche. The chocolate had been quickly ruled out as liquids were faster to test.

I had briefed Ned and Borelli on the people closest to Wanda and the unfolding of events. Borelli and their team had taken the names and brief statements of the ancillary crew and dismissed them, as they hadn't had access to Wanda's food or drink.

Ned used the dining room set to talk to those who remained: Lettie and Inchul, Dowling, Meg, Barney from props, the actor playing Alain Duchamp, and surprisingly, the restaurateur himself. After Ned called and explained what happened, Duchamp had rushed to the studio. The graying man was trim and attractive, but appeared distraught over Wanda's death.

Ned introduced himself and Borelli to the somber group as we sat around the large table. He bent his lanky frame to fit under it.

"Let's take things in order, please." Ned nodded to Borelli to take additional notes and flipped open his own notebook. His take-charge attitude pleased me. Borelli, coffee cup in his olive-skinned hand, sat next to Meg. I sat opposite Ned at the foot of the table to watch faces, with the others ringed around the sides. "Mr. Dowling?"

Dowling scowled. "Yesterday Wanda insisted she would only do today's scene if she had a piece of Alain Duchamp's famous Quiche Alain."

Heads nodded. Meg said, "I called the restaurant twice to make the request and made certain he knew it was for Toot . . . Wanda."

Duchamp pinched the bridge of his nose in grief, but clearly wanted any questions of responsibility cleared up. "I came as soon as you called, Detective. That was my standard recipe. Nothing like this has ever happened, and for it to happen to Wanda . . ."

His lingering accent was charming. I could see why Wanda had fallen for him.

"What makes it unique?" Ned asked.

"Most quiches have an egg-custard base with Gruyere cheese and usually bacon, or perhaps spinach or another twist. Mine mixes Locatelli cheese to add saltiness to the nutty Gruyere, and not only bacon, but also ground beef, sausage, and duck *confit*, along with mushrooms."

"A meat lover's version," Borelli threw in.

This garnered a withering glance from Duchamp. "It's hardly a pizza."

"Did you say mushrooms?" Ned asked.

"I assure you they are perfectly harmless. I used others from the same supplier's order last night without any illness."

Ned made a note. "You had a relationship with the deceased spanning years?"

"Over forty, on and off. More recently off." He shifted in his seat.

"So there was no love lost between you?" Borelli asked.

Duchamp drew himself up. "I had the utmost respect for Wanda's acting prowess, but we'd parted ways on a personal level."

"Yet you agreed to make your quiche when she asked," Ned said.

The chef nodded and bowed his head. "History." I knew he was thinking of his Tootsie.

Ned continued. "And you delivered it to Ms. Jackson's residence this morning?"

"To her house, but I didn't see Wanda. I'm sorry now I didn't."

Ned turned to Lettie. "You took possession of the box?"

"Yes, I answered the door. Wanda was excited. She would have tasted it right then, but I made her wait and put it in the kitchen." Lettie looked at me. "Would it have made a difference?"

I shook my head. "If the quiche was poisoned, she would have died at home instead. Or maybe in the car."

Ned asked, "The box traveled with her in your car?"

"We left fifteen minutes later, and it sat on the back seat between us," Lettie confirmed.

"And when you arrived at the studio?"

My turn to pipe up. "I was in the lobby with Meg. I saw Lettie bring it out of the car and hand it off to Meg after Inchul and I helped Wanda into her chair."

"I closed the trunk and pushed Wanda to hair and makeup, along with Trudy and Lettie," Inchul said.

"And I took the box to Barney, the prop master," Meg added.

Barney agreed. "Where I stowed it in our flower cooler while the actors rotated through hair and makeup."

Ned addressed Barney. "How long was it in that cooler?"

"Probably an hour. I was in the room the entire time, working on a flower arrangement for the soap, and no one came near it."

"Until I called for it," Dowling butted in, wanting his moment of importance in the timeline. "When we were ready to film."

"So you retrieved it?"

Dowling deflated. "No. Union rules. Barney had to bring it to the set."

Ned looked at me and I shrugged. He was learning the vagaries of studio life. He swiveled his attention back to Barney. "When Dowling called, you brought the quiche to the set?"

"Yup." Barney brushed his sandy hair off his forehead. "Took it out of the box, watched catering heat it in the microwave they have by their table, put a piece on the plate the set decorator chose, and added the fork. I stood watching the scene play out. The plate was right in front of me until the Alain actor took it into the frame."

The actor playing Alain agreed. "I was merely the carrier, all on camera."

Ned pinched his lips and rose. "Let's take a brief break. Please stay here."

Borelli met him on the bedroom set, out of range of being heard. Meg and I didn't hesitate and joined them. We all started to speak at once.

"Boss, seems to me—"

"Ned, I think—"

"What about—"

Ned cut us off with a gesture, then pointed to me and Meg. "You two don't even belong here." He saw my steam gathering and backtracked. "But I appreciate your inside knowledge. Borelli first."

"Seems to me that quiche was pretty well covered by witnesses once it hit the studio, which means the poison had to be introduced by Duchamp when he made it, Lettie or Inchul, or Wanda herself."

I was stunned. I'd never considered Wanda committing suicide, especially in such a public way. Could the Tootsie message have been a sign to Alain to poison the quiche? It felt wrong, and Meg agreed.

"We can rule suicide out," Meg said. "I heard Wanda tell the makeup gal today that her goal was to see her movie and book come out, and then her bucket list would be done and she could die happily."

I nodded. "She wouldn't end her life when her goal was in sight. Wanda was a fighter. Despite her extreme pain, she soldiered on."

"Then what was the motive to kill her? Alain Duchamp for revenge on a former lover?" Ned suggested. "Or was Wanda a mean boss?"

"No way," I said. "Lettie and Inchul seem devoted to her. They wouldn't have stuck around so many years if Wanda had been difficult."

"Unless they were in it for the money," Borelli said. "We should find out who benefits financially from Wanda's death. I'll get the team on that."

"If it helps, Wanda had no arguments with anyone here on set, though she didn't care for Dowling's attitude," I threw in.

"That narrows it a bit."

Ned herded us back to the dining room set and released Barney, the fake Alain, and Dowling. "Please be certain the officer at the door has your contact information."

Dowling looked unhappy to be dismissed and opened his mouth to protest, but Ned had his measure and cut him off, pointing to the door. I might have had something to do with that, since I'd previously been pretty verbal about the man's misogyny.

I watched Ned scrutinize those who remained: Alain Duchamp, Lettie Thompson, and Inchul Jones.

They were the people who'd been alone with the quiche. I ran through their actions and possible motives in my mind.

One of them was Wanda's killer.

***

Meg, Borelli, and I had retaken our seats when Ned's phone rang. He turned aside but I heard him thank Byron and ask him to text "the name," even as I thought long and hard, staring at everyone left at the table.

While revenge, jealousy, greed, even hate were all good motives for murder, so was love. And suddenly, as my eyes settled on Alain, I thought I knew who had killed Wanda.

Ned kept his phone out and addressed the group circled around him. "That was the ME. The rush analysis on the quiche came through." His phone pinged a text. "Wanda Jackson died from ingestion of"— here he consulted his phone—"tetrodotoxin."

I sucked in a breath and Googled the poison on my phone, even as my hunch solidified.

Alain grimaced. "Pufferfish?"

Ned turned to him. "Very rare. Serve it in your restaurant?"

The man's face paled. "Of course not. It's extremely dangerous. I would never use it."

"And yet, someone accessed this poison."

Lettie frowned. "I don't understand. What kind of poison is it?"

I expounded. "It causes paralysis of the diaphragm, increasing respiratory distress, tremors, excessive drooling, and convulsions, just as Wanda exhibited. In Wanda's case, her autopsy will likely show complete respiratory failure with cardiac arrhythmia." I blinked back my own tears for Wanda. Her last minutes had been fraught with suffering as she fought to breathe. It had to have been horrific, but at least it was mercifully brief.

Lettie wept. "Who would have done this?"

"Not you, Ms. Thompson?" Ned's voice was gentle. "Tired of seeing your long-time friend in terrible pain?"

Lettie's eyes opened wide. "No! I don't believe in euthanasia. I would never shorten her time."

"But you would," I broke in, turning. "Isn't that right, Inchul?"

He averted his eyes and dipped his chin to his chest.

"You couldn't stand to see Wanda suffer any longer," I continued. "Tell me, do you have relatives in the Asian community with access to pufferfish?"

His chin quivered as he met my gaze with a huge sigh of remorse, crying quietly. This was what had struck me earlier. Inchul had started crying at Wanda's first tremble. He'd kissed her cheek as though in farewell when he laid her on the bed. There had been obvious affection between them.

It made sense. I gave him a sympathetic look and nodded, urging Inchul to confess.

"Fugu," Inchul whispered, then cleared his throat. "It's called fugu in my culture. At the house I injected fugu extract into the quiche, to stop Wanda's suffering."

A gasp ran around the table.

Inchul appealed to Lettie. "You saw her pain. She was in agony every waking moment." He looked down again. "I couldn't stand watching the torture living had become for Wanda." Then, even softer, “I loved her.”

Before anyone could react, Alain Duchamp punched Inchul Jones right in the face. “That’s for my Tootsie. How dare you decide when she lived or died?”

Borelli sprang up and held the chef back from a further assault.

Ned handed Inchul a clean linen handkerchief to stem his bloody nose. “I think you need this more than me.”

DIET OF DEATH

By Ang Pompano

Pretending can backfire, in more than one way. Just ask Quincy Lazzaro, the culinarily challenged food columnist whose 'Cooking with Betty' alter-ego has to interview a diet guru.

An early morning call from Archie was never good. But since he was my boss, I answered anyway.

"Tolzer wants to end his feud with Betty. He's willing to do an interview."

Dr. Alan Tolzer, inventor of the Westport Diet, had a long-standing feud with Betty Ann Green ever since she panned his first book. The diet had taken love-handle-conscious America by storm after one of those panty-free celebrities announced to TMZ that it was the "hottest diet since South Beach." Now Dr. Tolzer was looking for publicity for his follow-up book, *The Enhanced Westport Diet*, touting an exotic kopi berry supplement. "Cooking with Betty" was just the venue he needed. Fair enough. We all sold our souls one way or another in the cooking industry.

I looked at the clock on the nightstand. 7:00 a.m.

I heaved a sigh. "Fine. I'll shoot an email with some questions over to him. Coffee first."

I could hear Archie clearing his throat on the other end of the line. "It has to be a face-to-face."

Archie must have gone out of his mind.

"How am I supposed to pull that off?"

I wrote "Cooking with Betty," a food column in *On-Topic Magazine*, in spite of being culinarily challenged. That's a nice way of saying I can't cook. I pulled it off with recipes given to me by my landlady, Mary Ticarelli. As if that wasn't enough on my plate, so to speak, I had to hide the fact that I was Betty. To the rest of the world, I was a guy named Quincy Lazzaro. No way I could hide that in a face-to-face interview.

"You'll think of something." He disconnected.

Lying was easy for Archie. It was almost a sport. I'm in the position I'm in now because of his lying, after he told me that I had to save him from his Siberian tiger of a father, publisher of *On-*

Topic Magazine, by filling in for just a couple of columns until Betty moved up to the New York area from Philadelphia. The couple of columns led to four when Betty had to wait for her kids to finish school. Four led to eight when her husband got sick. Every month it was one excuse after another until the tenth column. Then Archie informed me that Betty wasn't going to be moving to New York after all. In fact, she was dead. A car accident. On the way up from Baltimore. Her car hit a cow. When I heard Baltimore instead of Philadelphia I realized the truth. There was no Betty. But Archie assured me there was. Me.

"There's one more thing. He wants the interview this morning. You have a nine o'clock appointment."

***

On the way to the Westport Diet Institute, I gave Mary a call.

"Where are you? You went out early."

I don't know why I have to account for my whereabouts to my eighty-four-year-old landlady, but she feeds me well and gives me recipes for my column.

"I'm on my way to interview Dr. Tolzer."

"The diet doctor? I thought he hated you, or at least Betty."

"Not anymore."

"So, are you in drag or something?"

"Of course not."

"What will you do?"

"I don't know. I'll think of something. Listen, do you have a better tiramisu recipe? The editor said the one you gave me is too complicated. The steps need to be short and logical. Assume the readers are dummies. We want our dummies to be successful."

"I'll try. But I'm Italian. We don't use a recipe to make tiramisu. We just do it. You want me to come along and pretend I'm Betty? I am, kind of."

"I've got this," I told her.

The reality was I had no idea how I was going to pull this off.

***

I drove up the copper beech canopied driveway to the main house, a greystone mansion with more chimney-stalks and leaded windows than a palace. Beyond, Long Island Sound lay calm as a kitten on Paxil. No wonder they called this the Connecticut Gold Coast: prime real estate indeed.

I parked and followed a boxwood-lined path to an arched door. I rang and was buzzed in.

I found myself in a large paneled office furnished in leather and mahogany with views of Long Island Sound. It seemed like a shrine, decorated with mementos and pictures of Tolzer with every celebrity from Adele to Jay-Z. No one was in the room. In one corner was a breakfast tray with the remains of what seemed like a meal all too healthy for me. Not a carb in sight. Next to the plate was a discarded empty bottle labeled *digoxin*. Someone was taking heart medication.

As I was looking at the bottle, a young woman holding a stack of papers came out of a door marked *Conference Room*. My eyes moved quickly from the small rose tattoo that peeked above the low-cut neck of her blouse to the single thin braid in her long golden-brown hair.

"Oh! I didn't know anyone was here." Her look morphed from startled to fully composed in seconds. "I'm Megan Haskins, Dr. Tolzer's executive assistant." She sighed and tapped the papers on a desk until she had a neat stack. "And you are?"

"I'm here to interview Dr. Tolzer for the 'Cooking with Betty'" column."

"You? We were expecting Betty Ann Green."

"I'm her front man, Quincy Lazzaro. I gather the facts and Betty writes the articles. That's the way she does it."

"Oh dear. It's the feud, isn't it? I assure you all is forgiven on Dr. Tolzer's part."

"Betty's ready to move on. Still, this is how she does things."

Megan seemed overly nervous.

"But we had a board meeting this morning. We had everything all set. Betty was supposed to interview Dr. Tolzer. It's very important that we promote the new *Enhanced Westport Diet with Miracle Kopi Berries*."

The door to the conference room opened. Out stepped two very familiar faces. I recognized Irene White, a former Broadway actress who recently had been running the local summer playhouse along with her movie star husband, Jeffry Johns. The other familiar person, Jeremy Ponds, was an Olympic tennis player who blew up to three hundred pounds after retiring. He lost half of that weight on the Westport Diet and was now Tolzer's spokesman. A third person, a man with silver hair wearing an expensive suit, I didn't recognize.

The three of them seemed surprised to see me.

"This is Mr. Lazzaro," Megan said. "He's here to do the interview instead of Betty."

"Oh dear." Irene White frowned, then quickly recovered. "And he's in an exceptionally good mood this morning because he was so looking forward to talking with her."

"Why isn't Betty here?" Ponds didn't seem to be able to hide his disappointment.

"This can still work." The guy with the silver hair put out his hand. "Dr. Stephen Richardson. Head of research."

"Really?" If you Googled an image for surprised you would have seen Megan's face.

"Of course," Ponds said, recovering. "Let me go in and talk to him." He started toward a door with a plaque that read *Dr. Alan Tolzer*.

"No. He's exercising. Let me call first." Richardson pulled out his cell phone and punched in some numbers. He turned his back to us and in a soft voice spoke to someone.

"He wants to talk to Mr. Lazzaro."

Richardson punched speaker and handed the phone to me. Dr. Tolzer's familiar voice came over the speakerphone.

"Where's Betty?"

"She sent her associate, a Mr. Lazzaro," Megan said.

"Let me talk to him."

"I'm here, Dr. Tolzer," I said, trying to make my voice sound authoritative.

"You sound like a kid. Are you sure you can handle this? Where the hell is Betty?"

"As I said to your assistant, Betty's a very busy lady. She prefers to have me do the legwork. I gather the information, but the articles are all hers."

"That's ridiculous."

"It works for James Patterson." And it worked for me, too. "I understand you have a new Westport Diet Book," I said.

Tolzer's voice boomed out from the speakerphone. "It's not just another diet book. It's the *Enhanced Westport Diet with Miracle Kopi Berries*. The *Enhanced Westport Diet with Miracle Kopi Berries*! She'd better get that right, for God's sake."

"I will. I mean I'll relay the information to Betty. She's a stickler for accuracy."

"Is that why she panned *The Sugar Revolution? The Sugar Revolution* was about how I started it all," he said. "I invented the low-carb diet. I beat Atkins by two years. You didn't know that, did you? Why would you? Nobody gives me credit for that."

I had slammed *The Sugar Revolution* because the book wasn't very good. It seemed like a rehash of the low-carb diets that had been around for a while.

"That would be between you and Betty. Besides, I understood you wanted the feud to end. I know it's over on Betty's part."

"Good." His indifferent tone told me that he didn't really care what I thought as long as Betty was on board. She was the one who could help him push his books.

"May I come in and speak with you?"

"No. I still want to talk to Betty. I don't want this article botched up. A good mention will mean millions in book sales."

I tried distracting him with a question. "What's so miraculous about kopi berries? Do they attack fat or something?"

"I'll explain it all to Betty when I see her. So, you tell me, what's she like?"

"She's a good boss. Nice to work for."

"Bullshit. She wouldn't be successful if she were nice to work for. But that's not what I want to know. What's she's like?"

"Like?" I had no intention of getting into locker room banter with this idiot.

"Don't play dumb, man. You know what I mean. Forget it, then. I already know. Betty and I go way back. She was good then. I'll bet she's still good now."

The remark pissed me off and I almost launched a defense of her honor. For the sake of getting what I needed for the column, I tried to be diplomatic with this delusional egomaniac.

"Well then, you already know how she is. Busy, busy, busy. That's why she sends me to gather information. I'm sure you want her to write the best article possible. As you say, it could be worth millions. Now, what Betty would like to know is—"

"Look, I've had enough. Megan will give you a fact sheet."

"I was hoping for an interview."

"And I was hoping for Betty," he said.

I tried to reason with him. "Betty sent me to get the facts. It will be a great interview. I promise."

"Well, I guess you have me just where Betty wants me. I should have known she'd hold a grudge. I'll talk to you as soon as I finish my exercises. Megan, give him a fact sheet so he can ask some intelligent questions when he comes in. Better yet, give him the damned book so Betty knows what the hell she's talking about when she writes the article."

Irene, Richardson, and Ponds looked at each other and shrugged.

"He's mellowing in his old age," Ponds said as the speakerphone went dead.

"Come with me, Mr. Lazzaro. I have some advanced copies." Megan began to lead me away as the lights flickered and we heard a crash from Dr. Tolzer's office.

Irene screamed so loud that I thought I'd lose my hearing. Richardson and Ponds rushed to Tolzer's door. The rest of us followed them into the office where we found the doctor sprawled on the floor at the foot of an antique scale.

As Dr. Richardson began CPR, I almost backed into it.

"Don't touch that!" Irene shouted.

"What?" I jumped away, dumbfounded.

Irene pointed to the base of the scale. There were wires coming from the platform.

Dr. Richardson checked for a pulse, then worked on Tolzer a bit more. He checked for a heartbeat after another minute. Finally, he stopped and glanced at his watch.

"He's dead," he said.

I stood by Megan, who had a look of terror on her face. Ponds looked as if he were in shock. Irene was crying hysterically.

***

"He was murdered," Dr. Richardson said as soon as the police arrived. "Murdered by electrocution, in my professional opinion."

An officer named Anderson seemed to be in charge. She was tall and wore a dark headband that controlled a headful of short dreadlocks. Because I was nervous, I fixated on her badge, which wasn't a badge at all but a sewn-on patch in the shape of a shield. I wondered if there was some safety reason for the uniform design.

"What makes you say that?" she asked.

"It's obvious," Richardson said. "Look at the wires attached from the defibrillator to the overturned scale. Dr. Tolzer had been talking to us on the phone as he did his workout. He must have stepped on the scale when he finished exercising."

Anderson seemed skeptical. "Is the battery in a defibrillator strong enough to electrocute someone?"

"The machine in the office is a modulated AC system. It has a high-voltage transformer. It's always kept near the scale, so Dr. Tolzer wouldn't have realized that someone had tampered with it and attached it to the scale."

Anderson had the other officers take statements from each of us separately. After an hour and a half, we were free to go.

***

On the way home, I tried to figure out what seemed wrong with what had happened. Was it that Tolzer's voice seemed off a bit? Maybe it was because he had been exercising. Or maybe it was the speakerphone. And why did he give in and agree to an interview with me when he really wanted to talk to Betty? He had a reputation of being tough. Why did he cave? My imagination was going wild and I forced myself to calm down.

***

I tried to sneak into my apartment behind Mary's house, but she waited for me in front of her yellow foursquare. Caught. I tried to divert her attention as she sat me at a wicker table on the porch.

"How was your interview with the diet guru?" Mary wanted to know.

"You didn't happen to come up with a good tiramisu recipe?"

Mary chose to use her selective hearing to ignore the question.

"The interview with Tolzer. How did it go?"

"He's dead."

"You killed him?"

If I'm ever on trial, I have to remember not to have Mary as a character witness.

"I did not kill him."

She went inside, then came out with a plate of baked eggplant layered with cheese and tomato sauce. She put it in front of me. "How did he die?"

"There was a doctor there named Richardson. He declared him dead from electrocution. The police found evidence that someone had hooked up a defibrillator to the doctor's old weight scale. They think he had gotten on the scale after working out and got zapped. But I think there was more to it. I saw a heart pill bottle. I can't prove it was his, but maybe he had a weak heart."

"Well, it doesn't look good for a diet doctor to die of a heart attack."

"I guess not."

"Of course not. My cousin Lucy can vouch for that."

"What does your cousin have to do with it?"

"Everything. She had a catering business she ran from her kitchen to make ends meet. Her husband, Charlie, was a gambler. Never worked a day in his life. He died in the chair."

"The electric chair?"

"No! The kitchen chair. He was eating dinner. So, she dragged him outside and put him in a lawn chair under the grape arbor before she called for help."

"Why would she do that?"

She gave a wave of her hand as if I were a fool not to understand. "People talk! If they found out he was eating dinner, right away they'd say it was ptomaine. End of business." She slapped her hands in an up-and-down motion as if they were two cymbals.

It almost scared me that I got her point. Things started to fall into place. I didn't have the whole picture, but I called Officer Anderson anyway.

"When is a murder not a murder?" I asked.

"Mr. Lazzaro, I don't have time for riddles."

"I know. So, I'll tell you the answer. When there was no

murder." I explained my theory, that in spite of what Dr. Richardson determined, there was no murder. I told her how I had seen the digoxin bottle on the breakfast tray. "I think Dr. Tolzer was dead before Betty was even called to go to the Institute, and the wires attached to the scale were a diversion by the board of directors to make it look like murder."

I was pretty sure that Officer Anderson was ready to hang up on me.

"And they would set themselves up as murder suspects, why?"

"But they didn't. Did they? They were all there with me talking to Dr. Tolzer. They had intended Betty to be a credible witness. They got me instead, but that's a different story."

"That doesn't tell me why."

"Because if Dr. Tolzer died of a heart attack, it would be bad for the image of the Westport Diet. So, soon after his body was found, they came up with a plan to make it look like murder. Humor me. Look into it, please?"

Anderson did not say that she would. But she did not say that she wouldn't. All night I thought about Tolzer and my idea of what could have happened. The next afternoon, as I was concluding that I had to stop watching conspiracy theory TV shows, Officer Anderson called.

"I wanted to thank you for the tip. It turns out that you had something there. We interrogated everyone again and one of the suspects admitted that the doctor indeed died of natural causes."

"Which one confessed?"

"I really can't jeopardize the case by giving you details, but I will tell you that you were speaking to an actor and not Dr. Tolzer."

Of course. Irene White's husband, Jeffry Johns, had pretended to be Tolzer. He must also have made the scale crash to the floor so we could come running in after he left through another door.

"So, there was no murder and no crime," I said.

Officer Anderson's voice was confident. "There was a crime. We just have to figure out what it was."

That was a problem for the police. My deadline was coming up and I still had to find an easy tiramisu recipe.

DEATH AT THE WILLARD HOTEL

By Verena Rose

Even a wedding celebration is not safe from the political strife between pre-Civil War pro-slavers and abolitionists.

April 6, 1860
White Oak Plantation

My dearest brother,

I have the most wonderful news. Father has finally agreed to hold my wedding at the Willard Hotel. His fondest wish was to have it at the new Spotswood Hotel in Richmond, but happily for me, the building won't be completed in time for my ceremony. He didn't dare ask me to postpone my wedding. What if there's a war and Joseph has to go?

I know you and Father may never reconcile but I still want you at my wedding. You'll always be my brother and I want you there. Please change your mind and say you'll come. The day is set for Monday, May 14th at 6:00 pm. And do convey my warmest regards and invitation to Zeke and Jelena.

Your loving sister,
Beryl

***

April 13, 1860 – Thanksgiving Day
Washington City

Sitting around the table after a fine home-cooked meal, Horace Kingsley regarded his friends, Zeke and Jelena Wallace. "I've been meaning to talk to you about something."

"What is it, Horace? Nothing's wrong, I hope?" asked Jelena with concern.

Taking an envelope from his coat pocket, Horace handed it to her and said, "This is from my sister. Please read it."

Jelena unfolded the letter, read it slowly, glancing up several times as she did so, trying to read Horace's expression. "Well," she said gently, "surely you are planning to go. You won't be alone as Zeke and I will be happy to join you. Besides, your father won't want to cause any unpleasantness, not on your sister's wedding day."

Zeke nodded his agreement. "Of course we will go with you, Horace. Jelena has the right of it. I imagine the worst Cyrus will do is ignore you completely. He wouldn't dare cause a scene at Beryl's wedding."

"You know I don't care about Father's attitude. What is really going to hurt is seeing Mother and not being able to talk with her. You know he won't allow her to acknowledge my existence," Horace said sadly.

Zeke and Jelena exchanged glances of understanding. Jelena folded the letter again and laid it down on the table. Zeke regarded his friend's unhappy expression and thought to bring the mood back to something more pleasant. "So, tell me what you and Noah have been up to down at the Morgue? Any interesting cases lately?"

Shaking her head at what her husband had chosen as a diversionary topic, Jelena left the men to talk shop while she brewed a pot of coffee to enjoy with their dessert. She had a surprise for the two friends—she'd made whipped cream to top the pumpkin pie.

***

May 6, 1860 – Sunday
Baltimore Sun and Evening Star – Headline

WEDDING AT THE WILLARD

Beryl Kingsley, daughter of Cyrus and Celestine Kingsley, will be wed to Mr. Joseph Rutherford of Richmond, Virginia, at the Willard Hotel on Monday, May 14. Mr. Kingsley, a prominent Marylander, is the owner of White Oak Plantation on the Eastern Shore. Sources told this reporter this will be the wedding of the season. Mr. Kingsley has sent all his personal kitchen staff to the Willard to start the preparations for the post-wedding banquet.

We have confirmed with the Willard management that the entire hotel has been hired for the occasion. The hotel is expecting many honored guests from as far away as New Orleans, Louisiana.

No expense has been spared as we've also learned that Mr. Matthew Brady will be on hand to document the new couple's happy occasion.

***

May 10, 1860
Ebbitt Hotel, Washington City

At a back table in the restaurant at the Ebbitt Hotel, several men were having a quiet lunch and talking furtively in whispers.

"Do you think it's wise for us to be meeting in such a public place, especially since the Washington constabulary must be on high alert these days?" asked Isaac Gunn.

Nodding his head, Jeremy Strong said, "I agree, but we can't pass up this opportunity to cause real damage to the pro-slavers. There will be Southern politicians and land owners from all over the South at this wedding. Besides, the Movement has sent down their orders. All I *can* say is we are to infiltrate the kitchen."

***

May 14, 1860
Willard Hotel, Washington City

Horace Kingsley, accompanied by Zeke and Jelena Wallace, entered the Willard Hotel at 5:30 pm to attend Horace's sister's wedding. They were directed down the main hall to the Ballroom. As they drew near, they could hear the strains of a violin.

An usher stationed at the Ballroom door enquired, "Gentlemen. Madam. May I direct you to your seats?"

"Certainly. I am Horace Kingsley, brother of the bride, and these are my guests, Hezekiah and Jelena Wallace."

"Of course, Mr. Kingsley. Please follow me." The usher lead them down the center aisle of the ballroom until they reached the first row. "You are to sit in this row, Mr. Kingsley."

Looking uncertain, Horace said, "I'm not sure we're supposed to sit here."

"I was specifically instructed by Miss Beryl to seat you in the first row. You will be sitting with the groom's parents," replied the usher.

Jelena touched Horace's arm and whispered, "It seems your sister has thought of everything. Let's sit down and prepare to enjoy her wedding."

Once they were comfortably seated, Zeke began to look around with interest. "Horace, I didn't know your father was so well connected in Washington. I see Mr. Jefferson Davis and his wife, Varina, and the Vice President, Mr. John Breckinridge with his wife sitting in the second row."

"Father makes it a point to know all of the Democratic Senators and Congressmen who are pro-slavery. And it's no surprise that he would use my sister's wedding to garner their favor. I've also seen the Maryland Senator, John Pearce, and both of the Senators from Virginia. I'm sure there are many more of that party present, but I doubt he invited any of the Republicans."

Nodding, Zeke asked, "Did you read that the Republicans are holding their convention on the 18th to nominate their candidate for the presidency?"

"Indeed I did. This is going to be an important election. I don't envy the person who wins."

As the orchestra started playing, the room became quiet. All eyes turned to look up the aisle toward the doors. To the strains of Mendelssohn's Wedding March, Cyrus Kingsley led his daughter to the altar.

***

Running over and throwing her arms around her brother's neck, the beautiful new bride couldn't contain her pleasure. "Oh, Horace, I am so glad you came. Seeing you sitting there was the best of all wedding gifts."

"Beryl, how could I not come to your wedding? Now introduce me to your new husband."

Turning to the handsome young man standing behind her, Beryl said, "Horace, I'd like to introduce you to my husband, Joseph Rutherford. Joseph, this is my brother, Dr. Horace Kingsley, and these are his very good friends, Hezekiah Wallace and his wife, Jelena. Zeke is a Washington City police constable."

The new brothers-in-law shook hands and simultaneously said, "Pleased to meet you." Then Joseph turned and shook hands with the Wallaces.

Beryl took the arm of her new husband. "We must go to greet the other guests," she said, adding hesitantly, with hope in her eyes, "You are staying for dinner and dancing, aren't you? And we're cutting the cake later, too."

Not waiting for Horace to answer, Jelena took Beryl's hand and said, "Of course we are staying, my dear. Your brother wouldn't miss a dance with the new bride for the world."

***

Escorted to a table near the front of the room, Horace and the Wallaces found themselves seated with several of the Kingsley cousins. The cousins were polite and said their hellos, but it was obvious they didn't want to be at the same table with their abolitionist cousin.

Jelena, hoping to distract Horace, picked up the menu card and said, "We're certainly in for a sumptuous meal. Look at this array of fine Southern fare."

STARTER
Turtle Soup

MEATS
Prime Standing Rib Roast
Virginia Baked Ham
Southern Fried Chicken

SIDES
Corn Pudding
Roasted Potatoes
Sweet Potatoes
Mince Meat Pie
Pickles & Relishes

ASSORTED BREAD & ROLLS

BEVERAGES
Sweet Tea
Milk Punch
Coffee & Tea
Champagne for Groom's Toast

DESSERTS
Poinciana Cakes (Individual Cakes)

Bride's Cake

***

As the orchestra tuned up for the dancing to commence, Horace Kingsley felt a light tap on his shoulder. Turning, he found Elijah, one of his father's house slaves.

"Master Horace, you must come quick. Jupiter is terrible sick in the kitchen and I'm feared he's dying."

Horace stood up quickly. "Zeke, will you come with me?" Not waiting for an answer, he followed Elijah out of the Ballroom. "What happened?" he asked Elijah as they hurried toward the kitchen.

"Well, Master Horace, you knows Jupiter. He can't resist a sweet cake. He ate one of the Poinciana Cakes. Next thing you knows he falls down, grabs his middle, screaming."

As the three men entered the kitchen, they saw the entire staff standing in a circle. Pushing their way through, they found Jupiter lying on the floor. Kneeling down, Horace checked for a pulse and found that Jupiter was, at least for now, still alive.

While Horace was making his examination, Zeke Wallace turned to what appeared to be the head chef and asked. "Where are those Poinciana Cakes? We need to make sure they aren't served to the guests."

"Yes, sir. I'm Judah, I cook for Master Cyrus. I made all those cakes myself along with some help from Miriam. I don't understand why Jupiter would go and get sick from eating one. I've made this same recipe many a time for the Master and no one ever got sick."

"We can't take any chances with the guests. You said Miriam helped you with the preparation. What exactly did she do to help you with the cakes? I'll need to speak with her."

"After I put all of the ingredients together, Miriam separated the batter into the individual baking pans. She was to watch and make sure the cakes come out of the oven on time. That was earlier this morning and to tell you the truth I haven't seen her since," Judah said, shaking his head.

Horace came and touched Zeke on the arm and whispered, "Jupiter is dead."

"Did he say anything before he died?" asked Zeke.

"He kept saying the name Miriam, over and over. But I couldn't get him to say anything else."

Zeke looked around for Judah who had backed away, looking very disturbed. "Judah, I am a police constable and I need to start gathering information. Who is this Miriam? Is she a regular kitchen worker? Is she from Mr. Kingsley's plantation or does she belong here at the Willard?"

"I never saw her before coming here to cook for Missy Beryl's wedding. All I knows is that she was here when we come and we was told we could use her to help. I'm so sorry, Master Horace," moaned Judah.

***

May 15, 1860 – Tuesday
Washington Evening Star – Headline

WEDDING DISASTER AVERTED

Last evening at the Willard Hotel in

Washington City disaster was narrowly averted at the wedding of Miss Beryl Kingsley to Mr. Joseph Rutherford. Just before the dessert was to be served a kitchen slave was struck down with what appeared to be bad stomach pains.

Mr. Horace Kingsley, brother of the bride and also a doctor and the City Coroner of Washington City, along with Mr. Hezekiah Wallace a Washington City constable, rushed to the kitchen. There they found a slave named Jupiter belonging to Mr. Cyrus Kingsley lying prostrate on the kitchen floor. During the course of his examination, Mr. Kingsley wasn't able to fully revive the victim but he did hear him repeat the name Miriam several times before he succumbed to death.

The slave apparently ate one of the individual Poinciana Cakes that had been made to be given to each of the attending guests. The Chef, a slave named Judah also belonging to Mr. Kingsley, stated that he had prepared the batter personally but that a kitchen helper from the Willard had been charged with preparing the cakes for baking. Not long after the cakes came out of the oven, Miriam disappeared from the kitchen and hasn't been seen since.

The Washington constabulary are presently searching the city for the missing slave named Miriam. They believe she has information vital to discovering the identities of those involved in this near disaster.

Hezekiah Wallace, the Washington City constable on site at the time of the event, believes this to be the work of the growing abolitionist movement. He told this reporter that over the course of the last year there have been murders and suspicious deaths attributable to either the pro-slavers or the abolitionists, each group trying to harm the other. In this

> case, had the plot been successful, many of the most important men of the South would have perished.

***

Several miles south of Washington City, along the bank of the Potomac River, Isaac Gunn and Jeremy Strong sat on horseback looking down at the body of a young negro girl floating out into the current.

"I thought we were working for the abolitionist movement to free the slaves, not to murder them," said Isaac Gunn, shaking his head.

"It couldn't be helped. She could identify us and if they caught her, which they would have, she'd have no other choice but to tell them who we are," Jeremy said, trying to calm his friend down.

"Well, I still don't like it. The plot was a complete failure and the only deaths were two of the same people we profess to want to free. I think the Movement will have to function without me from now on." Isaac turned his horse back toward the city.

No one was near enough to hear the sound of the gunshot, nor to see the second body enter the water.

Author's Note

I have a passion for history and while sitting at the bar at the Ebbitt Grill in Washington, DC, reading a postcard with the establishment's history, I decided I wanted to write about the time just before and during the Civil War. This is my third story featuring Washington City Coroner Dr. Horace Kingsley and Constable Hezekiah Wallace. For each of my stories I've researched the locations and what would be appropriate for the time. In this story, which features a wedding, I researched what might be served at a wedding banquet in the 1860's, taking into consideration that Washington City was very much a southern city at the time. It was really fun making the selections and most of the menu features dishes we've all heard of and possibly eaten. There are, however, two items about which I'd like to share some interesting findings.

MILK PUNCH

First, the word "punch" comes from the Hindi meaning "five" and typically most punch recipes have only five ingredients. The vogue for punch had its start in seventeenth century England where it was introduced by the officers of the East India Company.

Milk Punch is a very popular beverage especially in the south. The original recipe calls for either rum or brandy, but I'm very partial to the bourbon version served at the BOURBON HOUSE in New Orleans.

POINCIANA CAKE

This cake probably originated in Florida where the Poinciana bush grows. The predominant flavor is lemon. The juice, rind, and zest are all used to flavor both the cake and its extremely sweet filling. The cake also features raisins in the batter and shredded coconut in the filling. The final preparation includes a typical frosting and sometimes candy leaves representing the leaves of the Poinciana bush.

For the purposes of my story, I have had small versions of the cake created to be given to each of the guests at the banquet.

DINING OUT

By Rosemary McCracken

Ollie Townsend enjoys being a restaurant reviewer. However, he may not keep his column—and those delicious perks—unless his reviews start getting better ratings in reader surveys.

"Ollie, a word."

Oliver Townsend sat up straight in his chair. "A problem, Bob?"

Bob MacGregor, *Toronto World*'s editor-in-chief, closed the office door and eased his bulk into the chair facing Oliver's desk. "You're doing a good job as entertainment editor. Balanced coverage—family fun as well as the artsy stuff."

Oliver wondered what was in the file folder MacGregor was holding. His boss wasn't usually this lavish with praise.

"Your restaurant column, however . . ." MacGregor opened the folder and jabbed at it with a stubby finger. "Our latest reader survey says it's one of the least-read columns in this newspaper."

Oliver rocked back in his chair. He wanted to keep the restaurant gig. Badly.

"Give me a chance, Bob." Oliver knew he was whining but he didn't care. "Readers need time to get used to me. Max Weinstein reviewed restaurants for twenty years, but I've only been doing it for six months."

"Six months is a lifetime in this business," MacGregor snapped. "Take a look at your reviews." He held up a newspaper clipping that was covered in red ink and read from it in a pained voice. "'The fried cauliflower was tasty.' Tasty? What kind of bullshit word is that?"

He was just getting started. "The words *amazing* and *awesome* irritate me more than a roomful of foodies. Are there no other words in the English language to denote the superlative?"

Oliver's heart was racing. *Amazing* and *awesome* usually hit the nail on the head.

MacGregor took another clipping from the file. "'Cooked up a storm.' A chef cooks up eggs, he cooks up bacon, but nobody has ever cooked up a storm."

MacGregor closed the folder and got to his feet. “Consider this official. You have been put on notice. If readership numbers don’t shoot up—and I mean way, way up— ‘Dining Out with Oliver Townsend’ is toast.”

Oliver took a deep breath as he watched MacGregor lumber down the hall. After thirteen years on the evening news desk, the entertainment editor’s job had been a most welcome change. Then things got even better. Out of the blue, Max Weinstein emailed MacGregor saying he wanted to “get away from it all.” Weinstein disappeared, and the restaurant column came Oliver’s way. The newspaper picked up the tab for dinner for two in fancy restaurants, which was a great way to impress a date. He straightened his shoulders and his tie. He was not going to give that up without a fight.

“Mr. Townsend.” A curvaceous brunette stood in his doorway, the cub reporter who had been turning heads in the newsroom for the past few months.

“Carissa,” Oliver said, running a hand through his thinning hair. “My name is Oliver, but everyone around here calls me Ollie.”

“Ollie.” Her face dimpled with pleasure. “May I come in?”

He gestured to the chair MacGregor had vacated.

She perched on the edge of it. “I just wanted to tell you how much I enjoy your restaurant column. The salmon you described at Neptune . . .” She closed her eyes as if in a reverie. “. . . I could almost feel it melting in my mouth. The way you write about food is an art.”

The kid was going overboard, but Oliver couldn’t help but smile at her. “What kind of writing do you want to do?”

“I’m in the lifestyles department right now,” she said, “and I’ve written some food-related articles: summer barbecues, making preserves, growing an indoor herb garden. But my dream, and the reason I got into this business, is to review restaurants. Like you.”

“Perhaps not exactly like me,” Oliver said, remembering what MacGregor had to say about his column.

“Of course not. I need to develop my own style. But I’d like to learn from the best.”

“That’s flattering, my dear.” He paused. “What are you suggesting?”

“Could I be your dinner date some evening? Observe you in action?”

“Hmm.” Oliver studied her for a moment. An attractive babe with an interesting proposition. “Would you like to dine at Pizzazz tonight?”

Carissa's face lit up. "Pizzazz! I've been dying to go there."

"Eight o'clock. Ask for Raymond Brown's table."

***

Oliver seated himself at the window table on the fifty-second floor of the Northshore Tower and sighed with satisfaction. For a few moments, he savored the view of Toronto's cityscape with Lake Ontario just beyond. Then he looked down at the white linen tabletop in front of him: polished silverware, sparkling glasses, gleaming plates, and a pale pink rose in a bud vase. Everything was just as it should be.

He checked his reflection in the window. His brown hair was combed back from his face, displaying silver at the temples. His finely tailored vanilla-colored suit marked him as a man of taste and discernment. He wasn't used to wearing such expensive clothes, but they looked damn good on him.

The maître d' appeared with Carissa, her luxuriant dark hair and golden skin set off by an off-the-shoulder black dress. "Welcome to Pizzazz, *mademoiselle*," he said, pulling the chair out for her.

"Carissa." Oliver liked the way her name rolled off his tongue. "You look lovely."

The maître d' placed two leather-bound menus on the table. Oliver nodded his thanks, and the man bowed and left.

Carissa's black eyes sparkled. "When I was hired at the newspaper, I never dreamed I'd be going on a restaurant review with you. Imagine being paid to go out to eat."

"I'm not paid to eat, my dear. I'm paid to write."

"I know that. And I want to learn from you."

"Would you like to review this restaurant?"

"I'd love to!"

"It will be under my byline, of course."

A waiter appeared with two martinis on a tray. "I hope you like martinis," Oliver said as the man placed the drinks in front of them.

"I do." Carissa clinked her glass against his.

Oliver raised his glass. "To a magnificent meal."

He took a small notebook and a pen from his breast pocket and slid them across the table. Carissa covered them with her napkin.

After some deliberation, they made their dinner selections. Oliver called for a full-bodied red from the sommelier's recommendations.

The wine arrived, followed by their starters. As soon as the waiter left the table, Carissa snapped two photos with her smartphone, and they tucked into the food.

"What do you think?" Oliver asked after they'd swapped plates.

Carissa sat up straight in her chair. "The goose *foie gras* was exquisite. A smooth texture and a wonderful musky taste. The sour fennel purée was the perfect accompaniment."

"The goat cheese soufflé?"

"Its appearance was off-putting. Collapsed in the middle."

Oliver chuckled. "Probably slammed on a table when it came out of the oven."

"Well, appearance was deceiving in this case. It was remarkably light and creamy."

Carissa jotted a few notes before the table was cleared. Their salads arrived and the waiter topped up their wine.

"The piattoni bean and dandelion?" Oliver asked after they'd sampled both salads.

"Naked coleslaw. But your green salad may be the best part of this meal. The balsamic vinaigrette was marvellously tart on the tongue."

She surreptitiously snapped photos of the main courses, and they picked up their forks.

"The duck magret was chewy, but the rhubarb sauce saved it. Sort of," she said when their plates had been cleared.

Oliver was impressed. Carissa wasn't letting her surroundings cloud her judgment. And those *bon mots*? He wished he'd thought of them.

"The lamb tagine?"

"Pedestrian. A hint of cumin, but no ginger, cinnamon, or turmeric. No bite to it."

"A forty-five-dollar travesty."

She inclined her head toward the window. "We're paying for the view."

Oliver looked up at the silver-haired man in a gray business suit who had appeared at the table. "I told you I'd be back, Marc."

The man gave him a smile that didn't reach his eyes. "And so you are. You ate well, I trust?"

Oliver placed a hand over his ample paunch. "I'm not hungry."

The man placed two small menus on the table. "Our dessert list." He set a silver tray with two truffles and a white envelope in front of Oliver. "A five-star review?"

Oliver glanced at the tray. "That will depend."

"You'll find everything to your satisfaction," Marc said and turned on his heel.

"What was that about?" Carissa asked.

"Marc Chastain, the owner. His way of saying hello."

"What's in the envelope?"

"His business card, I expect."

She gave him a dazzling smile. "Can we do this again?"

"Why not?" He opened a dessert menu. "We'll have something sweet. Then we'll head over to my place and see what kind of review you can write."

***

Six weeks later, Bob MacGregor appeared at Oliver's office door with a smile on his beefy face. "The numbers for 'Dining Out' were up in the last survey. Considerably."

Thanks to Carissa, Oliver thought. "I've been giving it my best shot," he said.

"You learned something from our little chat," MacGregor said. "I like that."

Oliver smiled as MacGregor ambled down the hall. Carissa had been a godsend. She knew her food and she certainly had a way with words. She was also a good-looking dish.

The telephone rang on his desk. "Entertainment. Oliver Townsend."

"You got a visitor, Ollie," the front-door security guard said.

"Who is it, Ronnie?"

"Tom Di Salvo."

The owner of Leonardi's, which he'd reviewed in today's paper. Oliver wondered what had brought him to the newspaper building. Probably to say thanks in person.

"Send him up." Oliver adjusted his cream-colored tie.

Minutes later, a tall, lean man walked into his office. In his black leather pants and matching jacket, his graying hair pulled back in a man-tail, Tom Di Salvo was the embodiment of rock-star hip.

Oliver smiled. "The president of the Di Salvo Restaurant Group. To what do I owe the honor of a visit?"

Di Salvo lowered himself into the chair across from him. "This." He pulled a section of the *World* from his black leather man-bag and waved it. "'The idea of dinner at Leonardi's is exciting, the reality is sadly disappointing,'" he read. "'This smart new restaurant left a sour taste in my mouth.'" He waved the section. "You accepted our gift and gave us this rubbish!"

Trying to hide his surprise, Oliver poured a glass of ice water from the pitcher on his desk. He raised the glass in a mock salute and sipped from it.

Di Salvo stuffed the newspaper back into his bag. "Print this." He threw a folded piece of paper on the desk and left the office.

Oliver scanned the page. "A retraction," he muttered.

He reached for the folded newspaper on his desk. He turned to the entertainment section and scanned the columns of newsprint.

"Damn!" A retraction was the last thing he wanted to run, but he didn't want to make an enemy of Di Salvo.

He scrunched Di Salvo's note into a ball and lobbed it at the wastepaper basket across the room.

***

"You seem down, Ollie," Carissa said after they'd placed their orders at Cricket that evening.

Oliver plucked the maraschino cherry from his champagne cocktail and popped it into his mouth. He bit into it and swallowed. "Tom Di Salvo paid me a visit today."

Carissa raised an eyebrow. "Is he as cool as everyone says?"

Oliver shrugged. "If dressing like Jagger did forty years ago is cool. The fool thinks his dad's money buys him style."

He sipped his cocktail thoughtfully. "Something went wrong."

"Went wrong?" Carissa asked.

"The copy was changed. 'This smart new restaurant left a sour taste in my mouth.' That's not what I sent in."

"You went over what I wrote last night," Carissa said. "Someone on the news desk must've changed it."

"I trained every one of those deskers when I was copy chief. No one would change an opinion piece."

"Someone with an axe to grind?" she asked.

Oliver waved a hand dismissively. "My concern is whether to print a retraction. That's what Di Salvo wants."

"A retraction?" Carissa's brow furrowed. "You can't go back on what you wrote, Ollie. You're the restaurant critic."

Oliver brought a fist down lightly on the table. "Enough. We won't let this ruin our dinner."

A waiter arrived with a bottle of Amarone. As soon as their glasses were filled, their starters arrived: *vitello tonnato* with capers and lobster bisque.

"Simply forgettable," Carissa pronounced when she'd sampled the thinly sliced veal.

Oliver slipped his notebook under her napkin. "We make a good team."

She lowered her eyes demurely, then looked up at him again. "Ollie, I don't suppose you'd visit my cousin's restaurant?"

Oliver lifted his gaze from his bowl of bisque. "Cousin's restaurant? The *World* doesn't review every eatery in town."

"Have dinner there with me. No obligation to write a review."

"I don't know, Carissa."

"As a favor, Ollie? I've been a help, haven't I?"

"What's this place called?"

"Diavolo."

"Italian?"

"Of course."

Oliver shifted uncomfortably in his chair. "How come I've never heard of it?"

"It just opened two weeks ago."

Oliver hesitated, wondering if he should tell her. "Carissa, the restaurants I feature like to give me a . . . token, shall we say, of their appreciation."

She didn't look surprised. "And should you decide that Diavolo is worthy of a review, my cousin will be happy to oblige."

"Do you know what I'm talking about?"

"It will be taken care of, Ollie."

The next "Dining Out" column wouldn't run until the weekend so Oliver dropped Carissa off at her apartment building after dinner.

"No nightcap?" she asked.

"I have work to finish at the office," he told her. "Write the review. I'll look at it in the morning."

***

The copy editors on the *World*'s news desk were shackled to their computers when Oliver arrived twenty minutes later. A woman with a mop of gray curls looked up from her screen, Martha Worsley, who had replaced Oliver as copy chief. "What brings you in here, Ollie?" she asked. "Restaurant run out of bubbly?"

"Who edited my column last night, Martha?"

She tapped her keyboard. "Trev," she called out, "Ollie has a question about today's restaurant column."

Oliver walked over to a man with a shock of ginger hair.

Trevor Manning looked up from his screen and smiled. "Hey, Ollie. What's the problem?"

"Can I get a printout of the unedited copy?"

"Sure thing." Trevor hit a button. "You went for the jugular in that piece. Good for you for telling it like it is."

"Make it snappy, guys," Martha shouted. "Deadline's in fifty-eight minutes."

"See you at Junior's?" Trevor asked Oliver.

He nodded and headed for the printer. He stuffed the two pages the machine spat out into his leather briefcase and took the escalator down to the front door.

Across the street in Junior's Bar, Willie Nelson was crooning "Blue Skies" from the jukebox to a nearly empty room. Oliver knew it was the lull before the storm; in another hour, the place would be buzzing with thirsty copy editors. Junior's had been his regular haunt after putting the paper to bed. He took his favorite booth at the back of the room.

"Look what we got here!" A plump young woman in a red miniskirt and black fishnet stockings smiled down at him. "Haven't seen Ollie Townsend since he started writing about frog legs and old cheese. Sorry, we only got Château Plonk in here."

"Get me a Corona, Sadie. And a shot of Canadian Club."

"That kind of day, was it?" She gave his shoulder a comforting pat before heading to the bar with his order.

Oliver took the printout from his briefcase and studied it. "'The idea of dinner at Leonardi's is exciting,'" he read out loud, "'the reality is sadly disappointing. This smart new restaurant left a sour taste in my mouth.'"

Carissa. Who else could it be?

The glasses on the table were empty and Oliver was about to call for refills when a figure slid into the booth across from him. "Seein' how the other half lives?" Trevor asked.

Ollie grinned at his old friend. "It's nice to be home . . . occasionally."

Trevor signalled Sadie for his usual glass of draft. Oliver pointed to his empties.

Trevor turned to him. "You've been seen on the town with Carissa Merlino. You sure know how to pick them, Ollie, although this one is on the young side."

"Carissa's a good kid, keen to learn the ropes. I took her on one of my restaurant reviews."

"I hear her family owned Raffaello's."

That was news to Oliver. "The swanky Italian place? It closed last year."

"That's the one." Trevor smiled at Sadie as she set drinks in front of them.

Oliver handed her a couple of bills. "For both of us."

"Thanks, Ollie," Trevor said, raising his glass. "You must've got a hell of a raise."

"You don't know the half of it."

"Funny thing," Trevor said, putting down his glass, "Max Weinstein was a softie with his reviews, then out of nowhere he slams Raffaello's. Business nosedives, the restaurant closes, and suddenly Max says *arrivederci*."

Oliver's stomach tightened. "All coincidence."

Trevor shrugged. "The chef—one of the brothers who owned Raffaello's—hung up his apron one night, headed home, and hanged himself. Left a note about bringing shame upon the family."

"Can't blame it all on one negative review," Oliver said.

"Yeah, who knows what else was going on in the guy's life," Trevor replied. "Anyway, that was the end of Raffaello's." He took a sip from his glass. "But someone has taken it over and renamed it . . . what, I can't remember."

Oliver had a sinking feeling in the pit of his stomach. "Diavolo."

Trevor snapped his fingers. "That's it."

Oliver threw back his Canadian Club. It burned all the way down. "Time to call it a night. I work business hours now."

***

On his drive home, he thought about Max Weinstein. New in his job as entertainment editor, Oliver had been working late; on his way out, he'd spotted cash in an open envelope on the restaurant critic's desk. He went over to check it out. The envelope held five one-hundred-dollar bills and a business card. Oliver had a chat with Weinstein about taking a cut on future envelopes of appreciation.

Weinstein had protested, saying he'd have to up what he charged. And that some restaurant owners might balk.

If they did, make an example of one of them, Oliver told him.

And that's what had happened with Raffaello's.

When Weinstein quit the paper and disappeared, Oliver lobbied hard to take over the restaurant reviews. And their kickbacks.

He gripped the steering wheel. Carissa knew. She'd seen the envelopes. She'd figured out his little scam.

His cell phone rang as he pulled into his parking space behind his condo building. He turned off the ignition. "Townsend."

"Good news, Ollie." It was Carissa. "We're dining at Diavolo on Friday night. Last sitting."

Oliver studied the brick wall ahead of him. "I . . . I don't know. I have work to catch up on."

"But you promised."

He couldn't recall having promised anything.

"We're a *team*, Ollie. You'd better play ball with me."

He sighed. What choice did he have? "All right."

"Cool! It will be a memorable evening."

***

"You enjoyed your dinner?"

Oliver looked up from his espresso to see a sad-eyed, mustachioed man in kitchen whites standing at the table. He and Carissa and two burly waiters were the only ones left in Diavolo's dining room.

"You outdid yourself, Vito," Carissa said. "Oliver, this is my cousin, Vito Merlino. I don't need to introduce you. Vito knows who you are."

Vito bowed. "I am pleased you are here, Mr. Townsend. May I offer you a liqueur?"

"A grappa would go down well," Oliver said.

"You like grappa?" Vito smiled. "It is an acquired taste."

Vito had removed his whites when he returned with three shot glasses filled with a clear liquid, a platter of cannoli, and three dessert plates. He took a seat at the table.

"Italian firewater," he said, handing a glass to Oliver.

Oliver raised the glass. "*Chin-chin*!"

Carissa passed out plates of cannoli.

Oliver took a bite of the tube-shaped pastry filled with sweet, creamy ricotta and wiped his mouth with a napkin. "This doesn't disappoint."

Carissa clapped her hands.

Oliver beamed at Vito. "Diavolo deserves a review in the *World*."

"I knew Ollie would love your food, Vito!" Carissa cried.

Oliver cleared his throat. "Here's how it works."

"Works?" Vito asked.

"Restaurants pay a fee to be reviewed in our newspaper."

"A fee," Vito said. "How much is your fee?"

"I'll write it down for you." Oliver tore a page from his notebook, scribbled a figure, and slid the paper across the table.

Vito stared at the paper and frowned. "Lotta money." He passed the paper to Carissa.

Carissa shook her head. "Integrity and accountability are the cornerstones of journalism, and you've breached them egregiously. Ollie, you're a disgrace to your profession.

"And you've been duping your readers," she added. "I've written your column for the past six weeks."

She produced her smartphone from her purse and placed it on the table. "It's all on here. What we said, and photos of what we ate."

Oliver gave her a ghastly smile.

"MacGregor will be interested," she said. "Your days at the *World* are over."

Oliver suddenly understood. "You wrote the negative review of Di Salvo's restaurant."

Carissa pulled a USB stick from her purse. "I wrote it in advance and put it on this."

"I didn't see—"

"We were working at your place. You were ready to send off

the review, but I asked you to get me a glass of wine. While you were gone, I transferred my file to your laptop and called it up on the screen. When you returned with the wine, I took a chance you'd send off what was up without looking at it again. I was right."

"But why Leonardi's?"

She gave him a sunny smile. "I couldn't resist the opportunity to take a swipe at Di Salvo. His restaurants have been our competition for years."

"That's why you were against a retraction," Oliver said.

She shrugged. "Why mess up a solid review?"

"I've had enough." Oliver started to rise, but he was pushed back down in the chair by the waiters.

"You had to be stopped, Ollie," Carissa said. "You were playing God. Like Max did with my dad."

Carissa's dad was the chef who hanged himself? Oliver groaned.

"We convinced Max to retire," Vito said. "Not smart to play rough with us. You asked me for money after Carissa helped you so much."

Carissa tucked the smartphone, the USB stick, and the page from Ollie's notebook into her purse. "*Ciao*, Ollie."

Vito clamped his left hand around Oliver's right wrist. "Come. We'll show you the kitchen."

One of the waiters took Oliver's other wrist, and they dragged him through the swinging doors. Terrified, Oliver saw a row of shining knives hanging above a massive chopping block.

Vito selected one of the largest blades and ran a finger along its edge. "We'll take you to Max."

"Max?" Max had retired while he could, smart guy. "W–where is he now?"

"At the bottom of Hamilton Harbor."

SNOWBIRDING

By Kristin Kisska

Cold Maine winters vs. sunny Florida beaches. Seems like an easy choice. Or is it? Lizzy and RuthAnne both think so.

~ Present Day ~
Lizzy

Ice scrapings fell from my windshield like shredded ribbons from last week's Christmas wrappings. It was a mite nippy, but nothing a Portlander would brag about. I crunched through the snow to attack the frost on the next window. Didn't care if my wicked old car's heater worked as long as the damned accelerator did. Tomorrow night, thanks to my roommate Joyce, I'd be taking my first swig of a lime margarita while walking barefoot on a Florida beach.

"What's taking so long?" I stomped feeling back into my feet, careful to avoid slipping on the cobblestones exposed inside the potholes. These old bones wouldn't survive another Maine winter, not even with a ferry-load of pocket warmers to thaw my creped hands and extra layers of flannel.

The phone rang inside, probably just another wrong number. Joyce's shadow crisscrossed the living room window of my soon-to-be-ex-apartment. It was hardly in Portland's most charming neighborhood, but at least I'd avoided the brunt of summer tourist traffic every year. Good riddance to this drafty excuse for a home. Couldn't wait to return the damned keys.

"Let's hit the road, already." No second thoughts for me. Last night, I bottle-dyed my grays, all ready for my fresh start. Maybe I'd find a job in Naples and live in sunshine and flip-flops forever. Didn't have anything to return to in Maine. No family to speak of, the downside of being a childless only child. Not even a bank account.

"Hang on a sec, Lizzy. I'm tryin' not to kill myself." Joyce refused to ever rig up to cover her too-hip-for-women-of-our-age fashions under anything as practical as a winter coat—dead giveaway she was from away. After locking the front door, she skated along the walkway's black ice in her high heeled boots, then handed me a paper bag packed with snacks and sodas for the road.

"We got ourselves a full tank of gas and the keys to your beach condo. Next stop, Florida." I shoved her over-stuffed duffel bag in the back and double-slammed the trunk to make sure it wouldn't pop open. The last thing we needed was to leave a trail of old lady panties on the highway. "All set?"

"Almost. Mind if we swing by the post office on the way out of town?"

"More mail?" Lordy, all she cared about was those insurance forms. At this rate, we wouldn't make it out of Portland before Valentine's Day. These past few days, I'd helped her sign so many forms, we could've paved the road straight through to the Gulf of Mexico.

"Don't get stubborn. It'll only take a minute or two . . ."

"Never mind. Sure." Hell, my brain was already in Florida, just needed my body to catch up. That gal was so dumb, she turned down my offer to pay rent for the beach condo. Just my car—beater that it was—to drive south and gas money. No need to play the lottery with Joyce around.

"Thanks, hon. I'll drive the first shift." Joyce's smile flashed her chin dimple, the first sign of road-trip excitement she deigned to share this morning. Hoped she wasn't regretting inviting me along.

I whooped and hollered as Joyce shifted into drive. "Go to hell, winter and pink slips and ex-husbands."

"Amen, sister." She gunned out of the parking lot, almost side-swiping a snow plow. "Buckle up, hon. We want to arrive in one piece."

~ Last Year ~
RuthAnne

"Should I take along my mother's brooch or not?" RuthAnne creaked open the lid of the velvet jewelry box. After transferring her summer wardrobe from her bureau to her suitcases, this heirloom was the last item to consider packing.

"It's exquisite." Jane, with the buttons of her navy cardigan fastened to her collar, stopped organizing her piles of paperwork and examined the piece of jewelry under the lamplight. "Did your grandparents give her that?"

"No, my father. He had it specially commissioned for Mother. It's engraved with their initials. I never met him." He'd left on a fishing excursion when RuthAnne was an infant, but never returned. All her mother's inquiries at the wharf and other villages Down East hadn't turned up any clues. This one piece of jewelry was her anchor—proof that her father had once existed.

"Bring the brooch along, hon." Jane's brow furrowed, but an instant later was replaced with a smile so bright it highlighted her chin dimple. She passed the jewelry piece back, squeezing RuthAnne's hands over it, then resumed her paperwork. "We'll have far more opportunities to get gussied up in Naples than Bar Harbor."

Whatever Jane's insurance job was, she enjoyed reasonable hours and could work from anywhere, be it swaddled in a quilt rocking on her frigid front porch or on a balcony overlooking the Gulf of Mexico. RuthAnne would welcome such a flexible part-time job. Well, maybe without so many papers. She wasn't partial to legal mumbo-jumbo. Or computers. Or even cell phones, for that matter.

"Yes. I think I will." RuthAnne wrapped the jewelry in her nightgown before zipping her suitcase closed. Decades ago, when a Boston fashion magazine featured the brooch, Mother had become quite the sensation among Bar Harbor's locals. But after only two generations, the heirloom's ownership would end with RuthAnne. With no siblings or children, she'd decided to bequeath it to the Woodland Museum where she volunteered as a tour guide. "Would you believe I've never been south of New England?"

Mother, may God rest her soul, would dance the jitterbug if she knew RuthAnne was embarking on this road trip. And a widow at her advanced age, to boot. Since Chip passed away, life had grown sedate with little to keep her occupied beyond volunteering, clamming, and pruning her dooryard plants, none of which was possible during Maine's winter months. Then Jane swept in like a tropical breeze. This surprise Florida vacation was shining brighter than the Egg Rock Lighthouse on a starry night.

"You won't be able to say that this time tomorrow, hon." Jane slipped an envelope into her pocketbook before rigging up in her winter coat. "Mind if we swing by the post office on the way out of town?"

"Of course." RuthAnne had already secured the last of the shutters and lowered the thermostat to save on utilities while she was gone. Since retiring, she'd scrimped every penny she could. "Hope we beat the snowstorm."

"If we hurry, we should be fine. The radio report said the roads have been salted." Jane handed her a paper bag full of snacks and sodas so they wouldn't have to stop for a while. "Did you tell anyone where we're going?"

"Just a change of address notification." No one to tell with Chip gone and her dearest friends relocated to assisted living communities. But now was no time to be wistful with visiting a beach made of sugar-white sand, if Jane's photograph of the Florida's clear turquoise water could be trusted, in her near future. The beaches she knew were similar to Maine's Sand Beach: a strip of coarse sand littered with driftwood, granite breakwaters on either side, pine trees along the back, and rolling dark surf with an occasional windjammer gliding by in the distance.

"Trust me, hon. The Gulf of Mexico is greener than your father's jade brooch. This will be the best winter of your life." Jane, rigged up in a fur-lined parka, helped her carry the last of her suitcases out to the car.

"I've heard of snowbirds—folks who flock south for the winter months—but I never dreamed I'd be one." Odd thing though, Maine's seagulls didn't migrate. Neither did true Mainers. Yet she was about to tilt New England's natural order on its side like a whitecap slamming a buoy.

Snowbirding.

RuthAnne deadbolted the front door and inhaled the crisp salty harbor air. She scanned the Frenchman Bay's horizon and bade a silent goodbye to the gulls squawking over the wharf, to her family's historic Victorian cottage, to Maine. "Look, Jane, I insist on contributing to your condo fees. After all, you paid me rent these months, and I may be staying with you for a while—"

"Stop. I wouldn't dream of it. We might as well have been born sisters. Besides, we're driving your car, and you're paying for gas. It's more than fair. But we shouldn't dawdle if we want to outrun that nor'easter." Jane stomped down the wooden porch stairs with her overpacked duffel bag, then out to the car.

RuthAnne followed, taking care not to slip on a patch of ice. Kicking off their trip by breaking her hip would be a bad omen. The car warmed while they finished loading the trunk.

"I'll drive the first shift." Jane shivered, though bundled in her winter coat, hat, scarf, and gloves as she shifted into reverse.

"Thank you for inviting me along. For everything. I . . ." RuthAnne's voice hitched as she warmed her hands on the passenger side heater. She planned to stay in Florida until the museum reopened to tourists next May. Otherwise, she had no reason to return home before Maine's peak clamming season. No one would miss her. A wicked clean break. Almost too clean. "I can't believe how neatly this trip came together."

"Buckle up, hon. We want to arrive in one piece."

~ Present Day ~
Lizzy

"Mind if I smoke?" The red brick buildings of Portland were long behind us. With every mile marker we passed on I-95, my spirits inflated as if I were one of those dang hot air balloons launched at the Crown of Maine. Any more euphoria and I'd float the rest of the way to Florida.

Twenty-two hours to go.

"Your car, Lizzy. Your rules." Joyce shook her head when I offered her a cigarette. "Tryin' to quit, hon."

Since when? We'd smoked together every damned night for the past six months. I hoped Joyce wouldn't turn too proper on me down south. Cracking open the window, I held the stub outside. I flicked through the radio dial but couldn't find much more than static. Nothing to see but snow-dusted pine trees and the occasional snowplow. Lordy, this was going to be a long ride.

"You still cold?" I nodded toward her hands. Odd for her to be wearing gloves, considering she'd slipped off her coat back apiece. Besides, the heater was cranking along just fine.

"The window draft chills the steering wheel. I'll take 'em off when it warms up outside."

Salt from the treated roadway splattered against the windshield as each mile melted into the next.

"So, tell me about that honkin' stack of forms you're always working on. Must be nice not having to punch a card in a time slot." Not that I'd collected a paycheck in six months, which was why I placed the classified ad in the *Portland Press Herald* for a roommate. Joyce had been the first to respond. When new employment never came along, she invited me to join her in Florida after the holidays. We'd be "snowbirds," she called it. I'd always wanted a sibling. This was as close to sisterhood as I'd ever get, so I jumped at the chance.

"Just work, is all. I process insurance claims. People get their money. Who needs an office for that?"

A few minutes drifted by marked only by the rumbling of my tires over potholes. Then another few. A flake or two hit the windshield.

Getting Joyce to talk today was proving painful. Her moods shifted worse than the Bay of Fundy's tides. We'd be stuck together in my car for a long time. The least she could do was help me out with the conversation.

"You're a cunning thing, Joyce." She'd never admitted her age, but I'd bet my overdue alimony check that she was at least five years younger than me. "Why didn't you ever get remarried?"

"No man's worth a ring. I knew better than to get hitched. My father left us for some other woman while I was still in diapers. We never heard from the asshole again. Not even a birthday card. Trust me, if he wasn't already dead, I'da helped him along for my mother's sake."

Lordy, I could relate. Men!

"My pops waltzed in and out of my life so much I thought our front door revolved like at a fancy hotel. He was always off on some commercial fishing expedition or other. Gone for weeks. Once, for a whole year. But wicked bad rumors had a way of following him back home. Affairs. Don't know why Mama let him out of her sight. Not me. The first time I caught Jimmy chasing skirts, I divorced him faster than a lobster trap could sink to the bottom of the Casco Bay. The best thing Jimmy ever gave me was my married name. Miller is a hell of a lot easier to pronounce than Wojciechowski."

That wasn't the only name I changed when I married Jimmy. As the child of immigrants and a less-than-practicing parishioner of Maine's first Polish church, I shed my given name—Elżbeta. Lizzy Miller became my all-American makeover. Too bad it didn't come with a steady paycheck and a man who kept his vows.

"Amen, sister." Joyce exhaled so loudly it could've been a groan. "No, Eric and I are much better suited apart than together."

"Eric? Your beau? Don't remember meeting him."

"You didn't. Haven't seen him for months. Maybe he'll drop by in Florida."

"How'd you get the beach condo?"

"Inherited it from my mom. She bought it after the divorce."

I flicked the cigarette butt out the window, then rolled it up. Twenty-one hours and forty-five minutes to go.

~ Last Year ~
RuthAnne

RuthAnne flinched whenever Jane took a turn a little too fast. But when she passed a snow plow on two-lane Bangor Road with an oncoming car speeding toward them, she muttered a prayer and braced for impact.

"Am I driving too fast for you, hon?" Jane gripped the steering wheel with gloved hands; there was still a bit of a chill despite having driven an hour.

"Perhaps you could slow down a dite." RuthAnne's car was

half her age, but still plenty old. Someone once referred to it as vintage.

"Your car, RuthAnne. Your rules."

When Jane eased up on the speed, RuthAnne relaxed again and adjusted the scarf covering her hairdo. "Thank you. Passing cars makes me nervous." Around Bar Harbor, she always drove ten miles *under* the speed limit. What was an extra hour or two on a long road trip anyway? Their objective was to arrive safely.

"We'll be on I-95 soon, hon. That'll be a smoother ride."

An hour or so later, they'd traveled beyond any signs and landmarks RuthAnne recognized. What had possessed her to take this trip? The truth was, not only had she never been out of New England, she'd never crossed the Maine border. But this road trip to Florida wouldn't be her only first this year. Last summer, RuthAnne had met Jane on one of her guided tours of the Woodlawn Museum. Despite the difference in their ages—Jane was at least a decade younger and spirited to boot—they shared a love of the Down East coastal region. Once Jane saw the panoramic harbor view from her front porch, she asked if RuthAnne had a spare room to rent. The payments eased her tight budget—Chip's illness and funeral expenses had drained her retirement savings—and the companionship revitalized her otherwise sedate existence.

Jane glanced over, then sighed. "You could use a spot of tea."

"Wouldn't that be lovely? I don't see a kettle or teacups in here, though."

"I wish!" Mirth twinkled in Jane's eyes. "But why don't you open a couple sodas for us, hon? You'll find a little surprise in the glove compartment."

Tucked beside her maps and a flashlight was a polished silver flask. One sniff of the contents tickled RuthAnne's nose, launching a wave of coziness through her body.

"Brandy? Oh, my dear, I shouldn't . . ." But as she objected, the bleak landscape whipping by her window chilled her bones. Or was she regretting leaving her home and all things familiar behind? The promise of Florida's golden sunshine tarnished in January's gray New England daylight. At least she'd brought along her mother's brooch.

"Treat yourself, RuthAnne. You're on vacation."

Perhaps a nip of brandy would help ease her nerves. "Are you sure? I expect you'll want to switch soon."

"I don't mind driving for a while. We'll make a pitstop in a couple hours. You relax and enjoy."

"You're so thoughtful." RuthAnne tentatively sipped the sweet, yet sharp cocktail. Oh, drinking by day was a new vice for her. Chip would've never approved. But where was he now? Locked away in heaven. A swig or two. What was the harm?

Warmth spread, first in her cheeks and then down her arms until her fingertips tingled. Her ankles sank into the floorboard. The winter sun took on a sepia-toned hue. Relax? Yes. RuthAnne could honestly say that she was relaxing. Drifting. It was delicious, except . . . except . . .

She flapped her turtleneck to catch some cool air. My, it was getting over-warm in there.

Oh, dear!

Why did it feel as if a strap was tightening around her chest?

~ Present Day ~
Lizzy

"Lizzy, hon, why don't you pop open a couple sodas for us? And I hid a little surprise in the glove compartment."

Joyce's smile had a mischievous glint. She was up to something, like that time she convinced me to forge names on her work forms. When her bonus arrived, we splurged on sparkly party dresses and went out for dinner in the Old Port District. My dress was packed in the trunk ready for another night out, this time in Florida.

Resting among my spare packs of cigarettes was a flask. Why hadn't I thought of that?

"Rum?"

"Treat yourself, Lizzy. You're on vacation."

"You're an angel." Or the devil. Either way, a cocktail or two would help the time pass quicker. Couldn't possibly be legal, but a glance ahead and behind us confirmed there wasn't much traffic on the highway. I drank a dite of the blueberry soda before spiking it all the way up to the aluminum rim. "Can I pour you some?"

"Not yet, hon. I'll have one when it's your turn to drive. But I'll take one of those lobster rolls."

"Mug-up. Cheers to us."

~ Last Year ~
RuthAnne

What's happening? The world around RuthAnne edged darker. *I can't breathe.* Oxygen. Precious, diminishing oxygen. That's all she craved.

Invisible weights crushed her lungs, though nothing but her

seatbelt strap tethered her. She tried to squirm away from whatever had her in its grip, but her arms wouldn't budge. If she focused, she could tap her little finger against the seat. Barely.

Noises invaded the black hole enveloping her, drowning her. Still, a whisper of a breath scraped past her lips.

Brakes squealed. Then metal slammed.

A blast of frigid air sliced her body.

"Is she dead yet?"

Who said that? A man. Had they been traveling with a man? No. RuthAnne hadn't spoken to any gentlemen in quite some time. A stranger, then.

"Think so. She was unconscious before I could pull onto the shoulder."

Ah, Jane. Dear, charming Jane. If only RuthAnne could somehow alert her that she was conscious, Jane would call for help.

An ambulance.

Police.

Please, somebody, help me.

RuthAnne tapped her pinkie. Once. Twice.

"Hand me your duffel. The rest area's a few miles down the road. Good spot to leave her car. I'll go on ahead and scope out the security cameras. If I text you a wink emoji, keep on driving. It'll mean cops or workers are there."

"Hang on a minute, Eric. RuthAnne packed some nice jewelry. Her father had it made."

~ Present Day ~
Lizzy

"Woah! Why'd you swerve, Joyce? You made me spill my drink." Syrupy soda and rum soaked the front of my cable knit sweater and seeped into the seat cushion. Crap. And just as I was about to indulge in my first swig.

"The asshole cut me off." Joyce laid on her horn and flashed her lights at him. "You really effed-it up this time, numb-nuts."

As the red pickup truck sped away, Joyce gunned the accelerator, thrusting me against my seat.

"What the . . . slow down!" I jabbed my foot at the floorboard, wishing there was a passenger-side brake like those for student driver cars.

Joyce flipped her middle finger over the dashboard at the truck. "This wasn't the plan, bastard."

"Don't tailgate the damned pickup truck. If he jams on the brakes, you're gonna rear-end him and get us both killed." I'd seen

Joyce fly off the handle before, but she was wicked overreacting. "Wait. Do you know him?"

"No." Instead of slowing, Joyce changed lanes to pull up beside him. What the hell? My poor, rusty sedan vibrated as the speedometer redlined.

"Stop the road rage!"

Joyce eased off the accelerator a bit, but the pickup truck slowed as well.

"Great. Now you've started something. I told you to cut it out."

"It's all over. See? The truck is staying a couple hundred yards away. The jackass learned his lesson. Pour yourself another drink, Lizzy. Relax."

"How can I relax while I'm sitting in a damned puddle and you're playing chicken with my car? Pull off the road. I'll drive."

"No, really, Lizzy. It's okay. I'll keep driving. We'll get off the next time we get to a rest area."

"When? In a hundred miles? I'll be glued to my seat by then. I might as well be a toddler who wet her pants."

Joyce let out a long breath before handing me an unopened can of soda. "Sorry. We'll get you cleaned up right away. Have another cocktail."

"Pull over. Now. My car, my rules. Remember, *hon*?" But Joyce made no effort to comply. "Why are you so obsessed with me drinking rum anyway? It's not even noon yet."

"Just wanna make sure you're enjoying yourself is all, hon. This was supposed to be a fun road trip. Florida is still a long way off." She handed me the flask of rum.

No one could tell me what to do. I rolled down the window and chucked Joyce's flask.

"What the hell did you do that for?"

~ Last Year ~
RuthAnne

"No way, Janet. Leave the jewelry with her stuff. We never take personal effects."

Janet? Why was this man calling Jane *Janet*?

"Her brooch might be worth something."

RuthAnne couldn't possibly have understood that correctly through the fog. She concentrated on twitching her finger. *Please, Jane, look over and help me.* Every breath struggled through lungs that refused to expand.

"This piece of crap?"

"Trust me, Eric. It's jade. Ol' man Borys didn't mind splurging on the good stuff for RuthAnne's mother, but not mine. I consider it a bonus for a lifetime of abandonment. Take it. We can decide what to do with it later."

No! How could Jane steal her mother's jade brooch?

RuthAnne tapped her finger again. Her breathing became faster, yet shallower.

A vision of the pin flashed in her mind's eye. Every nuance of the carved swirls in the single block of stone. The exact shade of translucent green. The white gold filigree surrounding the oval jade. RuthAnne had worn it on her wedding day as her Something Old, even more sentimental since the father she'd never met couldn't walk her down the aisle.

"Shit. Did you see that? Her finger. It's twitching."

"RuthAnne's alive?"

Oh, thank goodness Jane noticed. She must help her before it's too late.

"Put that goddamned gun away, Eric. If they suspect murder, the insurance company won't pay out."

"One way or another, this bitch is gonna die. Take care of it now, or I'll shoot her."

Pressure pinched RuthAnne's nostrils. Her jaw clamped shut. Her head forced into the headrest. She fought to part her lips, but warm hands squeezed them together.

Why, Jane?

"See you in hell, sister."

After a moment, the fire burning RuthAnne's lungs eased. Her fingertip relaxed, then stopped responding altogether. The vision of her jade brooch dissipated like Bar Harbor's mud flats at low tide when the fog creeped in.

Nothingness.

~ Present Day ~
Lizzy

Blue lights flashed in the rear-view mirror.

"Oh, no. Cops. Do you think they saw me throw out the flask?" If so, they could force us to walk a straight line and touch the tips of our noses. The sickly-sweet smell of blueberry soda and rum enveloped the car.

Joyce braked as the red pickup sped away. One of the cruisers flew by to chase it while the other two cornered us. She pulled off on the shoulder, then rolled to a stop.

"License and registration." Guns were trained on both sides of my car. "Hands on the steering wheel. No fast moves."

"Sorry, Joyce." I raised both hands in the air and said my prayers. Didn't realize littering was taken this seriously in New Hampshire, or Massachusetts, or wherever the hell we were.

"Janet W. Martin, we have a warrant for your arrest. Get out of the car."

They must've stopped the wrong car. No one named Janet Martin in here. But Joyce opened her door and stepped out.

"You have the right to remain silent . . ." A cop handcuffed her wrists, walked her to the waiting police cruiser, then shoved her head down as she crunched into the back seat.

What's going on? What was I missing? Arctic wind whipped around me from the still-open driver's side door, chilling my soaked sweater and pants.

Wait. Joyce's real name was Janet?

That phone call last night while Joyce packed the car. Some guy asked for Janet. Figured it was a wrong number, so I'd forgotten all about it. But why would she be arrested?

"Ma'am?" Bare knuckles rapped on the passenger-side window until I cracked it open. "I'm Agent Mulroney. You all right?"

"I'm fine." He flashed a badge at me, but I stared ahead at the blotches of salt staining the highway white. The barren trees on either side of the pavement stretched endlessly into a bleak horizon. Traffic zipped by us in the far lane, all heading south, the direction I wanted to go.

With averted eyes, he shook his head. "An ambulance is on the way for you. I'll follow you to the hospital and get your statement there."

"What the hell just happened?"

"I'm sorry, ma'am, but the driver is a known killer. She and her husband are wanted in a couple states."

I couldn't have possibly heard that correctly. Joyce, a murderer? But one look at his furrowed brow and clenched jaw, and I almost peed in my already-soaked pants. She must've lied about not being married, too.

"How . . . how'd she do it?"

"Poisoning by hemlock."

"Holy Mary, mother of God. I came *this* close to drinking her cocktail. You'll find her flask back there apiece in the grass. Did I save myself by my own stubbornness?"

After donning rubber gloves, the agent slipped my soda can into a plastic bag. "Your drink may have been poisoned. Don't touch your mouth."

"How many victims?"

"One other, that we know of. Older female of modest means.

We found her body in her own car at a rest area about a hundred miles south of Maine. Before leaving, she'd taken out a new life insurance policy and filed a change of address to a Florida beachfront resort for the winter. Janet and the victim have the same name on their birth certificates—Borys Wor . . . Wojcie . . ."

Memories of people butchering my maiden name with similar sputtering flooded my mind. Oh, how I dreaded all those Polish vowels as much as any nor'easter.

"Borys Wojciechowski?"

He nodded.

My heart sank to where my jeans scrunched into my Bean boots. *Oh, Pops.* Mama may have forgiven him his sins, but I sure as hell hadn't. I'd heard the rumors of his illegitimate children. Never, ever believed any of 'em. Until now.

My chin quivered. Dammit, I refused to cry in front of these cops or agents. "How'd you brainiacs finally peg the murders to Joyce—or Janet—or whatever her real name is?"

"She got greedy."

"Come again?"

"She pawned a jade brooch. The piece was unique enough that the shop owner looked into auctioning it. It was engraved. We traced the ownership back to her victim and identified both Janet and Eric Martin through the security footage from the pawn shop. Last night, we tracked his call to your home phone."

Ambulance lights strobed in the distance. With each flash, four thoughts throbbed in my mind. I hadn't been an only child after all. I'd been living with my sister—correction, my half-sister—for months without realizing it. She probably killed my other half-sister before I could meet her. And she had been planning to kill me, too.

"So, if it hadn't been for a piece of old jewelry, I was her next . . ."

Sweet Jesus, I needed a smoke. Now.

"…snowbird."

UP DAY DOWN DAY DEADLY DAY

By Ellen Larson

'For never was a story of more woe . . .'
William Shakespeare

Aly Mackey spoke in a reedy voice, easy to hear above the chatter in the room. "So pleased to see a new face, Chief. Tell me . . ." She swirled her ruby-red goblet and peered at me with great solemnity. ". . . what is your WOE?"

I experienced what my pre-teen daughter calls a free zone of disquietude.

As police chief of Meadow Rue, NY (population 781), I get paid to keep a cool head in tricky situations. But as I stood in the Municipal Building Community Room that evening in late April, waiting amongst the regular members of the Slim Janes for the Tuesday meeting to begin, I blanked.

Woe? Hm. Internet slang for a traumatic life event? Hard to picture Ms. Mackey, a retired history teacher soon to celebrate her seventieth, as a cyber nerd. A quote from Shakespeare? Or the Bible? I quaked. Being saved was not anything I had imagined when weighing the perils of joining the Janes.

"Actually, I'm in pretty good spirits, thanks," I said.

Ms. Mackey's stare seemed to have gotten stuck. I stared back, likewise frozen.

"Oh for Pete's sake, Aly." Tempest Whitehall materialized at my elbow, a stout ninja bearing a golden goblet come to the rescue. Tempest was one of those perpetually smiling women who are often underestimated by those who interpret their relentless good spirits as a sign of shallowness. "She's asking your way of eating. W, O, E. Get it?"

"Ah! I see." This I had prepared for. "Well, I don't think I eat more than I used to, but as the years go by I've put on a few pounds, and I can't seem to—"

"No, no," said Ms. Mackey, waving a hand in my face. "Your *regime*. Your *plan*. Weight Watchers, South Beach, Atkins . . ."

"Oh! What *diet* am I on!" I boomed, not realizing till it was too late that the chatter had died down.

Sissy Toogood, who operated a small business selling goat's

milk soaps, winced.

"Sorry," I said.

Sissy handed me an emerald goblet. "We don't use the D-word."

"Oh. I see."

"We prefer *way of eating*," said Ms. Mackey.

"Ah!" The Janes had gathered round, their communal curiosity no doubt piqued by my brilliant imitation of a fish out of water.

"There's lots of WOEs," said Ronnie, co-owner of the Meadow Rue Diner. No-nonsense Ronnie held no goblet of any color. "UDDD, IF, EOD, OMAD . . ."

"He's probably SAD," suggested someone from the group.

Again with the tragedy, I thought, but managed not to say.

"Standard American Diet," explained Tempest, her brown eyes twinkling. "Full of carbs."

"Tempest does keto," said Sissy, as if explaining something.

I gathered the shreds of my dignity and asked, "What do you do?"

"I'm eco-Atkins," she replied.

"Oh." So much for dignity. "Well, I see I'm going to learn a lot about di . . . about, uh, weight loss."

"Weight management," said Sissy.

"Weight management." I took a sip from my goblet. It was water. "Because to tell you the truth, I've never been on a di . . . I've never tried to l . . . I've never done this type of thing before."

"Don't worry, Chief." Tempest placed a hand on my arm. "You'll get the hang of it."

The Janes drifted away and the chatter resumed.

I stared at Tempest. "I just wanted to lose a few pounds."

Her lips twisted in comic sympathy. "Welcome to my world."

***

"Where's Becca?" asked Aly Mackey. "It's a quarter past and everyone is here. You'd think our chairwoman would be on time."

"I'll call her," said Sissy, whipping out her cell and drifting to a corner of the Community Room.

"You'll have to run the meeting, Tempest," said Ms. Mackey. "Seems the toxins have gotten to Becca again."

"You wish," scowled Ronnie. "We had lunch together. Rarin' to go. She'll be here."

"I'll step in if I have to," said Tempest. "But I'm sure . . ." She looked around till she spotted Sissy, at which point her face fell. "Uh oh."

I turned to follow her gaze and witnessed Sissy moving to the center of the room, her face streaked with fear.

"This is horrible!" she gasped. "Horrible! Becca is in the Watertown ICU. Anaphylaxis and heart attack. Severe allergic reaction! That worthless Milton was out playing golf so she lay there till four. If the mailman hadn't spotted her through the screen door, she'd be dead!"

And suddenly I was back in my world.

***

"Chief." Tempest rose to shake my hand as I entered her real estate office the following Friday. "Nice to see you again so soon. How's the diet?" She pointed to a chair.

"Should you be using the D-word?"

"I'm a rebel."

I sighed as I seated myself. "Well, in all honesty, I'm having trouble getting into the groove," I admitted. "Although I've cut back to one teaspoon of sugar in my coffee. That's a start, right?"

She gave me a calculating look. "I'll be honest with you, Oz. A man of your height and age should probably consume about two thousand calories a day. There are sixteen calories in a teaspoon of sugar. Do the math."

I treated Tempest to the police officer's side-eye. "You pulling a fast one? You rattled those numbers off pretty quick."

Tempest looked at me like I had just arrived from Mars. "I know the calorie count of any food you'd care to name. And the carb count, too."

"Celery."

"Sixteen calories per hundred grams, one and a half carbs."

"Steak."

"Two-hundred-seventy calories per hundred grams. Zero carbs."

"Baked potato."

"Seventy calories, twenty carbs."

"Seventy? That's not so bad. Wait. Does that include the butter?"

"Nope. Add a hundred calories per tablespoon for the butter."

"Darn. I like butter on my baked potato."

"Me too." She sighed wistfully.

I knew that sigh. "Do you miss it?" I asked.

"The butter? Heck no. I'm keto. I eat all the butter I want. It's the potato I miss."

"Really," I said before I could stop myself. I folded my hands on my stomach and was suddenly aware of the bulge that had not been there the previous spring.

"So, what can I do for you today?" she asked. "You gonna put your chateau up on the market?"

"Not likely. Becca's doctor called me to say she's holding her own. Still sedated, but they say no damage to the heart or lungs and what not. I thought you'd want to know."

"Thank heavens!" Relief washed over Tempest's cherubic face. "What on Earth happened? Do they know?"

I shrugged. "Still trying to put the pieces together, from what I gather. Looks like an allergic reaction, maybe to wheat. Do you know if she had any food allergies?"

"No idea. She was into health foods and supplements and all that. Very careful eater. Ronnie might know. They share recipes. But I can tell you this: she definitely did *not* have an allergic reaction to wheat."

"How do you know?"

"Because Becca's WOE is low-carb paleo."

"That actually doesn't help."

"Sorry. That's the one where you only eat foods that were available to our cave-dwelling . . . Okay, never mind. Let's just say she ate very low carb. And that means she never ate anything made with wheat."

"Huh," I said. I fixed my eyes on the painting on the wall behind Tempest's head. An Oneida longhouse built on the edge of a meadow, bright with flowers. "You know, I have to admit I don't get all this low-carb talk." I raised my hands, palms up. "Can you—?"

"It's simple—no, really. Okay, I'll make it simple. There are only three things you can eat that contain calories: protein, carbs, and lipids—that's fats to you, unless you're shy about using the F word."

"Wouldn't dream of it."

"You're learning. So you know what foods are fatty, right? Butter, cream, oils, cheeses, eggs."

"Right. And protein means meat."

"More or less. Also some beans and eggs again."

"So that leaves the famous carbs. Which I always assumed was sugar."

"Sugars or starches. Rice, potato, bread and pasta, fruit."

"I thought fruit was good for you. An apple a day."

"It's not about good or bad, Chief. Remove that way of thinking from your mind. No food is good or bad. It's about how much, how often, and in what combination. At least it is now. When we were kids, the commercial dieting world only considered how much. Calories in, calories out. More out than in, you lose weight."

"Makes sense."

"Yes, it does. For many people in many situations. But not for everyone. Because it makes you really hungry. In the Sixties, the solution was supposed to be low fat, because the more fat you eat the more you put on, right?"

"Makes sense."

"Does it? You're gonna want to study up on how your metabolism works some time real soon. But the sugar industry thought the fat-equals-fat argument was super. They promoted the idea that carbs were 'energy,' and everybody likes energy and hates fat. Which ended the country up in the type 2 diabetes epidemic we now face."

"So carbs are bad—sorry! So the pendulum swings, and rings a bell. Atkins."

"Right. The granddaddy of low carb WOEs. Ah, the simple days of the 1980s. It worked for a lot of people. Particularly because you can eat a lot of calories on low carb. I lost eighty pounds on Atkins. On the other hand, the original menu was limited. A lot of people got bored out of their skulls, including me. But clever people started developing other low carb WOEs that weren't so restrictive. Got it?"

"Got it. The acronyms. So, getting back to Becca . . ."

"We're almost there. The thing with low carb is that you have to do it religiously, or it doesn't work at all. Rice, potatoes, bread, and even that apple are never, ever on your menu. For example, I try to keep my carbs under twenty a day. Take our favorite, the potato. That's twenty carbs right there. Most foods have at least a couple of carbs in them, so there's no way I can eat a potato and then eat much of anything else."

"Okay, I hear you say that, but why? That's what I never got. What's the trick?"

Tempest rose and went to the mini fridge atop a filing cabinet. "Care for a Diet Coke? Diet Sprite? Diet anything? I stock a full bar."

"I'm good, thanks." I never cared much for the taste of a diet soda.

She pulled out a can of Diet Cherry Coke and leaned up against her filing cabinet. "Here's the deal. Metabolism 101. If you severely restrict carbs long enough—three or four days—your body runs out of stored energy."

"And you die?" I was suddenly aware that the noon hour was approaching, reminded by the gnawing sensation in my gut.

"Eventually. But it takes quite a while. In the meantime, with no immediate source of energy, the body changes metabolic gears and switches to the back-up plan. It converts stored fat into energy.

I mean, what the heck do you think all those fat cells were actually intended for, anyway?"

"Well, what do you know. I think I got it!"

"See? Now here's what you have to remember: when the body has no carbs and is burning up fat cells for energy, we call it being in ketosis. The fast track to weight loss while eating lots of good foods and not being hungry. But the catch is, to make it work, you have to stay in ketosis. And to stay in ketosis, you can't ever, even for one day, or one meal, pig out on carbs. Because if you do, the body will go back to metabolizing carbs, and all those fat calories you're gobbling will spike up your weight."

"I got it! What you're saying is, Becca didn't eat carbs, so she didn't eat wheat, because wheat is full of carbs!"

"Yeah." Tempest took a slug of her Diet Cherry Coke. "That's what I'm saying."

"But she might have broken her WOE. People do that, right? Even low carb people?"

"Yes, we do," said Tempest. "That's why we call it weight management and not a diet. But I'm telling you as an expert in the field, it's unlikely Becca would do that, as it is not her pattern, and that there is absolutely no chance on Earth that she would break her WOE during the Easter Feaster Challenge on the very day of a weigh-in."

"Easter Feaster?" It was like a new language. "Challenge?"

"A challenge is a commitment to rigorously follow your WOE for a period of time. It can be a way to regain focus, or to break a stall. Or just to participate with others, for fun. We do four month-long challenges a year. The Easter Feaster runs from March twentieth to April twentieth this year."

"A competition," I repeated. "The winner is the one who loses the most weight?"

Her eyes flickered. "We discourage that. We're a support group, not an Olympic sport. We set personal goals for our challenges and strive to meet them. But, yes, some . . . people . . . believe a competitive spirit can be of assistance in sticking to plan."

"Some people like Becca," I said. Her face told me I had it right. "Ergo, Becca did not eat wheat on Tuesday." I leaned back, making a steeple with my hands.

Tempest's logic was, if not irrefutable, at least an excellent working hypothesis. And as such it cast the circumstances of Becca's near death in an entirely new light. "What did Aly Mackey mean," I asked, "when she said the toxins were getting to Becca again? And then Ronnie said 'You wish'?"

"My, you're good," said Tempest quietly, as if to herself. She took another slug of soda. "Okay, I'll spill. But you didn't hear this from me."

"Deal."

"Aly was implying that Becca skipped the meeting because she didn't want to weigh in. Aly is also . . . competitive."

This was not what I had expected to hear. Which made the back of my neck tingle. "A bet? Lunch at the Waterfalls Bar and Grill?"

"No. We don't allow that. But we can't stop people from boasting. It may sound foolish, but people get extremely invested in their WOE. Aly is old school. A calorie-counting purist. That's all she does. Count calories. She thinks low carb is smoke and mirrors, a marketing gambit by the specialty food industry invented to separate the suckers from their money. Aly lives on a fixed income, whereas Becca spends a fortune on low-carb foods and substitutes."

The mind boggled. It had never occurred to me that I might have to spend more on food to eat less. "What are substitutes?"

"That's like using a lettuce wrap instead of pita bread, or almond flour instead of wheat flour. Becca is an amazing low-carb cook."

"That does sound good. Maybe I should try a low-carb WOE."

"I honestly don't think it's for you, Oz. It takes a lot of prep, and you're a busy man. And the restrictions can be tough. But I tell you what—you should do the Up Day Down Day Diet. It's easy and it works, and you can eat all your regular foods. Just—not much of them every other day."

My stomach growled. "How much is not much?"

"About five hundred calories for you."

I consulted the longhouse again. "That's not much."

"No, but you'd be surprised what you can do with zucchini and an egg. And the beauty is you're never more than a few hours away from a filling meal. Up Day Down Day is a great tool. It suppresses the appetite and is flexible. I sometimes use it myself, as it's perfect for maintenance mode."

"Maintenance mode?"

My look of wonder inspired another what-planet-did-this-man-come-from look from Tempest. "Losing those few pounds isn't like getting over a cold, Oz. You're one of those people who's put on ten or twenty pounds over time. Easily corrected. Obesity has not been a life-long problem for you. If you can commit to six or eight weeks of Up Day Down Day, you should be able to regain your fighting weight. Then throw in a down day or two every week to keep it off. I can email you the info."

"I'd appreciate it." The gnawing in my stomach was impossible to ignore. "Well, I better get a move on. Thanks for your time."

"You're welcome," she said. But when we rose and shook hands, she held on to mine. "Oz . . . it was an accident, what happened to Becca, right?"

"I assume so," I said. "Why do you ask?"

"Because if you just wanted to let me know that Becca was doing better, you could have called."

Busted. But . . . "Something you want to tell me?"

She released my hand, the perpetual smile fading. "It's pretty common knowledge that Milton married Becca for her money. He's . . . not a nice man. You didn't hear that from me."

"Hear what?"

The smile returned, and the twinkle. "See you at the Slim Janes this Tuesday?"

"I wouldn't miss it," I said.

***

I headed across the town square without really seeing the show of red and yellow tulips around the war memorial, for my head was filled with visions of metabolic processes and carb counts. Where had this information been all my life, I wondered? By the time I pushed through the doors of the Meadow Rue Diner, I had decided that I was sadly ignorant—and very hungry.

I took a seat at a back booth and picked up a menu.

Carbs jumped out at me: French fries, onion rings, hash browns, beans and rice, pie, cake, brownies, bread, bread, bread. And the fats I had been conditioned to fear. Egads. Cheese omelets, liverwurst sandwiches, onion rings again, avocado, cream, olive oil, butter, coconut custard, salad dressing, bacon, bacon, bacon. And there on the bottom third of the second page a small section I had never even noticed: Low Carb Fare.

"Morning, Chief," said Ronnie as she sailed up and parked it by my booth. "How's life treating you?"

"What's a veggie burger?" I asked. "Low carb?"

"Nope," she drawled. "Veggie burgers are pretty much all carbs. Vegetarians love carbs. Real burgers are low carb. Paleos love burgers. Protein."

"Of course." I put the menu down with a sigh. "Actually, I was hoping to talk with you. You got a minute?"

Her eyes widened in fear. "Is it Becca? Is she okay?"

"Out of the woods, according to her doctors. Gonna be fine. Didn't mean to scare you."

"Well, that's good, because as a matter of fact I want to talk to you. Cover for me, Chickie!" she called over her shoulder. "I'm takin' five." She planted herself on the green vinyl seat opposite and placed her palms on the table, elbows akimbo. "Is there any hope you're gonna tell me you arrested that no-good scoundrel Becca called her 'nutritionist.'"

"Hold on, there, Ronnie. What—?"

"Because it's clear as the nose on your face that whatever threw Becca into anaphylaxis whatchamajiggy had to come from one of those supplements 'Professor' Jewel had her taking. You hear about contaminated supplements all the time. Half the baseball players—"

I switched to my professional voice. "Slow down, please, Ronnie. I'm going to listen, but I need you to take your time and stick to the facts."

"Yeah, yeah, sure, Joe Friday." She exhaled rapidly, and moved her hands to her lap. "Look, I admit I'm upset. My best friend almost died three days ago. I told her Jewel was just a leech, suckin' her dry, but she was all about the probiotics and the beets and the green micronutrients and she bought whatever he sold her. By the case. To the tune of thousands."

"Wow."

"You gotta have those supplements tested, Chief, I'm telling you. I went over to her house Tuesday night to make sure that slacker Milton didn't throw them out. Sat on the porch and waited there till midnight for him to get home from the hospital."

"Smart thinking," I said. "You had lunch with Becca Tuesday, right?"

"Pfft. You're not very subtle, are you? Me neither. I've been over it a hundred times. We had avocado salad with pecans, her fresh-baked almond bread, and a chicken cold plate on lettuce." She counted off the items on her fingers. "I ate everything she ate, and even took home a piece of bread which I ate the next day. And as you can see, I'm just fine."

"Did she have any food allergies?"

"She never mentioned one. But obviously she wouldn't intentionally eat anything she knew she was allergic to. I'm surprised you didn't think of that. That's why it's gotta be Jewel! He should be arrested! He's a criminal!"

"Now, Ronnie. Why would he try to harm Becca?"

"I'm not saying it was intentional—or I'd be pointing a finger at that moocher she married. But negligence is a crime, isn't it? And at the very least, Jewel was negligent! What else could it be?"

"I don't know. But thank you. You're doing the right thing by telling me your suspicions. You're a good friend."

Ronnie curled her lip. "Good lord, will you cut it out with the support group drivel? You're just as bad as the damned Slim Janes. 'Oh, you're doing so well! Never mind if you fall off the wagon, everybody does! Oh, you look great. It's just a stall!' *Tch.* It's so patronizing."

"Not the sensitive type, either." I pretended to take a note. "In which case, pardon me for asking, but why do you go to the Slim Janes? You're not, y'know . . ."

"Fat?" she snorted. "I thought you were smarter than that, Chief. You're not drinking these days, but you still go to AA regular, don't you?"

"Good point," I said. "So you're in maintenance mode."

"That's right." She grinned suddenly. "Twelve years."

"What's your WOE?"

"This month I'm doing keto, so I could do the Easter Feaster with Becca. But as the years go by I get bored, so I often switch up. I throw in Stillman's or a potato hack every now and then."

"What's a potato hack?"

"Look it up." She stood and whipped a pen out of her pocket. "So what'll you have?"

I sucked in my lips as I perused the menu. So many choices. So many pitfalls. I had acquired enough knowledge to realize that there were a dozen different paths to weight loss, but not enough to pick one. Best to stick with the tried and true.

"I'll have the tuna melt. On whole wheat."

"Side?" she asked.

"Fries. And a cup of coffee. Black, two sugars." After all, it was only sixteen calories.

***

The Community Room was festooned with paper Easter baskets filled with eggs dyed blue, pink, and yellow. I sat in a folding chair that seemed slightly too small, nursing a water with a dash of lime in a turquoise goblet and watching the Slim Janes take turns recording their final Easter Feaster weigh-in. They made it look fun, applauding one another and calling out words of encouragement no matter what the result. Even the superior Aly Mackey, standing next to the physician's scale and verifying the numbers, had nothing but nice things to say. A sense of belonging stirred within me. What a gang.

I turned to Sissy Toogood, sitting to my left. "You didn't do the Easter Feaster?" I asked

"I did," she said. "But I don't weigh. Scale weight is passé. It's not reflective of true lipid-mass loss. I track BFP."

"Oh," I said. "What's—?" I began, but was interrupted by Ronnie's irritated twang.

“The scale is off, Tempest. It’s completely impossible for me to be up three pounds.”

“You’ve just stalled, that’s all,” said Aly. “Typical for low carb.”

Tempest shot Ms. Mackey an aggrieved glance, then turned back to Ronnie. “Never mind. You know it happens. Are you sure you’re in ketosis?”

“Well, I didn’t check, if that’s what you mean. I can’t afford keto strips.”

“Don’t be disappointed, Ronnie,” said June. “You’re a role model for all of us.”

Ronnie rolled her eyes. “Seriously, June. I could care less about three pounds. I’m trying to tell you that I know what I’ve eaten the past week, so your scale must be off. There’s no other possible explanation. I told you these modern body fat scales don’t work!”

The Janes took a hard right into a discussion about bioelectrical impedance and something called a DEXA Scan. But I didn’t even try to follow, for the back of my neck was tingling again.

“Excuse me,” I said, raising a hand. “Excuse me?”

The chatter faded and the Janes turned to me.

“Do you have a question, Chief?” asked Tempest.

“Believe me, you don’t want to know about keto strips,” cracked June.

“I need your help,” I said, putting my goblet on the floor. “Check me here. Isn’t it true that there *is* another possible explanation for Ronnie’s scale reading?”

Ronnie threw up her hands. “I am not in denial and I didn’t eat anything that would make me gain weight!”

“I’m sure you didn’t—intentionally.” I spoke slowly, searching my newly acquired knowledge for the right words. “But if you thought you ate some, uh, low-carb substitute, but were actually eating the real thing, ingesting lots of carbs, wouldn’t that, uh, throw you out of ketosis? And wouldn’t that result in an unexpected weight gain?”

“Yes, but I didn’t! I did all my own cooking and—”

“Except,” I raised a finger, “for lunch with Becca. Right?”

“Right. But that was a keto meal. Less than ten carbs,” said Ronnie, spelling it out for me.

“What about the bread?”

“Almond flour.”

“Are you sure?” I asked.

A hush fell over the room. I watched as they processed what I was implying. Ronnie, thinking it through behind her protective frown. Sissy, above it all but intrigued. Tempest, deep in thought.

Aly Mackey, staring at me with a puzzled expression.

"Almond flour has a distinctive flavor," said Sissy. "She would have tasted the difference."

"Not if it was cut half almond and half wheat," said Tempest. "Then it would taste like almond flour, but be chock-full of carbs. There's ninety-five carbs in a cup of wheat flour. If Ronnie's been eating bread like that, no way she could be in ketosis."

"Are you suggesting Becca intentionally sabotaged Ronnie's WOE?" asked Sissy.

"Of course not," said Tempest. "They both ate the bread. So they'd both be thrown out of ketosis. Becca wouldn't do that, especially if she had a wheat allergy."

"But I know who would!" Ronnie, face flushed and fists clenched, stepped toward Aly Mackey, still standing beside the scale. "Somebody who didn't know about the wheat allergy and wanted to win a stupid bet so much that she sabotaged Becca's WOE! How could you, Aly?"

I moved fast, putting myself between Ronnie and Aly Mackey.

"She could have died!" shouted Ronnie.

She tried to shove past me, left then right. I didn't try to stop her, just blocked her path and let her bounce off of me. Sometimes it's handy to have some girth. Most of the Janes stood in shocked silence, but Tempest went to Aly Mackey's side and took her arm.

Ronnie ceased her efforts and stared at me, breathing hard.

Having thus gained her attention, I spoke. "I know you're upset, Ronnie. But let's think this through. If somebody spiked Becca's almond flour with wheat, they had to have the motive and the opportunity."

"Aly's the only one with a motive," said Ronnie.

"A pretty slim motive," said Sissy. She glanced at me and blushed.

"But did she have the opportunity?" I asked. "Becca kept her house locked when no one was home, right?"

"Yes."

"And the bread was baked that morning, right?"

"Yes," said Ronnie reluctantly.

"Could Ms. Mackey have snuck into Becca's home that morning?" I asked.

"Impossible," said June. "Aly and I went to the co-op in Bounty last Tuesday morning to pick up our coconut butter."

"Then it probably wasn't Ms. Mackey," I said gently.

Tears gathered in Ronnie's eyes.

Aly Mackey went to Ronnie and put a hand on her shoulder. "I really didn't do it, Ronnie," she said.

"I know," sniffed Ronnie. "I'm such a jerk. I'm sorry. I don't know why you guys put up with me."

I eased backward as the Janes engaged in a group hug.

"Okay, that's nice," said Sissy. "But who spiked the bread? Who could possibly care whether Becca was in ketosis or not?"

The weekly Slim Janes meeting was no place to discuss such matters, so I stayed mum. But that did not stop my clever new friend, Tempest.

"We're assuming the motive was to bounce Becca out of ketosis," she said. "Isn't it far more likely that somebody knew about her wheat allergy and spiked the flour to try to flat-out kill her? And there's really only one person that could be!"

"That damned nutritionist!" burst out Ronnie.

"No, no," said Aly Mackey, patting her shoulder again. "It had to be—"

"Milton!" said the Janes, a Greek chorus arrayed in Easter colors.

"Milton!" echoed Ronnie. "To get his hands on her money! He could have cut the flour any time. Why I could stra—"

"Easy, Ronnie," said Tempest. "Careful what you say in front of the law. The scales of justice are mighty sensitive." She glanced at me and raised her eyebrows.

I nodded. "Well, ladies, duty calls."

"Will we see you next week?" asked Aly Mackey.

I tugged at my belt. "The weight of the evidence suggests you will."

THE SECRET BLEND

By Stacy Woodson

Too many things are going wrong for Jilly and her family's restaurant. With Valentine's Day approaching, her only hope to stave off disaster is a new menu—and a very secret blend.

Every Saturday, Frank shuffled into Marzoli's Ristorante near closing time. He'd wear the same check shirt and the same polyester pants. He'd prop his cane in the same corner, take a seat at the same table. And Jilly would bring him the same dish—Pasta Frittata.

She considered the choice pedestrian, and it wasn't on their menu. But she made it for Frank because he'd served with her father in the Korean War, the dish was his favorite, and in this small way she could honor their friendship.

Jilly made her way to Frank's table and placed the steaming plate in front of him. The smell of his Old Spice mixed with the fresh garlic and Parmesan cheese that wafted in the air. He reached for his fork—not much for words when there was eating to be done—and took his first bite. She loved the way his eyes closed, the serene look that crossed his face. Knowing her food stirred something inside him meant something to her. And for a brief moment, the stress she felt melted away.

"Jilly." Her brother's voice yanked at her. He strode through the dining room, tie half-mast, face flushed. "Did you see this?" Nick waved his iPad in the air—the Bay Area's *Winter Restaurant Guide* visible on the screen.

From the tone of Nick's voice, she knew the review couldn't be good. As much as Jilly didn't obsess over restaurant reviews, the negative ones always felt like a punch in the gut. Things had been bad enough with the bomb threat, the produce delivery mix-up, and the broken walk-in fridge. She didn't want to deal with something else—not today.

"It can wait until tomorrow." Jilly gathered dirty dishes from an empty table and pocketed the tip, making a mental note to give it to Mia, one of her servers, who had left early to visit her mother in the hospital.

Nick still hovered. "It's not a review of Marzoli's."

"What's the big deal then?" Jilly glanced at Frank's table, his glass of Chianti nearly empty. She should ask Nick to refill it. But the way he continued to stand there—too close, antsy—she knew he wasn't going to let it go.

She sighed. "Read it to me."

"Now?"

"It's why you brought the iPad in here."

Nick cleared his throat. "Finally, an exceptional dish . . ."

She tried to listen. But Walter Hess, the restaurant critic, was such a blowhard. Her mind drifted to things she needed to do—contacting the distributor about her produce problem on the top of the list.

Nick's voice weaved back in again. ". . . the fresh figs in the marinara sauce was an unexpected delight. And a welcome change to the overly salted sauces commonly found in dishes like these. A fresh, innovative choice in Italian cuisine, Benitos' Sweet Heart menu will not disappoint."

Jilly froze, dirty plates still stacked on both forearms. "Fresh figs?"

"Fresh figs."

Her Valentine's Day menu . . .

She'd planned something new, contemporary, a fusion of flavors, spent days perfecting each dish. Italian food that reflected North Beach's evolving landscape. A menu she'd planned to unveil next week. A menu she'd hoped would boost their declining business.

It couldn't be right.

She put the dishes down, took the iPad from Nick, and scanned the article—no different than what he'd read. She clicked on the link to Benitos' menu. Held her breath, waited.

A Sweet Heart menu filled the screen. The banner the same, the selections exact, a replica of the menu she'd created. One of the fastest growing Italian restaurant chains in the San Francisco Bay Area, Benitos was bulldozing their competition. And now it seemed Marzoli's was in their crosshairs.

"Benitos stole our menu?" The thought nearly hard to believe. And yet, there it was—hearts and all—in its full pixelated glory.

"Not ours anymore." Nick tapped the iPad screen. "They released it first. As far as the public is concerned, the menu is Benitos'."

Nick was right. If they announced something similar it would look like a weak imitation.

"They stole our menu," Jilly said again. Her fingers tightened around the iPad, knuckles white—the outrage still mounting. Someone from Benitos had broken into her kitchen. She felt violated, angry. And she didn't understand why her brother wasn't angry too.

Instead, his was face expressionless, like the cymbal-clanging monkey she'd had as a kid. "Sales are down, Jilly. The bill from the walk-in is huge. Now this?" He shook his head. "The restaurant's property value is still high. Maybe we should revisit selling the place."

"We're not selling Pop's restaurant."

Patsy, her *sous*-chef, emerged from the kitchen, earbuds stuffed in her ears. She wore a t-shirt that said *Spaghetti Created This Body.* It hugged her curves in all the wrong places.

Jilly clicked off the iPad, returned it to Nick, and hoped Patsy hadn't seen the review. Patsy had culinary school bills. The Benitos debacle could be enough to send Patsy looking for another job, and Jilly needed her.

"Oven is off, kitchen is clean," Patsy slung her tote over her shoulder and flashed her customary peace sign. "See you tomorrow, peeps." She headed to the front door—her pink ponytail swinging in time with her gait, the faint sound of Alice In Chains drifting from her ears.

Jilly picked up the dishes again and continued to the kitchen, Nick behind her. She walked past the stove where her father taught her to cook, the wooden stool she'd needed to reach the pans still in the corner. On the shelf above, the statue of Saint Lawrence—the patron saint of cooks—still looked down upon her. She'd always felt safe in here, the world filled with culinary possibilities.

Until tonight.

Now, she felt unsettled, edgy. Her childhood memories crowded out by the thief who had been in her kitchen. She placed the dishes in the sink and faced Nick. "We should call the police."

"The police?"

"You heard me."

"And tell them what? There's a culinary cat burglar on the loose?" He shook his head. "The San Francisco Police Department has bigger problems to deal with."

The SFPD certainly made that clear the day of the bomb threat. It happened in the middle of Sunday brunch. Marzoli's had a full house. SWAT evacuated the building, and then discovered it was a hoax. Jilly had to comp her patrons, and she still wanted justice. The SFPD traced the caller to a Club Sport near Washington Square, but went no further in their investigation.

"Our intellectual property was stolen. There has to be

something we can do," Jilly pressed.

"I'd love to go after Benitos, but collaring the thief won't get us out of debt. It won't boost our business. These are the real issues, Jills."

She hated when Nick called her Jills. That was Pop's nickname for her. "Don't mention selling the restaurant again. It's disloyal to Pop."

"This isn't about Pop. It's about business. If he were alive, he'd agree with me."

She didn't see it that way. Pop was a fighter. He'd survived turf battles from competitors and would expect them to do the same. "Valentine's Day is still a few days away. I'll think of something."

"One good night isn't going to be enough," Nick mumbled before he disappeared into the office and shut the door.

Nick was right. They would need something transformative. Her father's legacy and the livelihood of the people who worked for her were all at stake.

She glanced at the Saint Lawrence statue, made the sign of the cross, and prayed for an idea. But instead, Frank's face flashed in her mind.

Yikes.

She'd nearly forgotten about him.

Jilly grabbed a bottle of Chianti and hurried to Frank's table. He was leaning back in his seat, eyes heavy, his round belly nearly touching his empty plate.

"More wine?" She waved the bottle.

He glanced at his glass, smiled. "Why not?"

She poured him another.

"Keep an old man company?"

She hesitated, considered the work she had in front of her, the new menu she needed to create. But Frank was a widower. This was the night he went out and socialized. And she couldn't turn him down. She filled a glass and joined him. "How was the frittata?"

His face had that serene look again, the one that captivated Jilly. "Perfection."

She shook her head. "Perfection is ravioli stuffed with sweet cauliflower and mascarpone or semolina gnocchi with oxtail ragu or—"

"What's wrong with frittata?"

"It's old school."

"I am old," he said, a chuckle in his voice.

"No, Frank. You're a classic."

"Isn't that the same thing?"

It was her turn to laugh. "I've always been curious why you like frittata so much. For three years, every Saturday since Pop died, I think I've made it for you . . ." She squinted, tried to do the math. ". . . one hundred and fifty-six times."

"Someone has to keep an eye on you." Frank winked.

"Can't think of a better person." And she meant it.

Frank swirled his wine, studied the way the legs trickled down the glass. "Sunday dinner at Nona's," he finally said. "I order the frittata because that's what my grandmother made."

Simple dish. Simple answer. And simply disappointing.

She frowned.

"Not what you expected?"

Jilly shrugged. She liked the mystery better.

Frank leaned deeper into his chair. The legs creaked under his bulky frame. And Jilly realized there was more to it, something more behind Frank's simple answer.

"It was World War II," Frank began. "I was twelve years old. The men were fighting overseas. During the day, we hoped to hear news from the frontlines—a letter. Something. At night, we were afraid of it. Because at night the telegrams came—the death notifications."

Death notifications. The idea made Jilly shudder.

"We had no money," Frank continued. "My sister was still an infant, and my mother couldn't work. She took in tenants, sold Dad's Model T. I shined shoes in the Transbay Terminal after school, gave her the earnings. It was a stressful time—not knowing if my father was safe, not knowing if we were going to make it."

"Except Sundays," Jilly guessed.

Frank smiled. "I loved Sundays. We made the long walk to Nona's bungalow in the Oakland Hills. My mother and her sisters brought the few ingredients they had in their pantries. Nona blended them together and made the most delicious frittata. Some of my favorite memories are from Nona's table, eating frittata with my family—when being together was all that mattered."

She could almost hear the laughter, nearly feel the warmth. And in that moment, she was back there, too. A tear rolled down her cheek.

"Now don't go doing that." Frank pulled a handkerchief from his pocket; the check pattern matched his shirt.

She took it, smiled, dabbed her eyes.

Frank lifted his glass. "To Nona."

"To frittata." Jilly would never look at the dish the same way again.

They both took a sip and sat in comfortable silence. They'd

almost finished their wine when Frank spoke again. "Couldn't help but overhear your conversation with Nicky . . ."

Fascinated by Frank's story, she'd nearly forgotten about the Benitos thief.

"Figs," Frank scoffed.

"What's wrong with figs?"

He wrinkled his nose.

"They give the sauce a honeyed flavor and a nice texture," she argued.

Not that it mattered anymore.

Frank's eyes narrowed. "You have an enemy in your ranks, sweet girl."

Enemy . . .

She considered Frank's suggestion that one of her people had betrayed her. Her staff was small—all carefully selected—some even second generation Marzoli's employees. All loyal. She couldn't see it. "Someone from Benitos did this."

"Were there signs of forced entry?" Frank pressed.

When she'd opened the restaurant this morning both the front and back doors were locked, no different than any other day. "Someone snuck in between shifts," she decided. The menu proof for the printers had been on a flash drive in the office. Clearly labeled. Easy for someone to pluck from her desk.

Frank shook his head.

"I trust my staff," she said.

"Do you trust your brother?"

"Frank!"

"Seems awful eager to sell the place."

The restaurant had always been a sore point with Nick. He thought Pop's late nights at work drove their mother away. He didn't know the reason their mother left was Sal the grocer. Nick adored their mother. Pop made Jilly swear never to tell him. Despite Nick's resentment, she couldn't imagine he'd betray her.

"Not Nick."

"Loyalty is good thing, Jilly. Just make sure yours doesn't blind you."

***

After Frank left, Jilly cleaned up the dishes and went to the back office—a space she shared with Nick. After her father died, Jilly took over the kitchen and Nick the books. The arrangement seemed to work except when they were in the office together.

His desk sat opposite hers—a tsunami of papers and 49ers memorabilia. He liked to listen to music while he worked, and he streamed all his media services through his desktop—newsfeeds, social media, text messages, voice calls—a mirror of his cell phone. The bings and bongs drove her crazy. She was grateful he'd left for the day. He never stayed late when he had racquetball in the morning.

She got to work. First, an email to her food distributor about the produce mix-up. She wasn't able to offer two of her popular dishes tonight because of the failed delivery. Unacceptable. Then, she tried to sketch out concepts for a new menu, considering ways to leverage seasonal produce to make something new—something different.

An air raid siren blared.

She jumped, her body reacting before her mind processed the alert from Nick's computer. She inhaled, tried to steady her heart rate. The siren went off again.

She swung her chair around. On Nick's computer was a text from his girlfriend. And Nick's reply—one that made Jilly blush. She shook her head, powered down his computer, blew out a breath, and tried to focus on the menu again. But all she could think about was Frank's reaction to her figs. And her ideas suddenly felt inadequate.

At midnight, she gave up and decided to go home. She reached into her pocket for her keys and found Mia's tip money. She put the money in an envelope and tossed it into her drawer where Mia would find it in the morning. And then she saw the space where her flash drive, with her Valentine's Day menu, used to be.

Her shoulders sagged. So much hope had been contained in that small plastic stick. Hope for new customers. Hope for job security for her staff. Hope for Pop's legacy to endure.

All of it gone.

And now she wondered what else Benitos had planned. Stealing trade secrets was just one method of sabotage.

Sabotage.

Her mind tripped on the word.

Is this what was happening?

The bomb scare, the produce mix-up, the broken walk-in—she'd chalked it up to bad luck. But the timing of each event hit her bottom line in the worst way: the bomb scare during Sunday brunch when the restaurant was at capacity; the produce mix-up, ingredients for two popular dishes missing; the walk-in refrigerator—broken—the same day the health inspector made an unannounced visit; her Valentine's Day menu stolen, plagiarized, right before it went to the printers.

The events were too specific, the timing too perfect to be a coincidence.

Oh god.

Frank was right. There was an enemy in her ranks.

Faces of her employees flashed in her mind.

Who could be bribed?

Who would betray her?

These questions still needled at her long after she got home.

When she finally slept, she didn't dream about stolen menus or saboteurs. She dreamed about Frank, Nona, and the bucket of figs they pelted at her.

***

Maybe it was Frank's story or her twisted dream, but Jilly woke up the next morning and knew what she needed to do—with her menu, anyway.

For Valentine's Day, she wanted to create something special—a nod to Frank's family dinners. And hopefully a connection to other North Beach families, too. His story had reminded her that good Italian food came from simple recipes with minimal ingredients of the best quality. A concept she'd somehow lost in her modern cooking techniques and elevated menus. She dug through her father's old recipe box and sketched out some ideas, Frank's opinion the only one she trusted.

He agreed to meet her after Mass in front of Saints Peter and Paul Church. Jilly waited on the sidewalk and watched parishioners spill from the front doors. Snippets of conversation in English, Italian, Chinese, and Spanish floated in the air. Frank worked his way down the stairs, his cane deftly navigating each step.

They continued down Filbert Street and crossed Columbus Avenue to the North Beach Farmers Market, already in full swing. Together, they talked with the vendors, looked at fish, sampled vegetables. And Jilly told Frank about her fixed price menu: fish stew, pasta frittata, and chocolate-covered biscotti for dessert.

They returned to Jilly's apartment with ingredients for her recipes, tested her new menu, tasted each dish. Jilly played with the spices. When the last plate was empty, Frank wiped his mouth and smiled. "You have a winner here."

She grinned.

"Now what?"

"Advertise the menu, schedule a preview. Create enough buzz to make sure we have a full house on Valentine's Day." All tasks Jilly needed to do soon if she was going to generate enough momentum to be successful.

"What about your saboteur?"

"I have a plan."

***

Jilly called an all-hands meeting on Tuesday to discuss the new menu. She arrived at the restaurant early, hid the nanny camera in the statue of Saint Lawrence, and then posted an announcement on Marzoli's Facebook page:

Come Experience the Romance of Old Italy.

Celebrate Valentine's Day with secret family recipes that honor Italian tradition. Sneak preview Wednesday.

She printed the recipes and made sample dishes from her new menu—the same ones she'd tested with Frank. Jilly was at her desk when Patsy arrived.

"Traditional Italian?" Patsy pointed at Jilly's Facebook announcement still up on the computer. "What happened to Italian fusion?"

"I decided to go in a different direction."

"Two days before a reveal?" Patsy's voice went tight. Her team would need time to perfect the new recipes, to prepare—an expected reaction under normal circumstances. But now Jilly couldn't help but wonder if Patsy's response was tied to something more.

Before Jilly could respond, Mia walked into the office. Her curls bounced like a Pantene ad. "Hiya."

"Hope the visit with Ida went well," Jilly said, referring to Mia's mother and her father's former *sous*-chef.

"She is responding to chemo. We're hopeful." Mia smiled. "Thanks again for covering for me."

"Your tips—" Jilly reached for her drawer, but Mia waved her off.

"Grabbed them yesterday."

Nick appeared. And Patsy and Mia faded into the kitchen.

"Secret recipes?" Nick dropped his gym bag on the floor. His racquet and towel spilled from the top. He shoved them aside with his foot, pulled out his desk chair, and took a seat. "Nice marketing ploy."

"No ploy."

"Seriously?"

"You'll see when everyone gets here."

Nick swiveled his chair and faced Jilly, his expression like the cymbal-clanging monkey's again. "If tomorrow isn't a success, we need to talk about selling."

Jilly wanted to protest. To tell Nick they shouldn't give up. But the truth was, if her new menu didn't work, she had nothing left to give.

She nodded.

***

Twenty minutes later, Jilly stood in her kitchen in front of a table with her sample dishes and recipes, surrounded by people she once considered family. Now she wasn't sure who on her staff she could trust. She studied each of them, looking for some kind of tell, something that would reveal their betrayal.

But no one shuffled their feet.

No one avoided her gaze.

There was nothing.

She took a deep breath, pushed back her shoulders, focused on her plan, and prayed it was enough to flush out the saboteur. "Thank you for coming in early. I've thought long and hard about our Valentine's Day menu and decided to create a new experience for our diners. This year, our focus won't be on exotic recipes and romantic love, but on tradition and the love of family. I dusted off secret Marzoli family recipes. Tomorrow night at our preview, this is what we will be serving."

Jilly lifted the dome covers, walked through each dish, handed out copies of the recipes listing each ingredient—everything except the spices. In their place she'd written *secret blend.*

"In honor of our family, I've kept the spices a secret. Instead, each recipe has a premixed spice package."

"Like KFC," someone cracked wise.

She cringed at the comparison, but it was a good example.

The Marzoli staff filed through the kitchen—Nick the last to follow. They tasted each dish, then discussed them. Jilly watched, knowing next to the spice rack by the prep station—the one in front of the camera—she'd left a list with the spices that *supposedly* made up the secret blends. She'd hoped the allure of a secret—inside information—would be enough to entice the saboteur to make a move before the preview, before more damage to Marzoli's could be done.

Everything in place, Jilly went about her day avoiding the prep table. The order she'd placed at the farmers market arrived. She'd arranged deliveries from local vendors—their offerings the best—which eliminated her concerns about their distributor being compromised. She inventoried each order, marking off each item, and waited for the moment when she could return to the office and check the camera footage.

It was late afternoon before she was at her desk. Nick was gone. The office was empty. She eased the door closed, reached for the mouse, started to click on the camera feed, when Nick dragged

Mia through the door.

"I caught her taking pictures." He tossed a phone onto Jilly's desk. On the screen was an image of Jilly's secret spice blends.

Jilly's breath caught.

Mia ripped her arm free. "I can explain—"

She thought about Mia's sick mother, Ida's mounting medical bills. Mia's access to Jilly's office. Mia the perfect target for a bribe. It was possible. And yet Jilly couldn't see Mia as the saboteur.

"I hope Benitos was worth it, Mia," Nick seethed, a passion in his voice for their restaurant Jilly had never heard before. And it made her realize Nick really did care.

Mia frowned and her eyes went wide. "You think I took this for Benitos?" She shook her head. "God, no. I . . ." Mia looked at her feet. "It's . . . for my mother. She follows the restaurant on Facebook. She asked about the new menu. Few things make her happy since she's been sick. I just wanted to share it with her."

Mia looked sincere, the explanation plausible. Ida was a chef. She'd want to know specifics. But her explanation was nearly too perfect. Just like everything else. And Jilly knew what she had to do.

"I'm sorry, Mia." Jilly handed Mia her phone. "I'm going to have to let you go."

Mia gasped. "Let me go? But I need this job—"

"I'm sure Benitos will compensate you," Nick fired back.

Mia opened her mouth like she wanted to say more. But instead her shoulders slumped, and she left the office.

"What about the picture? The list of spices is still on her phone." Nick moved toward the door like he intended to rush out and intercept Mia.

"Don't worry about it."

His eyes narrowed. "The secret wasn't real?"

"It served its purpose."

***

The next night wasn't Saturday, but Frank was at Marzoli's. He wore a fedora. And with his cane, he had an old-world elegance. Jilly greeted him with a hug. "You came."

"I wouldn't miss your preview." He grinned. "I brought some friends from church."

It was a diverse crowd, a reflection of North Beach's evolving landscape. Just what she'd wanted, and a fusion menu wasn't what had brought them through the door.

Jilly walked Frank and his guests to their seats. "Is that Walter Hess?" Frank whispered, his gaze on a man with an over-waxed mustache at the table behind him.

Her stomach fluttered at the mention of the food critic's name. She tried not to stare. But as soon as the man turned his head, Jilly knew. "It's him."

Frank grinned. "Go get 'em."

Heart jackhammering, Jilly made her way to the kitchen. Patsy was expediting food, and Nick had volunteered to replace Mia in the dining room. Jilly motioned for both of them to join her. "Walter Hess is here. Table twenty."

Nick grinned. "I made a phone call. A buddy from my fraternity works at the paper—so I thought, maybe . . ."

"Who is working the order for table twenty?" Patsy called to her staff.

Nick's cell phone buzzed. He pulled it from his pocket. Typed a reply.

Jilly shot him a look.

"Relax, Jills. Everything is going as planned." He pocketed his phone, picked up a tureen of fish stew, and disappeared into the sea of tables.

Jilly returned to the pass-through. She checked each dish—sent some out, returned others. Ten minutes later, Patsy placed a platter of frittata in front of her. "Table twenty."

Hess.

Jilly's hands shook as she slid a fork into the pasta.

Please be perfect.

She tasted.

And it was perfection.

She reached for parsley—the garnish the final touch. She started to chop, but her hand slipped, and she sliced her finger.

Crap.

She glanced at the food—no blood in the frittata. *Thank, god.* But blood flowed down her hand.

She told Patsy to take over.

"You okay?" Patsy asked, as she worked the parsley.

"Nothing a bandage and glove won't fix." *She hoped.* Jilly went to office to find the first aid kit, blood now to her forearm. She looked for a towel, something to stop the bleeding, and remembered Nick's on the floor. She picked it up. And that's when she saw it—the Club Sport logo—stitched in blue.

She'd never made the connection that Nick played racquetball at the same gym where the SFPD had traced the bomb scare caller.

She wiped the blood, pressed the towel against her finger, opened the first aid kit, while her mind swirled around this new detail. The bomb scare, the produce mix-up, the broken walk-in, the compromised menu. All executed from an insider. She could still see Nick dragging Mia into the office, the passion in his voice—the conviction too perfect. Mia's story was true and Nick had seized the opportunity to frame her.

The saboteur wasn't Mia.

The saboteur was Nick.

Jilly's heart sank.

An air raid siren startled her. Jilly looked at Nick's computer, a text message from a name she didn't recognize. Followed by Nick's reply:

After Hess' review, she'll sell. Tell Benitos it's prime North Beach real estate. $5 million and they have a deal.

And now Nick was going to sabotage her review.

Jilly rushed to the kitchen. "Where's Nick?"

"Bringing Hess his order," Patsy said.

Jilly's stomach tightened. She scanned the kitchen, tried to determine what Nick had done. Her eyes went to the prep table, next to the spice rack, the salt cellar open, a ring of white granules where the food critic's plate of frittata used to be.

She rushed through the kitchen doors into the dining room and looked for Hess' table. Nick was halfway there, nearly a world away.

Jilly called his name, but he continued to move.

Please don't do this.

She followed, tried to reach him. But there were so many diners, too many tables. She locked eyes with Frank, her last line of defense.

Jilly tried to think of a way to signal him, some way he'd understand. She pointed at Nick and mouthed, "*Enemy in the ranks.*"

Frank frowned.

She tried again. "*Enemy in the—*"

Franks eyes went wide. He grabbed his cane, swung it forward, caught Nick's foot. Nick stumbled. He regained his footing, but the over-salted frittata flipped off the plate, and splattered against Nick, then slid to the floor.

"Oh, Nicky. I'm so sorry. I'm so clumsy these days." Frank pushed up from his table and winked at Jilly while he tried to wipe Nick's shirt.

"Stupid old man." Nick shrugged Frank off and took the empty plate back to the kitchen. Jilly grabbed another server to clean up the floor, then followed Nick.

Patsy called for another order of frittata as Jilly pushed through the kitchen doors.

"Frank—that bumbling old fool," Nick began. "Did you see what he did to me?" He slammed the plate into the sink and continued to the office. He found a fresh shirt behind the door, flung the hanger onto his desk, and continued to rant. "What did Pop ever see in that guy?"

"Stop," Jilly whispered. She couldn't stand to hear Nick speak, let alone hear anything disparaging about Frank.

Nick finished changing and tried to return to the kitchen, but Jilly blocked his path.

"What are you doing? I need to get back out there. I need to get Hess his order."

"Not you."

Nick frowned. "What's going on?"

"I know you're the saboteur."

Nick laughed. "That's ridiculous. Mia—"

"I know about the offer, Nick."

Jilly waited for him to make another excuse.

But he didn't.

Nick sighed and said, "I did this for you, Jilly. This place . . . it was becoming your life. Just like Pop's."

"No, Nick. You have five million reasons why you did it for yourself. Now get out of *my* restaurant or so help me—"

"Five million dollars. Come on, Jills . . ."

"Don't call me Jills. You insult Pop's memory."

Nick shook his head. "You deserve to end up like him."

Jilly could only hope for so much.

A few minutes later, Jilly carried a plate of pasta frittata to Hess. As she placed it on the table, she locked eyes with Frank and they both smiled.

FIRST OF THE YEAR

By Gabriel Valjan

Food critic Max was willing to give the restaurant a second chance at a positive review, surely a chance for the chef to shine. Why then isn't Max answering his door the next day?

Everyone has to eat, everyone has to die, and death had an appetite that morning. Mothers and cops have that special something that alerts them when something is wrong. Call it instinct. Max not waiting for me in his laced-up Nikes and sweats was the first clue something was off. He might've worked late last night at the Wolf & Lamb, but he was fanatical about fitness. It being the first day of the year was no excuse.

I peppered the doorbell like an obnoxious kid on Halloween. Nothing. I reached inside my pocket for my cell. A useless tactic since Max disliked talking on phones. Like me, he preferred face-to-face conversation. No answer. I pressed my face against the glass, aware that Max would spritz me with Windex before he cleaned the nose print.

Then I saw it.

A profanity later, I fumbled for my keys and rushed inside. His feet were in the hallway, toes up like the witch under Dorothy's house. The rest of him was inside the bathroom. My first thought was heart attack.

And there he was in front of me, inches away from the toilet, a gash to his temple, the blood crusted and a sweet scent around him like a halo. My training kicked in and I followed the ABCs of CPR, but it didn't matter. Max was dead.

I dreaded making the call. I recognized the voice as Garcia's, who had the misfortune to have been tagged to hump the calls to the desk. I conveyed the address and told him to send the body snatchers and requested two suits from homicide.

"Are you sure it's a 187?" he asked.

Guys in homicide called accidental, natural, or suicides The Junk because it wasted their time and talents. Garcia sighed attitude and told me he'd have dispatch send out two detectives and the coroner's transport team. He named the two investigators. It was my turn to sigh. I didn't like one of them and he didn't like me.

I waited in the library while the coroner's team did their thing. The senior detective put the new guy on me to do the IR. I guided him through the timeline for the incident report, explained that Max traveled a lot and he'd given me a spare key to collect his mail and water his plants. It hit me then. Max was dead. We ran daily, rain or shine, like the motto of the postal service.

We were an odd couple. The only thing we had in common was we were working-class Joes. I was a cop and he was a chef turned food critic. Max was a self-made man, a real polymath who had taught himself languages to read the cookbooks on his shelves; had learned wines well enough to become a sommelier, cheeses to be recognized as an *affineur* by the American Cheese Society. In his teens, he enlisted as a dishwasher and he worked every station on the line before he became executive chef and earned three Michelin stars at the precocious age of twenty-five.

We shared a love of crime fiction, hence those many books in his vast library. People compared Max to the French intellectual Foucault because of his bald head, the scowl, and intense stare—a comparison Max loathed. He preferred James Ellroy, the opinionated and self-proclaimed 'Demon Dog' of American noir fiction.

"Looks like a fatal fall. Happens all the time, especially after nights like last night," the senior detective told me. He had toured the five-bedroom restored Victorian while his partner took my statement.

"This isn't Junk," I told him. "Old people and the inebriated fall, but not Max. The man could hold his food and his liquor; it came with his job."

"Yeah, notorious food critic, I know." He scratched his ear. "We'll see what tox says about his blood alcohol level. No shortage of suspects if you're thinking foul play. Your friend made himself a lot of enemies."

True. Max's opinions had created and destroyed culinary careers, opened or closed doors to restaurants around the country. Max was honest as Lincoln about food he loved and about grub that didn't meet his standards. He said our jobs were alike. A detective had to be both a good writer and a talker. We both said and wrote unpopular truths. We both had the gift for irritating people.

Once, elaborating on M.F.K. Fisher's comment that each culture had one definitive ingredient to its cuisine—butter for the French, olive oil for the Italians—Max added that American culture could claim sugar as its identifier. Sentimental. Glycemic spikes in intellect, the crash and burn of fads. Americans lacked discernment, he said, and entered into evidence that most death-row inmates requested fast food for their last meal. “Your last hours on earth and you ask for chicken nuggets?” he’d asked a talk-show host.

The detective humored me. “There’s no crime scene here, no sign of forced entry or any indication of a struggle. Perhaps Mr. Essen took ill, once or several times during the night, and lost his footing on his last trip to the john. He misses the light switch, trips and he hit his head on the sink. Perhaps it’s a case of food poisoning.”

Perhaps was the word homicide used when they cooked theory.

“He’d have to have fallen forward to hit his head,” I said and lifted my chin. “You saw him, flat as an ironing board on his back. And don’t even suggest he choked on his own puke. Clean face, clean clothes, and clean toilet bowl. A sweet odor was present and that’s it. We both know vomit is acrid and bitter.”

“Swelling of the brain then?”

“Cerebral edema?”

“Won’t know until the autopsy is in. I know this is difficult. I get it. He was your friend.” The detective tapped my arm. I stared at his hand while he pronounced the formulaic “I’m sorry for your loss.”

They wheeled the gurney out. Crisp air crept into the hallway from the opened front door, and I heard the familiar, metallic sound of wheels against the steps in the descent to the dark car.

The senior detective idled up. “Heard you’re on mandatory vacation.” He smiled as if we were buds at choir practice, enjoying a cold beer after hours. “Word is you did a brake check and the mope in the backseat broke his nose against the cage.”

“Don’t believe everything you hear, Detective. For your information, a dog ran in front of me. It’s all in the report,” I said and walked away.

An autopsy could take days and a toxicology report, weeks. New Year’s Day guaranteed delays. The city was asleep, recovering from last night’s revels. Food poisoning had crossed my mind. Perhaps. An intentional poison was detectable, if—and only if—the lab had an idea which direction to set their chromatography machine. Homicide had to alert the pathologist of the possibility first, but that didn’t seem likely here. Intoxication and fatal slip and fall were the presumed cause of death. Occam’s razor stated the simplest explanation was often the truth.

Death from food poisoning seemed cruel poetry for a food critic. Max had explained over dinner once that the human body almost always rejected toxins. Somatic reflex causes us to spit the offensive food out. If poisoning was indeed the culprit, the ER would be busy with other victims of the Wolf & Lamb. I called in a marker from a friend of mine in forensics—the other kind.

"Harry, I need a favor."

I heard the groan of surprise in Harry Wexler's voice. I pictured the bureau's foremost forensic accountant tucking his head tortoise-like into his armpit. My reception was fine, but Harry's voice took on a scratch and whisper. "I thought you were on administrative leave."

"Temporary. About that favor, Harry."

"What do you need?"

"Financials on Max Essen and whoever owns the Wolf & Lamb restaurant. Max banked at First Union's main office, if that helps. You're on your own with the rest. When can I call back for a preliminary?"

"I'll have the electronic feeds in an hour, but any analysis on my end will be crude at best."

"I like crude. I'll even take vulgar."

Harry was adept at numbers and patterns, enough so that the DEA tried to poach him to work with them against the cartels. He declined after he learned the Spanish word for "stew." Harry's work took time and the Zetas had just the right recipe, El Guiso, for extracting information from their unfortunate guests. "Isn't Max Essen the food critic?" Harry asked.

"Was, and that should prop a warrant, if you need to do this by the book."

"You do know everything digital leaves a trail, don't you? Not all of us are unorthodox like you, or did you forget?"

"Live a little, Harry. I'll call you later."

***

The Supreme Court allows law enforcement to use lies to work a case and suspects. I did just that when I flashed my badge in the window. The waiter inside unlocked the door to the Wolf & Lamb. Brunch service started in a few hours. The kid's face dropped when I said Max Essen, critic extraordinaire, had come down with food poisoning. If a bad review from Max was the Mass Card, then a case of foodborne illness lit the candle and sung Vespers.

The kid offered me the choice of coffee or cold water. I chose water. He returned with a popover and a small dish with a knife. Freckles of sea salt dotted an oval of butter. The hybrid of bread and pastry in a tin with a handle perplexed me, but my confusion disappeared after I pierced the oversized but soft and flaky head and saw steam. I buttered it and took my first bite. "This is delicious," I told my new friend. He pushed an extra napkin my way. Waitstaff filed in behind me, reflected in the mirror behind the bar. I asked him if he had worked New Year's Eve. He had. "Can you tell me what Mr. Essen ate last night?

Saying he'd trawl through the previous night's receipts, he headed toward the swinging doors that led into the kitchen. I enjoyed the rest of the popover with greasy fingers and drank ice water from a glass beaded with sweat. The restaurant was quiet as a morgue, the voices in the back of the house distant. Firm leather banquettes lined the wall behind me; all the dark wood, exposed brick, and muted lights provided a study in shadows worthy of a Renaissance master. A door moved. I expected a manager. Instead, a chef in whites appeared. He introduced himself as Andrea, the *sous*-chef. I asked him how long he'd worked there and he answered "close to a year." His English didn't come out like broken eggs, but with a romantic cadence of genuine interest and concern for Max.

"I asked about the menu because Mr. Essen is ill, and I'm worried there will be more cases of food poisoning reported today."

"Impossible."

A one-word answer didn't invite debate. I anticipated attitude, expected a defensive huff and puff. Chefs were consummate control-freaks, sticklers for food prep and proper sanitation. Amateurs failed to cook chicken, pork, or seafood to correct temperatures. An eager boyfriend, short on time and hot for the bedroom, might not wash the greens from the store because he trusted the packaging claiming it was pre-washed. Not the men and women in white. The accusation that a chef's food had harmed a client amounted to an insult to their honor.

The *sous*-chef crossed his arms and shook his head. "Not possible."

"How can you be so certain?"

"The chef herself prepared Mr. Essen's meal, and he ate an individually prepared meal, different from the rest of the house."

"Different how?"

Andrea explained the owner and Max had come to an agreement. Max had savaged the Wolf & Lamb in a review. The restaurant sought redemption, an opportunity to make amends, and the owner upped the ante. Give her a week's notice, set the date and time, and Max could name five dishes or select a gastronomical theme, and the chef would execute the meal herself. Of course Max would pick one of the most stressful nights of the year. The *sous*-chef wasn't speaking loudly, but his impassioned defense attracted attention. Another man appeared, dressed in a tailored suit, which said *money* and *owner*.

"I'll take it from here," he said. The *sous*-chef bowed his head and disappeared. "I'm Nick Wolf, one of the owners. How may I help you?"

I showed my badge again. "Max Essen ate here last night and he's sick. Food poisoning is suspected. Andrea just explained the challenge between you and Max."

"Police? I though the department of public health investigated food poisoning." Wolf adjusted a cufflink on his sleeve and placed both hands behind his back to assert dominance. His body language didn't stop there. The exposed chest suggested fearlessness.

"DPH oversees restaurants, but Max is a dear friend."

"I see." Wolf said it like a schoolmaster who had just read a forged note from a student's parent. "A serious allegation nonetheless. Is Mr. Essen home recovering? I should call him. Oh, I forgot, he doesn't answer his phone."

"That, and there's another reason: Max is in the hospital."

Wolf's eyes flickered panic. "Sure it isn't the holiday flu? If you tell me the name of the hospital, I'll send flowers and a card; it's the least we can do."

"Flowers would be nice, but first I'd like to ask you some questions, if you don't mind."

"Certainly."

Experience has taught that either the vain and guilty or the naïve and stupid cooperated this easily. Wolf looked good for an MBA and probably had a CPA who charged the same hourly rates as high-end escorts. He had put too much thought into his sartorial elegance, and probably brooded over every single detail of the décor in the Wolf & Lamb, to be so dumb as to answer questions without a lawyer. Damage control is vital to a business' reputation. I trusted my gut on my read of Wolf. A man who named a place after himself had to have a healthy ego.

"You mentioned you were one of the owners. Who are your partners?"

"One partner. She. My soon-to-be ex-wife. Chef Caroline Lamb."

"Quite the literary name."

He relaxed, saw his chance for fluff conversation. "Maybe one in a hundred people know the name. I'm impressed. You know your literature."

"Besotted with Lord Byron," I said and watched his reaction. "I read a lot, especially crime fiction. You'd be surprised how often food makes an appearance. Nero Wolfe's personal chef. Sherlock

Holmes liked curried chicken. Sam Spade's favorite meal was lamb chops with a sliced tomato and a baked potato. Myself, I'm partial to Dorothy Sayers and Agatha Christie."

"Because they offer a woman's perspective?"

"No, because they were fond of poison. Sayers used arsenic in *Strong Poison*. Christie was more adventuresome and diverse. She stirred strychnine, cyanide, digitalis, and morphine into her plots."

Wolf paled and his lower lip dropped as if he was about to say something.

"Sorry to hear about the divorce," I said to change the subject. I twirled a finger in the air. "Does that mean the name of this place will change?"

"Our split is amicable. Are you married?"

"No, I watched my mother stay up nights waiting for my dad to come home. He was a cop. I promised myself I'd never subject a woman to that kind of anxiety."

"Admirable." Wolf said without any emotion.

No divorce in its early stages was amicable. It was only human to harbor disappointment, a grudge, and resentment. Partners in a failed marriage who remained business partners required uncommon delicacy and finesse. Max said chefs were descendants of warriors, men and women who transformed violence into an art with sharp knives. Every chef, he emphasized, favored one blade in their arsenal and worked it like a samurai wielded his sword. That's more finesse than a fountain pen inside a high-end suit.

"About this menu," I said. "What were the dishes? The theme?"

The holidays were a special time of year when Max allowed himself to indulge in some variation of pork or lamb. Max considered piglets and pigs cute, so he limited his intake to twice a year. Swine and humans, he remarked, behaved alike. One creature Max would never eat, out of respect for its intelligence, was octopus. I ruled out lamb. Max was sensitive to innuendo. He wouldn't dare ask for dishes that shared the same name as the chef. I wagered on pork.

"Mushrooms. Mr. Essen requested mushrooms."

Wolf's answer surprised me. He had to know what I was thinking. Mushrooms required a trained eye and nose. Several toxic fungi could pass for their edible cousins. The death cap in Europe, for example, resembled the straw mushroom. The infamous fungi came up in a conversation with Max after we'd watched an episode of *I, Claudius*. Agrippina, his wife, was rumored to have poisoned Claudius with them to enable Nero to wear the purple toga. I remembered the conversation for another reason. The intestinal pain from poisonous mushrooms was intense and would drive any sane person to the hospital.

"Can you go over the menu in detail?"

"I can do better," Wolf said. "I'll show it to you." His torso dipped behind the bar until he resurfaced with a piece of paper. "Here it is. Five courses with wine pairings. Chef Caroline created this feast and prepared all the dishes herself, per her and Mr. Essen's agreement. Nobody helped her."

"Not even her *sous*-chef?"

"Andrea presented Mr. Essen with his specialty, an *amuse-bouche*."

"A what?"

"It's a petite appetizer," Wolf said.

Wolf's tone was colder than the water in my glass. After years of friendship with Max, I knew what an *amuse-bouche* was. Max taught me how to braise, how to make *crêpes* and shirred eggs, and the perfect *panna cotta*. I was toying with Wolf. An *amuse-bouche* was more than just a morsel. The bite-sized pleaser was symbolic of the chef's approach to the art of eating.

"So Andrea served an *amuse-bouche*," I said. "Chef Caroline must trust him to create a starter that sets the tone of the meal."

"I wouldn't know. You'll have to ask her yourself."

"Where do you get your mushrooms from?"

"Locally sourced from a farmer named Martha, who is responsible for all my vegetables and greens. She's not here at the moment." The hands swept behind his back again. Nervous pride, or he was hiding something. "I oversee the orders for wines and meats myself," he said. "I have a *fromager*, who handles—"

"Cheese, I know. Give me some credit, Mr. Wolf. I learned a few things from Max." My cell trilled. I took the menu. "Excuse me while I answer this."

I stepped away, turned my back to the bar and read the menu. I said hello and heard Harry say, "Think I've got something."

"You think or you know?"

"I don't go off half-cocked like some people. What's new on your end?"

I scanned the menu. "Mushrooms and lots of them: maitake, black trumpet, morel, shitake, and porcini. Did you know mushrooms provide meatiness in a recipe, Harry? That's why people grill portabellas. The texture is like steak." I ran my thumbnail down the cardstock. "I'm impressed. Porcini with chocolate chantilly in the *pot de crème*. Inventive."

"Are you done?"

"Don't you want to hear the wine pairings?"

"The Wolf & Lamb is owned by a husband and wife, Nicholas

Wolf and Caroline Lamb. Their restaurant barely survived the 2008 financial crisis. Wolf used to work as a hedge-fund analyst, which throws shade on his character, in my opinion. Looking at the financials, I'd say he's saving for a rainy day. I also see some unwise personal loans to an organic farm, owned by an M. Kavanaugh. Big numbers."

I heard keyboard clatter and thought M stood for Martha. "Anything else?"

"Mrs. Wolf applied for a condo. This part is strange, though. She listed a previous address and it's not the one she shares with husband Nicholas. That address is . . ." Harry hit the keys hard, which meant he expected nerd nirvana. ". . . In Little Italy. Are we good?"

"Yeah, we are, Harry. Thanks."

I pocketed the phone, returned to the bar, and sat on a stool. I eyeballed the menu one last time then slid it toward Wolf. I'd give him the benefit of the doubt, that he was no expert on fungi, no mycologist. I smiled at him. He bared some teeth in a forced grin.

The front door opened and a woman walked in. She looked fast and hard over at the bar and pulled her purse tight against her. Her heels clicked across the flooring. A door to the kitchen opened and Andrea appeared, holding it open. She stepped into the kitchen and the door swung closed, creaking until we watched it stop moving.

"Your future ex-wife, I presume?"

"You want to talk to her?"

"Not really. I want to know how you did it."

"Did what?"

"Let's not play games with each other, Mr. Wolf. You and your wife are headed for divorce court. Things are tense between you. She walks in, doesn't say hello to you, and she can't wait to join her boyfriend in the kitchen."

"Boyfriend? That's absurd."

"Is it? As absurd as you and Martha together? Curious, but where does Andrea live?"

"In Little Italy, and you're off your head."

"Am I? Let's play a game of perhaps then." I expected and received an expression of confusion: eyebrows peaked and then lowered, eyes narrowed with suspicion.

I hammered him with theories. "Perhaps you're jealous. No executive chef entrusts their *sous*-chef with an *amuse-bouche* unless they're in complete agreement about food and flavors. Simpatico. And Andrea has scored plenty for someone who has worked here for less than a year. Chef Caroline trusts him, doesn't she? He knows her so well he's at that door waiting for her."

"Preposterous. Ever hear of a work schedule?"

"Perhaps you're afraid this divorce will ruin you. Financially speaking. A middle-aged guy like you can't just jump back into the nine to five. Those young bloods have more degrees, work for less coin, and they've got fire in their veins. Perhaps Martha's wholesome way of life isn't for you. All the granola in the world can't provide you with the standard of living you've grown accustomed to. No more expensive suits and—"

"What are you implying?" Wolfe asked. He had planted both fists on the counter. The veins on the top of his hands bulged.

"Establishing motive, Mr. Wolf. Call it revenge."

"Against whom? Caroline?"

"Perhaps against Max. He wrote that damning review."

"And might I remind you that he returned for a second meal."

"Which your wife cooked." I wagged my finger. "I get it now. I was wrong; it isn't revenge, it's spite."

Wolf stiffened, straightened out his spine, and glared at me. He had height on me, but I had decades of experience with every type of scum. His faux outrage might work on an accountant on the cube farm, but he never had to enter a dark alley or have the nostrils of a sawn-off shotgun sneeze birdshot at him. I wanted to threaten his privileged world.

"I suggest foul play, the medical examiner backs me up, and the DA will interview Caroline and Martha. Fur will fly, and I don't mean a cat fight. It'll be your hide and expect to lose some skin, too, Mr. Wolf. All your little secrets will surface. Whatever credibility you had going into divorce court vanishes. While you fight to salvage your reputation, she'll find the most vicious lawyer who'll hire the best bloodhound to find every dollar and cent you hid under the mattress or in a coffee can."

Not quite panic, but the screwed-up face of confusion. "Who are you talking about? Caroline?"

"Her or Martha. Does it matter? You used both women. You can, however, avoid the entire mess if you tell me how you did it."

Wolf reached behind the bar and picked the most expensive bottle of bourbon, 20-year old Pappy Van Winkle. He poured himself a shot and downed it. He whistled after the heat.

"I wanted to teach them a lesson." I asked who. He said his wife and Max. Martha had nothing to do with it, he insisted. I asked with what and he said, "With the wild onions."

"I'm listening."

"Wild onions are poisonous, if you don't know what you're doing. They're odorless and they don't make you cry." I asked how and he said, "They were in the fried mushrooms, and in the *bordelaise* with the steak *frites*. I changed the label on the crate when they were delivered."

"You poisoned Max."

"To embarrass Caroline. To give him an upset stomach like he gave me. So he'd have the trots at worse. So what? She receives one more bad review."

I googled wild onions on my phone. I scanned an article about almonds, carrots that could pass for hemlock, fox grapes, and plenty of other lethal *doppelgängers*. I read about wild onion, and the symptoms, for which there was an acronym: SLUDGE.

Wolf kept talking; they all do when they're nervous.

"A night in the bathroom for him and I'd fix that—"

"Better pour yourself a double, Mr. Wolf."

He poured himself that double, knocked it back like a barbarian. A tremor rippled through him and he clenched his eyes and opened them so I could lay the cold hard truth on him.

"The toxin in wild onions lowers your heart rate. In and of itself, that's not a terrible thing, unless you have a very low resting heart rate, which Max did from years of running."

He still had his hand curled around his glass. "What are you saying?"

"Max is dead, Mr. Wolf. His heart rate dropped like the proverbial stone. He hit his head, and that makes you responsible for his death."

He stared at me and his lips parted in classic disbelief. My cell phone pinged. I opened up the email. It was a notification that Max's latest article had posted to the web. People do speak from the dead. He must have emailed his editor before he died. I smiled as I scrolled through the article while Wolfe stood there. "What's so amusing?"

"The irony, the unexpected, and your bad luck, Mr. Wolf."

I pushed the phone across the counter so he could read it himself as I reached for my cuffs. "Max gave Chef Caroline a glowing review."

STICKY FINGERS

By LD Masterson

Her dead brother made a terrible mistake. Now she has to make good on what he owed or there will be consequences . . .

I hate funerals. Not that anyone likes them, I know. Except maybe little old ladies who go to socialize and partake of the refreshments. But I buried my husband two years ago and my only brother yesterday and I hated every minute of it.

And yet, the morning after is always worse. I'm alone in my kitchen, nursing a cup of coffee, looking out at a gray day. All the condolence wishers are gone, the twins are back in school . . . life goes on. But someone is left with the cleanup duty and, as Bobby's next of kin, that would be me. I have to go through and pack up all the bits and pieces of his life, sell or give away his possessions, and settle his affairs. At least it's only his personal affairs. When Mitch died there was so much paperwork—transferring ownership of Gemini Electronics to me, setting up the trusts for the boys—but Bobby was just a middle manager in R&D. Nepotism at its finest. Damn. He could have been so much more if it hadn't been for—

The doorbell interrupts my dark thoughts. A little early for visitors. Oh, please don't let it be more flowers.

I recognize him immediately. Large, heavyset, hard features that seem set in a permanent sneer. Ralph Gorman. A man Mitch fired three years ago for stealing from the company.

"Morning, Mrs. Russell . . . um, Julie. I apologize for just dropping by like this, but I couldn't get to the funeral yesterday and I wanted to tell you how sorry I was to hear about Bobby."

My first instinct is to say thank you and shut the door, but midwestern manners require inviting him in. I murmur a suitable response and wave him into my living room. I ask him to sit but he moves around the room, looking at the many framed pictures, family photos mostly, of Mitch and the twins. He stops and picks up one of Bobby.

"Yeah, that was a real shame. I read about it in the papers. A mugging gone wrong, they said. So, have they found the guy yet?" He glances up and looks at me. "The guy that did it?"

"No." My voice sounds tight and I try to relax. I don't like this man, but he did work with Bobby so it's not unnatural for him to be interested.

He wanders toward the kitchen and motions to the cupcakes on the counter. "Ah, that's what I smelled. You're baking early this morning."

If he's waiting for me to offer him one, he's going to be disappointed. "They're for a bake sale at the boys' school."

He turns to me and the thin mask of civility has slipped away. "Okay, Julie. Let's cut the crap. Where is it?"

I try to process his words but they make no sense. "Where is what?"

"You know what. We had a deal, your baby brother and me, and he backed out. But I know he had it and you're the only one he would have given it to. So hand it over."

"I don't know what you're talking about. What deal? What is it I'm supposed to have?"

"Don't play dumb with me, sweetie." He crosses the room in a few long strides, stopping too close in front of me.

I take a step back. "Listen to me. I have no idea what you're talking about. I hadn't seen Bobby for weeks before he was killed."

He frowns, like he's turning my words over in his mind, trying to decide if I'm lying, then goes back to wandering around the room, talking more to himself than to me. "So, he didn't give it to you. But he had it. He told me he had it, back before he tried to welch on me. And he didn't have it on him. That means he stashed it somewhere."

He turns on me with an ugly stare. "And he would have told you where."

I hate the pleading sound in my voice as I answer. "He didn't tell me anything. I swear. I don't even know what you're talking about."

"Well, then I guess you better figure it out. And quick. The people I'm working with don't like to be kept waiting. I'll be back tonight. And don't even think about calling the cops." He rests his hand on the double frame holding the twins' school pictures. "You just got finished with one funeral . . ."

I open my mouth but there are no words. Gorman goes out and pulls the door closed with a force that jars me out of my stupor. That asshole just threatened my children. I pull my cell phone from my pocket.

"Hey, Julie. How're you holding up this morning?" The sound of my best friend's voice is both calming and strengthening.

"Karin, I need you. Now."

"On my way."

I think she sprinted across our back yards; she's at the kitchen door almost before I am. She looks at me, steers me into a chair, and gets us both a fresh mug of coffee before sitting across from me. I welcome the brief time to gather my thoughts.

"Okay," Karin says. "Now tell me."

"Ralph Gorman was just here." I can tell she doesn't recognize the name. "A couple years ago. He worked at Gemini. Mitch had to fire him."

This time she nods. "Mitch found out he was stealing from the company."

"That's him."

"Ugh. I remember that guy. He was here at one of Mitch's company cookouts. What a slob. He ate everything with his hands, then he'd catch some woman's eye and suck the food off his fingers, real slow, like it was supposed to be sexy or something. Gross."

I'd forgotten that.

"So, why was he here? What did he want?"

Telling her helps me clarify the frightening visit in my mind.

Karin sits quietly until I finish. "But what could Bobby have that would be valuable to Gorman?"

The realization is chilling. "Oh God. Bobby worked in Research and Development. He had access to almost everything. We've got some new designs that would be worth a lot of money to someone who knew where to take them."

"And Gorman would know."

A silence draws out between us as I run through a mental list of possible targets.

"Julie . . . did Gorman say Bobby 'didn't have it on him,' those exact words?"

"Yes, he said Bobby told him he had it and he didn't have it on him . . ." Her meaning hits me, catching my breath. "He meant when he was killed. Bobby didn't have it on him when he was killed."

"And the only way he could know that is . . ."

"If Gorman killed Bobby. Oh, God, Karin. Ralph Gorman murdered my brother."

"You've got to call the police."

"No! I told you what he said. If I go to the police, he'll hurt the boys."

"But he can't hurt them if he's in jail."

"He won't be in jail. I have no proof of any of this. Even if they take him in for questioning, they wouldn't have enough to hold him. He'd be out there. With my sons. I won't risk it. I won't."

"Okay. No police. For now, at least." She chews her lower lip. "Then we need to figure out what Gorman's looking for. Could Bobby have come by the house when you weren't home? Maybe left something?"

I shake my head. "I don't think so. He's . . . he had been avoiding me the last month or so." The thought, which I'd managed not to put into words until now, tears at me. But it's true. My brother had been avoiding me.

I see the sympathy in Karin's eyes but she pushes on. "What about mail? Did you get any strange mail?"

"Oh Lord. There's a whole stack of mail on my desk. Condolence cards I haven't even gone through yet."

She moves quickly down the hall and returns with the stack of envelopes, placing half in front of me and taking the rest. "Okay, first let's just check for any that don't feel like a card."

I find it about halfway through. "This one."

"What? How do you know?"

"There's something inside and the return address is Valley Street. It's where we lived when we were kids. He just added a bogus house number. The street numbers didn't go that high."

Karin sets the other mail aside and watches as I open mine. There's a folded sheet of paper and a small key. The note is in the almost perfect handwriting Bobby was teased about as a kid. Too neat for a boy. Much neater than mine. Karin lets me read it to myself first.

Jules,

I'm sorry to have to write this but I screwed up. This is not a big surprise, I've always been a screw up but this is a bad one. I broke my promise to you. I've been gambling again. And losing. I wanted to stop but I kept hoping my luck would turn and I could get even so I didn't have to come to you to cover my losses, again. Of course, it didn't happen and I got in really deep.

Anyway, an old friend of ours offered to bail me out. Remember Sticky Fingers? You know who I mean. He found out about the chip we designed for you-know-who. He said he could get a pretty penny for it from their number one competitor and screw the company over in the process. Looks like he never forgave Mitch for firing him. Well, I guess I wasn't thinking straight because I said okay. I lifted the prototype and the schematics from work and told him I had them but then

I came to my senses. I can't do that to you. Or the boys.

I've left what I took in a locker at the place where I met my first true love. Remember? The locker number is the real house number. I know you're a lot smarter than me so you'll figure it out. I'm going to meet our friend tonight and tell him the deal's off. Then I'm going away for a while. Things aren't too healthy for me around here right now and I'm not letting you bail me out again.

Please tell the boys their Uncle Bobby loves them.

I'm sorry, Jules. You deserved a better brother.

Bobby

I pass the note to Karin and wait while she reads it.

"I'm sorry, Julie."

Anger bubbles up inside me and spills over. "That chip he stole was designed under contract. A really *big* contract. If Gorman had pulled this off, it would have ruined Gemini. Destroyed Mitch's legacy. Taken everything from our sons. How could Bobby have done this? Even thought of doing it?"

I get up and pace around the kitchen, ranting about everything we had done for Bobby, covering his gambling debts, getting him into therapy, giving him a good position in the company. Finally, I run out of steam and return to my seat. Karin hands me a paper napkin and I realize my face is streaked with tears.

"He didn't have to do this. I would have helped him." My voice is smaller now, anger giving way to regret.

"I know." She gives me a moment to settle then continues. "Do you know where he means? Where the locker is?"

I nod. "It's a gym downtown. He met a girl there . . . years ago. Fell really hard for her. They dated awhile but she chose someone else. He never quite got over her."

"And the number?"

"Yeah. He set it up with the return address. It's the real address on Valley Street. One-twenty-one."

"Okay. So you know what Gorman wants and where it is. If you give it to him, he'll destroy Gemini. If you don't, he could hurt you or go after the boys. And you still won't go to the police?"

I shake my head. "No. No police."

"Well then . . . what do you want to do?"

***

I hear Karin coming in the kitchen door as I close the dishwasher.

"Any sign of him?" I ask. It's dark now but I have no idea

when Gorman will get here.

"Uh uh. And no strange cars parked on the street." She stops at the sight of two dozen frosted and decorated cupcakes on the counter. "You finished the cupcakes?"

"The bake sale's tomorrow." She arches one eyebrow at me and I shrug. "I needed to do something. To keep busy. Are we all set?"

"All set. I took the boys to Mitch's mom's. They were delighted at the unexpected sleepover. I don't think she makes them do homework. She said for you to get some rest."

It was the excuse I gave my mother-in-law earlier . . . that I needed to rest. The twinge of guilt is fleeting. She loves having them.

"And Jack's gone to Trevor's meet. It's clear out in Fairfield. They won't be home till late."

"Thank you, Karin."

"Yeah, yeah. Now . . . have you figured out what we're going to do?"

"I'm going to lie through my teeth. I'm going to tell him I have no idea what it is that Bobby had for him or where it is now. Then I'm going to offer to pay him back for whatever debts he covered for Bobby. If I can make him believe I can't give him what he wants, maybe he'll figure breaking even is better than nothing."

"You're going to pay him off?"

I could hear her unspoken thought. This guy killed Bobby.

"I'm going to try to buy some time."

"Okay. What do you want me to do?"

"I want you in the bedroom. Gorman wants something from me so I don't think he'll try to hurt me, but if you hear things getting ugly, call 9-1-1."

We don't have to wait long. At the sound of footsteps on the porch, Karin ducks into the nearest bedroom. I open the door and motion Gorman inside.

"Mr. Gorman, would you like a cup of coffee?" I'm trying for a tone of strained politeness. It seems to work.

"Sure, Julie. We can do that."

We move into the kitchen and he sits at my table. His back is to the counter, which is covered with cupcakes. The block of kitchen knives by the coffeemaker beckons invitingly as I fill the mugs. I put the mugs on the table and sit across from him.

"So, Julie, what have you got for me?"

"Mr. Gorman," I can tell he likes this gesture of respect, or fear, "I don't have what you want. I don't even know what it is that you want. Bobby didn't give me anything. He didn't send me anything.

Whatever it is he had for you, I don't know where it is." I glance nervously past his hulking presence, to the coffeemaker, the knives, and the cupcakes.

The false smile drops away from Gorman's face. "Don't give me that crap. I—"

"Please. If Bobby took money from you for something and didn't deliver, I agree that's not fair." I look toward the counter again and quickly back. "And you should be . . . compensated. I can't give you what he had, but I can repay you. Whatever you gave him."

I break off when I realize Gorman is no longer looking at me. He's turned toward the counter, looking at . . . the knives? Is it time to scream for Karin?

"You frosted those cupcakes." There's accusation in his voice.

"Yes. I told you. They're for my sons' bake sale tomorrow."

A sly grin spreads across his face. "I gave you one day to find what your brother owes me, even gave you a little nudge with those brats of yours, and you spend the day making bake sale cupcakes." He stands and steps to the counter. "I don't think so."

"No. Please don't . . ." But even as I speak, he takes the first cupcake and crushes it in his meaty fist.

"What are you doing?" I try again. "Stop that."

He moves from one frosted cake to the next, crushing each one and rolling the crumbled mess in his fingers. He finds it on the seventh try.

"Well, well. What have we here?" He rubs the cake off the small key and turns to face me. I watch as he proceeds to suck the frosting from each of his fingers in turn. Karin was right, it's some kind of sick turn on for him. I watch in disgust until he's done.

"So . . . you thought you were clever, huh? Next time you want to hide something from someone, try not looking at it every other second." He laughs heartily as I slump in my chair. "Now why don't you be a good girl and tell me what this key goes to?"

"It's a bus station locker," I tell him, my voice flat with defeat. "Fifth Street Station. Box seventy-two."

He drops the key in his pocket, pulls out his cell phone, and makes a call.

"I got it. Never mind from where, I told you I'd find it, and I found it. I'll be there in an hour. Yeah, and you better have my money ready."

He walks into the living room and picks up that same picture of the boys. "I don't have to tell you again about not going to the cops, right?"

I shake my head.

"Right?"

"No, you don't have to tell me."

Karin is in the kitchen before Gorman is off the front steps. She stares at the mess of destroyed snacks. "You put the key in a cupcake? Why?"

"It seemed like a good idea. Besides, it wasn't the key Bobby sent me. It was just an old file drawer key I don't use anymore."

"And I heard you send him to the bus station so the key is a moot point anyway. But what happens when he gets there and nothing works? You know he's coming right back here."

"No, he won't be back."

Karin narrows her eyes at me. "How do you know?"

"Because there was enough poison in that frosting to kill a man ten times Gorman's size." I flash her a look of wide-eyed innocence. "Did you know you really *can* learn to make almost anything on the Internet?"

She can't quite stifle a snort of laughter.

"I knew if I could point him at the cupcakes, he'd end up with his fingers in the frosting."

"And he was bound to lick them clean."

We stand there for a moment in quiet celebration. I suppose I should feel guilty, but Ralph Gorman murdered my brother and threatened my children. This was justice, plain and simple. I can tell Karin agrees.

"Come on," she says, reaching for a trash bag. "Let's get this mess cleaned up."

"And after that, you can help me bake a fresh batch of cupcakes for the bake sale tomorrow."

THE CREMAINS OF THE DAY

By Josh Pachter

When is a donut not just a donut? When it's a hole 'nother story.

I blame it on the Bossa Nova.

As I said just the other night to my husband Ed, who teaches English Lit at the University of Northern Iowa, the Bossa Nova donut from Mojo Donuts—right next to Cup of Joe on Main Street downtown—is a thing of beauty and a joy to behar. Ed, of course, first pointed out that the actual Keats quote, from something called "Endymion," is "a thing of beauty is a joy for ever," and not "a joy to behold," and, second of all, that he agrees with eighteenth century lexicographer Samuel Johnson, who ought to know what he was talking about, that puns are the lowest form of humor.

That may be, I riposted, but Dr. Johnson died more than two hundred years ago, while the great Alfred Hitchcock—who is also currently dead but was much more recently among the living and to this day, dead or not, continues to run a top-notch crime-fiction magazine to which I subscribe—once called puns the *highest* form of literature.

But I digress. The Bossa Nova donut is, if truth be told, a common or garden variety Boston cream with hundreds and thousands of multicolored sprinkles dotting the layer of chocolate icing on its top, and it is the sprinkles, the jimmies, the hundreds and thousands, that turn it from an ordinary donut into a work of art.

I know, I know: a cop who loves donuts. Clichéd, am I right? But what do you want me to say? I *am* a cop, and I *do* love me some donuts . . . especially the Bossa Novas from Mojo. I would eat one every day, if I wanted to weigh three hundred pounds, but then I'd get kicked off the force, and where would a three-hundred-pound woman in her fifties find a job that allows her to drive around Cedar Falls all day every day, only stopping once in a purple-and-gold moon to write a twenty-dollar ticket to some UNI student who runs a red light or parks beside a fire hydrant? So I only treat myself to a Bossa Nova on special occasions.

And today certainly counts as a special occasion: it's a

beautiful April afternoon; the last of the winter's snow has finally melted; I've just come from the Conway-Markham Funeral Home in New Hampton, where I've picked up the ashes of Ed's dear departed Aunt Penelope, and I'm on my way home to decant them out of the cardboard boxed Ziploc baggie they came in and into the cremation urn we bought online from One World Memorials and set that Classic Pewter container ("with minimalist black banding and a threaded lid for a secure closure") on the mantel in our family room, so Aunt Penny can glare down at us daily in death as she glared up at us weekly (but not weakly) in life when we visited her every damn Sunday for the last ten years for lunch at Shady Pines, where she retired—after a four-decade career as a third-grade teacher in Pella, a hundred plus miles to the south and far enough from the Cedar Valley to limit her pre-retirement glaring to Christmases and Easters—to be closer in her old age (and her cold rage) to her only living kin, my Ed.

Anyway, Penny finally bought the farm, leaving specific instructions regarding ashes to ashes, and now Messrs. Conway and Markham have done their thing, and instead of paying their outrageous fifty-dollar delivery charge I simply swung by during my lunch break to fetch the cremains myself.

As the crow flies, Mojo Donuts is not on my way from Conway-Markham in New Hampton across the Cederloo line to our humble abode in Waterloo, but my caffeine low-level light is flashing, and it isn't much of a detour to swing by Cup of Joe on Main for a refill—and, as noted above, it is a special occasion, so, leaving Penny's box buckled in on the passenger seat of my patrol car, I duck next door for a donut.

And, as has also been previously stipulated, I blame what happens next on the Bossa Nova.

Or, to be more specific, on those damn sprinkles. Holding the steering wheel with my left hand and the donut in my right, I'm taking the scenic route past George Wyth State Park on 218 and heading for home. I take a big bite of Mojo just as my front right tire bumps through a chuckhole the good men and women of Iowa DOT haven't yet gotten around to filling—and, wouldn't you know it, scatter sprinkles all over my uniform shirt and gun belt.

What I *should* do is pull over onto the shoulder and clean up the mess. I keep a pack of Handi Wipes in my glove compartment for just this reason: those sprinkles are not exactly glued onto the chocolate, and I *know* there are potholes on 218 in the spring.

What I *do*, though, is pure dumb Pavlovian reaction: I jam on my brakes.

In and of itself, that ought not to create a problem. I-218 is not exactly a major thoroughfare, and on an ordinary day I can drive from the cop shop in Cedar Falls all the way home without seeing another car.

Today, though—wouldn't you know it?—I am not alone on the highway. In fact, unbeknownst to me, focused as I am on my Bossa Nova and the road stretched out before me, a 2011 powder-blue Honda Fit is tailgating my Crown Vic at the moment of truth, and when I hit my brakes it rear-ends me but good.

My memory of the moments after the impact is hazy at best, but as I reconstruct the ensuing sequence of events, when I screech to a halt and the Fit smacks into my back bumper, my donut and Aunt Penelope's box both continue traveling forward at approximately fifty-five miles per hour, which is the speed I am driving when I slam on my brakes. My right hand, now unencumbered by donut, instinctively lunges out and somehow manages to arrest Aunt Penny's box before it can explode into my windshield. In about eleven different kinds of shock, I manage to set the box back on the passenger seat where it belongs and wrestle my patrol car onto the shoulder. The engine sputters and dies, and I am enveloped by what would be a great silence if it wasn't for all the screaming.

I work my jaw, flex my fingers, move my head from side to side, and determine that none of my more important body parts seem to be broken. Who, then, if not me, is doing all the shouting?

It's at this point that I realize what has happened: I've been popped from behind, and the driver who popped me is shrieking in agony.

I manage to unbuckle my seat belt. My door doesn't want to open, but I'm able to force it loose. I get out of the car, lick my lips, and turn back to face the music. The Honda Fit is looking fit for the junkyard: its entire front end is smashed in, and the screaming is coming not from its driver, who is slumped across his steering wheel and not moving, but from his horn, which his head is pressed against and therefore causing to blare.

The driver is a youngish Caucasian—maybe twenty-four, twenty-five. Long greasy hair that droops down over his collar, a scraggy mustache. I can't see the color of his eyes, because the lids are closed. He's dressed in blue jeans and a chambray shirt, its sleeves rolled up to reveal a line of barbed wire tattooed around his left bicep. No visible scars or other distinguishing marks.

The driver's-side window is shattered, so I reach in—careful to avoid the shards of broken glass—and press my fingers to the side of the man's neck. I feel a strong pulse throbbing. He's not dead, thank goodness, just knocked cold by the crash.

I hurry back to my shop to see if the two-way is working, so I can radio in for an ambulance and a couple of tow trucks. As I reach for the handset, it crackles into life.

"Calling all cars," I hear. "Be on the lookout for a blue 2011 Honda Fit. Driver just stuck up the Cedar Falls Community Credit Union on West Fourth and is armed and dangerous. Do not approach without backup."

"Huh," I say out loud, and I scuttle back to the Fit to examine the inside of the vehicle more closely. There is a ski cap on the passenger seat in front, and in April that is clearly not a wardrobe choice but a disguise. Peeking out from beneath it is what looks to me like a Taurus 709 Slim semi-automatic 9mm handgun. There are two bulging money bags on the floor in the back, stenciled with the letters *CFCCU*.

I check on the driver. He's still breathing, but I see no need to cuff him. He's not going anywhere, not for a while yet, anyway. I reach across him and confiscate his weapon, just in case I'm wrong and he regains consciousness sooner than I think he will, and then return to my radio.

***

Later, I'm sitting in the family room with Ed and I tell him the whole story.

"You captured a bank robber," he says proudly, scooching up beside me and snaking his arm through mine. "You're bound to get a commendation out of this, Frannie. I'm amazed you had the presence of mind to rescue Aunt Penelope from your car before they towed it away."

We both gaze up at the mantel, where what's left of Ed's aunt rests in peace—and I have to acknowledge that the minimalist black banding on the Classic Pewter finish truly does lend both the container and our humble home a touch of class.

"Well, you know what they say," I murmur modestly. "A Penny saved—"

"Don't," Ed warns me.

"—is—"

"Francine," he begs. "Please, no!"

But I can't help myself. A pun my soul, I can't.

"—is a Penny urned," I say.

HONOR THY FATHER

By Harriette Sackler

A selfish man, Abraham gorges himself on good food while his family struggles to survive. When he pays the price for his gluttony, his eldest son struggles to understand what happened and what kind of man his father really was.

New York City, 1911

Jacob's body tensed when he heard his father's heavy footsteps climbing the tenement's wooden stairs. He knew he was violating one of the Lord's sacred commandments, but he could not honor the cruel man who was his father. Abraham was, at best, indifferent to his wife and seven children. Unfortunately, for most of the time he graced them with his presence, he was abusive. It took very little or nothing at all to provoke him to pull off his belt and use it on his children or wife, leaving them with bruises.

Abraham slammed the door behind him as he entered the apartment. Hanging his coat on a peg nailed to the wall, he didn't even acknowledge his son's presence as he strode to the battered wooden table and set down the packages he carried. The smell of corned beef and sour pickles made Jacob's mouth water, but he knew none of the food would be offered to him.

"Gertie," Abraham bellowed, "bring me tea!"

A moment later, Jacob's mother appeared from the rear of the apartment and silently poured hot water from the kettle over tea leaves she had placed in a glass. Along with a small bowl of sugar cubes, she placed the hot beverage in front of her husband, then left the room to tend to her other children.

Jacob, sitting on a bench several feet from his father, quietly watched as Abraham ate the tantalizing meat that was layered on thick rye bread. This was a daily ritual. And, while his family ate the thin soup and bread that Mama prepared for them, Papa never offered his brood the smallest bite of his dinner.

When Abraham had devoured every bit of the sandwich, he turned to the second package he'd brought home. Inside were several slices of lemon-scented pound cake, lightly dusted with powdered sugar. Without delaying to savor the delicately scented dessert, Abraham greedily stuffed two slices of the cake into his mouth, barely taking time to chew. He wrapped the remainder of the cake in its package and placed it on a high shelf over the sink, out of the reach of his children. He could have left it on the table, because no one in the family would have dared to sample the delicacy. Without one word to Jacob, he headed for his bedroom.

***

What seemed like hours later, Jacob woke to the sound of moans from his parents' room. His two brothers continued to sleep soundly next to him. All of a sudden, he heard his mother call his name, and he jumped up and ran to their room. His father was lying on the bed, sweat covering his face, which was white as snow. His limbs twitched, and the smell of vomit assailed Jacob's nose.

"Jacob, we have to get your father down the hall to the toilet. I don't know what's wrong with him, but it came upon him suddenly, and he's very ill. Maybe something he ate made him sick."

"Of course, Mama. Do you want me to wake the other boys?"

"No, no, let them sleep. I think we can manage on our own."

With great difficulty, Jacob and his mother half carried and half dragged Abraham out of the flat and down the hall to the toilet room shared by the families on the floor. His father's senses seemed to have deserted him, and all he could do was moan in what appeared to be intolerable pain. This only lasted a few moments before Abraham's body convulsed one last time, and then went limp. His breathing ceased, and his lifeless eyes lost their light.

***

In keeping with Hebrew custom, Abraham Levine was laid to rest the following day. The rabbi arranged for him to be buried at Mount Richmond Cemetery, which was managed by the Hebrew Free Burial Association for poor Jews living on the Lower East Side. Jacob and his mother made the long trip to Staten Island to bid Abraham farewell. No tears were shed, and this would be the one and only time they would visit the grave. The younger children remained at home under the care of Aunt Minnie, Gertie's younger sister, who lived several tenements away. Minnie despised Abraham for the pain he caused his wife and children. Although Minnie, like her sister, was in an arranged marriage, as was the custom in the old country, her husband was a good and kind man and did his best to provide for his family. Gertie hadn't been so lucky. She, a loving and wise woman, deserved a far better man than the selfish brute who made her life a misery. Minnie had pleaded many times with her sister to leave Abraham, but Gertie would not. "For better or worse, marriage is for life," she argued.

Even though the exact cause of Abraham's death was unknown, there was no legal requirement for a formal investigation. The police paid little attention to the demise of Lower East Side residents. The poor were largely ignored, and their deaths were a daily occurrence. Most importantly, they had no money to pay the bribes required to entice law enforcement to undertake a formal death inquiry.

But Jacob was puzzled. It seemed his father's death was so sudden and agonizing that something unnatural had happened to him. But what? The only explanation that made sense was that Abraham had been poisoned, either accidentally or intentionally. How and why were the questions to be answered. In his heart, Jacob knew that his father's death was a relief and, aside for the need for the family to bring in more earnings, life would be easier without Abraham. But the death was a puzzle that he wanted to solve.

***

Visitors had come and gone all week, paying their respects to the Levines. Aunt Minnie and her husband greeted guests, thanking them on behalf of the bereaved, and graciously accepted the offerings of homemade food that were brought to the house, as was the tradition.

"Condolences to you and the children, Gertie."

"May Hashem, the good Lord, watch over the family and grant you peace."

"Abe will continue to live in your memories."

When the shiva, or week of mourning, was over, Jacob turned his attention to learning about his father's last days. Even though they shared a dwelling, Abraham had been a stranger. One evening, Jacob sat at the kitchen table after his mother and siblings had gone to bed. He thought about the many aspects of his father's life that he knew nothing about. How was he regarded by his coworkers? Did he engage in the pursuit of vices like gambling or drinking? Did he betray his wife with other women? Anything was possible.

But first, the cause of his father's death needed to be uncovered. Abraham had seemed well when he arrived home that evening. He had become ill during the night, several hours after he had eaten his dinner. Was there a connection? Jacob knew that his father stopped for a sandwich at Greenberg's Deli every night. It was the most popular delicatessen on the Lower East Side, and Jacob had never heard of anyone becoming ill because of the food. But what of the cake Abraham had brought home? He knew it hadn't come from Greenberg's, since the deli didn't offer pastry on its menu. Had it come from a local bakery? His father rarely brought baked goods home.

Deep in thought, something niggled at Jacob's brain. Something about the cake. He remembered that his father hadn't eaten it all. Yes. He'd put the remaining slices back in the wrapping and placed the package on a high shelf over the sink. Jacob quickly rose and dragged his chair over to the sink so he could reach the shelf. Abraham had been a large man, tall and muscular and his son had not yet reached his height or breadth. Balancing on the rickety chair, Jacob reached for the package, then pulled his hand back. Jacob's stomach turned as he looked at it. The cake and the paper it was wrapped in were covered in dead insects. The only remedy to alleviate the plague of the small creatures that infested the tenements was poison. So, without doubt, the cake was tainted, and certainly not by accident. Someone had meant to poison Abraham. At that moment, Jacob could only thank the good Lord for his father's selfishness. For if he had shared the dessert with any members of the family, they, too, would be in their graves.

***

Except for the two youngest children, the family was working harder than ever to earn enough to pay their rent and buy food without the few dollars Abraham had grudgingly given Gertie each week. But even the longer working hours didn't put a damper on the new-found freedom the family now enjoyed. The children, no longer in fear of a hard slap across the face if they dared to disturb their father, played and laughed in their flat. And, Gertie, seeing her children enjoying life, smiled and encouraged them. The lines and furrows on her face had even diminished.

***

Over the next several weeks, Jacob spent every spare moment, and there weren't very many of them, looking into his late father's life. He had created a list of people who might shed light on the activities in which Abraham had been involved. He started with the supervisor at Strauss and Sons Fine Suits where Abraham had been employed as a pattern cutter since he arrived in America eighteen years before in 1893. Mr. Schwartz, an elderly man with stooped shoulders and thick-lensed eyeglasses, offered his condolences to Jacob and showed him a seat in his cramped office.

"How can I be of service, young man?" he asked.

"I wonder if you would be so kind as to tell me a bit about my father's work life. Was he a good worker? What did you think of him? Did he spend time with anyone here? Any information you can offer would be helpful."

Mr. Schwartz considered the questions before responding.

"I was the one who hired Abraham many years ago. He was an excellent pattern cutter and was one of our highest paid workers. Mind you, he would never be wealthy, but not so poor either. He was not a friendly man and kept to himself. He came to work on time every day and never left early. The only person I saw him spend time with was Agnes Feldman, but not of late. One thing I have to say is that your father had a very bad temper. When he had trouble cutting a pattern, he would raise his voice and pound on the table. But since it didn't happen too often, I didn't feel the need to talk to him about it. I think that's about all I can tell you."

"Thank you for your help, Mr. Schwartz. Can I speak with Miss Feldman?" Jacob asked.

"Well, she's working right now, but I can tell her you'll be waiting for her in front of the factory at six o'clock. Stand right outside the door. And it's Mrs. Feldman. She's a widow who lost her husband a number of years ago."

***

When Jacob met with Mrs. Feldman, he was shocked to learn that she had kept company with his father for the better part of a year. This revelation made him sick. Abraham had taken her out to dinners and bought her gifts. She enjoyed his company and assumed he was unhappy at home. But after they fought one evening and he became abusive, she told him that their relationship was over. Although they worked in the same building, she never spoke to him again.

Jacob was disgusted to learn of his father's infidelity. What else would he uncover about Abraham's secret life?

***

Jacob visited other places over the next few days. When he stopped at the bakery that was located midway between the factory and their tenement, Jacob learned that his father often stopped there on the way to work to purchase two buttered rolls for his lunch. He never bought pound cake, and besides, they didn't even offer lemon. The proprietor remembered his father well because Abraham came into the bakery at exactly the same time every day and never ordered anything but the rolls. Jacob couldn't imagine where his father had gotten the cake that had ended his life.

At the neighborhood tavern, the owner and several patrons remembered his father well. He would come in several times a week, order a whiskey, then would leave shortly thereafter. That was unless he joined the poker game in the back room. But Abraham didn't play for long and never lost a great deal of money.

He wasn't terribly friendly and rarely joined in conversation with the other men.

It appeared that the mystery of his father's death would never be solved. Jacob would have to set it aside and move on with his life. After all, Jacob, as the eldest son, was now responsible for the welfare of the family. His responsibility was great. He needed to look to the future and not the past.

***

Several weeks later, Jacob returned from his job as a clerk at a dry goods store to find his mother sitting at the kitchen table, staring at the wall, her face as pale as death.

"Mama, Mama, what's wrong? Are you sick? Tell me! What can I do to help?"

Gertie shook her head as though waking from a trance and turned to look at her son. Then she wordlessly handed Jacob a wooden box that had been on the table in front of her. Puzzled, Jacob took the box from his mother and opened it. His face turned as pale as Gertie's.

"Mama, where did you get this?" Jacob asked as he gazed at all the money stacked in neat piles inside the box.

"I thought it was time to clear out the chest of drawers that held your father's things. After all, I could use the fabric to make clothing for you and the other children. In one of the drawers, covered by Abraham's shirts, I found that box. I don't know where he got all this money. Did he steal it? Or save it from his wages instead of making a better life for his family? I feel numb! To think he had this money hidden away while we were forced to survive on so little. To think I was married to such a godless man!"

It hurt Jacob's heart to see his mother in such pain.

"Mama, he's gone now. The money belongs to you. It no longer matters where it came from. Life can change for us. Maybe Hashem, the good Lord, is watching over us after all."

"Jacob, my son, that someone so young should be so wise. If this is God's plan, who are we to refuse?"

***

Minnie Cohen hummed an old Yiddish tune as she busily prepared Shabbat dinner for her sister Gertie's family and her own. She would have liked her family to sit down for the meal with her sister's brood, but their two flats were just too small to allow them all to eat together. But when Gertie moved to a larger place, they could all celebrate the Sabbath together.

So Minnie was cooking enough for everybody. Two chickens were roasting in the oven, along with potato kugel and challah. Soup, brimming with vegetables, simmered on the stove. She had just finished preparing dessert, which would be next to bake in the oven. She remembered the last time she'd made lemon pound cake, sprinkled with powdered sugar, that she gave to Abraham as he walked by on his way home the night he died. And she smiled.

KILLER CHOCOLATE CHIPS

By Ruth McCarty

The chief knows repeated domestic abuse can't be resolved easily, even when accompanied by a chocolate chip cookie.

Chief of Police Erin Donnelly stared at the box of walnut chocolate chip cookies Abby Jones had dropped off at the station. Third box of homemade cookies that week. All because Erin had responded to a domestic call at Abby's bed and breakfast, the Rose Trellis Inn, and arrested Abby's husband for allegedly choking her, even though Abby's neck wasn't even bruised.

A classic he said/she said case and Erin wasn't sure it would hold up in court. Several of the guests had heard Abby and her husband arguing and they said she gave as good as she got. Erin had gone to high school with both of them, so she knew about the on-again/off-again relationship they'd always had.

Erin didn't need another cookie, even though they smelled and looked delicious. She reached into the box. "Just one more. That's it," she said aloud, but she knew better. If the guys at the station didn't gobble them up soon, she would eat each and every one.

Reggie Jones had been released on bail that morning, and Abby had come bearing gifts and asking for extra protection. "He's going to kill me next time. I just know it," she'd said, swiping a balled-up tissue at her eyes. "He's burning mad that I filed the protective order against him. Thinks because he's half owner of the inn that he can come and go as he pleases."

Erin had explained once again how the Maine Protective Order worked. "You know Reggie's excluded from the home, school, or work of the protected person, and since you live and work in the same place, he won't be allowed anywhere near the inn. He hasn't contacted you, has he?"

"Nope. But I know the minute he has a few whiskeys he'll be right there in my face. And you know he has a gun."

"We took his gun when we served the order. He's prohibited from possessing a gun."

"And you of all people know that his hunting buddies have more guns than a Remington factory."

It was true, Erin knew. She'd bet most everybody in Prosperity had multiple guns. Some registered, some not. They had confiscated the only gun registered to Reggie, but her gut told her he had more stashed somewhere besides the inn. The thought had haunted her all day. Would their domestic spat escalate into murder?

It had been a long day at the station and she was exhausted. Two of her officers were on light duty due to injuries and one more had taken a bereavement leave to attend his mother-in-law's funeral in Connecticut, so Erin had helped out on several of the calls.

She'd responded to a 9-1-1 overdose call because she was closer to the location than the paramedics. She'd arrived right before them, and administered a shot of Narcan to the victim's thigh. As chief, she had made sure each cruiser was equipped with a Narcan kit. Alcoholism and drug abuse ran as wild as blueberries in Maine, and Prosperity hadn't missed the season.

Before heading to her cottage on Backwater Pond, Erin decided to stop at the Rose Trellis Inn to check on Abby and buy a home-cooked meal to eat later.

The dining room had a smattering of tourists, and a few of the locals sat at the bar. After saying hello, Erin walked through the narrow hallway to the well-stocked kitchen. Bowls of apples, peaches, bananas, potatoes, mushrooms, and onions portrayed a still life display on the granite island. Copper pots and pans hung above a commercial size gas stove.

Abby was busy poring over a dog-eared book. She looked up and jumped out of her chair.

"Gawd, you startled me," she said, and slammed the book shut.

"Oh, sorry. I thought you heard me coming. I hope you didn't think I was Reggie."

Her hand went to her neck. "Just didn't hear you."

"Something smells amazing. What do you have in the oven?"

Abby wrung her hands, walked to the oven, and opened the door. Erin spied a frying pan-sized chocolate chip cookie. You would think with all the cookies she'd eaten that day that looking at this gooey treat would make her sick. It didn't. The smell of chocolate made her stomach growl instead.

"Now don't get mad," Abby said. "It's a special cookie I made for Reggie. Gluten-free. You know what happens with his celiac disease. Vomiting—"

"Are you kidding me?" Erin heated with anger. She couldn't believe what she was hearing.

"I was going to stop by the station tomorrow and drop all the charges. And cancel the protection order."

"Why the hell would you do that?"

"Well, you know Reggie and me always make up," Abby said, rubbing her arms. "And I can't run this place without him."

"Just this morning you were afraid he was going to kill you," Erin said through clenched teeth. "What about him choking you the other night?"

Abby looked out the window before turning back to Erin, but couldn't look her in the eye. "I may have exaggerated a bit."

Erin balled her hands into fists to keep from yelling. "This has to stop. I'm going to recommend to the judge that both of you get counseling. You can't keep doing this."

Abby sort of smiled. "You're right, Erin. I totally agree. This has to stop. Now is there something I can get you before Reggie gets here? I have some leftover stew in the fridge."

Erin shook her head and tried to reason with her. "You can still keep him out of here. You don't really need him, you know. You can always hire someone to help you around the inn. Lots of people are looking for work now that the summer is almost over."

"And what will I do in the fall when the last of the tourists have left? Or in the middle of winter when I have no money coming in? Chop wood myself?"

Erin knew that winters in Prosperity were hard for a lot of the residents. "This is it, Abby. Next time I arrest both of you and I'm not going to drop any charges."

"Can I send you out with some cheesecake then?"

Erin put up her hand and walked out of the kitchen, down the hallway to the grand front door. She pulled it open and nearly ran into Reggie. "You touch her one more time and you're going away for good," she said and kept walking.

"We're going to make it work this time," he yelled after her. "I swear. Abby called me last night and we talked for a long time. I love her, ya know."

"Yeah. Right. You both need counseling," Erin yelled back.

"Okay. We can do that."

Erin got in her car and sat there, staring at the inn. She knew she'd be back.

***

The 9-1-1 call came into the station in the middle of the night. Nessa Sullivan was on dispatch and called Erin after sending an ambulance to the inn.

"Just wanted to let you know we got a call from the Rose Trellis Inn—"

"Son of a bitch," Erin said. "Took less time than I thought."

"No, wait," Nessa said. "It's Reggie Jones. Sicker than a dog. Abby said he couldn't stop vomiting and had diarrhea so bad she couldn't get him to the emergency room."

"Oh. Good. Well, not good," Erin said. She thought about the celiac disease Abby had told her he suffered from. Looks like that special chocolate chip cookie was wasted on Reggie. "Thanks for letting me know, Nessa."

Erin tossed and turned for almost an hour. Finally, she gave up and drove to the hospital to see how Reggie was doing and if Abby needed a ride home.

As she drove up, the emergency department lights glared bright in the black Maine sky. Erin parked in a space reserved for police or clergy. She hoped no one would be needing a priest or rabbi that night. Automatic doors opened into a waiting room filled with patients. She heard a child crying, sounding much like her nieces when they were little and feverish and wanted someone to hold them. A father was sprawled on a chair, softly snoring while the mother rubbed their child's back, murmuring soothing sounds.

A citified woman on a cell phone yelled above the noise saying, "Yes. A heart attack. And we're in this backwoods town."

Erin ignored her and walked to the window where an RN she knew by sight slid open a window and said, "Chief Donnelly, what can I help you with? Are you here for the DUI?"

"No. I'm actually here to talk to Abby Jones. She still here?"

The nurse looked at her screen and said, "They're in four." Then she buzzed Erin in.

"Thanks."

The smells of the emergency department reminded Erin of the nursing home where her mother had recently been a resident. She avoided looking in the rooms and knew she had arrived at four when the overpowering smell hit her. The curtain was closed, so Erin said softly, "Abby, it's Erin."

Abby pulled the curtain aside. She looked horrible, and if Erin didn't know better she would have thought Abby was the patient.

"What are you doing here? We didn't do nothin'."

"I know. I got a call that an ambulance was heading to the Rose Trellis Inn and wanted to check on you. Reggie okay?"

"This is the worst attack he's had. Couldn't stop vomiting or shitting. Smelling up the goddamn inn."

So much for her being worried about her husband. "What do they think caused it?"

"Well, I don't know. Don't know where he ate the last few days. Maybe it's what they fed him at the jail." She crossed her arms and raised her chin toward Erin. "Bet they didn't give him gluten-free meals."

"You know, Abby, I'm sure they would have. We have a policy about checking for allergies."

"Well, all I know is I'm going to be a mess in the morning and I have to have breakfast going by six."

"Are they keeping Reggie overnight?"

"Don't know yet. They're giving him fluids now."

"Well, he's in good hands here. Let me take you to the inn. When they discharge Reggie, I'll send someone to drive him home."

"I'm dying here," Reggie moaned, and Erin knew the diarrhea hadn't stopped.

"Look. I can't go home now," Abby said.

Erin guessed she wished she'd never let Reggie come back.

"I'll swing by Dunkin's in the morning and bring coffee and donuts to the inn for you, tell your guests what happened."

She snorted. "If there's any guests left after the smell."

***

At six o'clock, Erin drove to the Dunkin' Donuts and ordered a few Box O' Joes and a few dozen donuts. Whatever had possessed her to help was beyond her. Abby had been a classmate, not a good friend. And Reggie had just been the skinny boy in algebra class.

After setting up the coffee and donuts in the dining room, she went to the kitchen to see what she could throw together for a fruit plate. She grabbed a few apples and a couple of the peaches and put them in an empty bowl she found on the counter. Then arranged a couple of the bananas on top. She looked at the potatoes and onions. Nothing quick she could prepare with those.

Abby's kitchen had lost the fresh-baked smell from the night before. Now it smelled more like bleach and dish soap. She opened a few cabinet doors, looking for any leftover cookie. Reggie must have eaten the whole thing. No wonder he got sick.

Hearing noises in the dining room, Erin went in and told the few guests what had happened. Strangely enough, one of them was the citified woman from the emergency department and she wasn't happy about not getting her home-cooked breakfast.

Erin heard a door slam in the back of the house. Had Abby come home after all? She walked back to the kitchen to find an elderly, hunched-over woman putting on an apron. "Do you work here?" Erin said.

The woman nodded. "Housekeeping. I come in most mornings to clean the kitchen, change the beds, and clean the rooms. At least in the busy season. Looks like the kitchen won't need me this morning."

Abby hadn't mentioned she had help. "Abby's at the hospital with Reggie. She should be home later this morning."

***

Erin was glad that Ian McDermott, her chief deputy, had returned from bereavement leave and she would finally have a day off. She headed home to get some much-needed sleep.

When she woke, she checked in with Ian, told him about Reggie. They talked a few minutes before ending the call.

The more Erin thought about it, the more she wondered what had made him so ill. She doubted binging on a gluten-free cookie could be the cause. What else could he have had to eat? And where? She scowled. The doctor on duty would surely call the health inspector if he or she suspected food poisoning. Right?

Erin decided to take a shower, then swing by the hospital.

***

Reggie had been admitted. Still had vomiting and diarrhea, Abby told her, when she entered his room. "Thanks for getting the donuts."

"Now we're even with the cookies," Erin said. "Did Reggie tell you what he ate yesterday?"

"Yeah, he did. Why?"

"I'm wondering if it could be food poisoning."

"I told you it's his celiac disease. He never watches what he eats."

"Did you talk to the doctor about it?"

Abby drew in a breath and turned red in the face. "Look, I appreciate you helping, but you really need to leave. It's just his freaking disease."

"Okay, then," Erin said. She headed out of the room and to the elevator, unable to shake the gut feeling that there was more to it. She headed down to the cafeteria, bought a coffee and a chocolate chip muffin, and sat at a table way in the corner, facing the door.

She took a bite, and thought back to Abby's kitchen that morning, smelling like bleach. Had Reggie gotten sick in the kitchen? Didn't seem likely. He would have instinctively run to the nearest bathroom.

No trace of the leftover cookie. No cast iron pan in the sink. The look on Abby's face when Erin had entered. Her slamming the dog-eared book closed. Had Abby purposely caused Reggie's illness?

Erin pictured herself back in the kitchen. The smell of the cookie baking. Abby giving her a quick look in the oven, knowing how much Erin loved her cookies. Making sure she told Erin this cookie was only for Reggie. Gluten-free, yes. But what else was in it? What wasn't there?

Erin jumped up and ran to the emergency department, asked to talk to the doctor on duty. Told her what she suspected.

Erin waited outside Reggie's room while they informed Abby they were taking him for tests. After they wheeled him out, Erin entered.

Abby paled. "Why are you still here?"

"You knew he wouldn't stop abusing you."

Abby opened her mouth to say something, then snapped it shut.

"They're testing him for amatoxin poisoning." Erin watched Abby's face. Her eyes widened, but she still said nothing. "I think you know what they'll find."

Abby crossed her arms and looked at the floor.

"Destroying Angel."

"I don't know what you're talking about," Abby huffed.

"I think you do. Symptoms include vomiting and diarrhea that slowly go away, but the damage keeps on going until the liver is destroyed—"

"It's his celiac!"

"No. It's the mushrooms missing from your kitchen. The ones that were there yesterday. You kept a few in case your first dose didn't work. He wouldn't have seen them in the cookie. Wouldn't have tasted them with all those chocolate chips. But you knew I saw the mushrooms and that I would remember them when Reggie died, so you got rid of the rest."

She shook her head. "I should never have let you in the kitchen. Leave it to you to solve yet another murder from our class."

Erin said, "He's not dead yet."

"No, but he will be, if my cookbook is right." She stood, stuck out her hands so Erin could cuff her. "Maybe they'll call me the Angel of Death."

ILLUSTRATION DIANE NETTLES

SUSHI LESSONS

By Edith Maxwell

Can sushi mend a failing relationship? Nicky's bartender friend Kiki knows a thing or two about dealing with men troubles.

The truly creative can always find more than one way to teach a lesson.

In the Yoshinoya *sushi-ya*, Nicky plucked the next small plate from the conveyor belt as it passed and set it on the stack of empties in front of her. The white porcelain held two pieces of *maguro* sushi. The rich red tuna melted in her mouth, the vinegary sweet rice was piquant on her tongue, and the chef had applied exactly the right-sized smear of sinus-clearing wasabi in between.

She winced when she glanced at Terrance's stack of plates—twice as high as hers—and the little dish of extra wasabi next to them. His Navy income as a seaman and her part-time paycheck from Business English Center were going to suffer from this splurge. Still, it was the anniversary of when they'd met two years earlier, and they'd taken the train into Tokyo to celebrate. Not that Yoshinoya was a fancy restaurant. Conveyor belt sushi places were the equivalent of McDonald's here. But it was all they could afford. She drained her glass of Kirin beer.

"Ter, we should learn to make sushi ourselves. How hard can it be?" She gazed up at her boyfriend, his legs way too long for these short stools. His big blue eyes, now-cropped blond hair, and luscious lips had made him a target for giggling schoolgirls wanting the apparent movie-star's autograph ever since he'd been stationed in Japan.

He raised a single pale eyebrow. "You always think you can do better. Go ahead and try."

She pressed her lips together as she signaled for the waiter to count their plates and give them their bill. They made their way toward the train station where they'd catch the Odakyu-sen back home.

"Five months, Nicky. Five months 'til I get out. You ever been to the Greek islands?"

"No, but I'd love to visit them."

"That's going to be the first stop on my trip." He sauntered with hands in pockets.

MY trip? Nicky wasn't included?

"I want to see Sweden, too, and Egypt. You know, with my family's history of heart issues, I plan to travel all over as soon as I'm discharged in case I don't get a chance later."

His father had died of a heart attack in his forties, but Terrance had been healthy ever since she met him. Nicky wanted to say, "But what about me? Don't you want me to travel with you?" She kept her silence. It would only sound whiny, and he'd already given her his answer by not inviting her to be part of his grand plans.

She glanced up sharply to see him exchange a rakish smile with a young woman who looked maybe five years younger than Terrance's—and Nicky's—twenty-three. The girl wore a short tight skirt, knee-high boots, and heavy eye makeup.

Nicky knew if she said anything about his flirting with other women he would calmly protest, "Of course I'm with you, babe. Doesn't mean I'm dead, does it?"

***

"See you in the morning, babe." Terrance planted a perfunctory kiss on Nicky's lips late the next afternoon.

Don't call me babe. She wasn't quite sure when their passionate relationship had devolved into unfeeling pecks and oblique criticisms, at least on his part. It seemed sudden but must have been a gradual slide when she wasn't paying attention.

She watched him bicycle off to the small Kamiseya naval base in the November near-twilight for his night shift, then returned to perusing the *Mainichi Daily*, one of the two English-language newspapers.

So Jimmy Carter had pulled it off, the first Deep South president to be elected since the Civil War. More power to him. It'd be good for the country to have a Democrat back in office, too.

Nicky didn't have any English-conversation classes to teach on Wednesdays or Thursdays and she'd been wanting to hack back the *wisteria floribunda* plant in front of the little house they rented in the commuter town of Minami-rinkan. Without its leaves or the fragrant lavender-colored blossoms of the spring, the gnarled and twisted branches loomed ominously outside the front door.

Except it was impossible to tame the plant without pruners or loppers, which this rental cottage evidently didn't supply. She settled for collecting the pendulous seed pods into a plastic shopping bag. One of them exploded with a puff of powder, releasing a round brown seed the size of a stone in the game of Go, or as they called it here, *igo*.

Inside the house Nicky stared at the pods, barely seeing them. She'd left a budding career as a landscape architect in her home state of Indiana to follow her heart—that is, Terrance—to Japan. She was good at coaxing classes of businessmen to actually speak the language they'd studied the grammar of for so long, but her true love was plants. Researching growth patterns, shade and soil needs, varieties of colors, and more let her be creative in other people's gardens in a way teaching conversational English couldn't even begin to approach.

Sighing, she turned to the book on making sushi she'd picked up at the English-language bookstore on the way to the train the day before and began reading about the proportions of ingredients for the rice, which fish to buy, and how to slice it.

***

Kiki-san poured more Asahi beer from the liter bottle into the small glass in front of Nicky where she perched on a bar stool that evening. Nicky had learned by now one didn't pour one's own drink in Japan. The tall bartender and proprietor set down a small dish of kimchi, the Korean spicy fermented cabbage that was a perfect bar snack. She added a pair of black enameled chopsticks, which in Japan always tapered to points. Nicky often walked down to Kiki's when Terrance worked night shift. She felt safe with a woman proprietor, knowing Kiki wouldn't let any local men harass her. Kiki thought it was entertaining that their names were so similar, even though she pronounced hers "kee-kee."

"*Arigatoo*." Nicky thanked her as she lifted the glass. "*Kampai*."

Kiki smiled through her heavy makeup. "*Kampai*. How are sings, Nicky?"

How are things. "They're okay."

The bartender peered at her. "What you mean, only okay? Terrance-san, he not treat you good, I sink."

"Sort of. It's nothing serious." Nicky had the urge to unburden herself to Kiki. She didn't have any women friends here and it was hard to be around only men all the time. Terrance, his Navy friends, her students. But she restrained herself. "I'm trying to learn how to make sushi."

"Good, good. You go *sakanaya* next door, ask *Obaa-san*. She teach you."

"Grandmother? Your grandmother works at the fish shop?"

Kiki threw her head back and laughed, but her red-dyed hair didn't budge. "No, just old lady."

"I'll go tomorrow." Nicky ate a bite of kimchi, then sucked in air. "Man, Kiki, this batch is super hot. Way too spicy for me."

"I know. I make it that way."

"Terrance would love it," Nicky said, fanning her open mouth. "He's a Californian."

Kiki leaned over the bar. "One time I put *gaidoku* in kimchi for bad man who, how you say, follow me all atime, call me all hours, don't go away."

"A stalker?" Nicky's eyes went wide. "What's *gaidoku*?"

"He never come back." She slapped her hands together in a dusting motion. "I say, good riddance."

***

Nicky left Terrance sleeping the next morning and paid a visit to the fish shop. She passed Kiki's bar, dark and locked with a sliding metal grate across the front that protected it until she opened at the end of the day.

Nicky had bought fresh fish at the *sakanaya* before but had never paid much attention to who was behind the glass case. Usually a young man had taken her yen. But sure enough, a bent-over little woman with a white headscarf tied over white hair and wearing a lab-type coat to match, stood at the back counter wielding a dangerous-looking knife. The young man was nowhere to be seen and Nicky was the only customer.

Obaa-san turned at the jangling of the bell on the door. "*Hai*!" she called out.

"*Ohayoo gozaimasu*," Nicky greeted her. Strictly speaking it meant something like, "Early is, nicely," but it was the morning greeting.

"*Ohayoo*."

"*Ano, anata wa Igirisu o hanashimasu*?" Nicky thought that was right. The little particles that went between words often tripped her up.

"Yes-u, I speak-u Ing-gi-rish-u."

Most shopkeepers in this area where so many American Navy personnel lived had at least one employee who spoke a bit of the language. It wasn't often the older ones, though.

Nicky spoke slowly. "Kiki-san said you can teach me to make sushi. I want to learn."

Obaa-san nodded, holding her hand up to hide her smile. "I teach. We start now?"

"Why not?"

***

Nicky had never had a worse Thanksgiving.

"Can't you ask for it off?" she'd pleaded with Terrance the week before. "It's Thanksgiving, Ter."

He'd shrugged. "Doesn't mean anything to me. I told Deser I'd take his shift. He's got kids and a wife."

All she could do was stare. Terrance had her, and he knew Thanksgiving was her favorite holiday. It was bad enough they couldn't get a turkey, and the only pumpkin pies available in the commissary were cheapo frozen ones. Now he was abandoning her, too. Because they weren't married, Nicky couldn't go on base without him, even if she'd wanted to attend the mess hall version of the family meal, which she didn't. And out here on the economy—as the Navy called anywhere off base—the third Thursday of November was just another work day. When had he stopped needing her? When had he stopped caring if she was happy or not? More to the point, why did she need him to need her? That was the hardest question to answer.

So she stayed home alone and made a new batch of sushi, her hurt hardening into resolve to be more creative in her search for happiness.

Obaa-san, who had said her name was Haruko Watanabe, had taught Nicky the correct proportions of vinegar and sugar to heat up and pour onto warm medium-grain rice. She'd showed Nicky how to pack a small log of the fragrant sticky rice into her left palm with her right index and middle fingers. She'd instructed how to mix the powdered wasabi with a little water into a smooth green paste, and how much to swipe across the log before topping it with raw fish.

The cutting of the fish Nicky left to the old woman. Whenever she walked in now, Haruko-san no longer covered her smile when she called out greetings. She always asked how many people Nicky was making sushi for. Her answer was never more than two, but the fish lady would nod and proceed to cut perfectly sized slices of tuna, salmon, octopus, and other offerings. Nicky sometimes purchased a few cooked shrimp, a half dozen slices of cooked eel already in its thick sweetened soy marinade, or pickled mackerel to go with the raw fish.

But sushi wasn't the only thing Nicky prepared that Thanksgiving.

***

That evening found her in Kiki's bar again. "No, I want something stronger than beer tonight," she said when Kiki set the usual bottle of beer in front of Nicky. She needed real alcohol tonight.

"Whiskey?" the older woman asked as if she already knew the answer. She turned away and brought back a squat unopened bottle of Suntory. "You buy bottle, I keep here for you." Kiki smiled and waved her hand toward the rows and rows of bottles in all stages of full and empty behind her, each labeled with a different name written in kanji, the Japanese version of Chinese characters.

Nicky took a deep breath. "Perfect."

"Mix-u?"

Nicky blinked at her. "What?"

"You want gingeru, supuraito, Coku?"

Oh. Kiki was asking if she wanted ginger ale, Sprite, or Coke to mix with her whiskey.

"No, thanks. Just ice." Nicky looked around. The place was devoid of other Americans tonight, and not that many locals, either, only one booth of red-faced men across the room.

Kiki set down a squat glass full of ice cubes and poured generously from the bottle. She uncapped a marker and wrote two characters on the label. "See? *Ni-ki.* Your bottle. It's means two spirits. *Ni ki.*" She grinned.

"*Doomo.*" Nicky took a sip. The whiskey warmed her all the way down.

"You don't look so good again. Wassa happening?" Kiki leaned both elbows on the bar.

"I might be going home soon."

"Man trouble?"

The whiskey emboldened her. "Terrance doesn't want me anymore. Maybe he's seeing someone else, maybe not. But if he isn't now, he will be soon."

"Thas-a bad."

Nicky nodded once. "Can I buy a jar of kimchi from you? I'm making him a special birthday dinner next week."

Kiki regarded her with tilted head. "I give to you tomorrow. We friends." She winked a heavily made-up eye. "But careful. Extra hot."

***

On the first day of December Nicky let Terrance sleep as long as he wanted. It was his birthday, and by some quirk he didn't have to work again for two days. She'd bought an expensive selection of fish from Haruko-san and had prepared the rice. When Terrance had been on base last night, Nicky had taken the bag of wisteria pods across town and thrown it in a dumpster.

The man could have won the Guinness world record for Healthiest Man Alive, apart from his family's heart history, that is. He never caught even a cold. Maybe if he felt sick, he would realize he needed her to take care of him. She knew how toxic the saponin *wisterin* was. Six seeds, which she'd ground into a powder on Thanksgiving night, wouldn't kill him and shouldn't affect his heart, either. On the other hand, he wouldn't feel at all well for at least a week. She'd be willing to stay in Japan until he got out of the Navy if their relationship was restored. But just in case, she'd also charged a one-way ticket home.

Now she mixed the seed powder into the dry wasabi and created the paste. Any taste the seeds had would be masked by the strong wasabi, as well as the flavored rice and the fish itself. She arranged more than a dozen pieces of assembled sushi in the round dish she'd bought and added a little pile of candied ginger. She also made two *nori maki* rolls, one with a generous dose of wasabi smeared next to the skinny spear of cucumber. She used the bamboo mat to wrap the thin crisp seaweed tight around the rice, then sliced his crosswise and arranged it on another plate. She set both dishes aside and scraped the rest of the wasabi into a little soy sauce dish. He always asked for extra when they ate out.

Nicky washed her hands and made a much smaller array for herself, all without wasabi. She spread a piece of classic indigo-and-white *ikat*, their sole tablecloth, on the small table. She laid out his plates and the wasabi, and her own, with a pair of chopsticks for her and a fork for him, plus the bottle of soy sauce and a little dish for each. It looked like a lot of food, but Terrance always awoke ravenous after night shift. She lit a fat scent-free candle and placed it on a small plate on the table.

After she set a pot of water on the stove to simmer for warming the little ceramic vases of sake she'd already filled, she placed two small sake cups on the table. It was nearly six o'clock and already dark outside. Maybe she should wake him.

Two strong arms encircled her waist from behind. "What's all this?" Terrance asked in a voice still husky from sleep.

Nicky eased out of his embrace and faced him, mustering a smile she hoped looked normal. "Happy birthday."

His face lit up. "I'm . . . speechless. Look at all this. You did learn to make sushi. Is it any good?"

He said that every time. She bit back her retort. "Are you ready to eat?"

"Let me just wash up. I'll be right back." He kissed the top of her head, which only came to his shoulder, and headed for the bathroom.

Nicky checked the table and snapped her fingers. She dished some of Kiki's kimchi into a bowl and set it at Terrance's place, too.

A minute later he was back, face washed and hair damp. After he sat opposite her, she poured sake for each of them and held up her cup.

"*Kampai*, babe," he said.

She mentally gritted her teeth. "*Kampai.*" The warm rice wine was strong and just what she needed to get through this meal.

He picked up a piece of salmon sushi with his fingers and dabbed even more wasabi on top of the fish, exactly as she'd known he would. As he always did. He popped it into his mouth and swallowed, then downed three more pieces in succession. He finally focused on her separate plate.

"Is yours different somehow?"

"I have a canker sore brewing. Wasabi would kill me right now. So would kimchi. It's all for you." Nicky smiled. She refilled their sake cups and drained hers again. He hadn't learned the protocol and did not do as Japanese do—fill your drinking companion's glass.

He plowed through his meal as usual, alternating popping sushi into his mouth with forkfuls of kimchi. At one point he picked up a piece of *nori maki* and then set it down again. "Whoa. I think I'm eating too fast. I'm getting dizzy."

Poor thing. Dizziness. She checked one expected symptom off her list.

"Maybe some nice spicy kimchi will fix it," she suggested.

"Yeah." He forked in another mouthful of kimchi. He clutched his stomach. "Shit."

"What's the matter?" Nicky tilted her head.

"Cramp. Shtomach . . . Shtomach . . . cramp. Got a cramp."

"Take a deep breath. Sometimes that helps." Impaired speech and intestinal cramps? Also symptoms.

He sat up straight. He inhaled and exhaled. "Yeah. Thanks, babe." Spittle flew out with the gratitude.

She started to pour him more sake, but he covered the cup.

"No, I had 'nuff." He got a confused look on his face. "Nuff . . . stuff. Whassit called? Sha-key. Yeah, shhha key."

Confusion. Another symptom. "You sound kind of funny, Terrance. Maybe you should go back to bed. I bought your favorite chocolate cake, but it'll keep."

"Don wanna wase all this ssuuushi." He popped in the last piece.

"There you go. Nice job. Clean plate club," Nicky said cheerily. She poured herself more sake and drained the cup of the now cool wine. The vase was empty, so she carried it to the stove, filled it from the bottle, and exchanged it in the pot for the full warm one.

When she turned back to the table, Terrance was on his feet, a blank look on his face. As she watched, he fell straight over backward. His head whacked *thud* on the wooden floor. He lay still and limp.

What? Nicky rushed to his side. "Terrance!" Passing out was definitely not a symptom, not from only six seeds. She knelt next to his head. His eyes stared, but he didn't see her. She couldn't feel a pulse in his neck. Death wasn't a symptom, either.

***

Kiki glanced at Nicky's rolling suitcase an hour later, at her jacket, at her shoulder purse slung across her chest, at her stuffed backpack. "So you leaving?"

"Yes. I, um, can't take it anymore. I need to get back to the work I love." Nicky was breathing hard, her words rushed and nervous.

"And maybe find good man who rubu you, too."

A good man who loves me? "Maybe."

"Terrance okay with you go?" The bartender raised her slivers of painted eyebrows.

Nicky shook her head once, slowly. She beckoned Kiki closer. "What did you put in that kimchi?" she asked in a raspy whisper.

"*Gaidoku.*" Kiki looked entirely satisfied with herself. "Poison."

Nicky inhaled sharply. "But I only wanted to make him sick!"

Kiki looked around. She made a tamping motion with her hand. "Talk soft."

"I'd already dosed his birthday dinner," Nicky went on. "And his father died of a heart condition. Kiki, you killed him." She stared at the woman, eyes wide, nostrils flared.

"We kill together. I guess he learn his lesson, yes? Now he not bother you." She touched her nose with her index finger. "Me, I help you, Nicky."

"But I didn't ask for your help."

"He not nice to you. I take care of business." Kiki shrugged. "You leave him there or you call the fuzz?"

"I didn't call anybody." In fact, she'd left a note on the table for him. It was dated today but with four p.m. as the time. It said she was desperately homesick and was leaving on the next plane she could catch. It was a terrible thing to abandon his body, but there had been no saving him. He'd been dead as soon as he hit the floor. *Wisterin* alone would not have caused his death. She wasn't sure she wanted to know what kind of *gaidoku* Kiki had added to the kimchi. The Navy had Terrance's health records. They would assume he died of sudden heart failure on his twenty-fifth birthday.

After she'd hurriedly packed, Nicky had slipped out the back way in the darkness and didn't think any neighbors had seen her.

She'd dropped the trash bag containing his dishes, fork, and anything else that had touched the *wisterin* in a dumpster behind Kiki's place before coming inside.

A new customer hailed Kiki from the other end of the bar.

She bowed to Nicky. "You take-a care, now. Write me postcard from America."

THE MISSING INGREDIENT FOR MURDEROUS INTENT

By Elizabeth Perona

Francine is worried about Mary Ruth's "blind date," who seems to have learned way too much about her friend. Will taking a baking class together confirm her suspicions of the man?

"I can't believe you've hooked me into doing this again," Francine McNamara said to her friend, caterer and minor celebrity chef Mary Ruth Burrows.

She responded with feigned innocence. "Doing what?"

Francine rolled her eyes, a gesture usually reserved for their friend Charlotte who often landed them in trouble on their way to solving mysteries. "Asking me to be your wingman on yet another blind date at the cooking school."

"It is *not* a date."

"Then what is it?"

"More like a trial run *before* a date. Like a speed dating session."

"So it is a date. You just used the word 'dating.'"

The two septuagenarians waited on a park bench for the Sur la Table kitchen store at the outdoor Clay Terrace shopping mall in Carmel, Indiana, to open. It was 9:45 a.m. and the ever-present buzz of highway traffic on nearby US-31 could be heard. They'd arrived an hour earlier and breakfasted at nearby Café Patachou. Confident they'd be sampling the croissants they would learn to make in class, Francine had avoided Patachou's wicked buttery cinnamon toast and opted for a bowl of healthy whole grain porridge. But now she found herself salivating over the heavenly scent of baked pastries emanating from the store.

Mary Ruth continued to be defensive. "Also, it's technically not blind. I know what he looks like, thanks to ourtime.com."

"If he's not catfishing."

"What's that?"

"Pretending to be somebody else online."

Francine observed three women hurrying around the corner of

the building heading for the Sur la Table door and making animated conversation. They were of different generations: one in her seventies with a pile of gray hair swept up on top of her head and held in place by an industrial-sized hair clip; a second in her mid-forties dressed in worn black jeans and a simple white tee shirt, and a tall early-thirties woman in a Sur la Table uniform of black polyester slacks and a black tee. Upon spotting Francine and Mary Ruth, the women pulled up abruptly. A quick conversation ensued before the youngest hurried back around the side of the building where Francine knew the employee entrance was. The older one put her hand to the store window and peered inside. The third tried the front door. It didn't budge. She strolled over to Francine and Mary Ruth on the bench. "You probably already tried the door, didn't you?"

Francine nodded. "We did."

She shifted from one foot to the other. "I'm Nancy," she said.

"Nice to meet you," Mary Ruth replied before introducing herself and Francine. "I'm sure the store'll open in a few minutes." She scooted over to make more room on the bench. "Would you and your friend like to sit down?"

"Oh, we're not friends," Nancy said, nervously eying the older woman. "We just met in the parking lot and walked in together because we guessed we were going to the same place."

The older woman gave up standing by the door and also approached the bench. "It sure is hot and humid out here," she said, sounding annoyed. She turned to Nancy and fisted a bony hand onto her hip. "We could have stayed at Waffle House longer and had more coffee."

Francine raised an eyebrow.

Nancy's eyes widened in alarm, but just then a male clerk in a black apron pushed the door open. "Good morning," he said, motioning them in. "Are you all here for class?"

They all responded with a "yes" and made their way into the store. Nancy and her purported non-friend hurried toward the back where the class would be held.

"We're still setting up the stations," the clerk called to them. "Feel free to look around."

"We'll wait," said the older woman. But Nancy slinked away and headed toward the cookware section.

Through the large windows in the kitchen doors, Francine could see the staff setting up. She breathed in the scent of baking pastries. "I'd like to get in there myself," she said, "but mostly to sample the croissants they're baking."

"It does smell good." Mary Ruth poked around the

Independence Day clearance merchandise on a table near the front of the store. Then the front door opened, and she surveyed five new possible classmates. “There are no men here,” she whispered to Francine. “I hope my date hasn’t stood me up.”

“I thought he wasn’t a date.”

“You know what I mean!”

I’m afraid I do, thought Francine.

Less than ten minutes later the door opened again and a nattily dressed man in white slacks, a pink polo shirt, white Nubuck shoes, and a blue seersucker sport coat walked in. He had a full head of white hair, dark brown eyes, and a tanned face. A cooler hung from a strap over his shoulder. Mary Ruth poked Francine in the ribs. “That’s him,” she whispered. “Oh, look, he’s brought my favorite flowers!”

Francine could see he was carrying a small bouquet of Gerbera daisies. “You have a favorite flower? I’ve known you for fifteen years and I didn’t know you had one.”

“Well,” she said, waffling, “I really don’t, but he asked at some point and I had to tell him something.”

Francine frowned at her. “Really? What else have you shared with him?”

But Mary Ruth was already hastily making her way over to meet him. She bumped into the table of star-spangled sale items, making her date’s head swivel in her direction. He calmly headed toward her with his hand extended.

“Ah, Ms. Burrows,” he said. His voice had a musical quality. “Blaine Forrester, at your service.” He did a little bow. “I brought you flowers,” he said, and handed her the bouquet.

“Aren’t you sweet?” she said, beaming. “And they’re my favorites! But please call me Mary Ruth.”

He took her free hand in his and kissed it. “Good to make your acquaintance, Mary Ruth.”

She gazed up into his eyes.

“Has anyone ever told you how beautiful your eyes are?” he asked.

Francine could hear Mary Ruth take in a sharp breath. *I can’t believe she’s buying this nonsense*, she thought. She slipped behind Mary Ruth, pretending to text something on her iPhone, and unobtrusively snapped a photo of him. She texted the photo to their mutual friend, reporter Joy McQueen, along with an eye-rolling emoji.

Since it was obvious no introduction would be forthcoming, Francine coughed.

“Uh, this is my friend, Francine McNamara,” Mary Ruth said,

stepping to the side so Francine could shake his hand. "She'll be one of our tablemates when we make croissants."

Francine noticed that he was about her height, five-ten. But though they could see eye-to-eye, his were still fixed on Mary Ruth's. "Nice to meet you," Francine said pointedly.

"Likewise," he replied.

Mary Ruth juggled the flowers. "I don't know what to do with these," she said. "I'm afraid to put them in the car where they'll get hot. I wonder if I could get someone to put them in the refrigerator in the kitchen for me."

"Not to worry," he said. "I brought an insulated cooler with me. We can store them in there until afterwards."

Francine stared at the cooler with curiosity.

"It's a surprise, for later," Blaine said as if he could read her mind. "Something else I know my date really likes."

Aha! Francine wanted to say. *So it is a date*! But instead she worried about what all Mary Ruth had shared with him. For this being a "trial run," Blaine seemed to know a lot about her. Francine had to wonder how long they'd been socializing online.

The silence again became awkward. "Do you cook much?" Francine asked.

"I know how to make a few meals for myself," he said. "But I've never been much of a baker. Hoping to pick up some tips."

"I'm sure you'll catch on quickly," Mary Ruth said. "And if you don't, I could tutor you." She giggled.

Francine bit her lip in annoyance.

Blaine took the flowers and placed them in the insulated cooler. The open lid hid the inside from Francine's view, though she tried to peek. Blaine moved quickly to zip it up.

More people poured through the front door. Those registered for the croissant class were told the kitchen was now ready for them. When they filed in, the instructor, a young black woman with Michele Obama hair and a perky voice, advised them to self-divide into teams. Mary Ruth, Blaine, and Francine went to one table and were joined by the argumentative older woman they'd met earlier.

"I'm Mabel Fisher," she said.

Blaine seemed unnerved by her inclusion in their group. "You!" he said in a nasty tone.

Mabel flinched. "Do we know each other, sir?"

He studied her face. "Oh, I'm sorry. You look like someone I once knew. I thought you were her. Forgive me." But he still seemed unsettled.

Francine looked about the room. There were sixteen people and four stations. Each group needed four people; all the more reason for Mabel to have joined their group. Francine noticed that Nancy had joined a group as far away from theirs as she could get. *They must not get along when they bake*, she thought.

The instructor got them started. Holding up pre-measured containers of each ingredient set out for them, she identified each and explained how they would be used. "Now, the first thing we need to do is get the dough started," she said. "So get going!"

"Actually, the first thing we need to do is have a Bloody Mary," Blaine said, just loud enough for their group to hear. "Mary Ruth's favorite!" He unzipped the cooler.

Francine glared at Mary Ruth. "Favorite drink?" she mouthed.

Mary Ruth looked away.

"Oh!" Mabel squeaked. "We must have been thinking along the same lines. I brought mimosas." She indicated her large tote.

But Blaine was already pulling out unopened bottles of Hoosier Mamma Bloody Mary Maker and Mogul craft vodka. "Let's save your mimosas for later, for celebrating after class." He appropriated four empty water glasses at their station and mixed a cocktail for each of them.

Francine knew from previous classes that they were allowed to bring in adult beverages, but she didn't think that would happen at ten in the morning. She felt a little uncomfortable imbibing that early with strangers, but she didn't want to appear unfriendly. She was beginning to think doing so would only alienate Mary Ruth, who seemed to be already under his spell.

"To a successful outcome!" he toasted, clinking his glass with the one he'd given Mary Ruth. He raised his glass to the others.

They all took a swallow, though Francine waited for Blaine to take his before she sipped hers. It tastes normal, she thought. *And Hoosier Mamma knows how to make good Bloody Marys.*

It wasn't until Mary Ruth directed Francine, Mabel, and Blaine to combine the ingredients for the croissant dough and knead it that Francine noticed Blaine had already drained his Bloody Mary and mixed another for himself. *This guy's a lush*, she thought. She stored that information to share later with Mary Ruth.

When they were finished, kitchen helpers swooped in, wrapped the dough in plastic wrap, and moved it to the kitchen for refrigeration.

"That was step one," the instructor said. "Our next step is to ready the butter block. But before we do, I want you to taste what this butter block is going to do for the croissants. I'll need a volunteer."

Before she could even get the request out, Nancy was already moving toward the front. "I'll volunteer," she said.

"I like your enthusiasm," the instructor responded. "What's your name?"

"Nancy."

"Class, Nancy will be distributing basic croissants for you to taste. We made the dough last night and baked these this morning before you came in." Nancy was given a tray of croissants cut into pieces. She walked them around. Each student took a piece, served on a napkin. Francine's group was last.

"Here you go," Nancy said. Instead of allowing them to take their own piece, however, she handed one to each of them. Francine's sample, as well as Mary Ruth's and Mabel's, were on white napkins. Blaine's was on a vanilla-colored napkin, like they'd run out of white and had to substitute. Nancy picked up the empty tray and returned it to a kitchen helper. The helper looked to be the third member of their original group, the tall young woman.

Francine's iPhone buzzed in her pocket. She bit into the croissant, placed the rest of it down, and pulled out her phone. It was a text from Joy.

OMG! Is that really MR's date? Don't let her get involved. He's a scumbag. A dangerous one.

How do you know? she texted back.

There was a pause. The iMessage bubble indicated Joy was typing. Francine looked up and found everyone effusively praising the rich butteriness of the croissant. Everyone except Blaine, who, like her, had only eaten half of his. He licked his lips, frowning at the taste. He set the rest of his croissant down.

Francine's phone buzzed again. Joy had sent a connection to a website. Francine only had time to click on the link and study the photo. It was definitely Blaine. The headline said something about being an unlucky widower.

Before she could read more, the kitchen helpers distributed a butter block and the instructor had them working it into dough that had been readied the night before by the staff. They learned a folding technique that enabled them to build layer upon buttery layer within the dough. Each member of the group was to take a turn folding and rolling. Mary Ruth volunteered to go first since she was already familiar with the technique. Blaine finished his second Bloody Mary and focused intently on her hands as she demonstrated. Francine sighed but shrugged off Joy's warning, figuring she'd have plenty of time to discuss Blaine with Mary Ruth before any future dates.

After the layering was completed, the dough was wrapped and sent to the back for more refrigeration. They took a brief break.

"Are you enjoying this?" Mary Ruth asked Blaine.

"Very much," he said. Then he yawned and excused himself to the restroom.

"Blaine seems less than enthused about the class," Mary Ruth said, disappointment in her voice.

"Maybe he doesn't like croissants." Francine pointed at the half-eaten pastry on his napkin.

"You haven't finished yours either, Francine, and I happen to know you love them."

"Oh, I was distracted." She popped the remainder in her mouth. She closed her eyes to concentrate on the flakey goodness. "If these were any richer," she said, "they would be under lock and key at Tiffany's. It can't be the croissant he doesn't like."

Blaine returned from the restroom.

"We're concerned you don't like croissants," Mabel said, sliding the napkin with the half-eaten piece toward him. "Can't you taste the butter in it?"

"I thought it had a rather odd taste," he told her. "Something I've had before but can't place."

"The rest of us thought it was heavenly. Try it again."

He took another bite and swallowed. His mouth momentarily pinched like the taste was bitter, but he gamely shook it off. "Delicious," he said agreeably. "Definitely buttery." He mixed another Bloody Mary and sipped it.

The instructor ended the break. "We're not just making plain croissants today. We're also making chocolate!" she announced. "But before we build the chocolate to wrap the dough around, Ashley will be distributing some chocolate croissants for you to try. I think you'll agree making your own chocolate gives you a better flavor." Ashley turned out to be Mabel and Nancy's third companion.

While they waited for their sample, Francine finished her Bloody Mary and immediately regretted it. Now she'd be tasting chocolate on top of the tomato juice. But the sweet smell of chocolate baking in the kitchen made resisting the sample impossible.

Francine's station was last again, and when Ashley got there, she had three half-pieces and one whole chocolate croissant left. "Looks like it's your lucky day," Ashley told Blaine, and tilted the tray so the whole croissant was closest to him.

"Looks like it," he said. He smiled and took it.

They ate their samples. "I like this one better," Blaine said. "The chocolate is amazing." Still, he didn't finish it.

Francine nibbled off the buttery edge of hers to try to cleanse her palate, but when the lesson started again she rolled the remainder in a napkin and slipped it into her purse for later.

The instructor explained how to make a thick, spreadable chocolate by using a chopped-up chocolate bar, cocoa mix, and hot water. They hadn't been at it long when Blaine headed again to the restroom. His gait was unsteady.

"I'm worried about Blaine," Mary Ruth said, frowning.

"Probably just needs some sleep," Mabel said.

Francine shook her head. "I'm a retired nurse. I wonder if he isn't taking a drug that's interacting with the alcohol. He's had a few Bloody Marys."

"He doesn't seem like the type to take drugs," Mary Ruth said.

"I don't mean illegal drugs," Francine said. "A prescription. Maybe something for anxiety."

"The only thing he seems anxious about is getting to the restroom," Mabel said, turning back to the station. "We need to finish the chocolate."

Since their group was already behind, Mary Ruth stepped in to catch them up.

Several minutes passed and Blaine had not returned. "I wonder if something's wrong," Mary Ruth said.

The three women watched through the double doors. Some kind of commotion was brewing. A harried clerk hurried toward the back of the store with her supervisor in tow. The clerk waved her arms, accentuating what she was saying.

"Isn't that the direction of the restroom?" Francine asked.

Mary Ruth handed Francine the spoon she was using to stir the thickening chocolate mixture. "This can't be good," she said. She opened the door and followed a crowd toward the back.

Francine stirred the chocolate, thinking. She turned to where Mabel had been only to find she was over conferring with Nancy. The two looked worried. On impulse, Francine slipped out her phone with the non-stirring hand and snapped a photo of the women. Deciding the chocolate was thick enough, she set down her spoon and texted Joy.

Can you find out if these women are connected to Blaine in some way? She had no idea if it were possible to run a facial recognition program to find out who they were, but she knew if anyone in her circle of friends could do it, it was Joy.

The wailing sound of approaching sirens could be heard and a nervous buzz started up. The instructor left the classroom to find out what the emergency was all about.

Paramedics from the Carmel Fire Department arrived and rushed back toward the restroom. On a hunch, Francine made her way back to Blaine's space to look for the remaining piece of his chocolate croissant.

But it was gone, already swept away by the kitchen staff. Francine thought about tracking down Ashley, the kitchen helper she'd seen in the company of Nancy and Mabel earlier, but she was nowhere to be found. Disappointed, she turned around to find Mary Ruth returning.

"Blaine's been in the restroom all this time," Mary Ruth said, wiping a bead of perspiration from her forehead. "An employee became concerned when the next person in line pounded on the door in frustration and no one answered. They found him passed out on the floor. They called 9-1-1. The paramedics are back there now."

"What do they think is wrong with him?" Mabel asked. Francine saw that Mabel, Nancy, and now Ashley had crowded around them.

"Overdose, they think. A customer who is a nurse checked him over and said to call 9-1-1 immediately. She said his heart was beating very, very slowly and his breathing was shallow."

"Oh!" said Mabel, sharing a worried look with her companions. A few minutes later, Carmel police arrived, followed closely by an official-looking man in a blue blazer.

"That's the Hamilton County Medical Examiner," Ashley said. She pointed to a plain-clothed woman with a police badge pinned to her shirt. "And that's Detective Sergeant Granger."

This cannot be good, Francine thought.

Granger pushed open the doors to the kitchen, accompanied by the instructor, who pointed her toward their group.

"Here it comes," Mary Ruth said. "We're going to be interrogated."

Granger had close-cropped hair, a thin face, and a baritone voice. She made her way over. "I understand Mr. Forrester was in your group," she said.

Francine waited to see what Mary Ruth would say.

"He was my, uh, guest," she said. "Not a date. Definitely not a date."

The detective narrowed her eyes at Mary Ruth. "Meaning what?"

"He was her *blind* date," Francine said, then mouthed '*Get over it*' when Mary Ruth glared.

Granger turned to Francine. "He was blind, or it was a date, sight unseen? Just to be clear."

Mary Ruth exhaled noisily. "Not blind. I found him on ourtime.com. This was the first time we'd met. I really don't go out that much, but when I do I always make sure it's in a public setting like this."

"So you didn't know him well. Did any of you? Was he acting strange in any way?"

They relayed his consumption of the three Bloody Marys. The detective examined the cooler and took it as evidence, even Mary Ruth's flowers. "I'd like to talk to you alone," Granger told Mary Ruth.

While they stepped aside, another officer took statements from the rest of the class and the staff. No one must have offered much because he completed the task in fifteen minutes. Moments later Blaine was wheeled out and placed in the ambulance. Based on the fact the paramedics were no longer working on him, Francine feared the worst. "I'm pretty sure he's dead," she said aloud.

Nancy joined Mabel, the two women perching on the stools near Francine at their cooking station. They looked nervous.

Francine's phone sounded. It was Joy returning her text.

It took a while to find this. One of the women appeared in a photograph taken outside the courtroom where a murder trial against Forrester was heard. Court reports said relatives of his late third wife testified he was a 'black widower.' Three wives to date, all reasonably wealthy, and they died under circumstances that could be considered suspicious. It was a hung jury and the judge declared a mistrial.

Francine recalled Blaine had thought he'd recognized Mabel. If she was related to one of the earlier wives, that could explain the resemblance and why it disturbed him. It also might explain something else.

He got away with murder and with their money? Francine texted.

Yes. The prosecution isn't going for a retrial. And let me tell you, I would bar the door to keep Mary Ruth from dating him.

Francine gave Mabel a suspicious glance, which Mabel noticed. "What?" she asked.

Francine tried to decide how to reveal her suspicions. Then she remembered the remaining chocolate croissant sample she had in her purse. It might do for what she had in mind.

She pulled her stool up to make a triangle with the two women. "This was not an accidental overdose, was it?" she said calmly.

They flinched like electricity had gone through them. Francine knew she'd touched a nerve.

"What do you mean by that?" Nancy asked defiantly.

"Yeah," Mabel said. "You act like we would know something about it." She spoke with only enough volume that the three of them could hear.

“I could see this happening in two ways. Let me try out Scenario One on you,” Francine said. “A hung jury recently saved Blaine from the charge of murdering his third wife. It looks like there won’t be a retrial, so no jail time and he’ll be keeping a big chunk of money he inherited from his three deceased wives. What if some friends and relatives didn’t like the outcome and decided to seek revenge? What if they spent a great deal of time studying him and knew his weak points? What if they learned he was going to be here today and had time to execute a clever plan?”

Mabel and Nancy sat stone faced.

Francine continued. “It would be no secret, not to anyone who knew the situation, that Blaine was a drinker. He wouldn’t turn down a mimosa in the morning, which you were prepared to supply. Only he did you a favor by bringing his own Bloody Marys. Alcohol is known to have fatal interactions with the right combination of other drugs. If a conspirator knew, for example, that Blaine had a problem with anxiety, the effects of the alcohol could be enhanced by adding an anti-anxiety drug to his piece of croissant. Are you following me?”

“How could someone have made sure he got it?” Nancy asked.

“Simple. By handing the sample to him. By making sure it was marked on a napkin of a slightly different color.”

“But if he ate the whole sample, there’d be no proof,” Mabel said. “No evidence.”

“Correct. Then through a second sample, a chocolate croissant for instance, one could feed him a different drug to interact with the alcohol and the anti-anxiety medicine. It would further depress his breathing and his heart rate. I’m guessing a prescription pain killer, maybe hydrocodone, which would be fairly easy for an older adult to get.”

“But that’s not how the class works,” Nancy said. “There’s no volunteer requested to give out the second sample.”

Francine turned to her. “You’re right. The kitchen staff would have to be in on it. Someone like Ashley. The pain killer would be less noticeable if mixed in with the chocolate, and more of it could be inserted, making for a deadly combination.”

“But if he finished the chocolate croissant, there would still be no proof of anything,” Mabel argued. “Prescription drugs would be detected in a tox screen, but since they were prescribed to him, they would be expected to be found in his bloodstream. It would be marked an accidental overdose.”

“*If* he finished the chocolate croissant,” Francine said. “But he didn’t.” She pulled her sample from her purse and cradled it in her hand. “I wonder if the police tested this, what they would find.”

She slipped it back into her purse.

Nancy and Mabel looked at each other wide-eyed. Finally Nancy crumbled. "Please, we didn't mean to kill him. We didn't know he would bring Bloody Marys and then drink so many of them. It threw off what we thought would happen. The plan was to give him a real scare. Convince him to give some money back by demonstrating we could get to him whenever we wanted. And threaten to finish him off if he ever married again."

Mabel leaned forward. She had tears streaming down her cheeks. "He killed my beautiful, vibrant sister first. Then he killed Nancy's aunt, who was a brilliant artist, and then Ashley's philanthropic grandmother. He's devastated the families of three amazing women. And your friend could have been next. Please don't give us away." Nancy handed her a tissue. Mabel tried to regain her composure.

Francine thought about Mary Ruth. She and Blaine had been in contact for longer than Mary Ruth had led her to believe. He'd clearly cast a spell over her. Could the Summer Ridge Bridge Club have talked sense into her if he'd tried to marry her? Would she have resented them for trying to interfere, and married him anyway? Mary Ruth was a stubborn woman.

Her sense of justice was conflicted. From Joy's text, she had reason to believe Blaine Forrester had it coming. He'd been careful enough that the law couldn't convict him. And the women hadn't intended to kill him, so technically it was manslaughter, not murder. And he'd brought the Bloody Marys himself. So in a sense, it *was* an accidental overdose. He'd done it to himself.

"Of course, I could be mistaken," Francine said. "It could be Scenario Two. In that circumstance, it was a simple, accidental overdose from a deadly combination of self-administered drugs. I just need to think about it." She patted her purse. "But I know the law would go easier on you if you confess before you get caught."

Mary Ruth returned at that moment with the detective.

"You can leave now," Granger told them.

Francine noticed Ashley sidled up to Nancy and Mabel on the way out. Anxious words were exchanged in hushed tones, and they all glanced back at Francine. She gave them a little smile, held up her purse again, and waved.

Let them be nervous for a while, she thought.

She hoped her bluff would cause the conspirators to confess. A confession would alleviate her from the burden of knowing what they'd done but not reporting it. Because she didn't think she could do that to them.

After all, the real proof was already gone—Blaine's piece of chocolate croissant was the missing ingredient she needed to prove it was murder. Any good defense attorney would nullify her testimony that they'd confessed to her. At worse, the defense would characterize Francine's testimony as the senile ravings of an old biddy—and the defense would emphasize 'old'—coupling it with her previous notoriety as an amateur sleuth, however successful.

More importantly, though, Blaine's death resolved any future threats he might have posed to Mary Ruth. Or any other woman.

Before starting the Prius to return to Brownsburg, Francine texted Charlotte.

I have the most interesting dilemma to share with you. It's about a mystery solved, a moral conundrum, and a missing ingredient to demonstrate murderous intent. See you soon.

IT'S CANNING SEASON

By Adele Polomski

Good fences make good neighbors. But so would drapes or a screen of trees when you have an uncouth neighbor like Earle.

I took a swig of Mylanta and winced. My late Aunt Fiona tried to warn me about Earle. I'd listened, of course, but I don't think even she knew how bad things could get.

"Virginia, that neighbor of mine is a man who's been on a dark path for a long time." A litany of Earle's sins against established rules of decency included his "compost pile." I stared out the window at the unholy collection of everything regular folks put out for the garbage truck. "Just ignore him," she'd warned. "And don't ever leave Jeffrey alone with him. I don't like the ugly way Earle glares at him when he thinks I'm not watching."

I'd moved to Trouble Creek in Florida last May after my aunt bequeathed me Jeffrey, her five-year-old cockatiel. The house, a nice old Florida style with an abundance of windows, legally belonged to the cockatiel. My aunt, who'd been a successful attorney, granted me the privilege of managing the estate. In exchange for taking care of Jeffrey, I was able to live in her spacious home and work in her well-appointed kitchen. Jeffrey, by all accounts, was happy with the arrangement.

Earle's home reportedly sported a collection of taxidermied animals and birds. I'd been visiting Aunt Fiona when I'd heard Earle express a desire to add Jeffrey to his collection. "When the time is right, of course, Miss Fiona. Like the next time he's on one of his squawking streaks in the middle of the night." Earle exploded with hoots of derisive laughter. Aunt Fiona never spoke to Earle again. "Some men don't like birds," she'd told me. "Or any other creature they perceive as weaker. Best you steer clear of Earle."

When I smelled smoke, I feared something in Earle's nightmare of beer cans, old tires, stained pillows, fast food wrappers, roaches, rats, and rotten food had caught fire, but it was only Earle grilling something on old metal fencing over a rusty barrel. The smell wasn't unappetizing until I spotted the ibis carcass left to rot atop

Earle's "compost" pile in the middle of an old TV. The breast meat had been roughly hewn away and set to char on the smoky grill. The rest of the bird, the open blue eye, bright red legs, and that shiny, raw chest cavity, still plagued my nightmares.

Earle, never generous of spirit, saw me watching and offered his fork of partially gnawed ibis breast. I recoiled, not only because his hands were filthy, and they were. "Go on. Tastes like chicken, I swear. I bet that noisy white bird of yours tastes like chicken, too."

He gave a sharp bark of laughter and a surge of anger made me want to slap Earle's oily face, then strangle him and leave his carcass to rot atop his trash pile.

I loved Jeffrey, who embodied everything gentle, playful, friendly, and highly intelligent. None of those characteristics applied to Earle. Over my seventy-two years, however, I've learned that a patient woman picks her moments. Maybe nature would give me a hand. Eating wild birds could bring on a nasty case of salmonella.

I didn't try to stop Earle, and neither would the state wildlife commission. The ibis was a protected migratory bird, but Earle was a fifth generation native Floridian and poaching was a longstanding family tradition. Lately, he'd taken to "harvesting" alligator eggs. It's not easy to get alligators to nest in captivity, so eggs were in high demand by Florida alligator farmers. Seventy bucks an egg wasn't chump change, especially to a chump like Earle.

Earle did have one unfortunate habit I could not overlook. Every evening, he slurped cheap canned beer and lounged in the nude on his red velvet chaise while enjoying porn on the widest wide-screen TV ever made with the volume turned all the way up. My kitchen overlooked his sitting room and he lacked draperies.

During canning season, which was almost year-round in Florida, I spent most evenings in the kitchen prepping and boiling vegetables from my garden to can for sale on the internet. My customer base, predominantly female, was provided through my website, designed by a computer engineer I'd taught in third grade some forty years ago. She was the kid whose folks never came to parent teacher meetings. The other teachers shrugged that fact away, but one day I paid the mother a visit. It took a long time before the mom came to the door. She only opened it after I told her who I was. I took in the bruises, the misshapen nose. Maybe she'd been beautiful once, like her daughter, who had since developed into a warrior for social justice, and a friend.

Given the heat in the kitchen, I kept the windows open. Air conditioning wasn't ideal. Jeffrey, like other birds, didn't have much of a sinus and was sensitive to cold air. He didn't mind the heat or humidity, and I'd grown accustomed to it.

Once, I'd offered to sew Earle a pair of drapes if he purchased the fabric, and he said, "Yes, ma'am. That's a good idea." Did he ever get himself over to the fabric section of Walmart? No.

About a week after the ibis incident, I showed up at his door around five in the afternoon, suggesting a screen of pines. "An Arborvitae. It's called Green Giant. Grows fast. You can get it at the Home Depot. You'll enjoy the privacy. For like the next time you want to do something . . ." Illegal? Uncouth? My mind settled on ". . . nasty." That covered a lot of Earle's bases.

Earle rubbed the back of his darkly tanned neck and said, "Well, go ahead. I guess I'm okay with it." He started to close the door.

"It'll cost about a hundred dollars."

He shrugged. "You wanna plant some bushes on my property, go ahead. I got no problem with it. Right now, I got somethin' more important to attend to." He sniggered. We both knew what he meant.

I scurried home, angry with myself. I should have said something like, "Listen up, Earle. Boorish male behavior is now considered sexual harassment." Somehow, I don't believe Earle would've gotten the gist or cared.

The more I thought about it, Earle's getting off on my agitation went right along with poaching alligator eggs, killing protected bird species, and piling garbage all over his yard. Men like Earle did whatever they wanted because they could.

My aunt was a religious woman and part of our agreement included monthly inspections by the pastor of the local Faith Christian Church. Aunt Fiona had so enjoyed spending time with old Reverend Johnson, a spike-straight man with a pinched face who passed away close to a year after we'd met. The new pastor, a young man with a rash of inflamed pimples on his chin, drove out to tell me the sad news. He spoke with a lilting Australian accent. "Housekeeper reported he died in his sleep, lucky man. It's a good way to go, to meet your maker." He gave a light cough and asked after Jeffrey. "The cockatiel? He's all right then?" he asked without asking to step inside.

I told the young reverend that Jeffrey was just fine, and that first time he took off without inspecting our home. I guess I looked harried and overburdened, my face bathed with sweat. I'd been busy in the kitchen, desperate to finish before Earle hit his chaise for the evening.

This time when the reverend knocked, I opened the screen door wide and invited him over the threshold. "There's a situation I need your advice on, Reverend. It's nothing to do with Jeffrey." The cockatiel sat on my shoulder, quiet. Not a good sign. Jeffrey chirped when he was happy.

"Does it bite?"

Jeffrey put his head down, ruffled his feathers then flapped his wings. He wasn't taking to our new pastor. "It takes him time to get used to new people." Jeffrey hissed and the young reverend took a step back. "Don't go. I'll just take him back to one of his playrooms and we can chat. I have a problem I'd like to speak with you about."

I talked and he listened earnestly and politely as I told him about Earle. Not about the ibis incident. Or the poaching. Or the four-foot alligator he had staked in his back yard for a whole afternoon without food or water while he waited for some ridiculous "hunter" from Minnesota to come and shoot the creature in the back of the head in exchange for a cash payment of twelve hundred dollars. I felt sick about that still. I should have done something. But if I'd called the sheriff, I truly believe he'd have turned a blind eye, and Earle could see fit to retaliate against poor Jeffrey. I couldn't risk that. Jeffrey was like the son I'd never had, which admittedly sounds crazy but it's true. I'd never wanted children and now I was sad about that, though I knew I'd made the right decision given the man I'd married.

"Well, you see, he's refused my offer of draperies and he won't pay for an evergreen screen. Reverend, surely you recognize Earle's lustfulness as a problem. I'd appreciate if you'd have a word." Sweat broke over the reverend's putty-like skin. He coughed into his fist and looked pained.

"Part of your job is offering counseling to those who have lost their way, isn't that right?"

"Your aunt, did she have this problem with your neighbor?" he asked, breathing like someone who'd just run a race.

"Aunt Fiona doted on Jeffrey and could ignore Earle, but I run a small, boutique internet business and I need to use the kitchen."

The reverend stood, and with a long, thin finger pushed aside the yellow-checked café curtains. I joined him. Sunlight fell on Earle's stained red velvet chaise. "The curtains don't help. I can still hear everything. And if there's a breeze and the curtains blow in . . . it's disturbing."

"Have you tried talking to him yourself? About this particular problem, specifically?"

"You know what I'd get. Evasions and denials."

The reverend tugged at his conical collar, his pronounced Adam's apple bobbing in his skinny throat. "I'd be happy to talk to your neighbor if he were a parishioner. It would be awkward for me to knock on his door and introduce myself and ask him to . . ." His speech was quick and breathy, his face full of sweat.

"He gets a thrill knowing he's naked and I'm an easy target. Let's just call it what it is. Elder abuse. And don't ask me to turn up the radio or television. Jeffrey enjoys peace and quiet."

I expected the reverend to advise me to contact the sheriff, who would laugh and tell me that, since I hadn't been physically assaulted, Earle was free to do whatever he liked in his own home.

And there it was. Earle, like a lot of men, did whatever they wanted because they could. They were entitled. A black anger swarmed up. I tamped it down, reminding myself that this reverend was not the problem. He sucked in a breath and whistled it out.

"I know it's warm in here. Or might it be the unsavory subject matter?"

"Virginia, I have to go." He stood and took a breath, sucking it down. "But trust in the Lord and your sins will be forgiven." Then he took off, wheezing as if suffering from a punctured lung.

I didn't wave as his white, battered Chevy Nova tore out, churning up a rooster tail of dust on the packed dirt road that led out of our clearing. I tried to steady my own breathing, taking comfort in his parting words. I tried to do what I thought was right. Maybe God would see it the same way. Maybe not, but I'd be able to make a case for myself.

I opened the playroom door and Jeffrey flew out in a powdery whir. For people deathly allergic to bird dander, open windows aggravated the problem by blowing the white dust around. I had three air purifiers going, but that didn't help folks like the reverend. That gave me an idea, admittedly a long shot, but what the hell? I unplugged the air purifiers.

Jeffrey sat on my shoulder, bobbing his head up and down as I sliced a banana. I offered him a piece, then peeled and sliced an orange. Jeffrey liked a choice of snacks and I didn't mind. I loved Jeffrey. I liked taking care of him in this house. I wouldn't let Earle hurt Jeffery and I wouldn't pay for a screen of trees that was his responsibility. It wasn't fair. The law applied to everyone, Earle included.

***

A couple of days later, I invited Earle over for lemon meringue pie. His eyebrows shot up and his jaw dropped with astonishment, but he accepted. The filling tasted a shade too tart, but Earle nipped up every crumb of that pie himself with gusto, but not like an untamed beast let out of its cage. More like a man who appreciated fine home cooking. He washed down the pie with several cans of beer brought over for the occasion. Jeffrey perched in his cage in my bedroom with the cover on, quiet for once. I remembered the ibis and wouldn't put temptation under Earle's nose.

We talked about the weather, and my garden, which he said he admired. "I see you planted some bushes between our houses," Earle said.

"Shrubs," I said in a starchy voice. "Elderberries."

Earle sipped his beer, his pinky finger curled like a cooked shrimp. His beard boiled around his face, clean and crumb free. His shirt was stained but didn't stink of sweat. He'd put in some effort, which I appreciated. And I learned something that afternoon. Earle didn't suffer from a deadly allergy to bird dander. He thanked me and took his leave. I plugged in the air purifiers.

In my imagination, our shared time together and the lemon meringue pie turned Earle around, civilizing the wild hog in him.

Wrong. That evening, right on time, he flipped on his TV and got to work.

The following morning, I dropped off a jar of strawberry preserves.

***

Three weeks later, I puttered in my garden, tending to carrots, green beans, and bok choy, Jeffrey's favorite. Without warning, Earle poked his big head over his rickety picket fence held together by weeds and wild honeysuckle. In a thoroughly annoyingly, friendly way, he asked if I might have a word. "Inside."

"I've spent the morning canning. My kitchen feels like a sauna. Can we do this another time?"

"It's somethin' serious. Come by my place and we'll have the bonus of your old bird not interrupting us."

Curious, I washed my hands in the rain barrel and accepted.

Earle lived in a small, white, one-story house with a detached carport. Both needed a good once-over with some paint. Inside, the wood-paneled interior was close and untidy but not dirty, though the air smelled of unwashed feet and stale sweat. Better than what I'd expected. The décor represented Earle's idea of what a modern Florida cracker bachelor's man cave should look like. Old furniture straight from a funeral parlor catalogue, grimy from seasons of dirt. A fake Persian wall-to-wall carpet like the one at Denny's. No window treatments, not even a cheap roller shade. The homemade examples of taxidermied animals were disconcerting, especially the flamingo with the feathered body and Dollar Store plastic head.

I waited while Earle retreated to his kitchen. He came back with a foggy glass jar half full of a murky green liquid. "Mint tea. From the dried leaves you gave me."

It looked more like pureed snapping turtle guts, but I thanked him for his hospitality.

He held a can of beer and led me into his family room. I'd rather have sat on a snake and donated a kidney than have gone near that chaise so I said, "Let's go back to the kitchen. You got any ice?"

He said okay, nervous like. Sweat on his forehead glistened like bugle beads. Made me remember my old life. Being on pins and needles all the time, not sure if what I did, didn't do, said, or didn't say would earn me a beating. My husband needed me to share the pain of his bad day, to absorb some of that for him. I didn't have a choice. So many women didn't and still don't. Men like Earle and my ex-husband were entitled. Enduring that kind of violence either made you scared of everything or fearless because you got to the point where you no longer had anything to lose. It might have been different if we'd had children. Now, I had Jeffrey. I had plenty at stake.

When we were seated at a none-too-clean Formica kitchen table, Earle asked about the jam I'd put up after the county's last strawberry festival. "Virginia, was there anything, well, unusual in it?" His voice was low, conspiratorial. "Something that could make someone sick?"

I pretended to be confused. "Whatever do you mean?" I pushed the tea away, untouched.

Earle scratched his cheek. "Anything you can think of? The sheriff may want to know."

"Why would law enforcement give a fig about my jam? It's a traditional recipe, Earle. Strawberries and sugar. That's about it."

"Gave that jar you left on my porch to my handyman to say thanks, and he didn't show up to finish the job."

"Is he the one who wore his grimy work pants real low on his hips?"

Earle scratched his cheek. "I suppose. When he didn't show up to finish, I called his number and someone at his house said he was dead."

"I don't understand . . ."

"He died after eating your jam. Or preserves. Or whatever you want to call it."

"How do you know that?"

"Whoever answered said they found an empty jar of strawberry preserves on the floor and that was about all the food left in the house."

"What about his wife?" I asked, my voice a shriveled whisper. "He had a wife and child." I'd overheard him saying the wife was a "fat cow who couldn't cook his eggs right" and he called his little boy a "homo in the making." Neither was spared the backside of his hand "every now and then."

"His wife left him a couple of weeks back. Went to live with her mother. Took the kid too. A sickly little thing if I remember right."

An inexpressible sense of relief passed over me. I took a deep breath to settle my voice. "Earle, it could have been anything that got your friend. A heart attack, an aneurism. Congestive heart failure." A bad batch of strawberry jam. Botulism wasn't as rare as the CDC thought. Only underreported.

For example, take Old Reverend Johnson who had reportedly passed in his sleep. Unlike the new reverend, who would never likely visit again, Reverend Johnson had managed to make a nuisance of himself. I greeted him politely and made sure I always had some fancy dessert on hand. While he enjoyed his third serving of crème caramel, he'd remarked, "Jeffrey's quite affectionate with you, Miss Virginia."

Only once, without thinking, I'd made the mistake of sitting beside him on the sofa after offering him a lackluster strawberry rhubarb pie because I hadn't had time to make something more complicated. He'd put his hand on my knee and said, "There's a tad more dander around than when Fiona was behind the helm."

All it would take was one word from the reverend to Aunt Fiona's attorney about how my care of the cockatiel was less than stellar, and I'd lose Jeffrey and my home.

A cold fury spread through me like a draught of cold water trickling down my gullet. I stood and brought him a second slice of strawberry rhubarb pie, this time with a generous dollop of vanilla whipped cream. I swallowed my dark anger, thanked him for his good advice, and sat in an armchair out of the reverend's reach. Jeffrey flew in to perch on my shoulder. The cockatiel played with my hair and tried to groom my eyebrows, which was strange, but he was extremely gentle. When he bent his head, I'd softly patted his back. "Jeffrey and I are getting on very well, I think."

"But it really isn't up to you to decide. Is it, Virginia?" he asked, licking his fork in a manner I found lascivious.

I sent him home with a jar of canned sweet corn and that was that.

Earle looked at the ceiling, seeming to think on it. "I guess you're right. There are lots of things that can kill a soul."

Amen to that. Speaking of which, "Earle? Do you care for elderberry wine? I'm thinking of putting up a batch." The seeds, stems, leaves, and roots of the black elder are all poisonous to humans. The berries were particularly toxic when raw. "I'll have you over as soon as I whip up a batch. Some folks say its flavor is something akin to battery acid, but I have a hunch you may like it."

"Virginia, you don't imbibe. Why would you bother? And what do you do with all the garden stuff I see you puttin' up? Can't be fun, all that work."

"It's not," I admitted, "but it makes me feel good." I consider it a public service. The dead handyman didn't worry me. We were living in a Podunk county and they didn't have a CSI team like on TV. They'd chalk it up to something, but not botulism. I was certain about that. And even if they did? Well, mistakes happen. Jeffrey squawked and Earle pointed a finger pistol in the general direction of my kitchen.

"I didn't realize how Jeffrey's voice carries."

Earle shrugged. "It's a pain, for sure, but we all got our crosses to bear, I guess."

Maybe, I thought. *Maybe not*. "I better go home and water those elderberries.

THE GOURMAND

By Nancy Cole Silverman

A gourmand loves eating and frequently overeats, which is certainly true of Big Keith. Strange that three of his wives died of food-related accidents.

I knew when I first spotted Big Keith, balanced on two stools at the chef's table reserved for VIPs in the kitchen at Bottega Louie in downtown Los Angeles, that this was a man with whom I could have my way. Keith was a food critic for the *LA Times*, and I was a struggling, thirty-two-year-old actress waiting tables. He had a bib around his neck to protect his expensive, blue pin-striped suit and had ordered the chef's signature dish, branzino with carrots and charred lemon with capers. He took a bite and smiled at me, the type of smile that told me the man had an appetite for something that wasn't on the menu.

And . . . being that an actress is always in search of her next meal, and my career had dead-ended after the failure of my last B-list movie, I was looking for the role of a lifetime: Hollywood wife.

They say the way to a man's heart is through his stomach. While I had always considered myself to be culinarily challenged, as a waitress/actress I did have access to some of L.A.'s best kitchens. And with a server's knowledge of their exotic menus and a few ideas of my own on presentation, I came up with a plan I hoped might close the deal and invited him for dinner. Oysters on the half shell in my teddy. Lobster Newberg a-la-naked in front of the fire. A sinfully sweet chocolate mousse at bedtime along with an expensive bottle of Dom Pérignon. All of which I cleverly brought home and transferred into my own newly purchased chef-ware and served hot from the oven—as if I had made it myself—to his waiting lips and welcome arms.

Three months later Keith and I were married at an elaborate beachside wedding at Nobu, an exclusive Peruvian-Japanese fusion restaurant in Malibu, where the only thing more awesome than the million-dollar view was the food.

I might have been happy with my life as the wife of a famous restaurant critic had I not learned soon after we married that I was not the first Mrs. Keith Van Buren . . . but the fourth! And while life was better than I had planned—a lovely Beverly Hills home, a lavish lifestyle that included personal appearances and dinners out, sometimes three, four, and five nights a week—I began to suspect the reason I knew nothing of my husband's previous wives or why he never spoke of them was because they were . . . dead.

But insured.

Thus, the beautiful home, the expensive imported cars with personalized plates—FOODIE1 and FOODIE2—and a closet full of hand-tailored, oversized thousand-dollar suits. Food critics seldom make the big bucks. But a critic with an insured wife, who had met with an untimely death, did. And Keith had three of them, all of whom had died accidentally.

Or what looked to be accidental.

Their mistake was the same as mine. A hurriedly signed prenup along with a stack of documents that included joint title to the house, bank account, and a multimillion-dollar life insurance policy. All of which I'm sure they had signed as quickly as I had, anxious to marry for the love and security of a big man with a big name and a big appetite for an even bigger lifestyle. They didn't call him Big Keith for nothing.

Now there are some who will say I should have known marrying Keith was a high-risk proposition. After all, in addition to his being twenty years my senior and grotesquely overweight, there were those three ex-wives (or more correctly, deceased wives). But I didn't know about them at the time and what woman didn't think she could change a man? Particularly when presented with a four-carat diamond marquise like the one Keith put on my skinny ring finger.

However, once I had learned about my predecessors' deaths, I couldn't help myself. My curiosity got the best of me and I decided to learn more about them. Specifically how they died. Their obits were easy enough to Google.

The first Mrs. Van Buren had died after choking on a chicken bone. The paper reported Keith had prepared a mushroom *coq au vin*, and as they dined, his wife began to show signs of choking. Keith had performed the Heimlich maneuver. Unfortunately unsuccessfully. The article went on to say they'd had a harmonious relationship. His wife traveled with him frequently, and the two were looking forward to celebrating their second anniversary.

Okay, so maybe the jury was out on that one. And perhaps the first Mrs. Van Buren's death had been accidental. Albeit, I believed a fortuitous death, and the beginning of Keith's plan for a series of insurable, disposable wives.

However, it was clear to me that the second Mrs. Van Buren

hadn't died accidentally at all. She had been poisoned. Keith had taken his wife on a trip to Japan where he was to do a *PBS* special on the training of fugu chefs who prepared and served deadly poisonous blowfish. *Unfortunately*, the article read, *the chef made a mistake, and Mrs. Van Buren, who had agreed to be Keith's taster, expired before she had even finished her meal.*

And the third? The poor woman died tragically when she experienced an unexpected allergic reaction to shellfish. Note to self: avoid sushi restaurants.

It wasn't that I was overly suspicious. But on the eve of our first anniversary—when I should have been shopping for a new dress to wear to Spago, where Keith and I had been asked to dine with the famed chef, Wolfgang Puck—Keith had accepted an assignment to judge a food truck competition. Food trucks had become the popular mobile cuisine for today's busy millennial-on-the-go, and Keith's job was to determine if the truck force of *Asian fusion meets Tex-Mex* was worthy of the three Michelin-Tire ratings the trucks had given themselves.

Now I have to say, I'm hardly a food snob, and probably wouldn't have given the food truck stop a second thought had it not been for the food poisoning I got that night. I spent the next day, *my anniversary*, convinced I was about to die, and that Keith had planned it all. I never did find out if it was all just a coincidence, but from that day forward I told Keith I'd eat nothing he hadn't sampled first. Of course, I didn't tell him why or that I was growing ever more suspicious he had murdered the previous three Mrs. Van Burens. Only that as a food critic, I trusted his judgment more than my own and I'd enjoy whatever he ordered for me. Provided, that is, he tasted it and explained it to me first. I figured between the time Keith took his first bite and explained the texture, seasoning, and history of the food—the only thing Keith did better than eat, was talk—that if he hadn't dropped dead after explaining it to me, it must be okay.

Then one night, while my husband and I were out, somewhere between the chateaubriand and the fresh-faced young waitress who Keith couldn't take his eyes off of, I became convinced my time was running short and Keith was planning to kill me. And, if I were going to survive my husband's ever-growing appetite, I'd need to take matters into my own hands, or more correctly, into the hands of some of L.A.'s more renowned chefs. I decided I'd feed him to death.

***

I began with my plan the very next night at Michael's in Santa Monica, where we dined beneath the stars on the restaurant's canopied, courtyard patio. We had just completed Michael's world-famous pappardelle, rabbit legs with porcini and thyme along with an order of cavatelli, braised shitake mushrooms, and asparagus with Parmigiano-Reggiano, when I leaned close to Keith and whispered suggestively into his ear, "Why don't we take an extra order of foie gras home . . . *for later*."

Keith had long considered goose-liver pâté to be an aphrodisiac and used to tease, *"A little pâté in the evening, and . . ."*—as long as I was on top—*". . . we could pâté forever."*

I should probably explain that despite the enormous quantity of calories we consumed, I have always been blessed with the metabolism of a hummingbird. No matter what I put in my mouth, be it sweets, fats, or forbidden salty foods, I've never gained an ounce. Keith, on the other hand, in our first year of marriage, had ballooned to more than three-hundred pounds. Together we were the reverse of Jack Spratt and his wife, with Keith the forever enormous-and-getting-bigger-by-the-day-fatty and me, his perpetually slim bride.

Don't hate me.

I truly believed I was fighting for my life, and despite all the late-night snacking and pâté-ing, Keith wasn't slowing down. The man had the constitution of a prized bull. The heavier he got, the more popular he became and the more hand-tailored suits he had to order to cover his growing girth. It was as though his added weight confirmed his fine taste in gourmet dining. Food aficionados throughout L.A. began to seek him out. Suddenly Keith was everywhere. On billboards. On TV. On radio. And for me, the only discernible difference, aside from the fifty plus pounds Keith had gained since our marriage, was a slight case of sleep apnea about which I said nothing and suffered silently through his endless nights of snoring like an overweight walrus.

I was beginning to think of my relationship with Keith as a kind of race, with the finish line being death. His or mine. I wasn't sure which might come first. In reality, I didn't think Keith, with his high blood pressure and Type 2 Diabetes, could go on forever. But he wasn't slowing down. And neither was his popularity, his voracious appetite, or his wandering eye. I had to do something.

So I upped the ante. I suggested we increase the number of nights we dined out and the number of meals we ate to satisfy the growing number of review requests Keith was getting from his fans. With a little more gentle coaching on my part—"Try a little more of this, darling" and "Oh, have you tasted that?"—I believed my husband would do what he loved best, and eat himself to death. And I'd be free.

I suppose I could have left Keith. But in my defense, with little over a year of marriage under my belt, why would I? As a divorcee, I would have nothing. And I considered Keith's new improved popularity to be my doing. My insistence we dine out more often, sample more and increasingly caloric foods, and accept more gigs was my doing. If I divorced him, what would I have? Nothing. But as a widow? Everything would be mine.

I'm no saint. But I'm not stupid.

But six months into my campaign to feed my husband to death, I realized he was growing ever more ravenous. This I discovered when he returned home from a late-night publisher's meeting with the *Times*, tasting of hot buttered rum and smelling of garlic mixed with the faint aromatic scent of Chanel.

That's when I knew. No visit to Crustacean in Beverly Hills for their fried catfish, no trip to Korea Town for Seongbukdong's braised short ribs, and no dessert from the Grill On The Alley, not even their Key lime pie, was going to do the trick. I had to get creative.

So I volunteered Keith to judge the Southern California Mystery Writers Chili Cook-off. What better person than Big Keith to do the job? I flattered his ego and off we went. While Keith was a big hit and sampled every type of chili from beanless to five-alarm, I became like many celebrity wives, extra baggage. Sensing he didn't need me, I found a small table and at Keith's suggestion, grabbed a bowl from the kitchen and waited for him. Which might have been fine, had I not had a terrible reaction to the chilies. By the time I got home, my mouth was tingling, my lips had swelled, and I went quickly as I could to the bathroom where I spent the evening with my head over the porcelain bowl, certain Keith had once again tried to kill me.

I was convinced my time was growing short, and with the approaching holidays, I suggested Keith increase his review schedule. There was no reason why we couldn't cover two, possibly even three restaurants in a day. This was genius on my part. Not only were we able to accommodate more restaurants, but it had the desired effect on Keith's slowing metabolism. I could see it in the way his clothes fit, the puffiness around his eyes, and the way with which he moved. He was slowing down.

Voila!

So, on what I thought had to be our final evening, after Keith had bid goodnight to the chef at Petit Trois, the third restaurant we had dined at that night, I suggested we be adventurous and try a new little Italian place I had heard about in Brentwood. I convinced Keith, despite the late hour, we should stop by. If for nothing else than a nightcap. A glass of white wine and the escargot, which I had heard, *were to die for*.

Of course, I knew the minute we had walked in Il Piacere and Keith smelled the French onion soup, that it wouldn't be just the wine and escargot. We ordered the soup and a double order of the escargot, and when it arrived Keith teased I'd better check his cellphone and make sure his cardiologist was on speed dial.

"No problem, darling, you've got me."

Keith smiled and patted my hand. "Yes, I do."

We agreed I should drive home, and Keith fell asleep in the car. His breathing was irregular, his skin clammy and wet to the touch.

I helped him to bed. "No pâté tonight, darling. You're too tired."

He mumbled something.

"Yes, dear," I said, and kissed him on the cheek.

I left his side and went to change into my favorite silk nightgown, then returned and snuggled into bed next to him, convinced the end was near. Along about three a.m. I thought I heard his breathing stop. I placed my hand on his heart. No, dammit, it was still beating. I put my head on his chest and he took a deep breath and began to snore again. I pulled away. Or tried to anyway, but . . . I couldn't move! My negligee had caught beneath his body and try as I might, I couldn't wrest it free. "Keith!" I yelled. But he couldn't hear me for his snoring. And then he turned over. On top of me! My slim body trapped beneath his enormous bulk. My screams smothered. I flailed with my one free arm. Hitting the bed. Hitting him. But to no avail. The harder I hit, the louder he snored. I couldn't breathe. My lungs were about to burst from his weight on top of me. "Keith . . . Kei . . . Ke . . .!"

If only I hadn't ordered that last esgargooooooooooooooooooo.

THE BLUE RIBBON

By Cynthia Kuhn

In Crocus Lake, people take their pies seriously.
Maybe too seriously . . .

I'd never seen the point of holding a grudge.

As far as I could tell, resentments tended to weigh on a person, like stones sinking slowly through the cold green waters of a northern lake. Too many and you've got yourself a wall.

Delia Burns, however, was fueled by indignation. The smallest thing could set her off: a perceived slight at a social event, a greeting returned with less enthusiasm than her own, a lack of credit where she thought some was due. Delia's perpetual sense of outrage prompted her to dream up blistering revenge schemes that she confided to me daily.

We worked together at the most popular shop in Crocus Lake. She'd opened the Blue Ribbon Bakery twenty years ago and offered me a job after the town had blended two high schools into one, eliminating my principal position. I could have fought to stay, but the other candidate was younger and therefore cheaper, so the die was already cast.

Not much to be said about that.

Delia and I had been best friends since first grade—for six decades, I'd played Ethel to her Lucy. She'd kept me by her side no matter how many accolades she acquired: class president, head cheerleader, valedictorian. Not everyone appreciated her blazing ambition, but it was generally understood that once Delia set her mind on something, you'd better do what she wanted or get out of the way. She'd been bossing us around from the playground to the town board, where she now ruled meetings with an eager gavel.

People occasionally asked how I put up with her.

"True friendship," I always replied, "endures."

***

I closed the cardboard lid over the cherry pie nestled in the box that would be picked up within the hour. It had turned out perfectly, following my mother's recipe. Reading her spidery handwriting on the index card made me feel closer to her.

A cloud of spicy perfume announced Delia at my elbow. Her

copper hair was a darn near exact match to my own—or at least the color mine used to be. I'd taken the path of least resistance, avoiding the salon and throwing my white hair into a braid every morning. But Delia had gone red so long ago that it was impossible to imagine her any other way.

"Who is that pie for, Ellie?" She slammed a tray of éclairs onto the counter.

I hesitated.

Delia glanced at the top of the box, where I'd written *Ellie Sweet* in neat cursive, and nodded. Then she slid open the door to the display case so hard it stuck at the far end.

I moved past her, scooping up a damp cloth to wipe down the bistro tables. As I headed toward the front of the bakery, I noted several items piled haphazardly on the opposite sidewalk and tried to determine what they had in common.

"Annie's changing the window again," I said over my shoulder. Usually Delia and I enjoyed guessing what theme the shopkeeper was going for.

There was no answer—just the sound of a cardboard box closing. I twisted slightly and caught a glimpse of a second white square next to the one I'd left on the counter. Delia was writing with a marker. I didn't even have to see it to know that her name was in large dark capital letters, or that she'd added underneath, in parentheses, *Reigning Champion.*

I turned my attention to the store across the street. Lakeview Treasures was filled to the brim with souvenirs celebrating upstate New York. Annie earned a good living off of the steady stream of tourists drawn to the lake on one side of town and the mountains on the other. Further enticing visitors were charming festivals and special events advertised in a variety of travel publications.

Like the famous Lake Bake, one of the oldest contests in town.

Which Delia had won for twenty-nine years straight.

Although she was capable of submitting intricate cakes or sophisticated pastries, the Lake Bake required the same item from all competitors: a pie. It was a beloved tradition, and I'd often wondered if Delia hoped that her victories somehow balanced the widespread distaste for her forceful personality. She varied the fruits in her pies every year, and people fell over themselves predicting which one she'd choose, as if it were a matter of great importance.

Her contest triumphs had propelled her to start a bakery when she needed to make a living after her husband died. I was glad about the Blue Ribbon, despite the fact that opening a bakery had been my dream from kindergarten forward. And that her husband had been my own fiancé until Delia decided she wanted him.

Anything Delia did was performed with such excitement and entitlement that I found myself swept along like a tiny pebble caught in the tide.

***

Delia had lined up her golden trophies on a high shelf so that customers could see but not touch them. Many was the day I'd admired their glint in the sunlight as I listened to her rejoice in how her secret ingredient had never let her down, and how proud Cal would have been about the winning his wife was doing. And I'd agreed that yes, one more trophy would be terrific, and yes, it really was remarkable that someone could win thirty years in a row, and yes, it probably was a world record.

I had cheered her on.

I had applauded her success.

I had smiled when she showed me her apron, newly embroidered with *Winner* in crimson thread—even if mine, unadorned by any word whatsoever, suddenly seemed to whisper *Loser*.

And then I'd entered the contest, too.

I'd decided to do it the moment I found my mother's recipe card tucked into the book she'd been reading in the big house that was all too quiet now. The memories rushed over me in relentless waves.

If only I'd taken her back to the doctor earlier. But Delia had said my mother was exaggerating her symptoms for attention. It had happened with her parents, she'd said. Checking out every little complaint was not worth the time and money. Trust her, she'd said.

So I had. Until it was too late.

***

The next day was a blur of measuring, mixing, kneading, rolling, and baking. We glazed this, we iced that, we started all over again. I tried to talk to Delia about the contest, but when I opened my mouth, I ended up complimenting her choice of fillings or blurting out ill-conceived frosting strategies.

What I needed to say remained submerged.

Our exchanges were excruciatingly polite, yet our attempts to avoid one another led to awkward choreography. We were in the same place, but we were no longer in it together.

It was almost a relief when Delia dragged me into the office, gripping my arm tightly enough to bruise it.

"Look!" She pointed at the computer screen with a blood-red talon. "The finalists have been posted."

My name below hers appeared to glow. I was transfixed by the sight.

Her fingernails drummed expectantly on the desk. When I eventually mustered up the courage to face Delia, she put her hands on her hips and fixed me with a blue glare.

For the first time, I read danger there.

Concentrating on keeping my voice steady, I congratulated her.

"Congratulations?" she hissed. "Why on earth would you do this to me?"

The words emerged slowly, as though they were swimming up through dark water. "It wasn't about you. For once."

Her intake of breath was so sharp it could have cut glass.

***

The morning after our second round of pies had been picked up for judging, customers flowed into the bakery chirping about the contest and wishing us luck. Delia and I spoke with every last one.

We never said a word to each other.

It was just after closing when the battered black phone on the wall rang. I wiped the flour off of my hands by sliding them across my apron and picked up the receiver.

"Blue Ribbon."

"Ellie," said the mayor, who supervised the Lake Bake. "I'm sorry to tell you, but we have a situation. The judges who tasted your pie all took sick."

I gasped.

His deep voice rolled on. "Like dominoes. One right after the other."

"What in the world—"

"Couldn't say, but I wanted to give you a heads up. As a courtesy."

"I'm so sorry to hear that." After a beat, I added, "You know I didn't—"

"Of course not." He paused. "It's going to be quite the story around town, I expect. You can kiss your chances of winning the contest goodbye."

"I don't care about that," I told him. "I just want the judges to recover."

"Good. We'll provide an update soon." He cleared his throat. "But this may affect the bakery, too. People could be afraid of eating there for a spell."

After thanking him for the call, I hung up the phone and gazed around the room as I processed what the mayor had told me. My eyes rose to the trophies spanning the wall like a gilded army poised for battle.

And then I knew.

The door banged against the brick wall as I hurried out into the alley, where Delia was pulling an item from the trunk of her car. I stumbled down the steep concrete stairs, avoiding the patch of ice that lingered on the steps all winter, no matter how many sunny days we had.

She beckoned me over as if I was not already charging in her direction and held out a small plastic bag. "Blue ribbons," she said, pursing her lips. "One of us is going to win this contest. We might as well decorate. Play up the name of the bakery."

I shoved the bag into my apron pocket. "Listen. The judges are sick. The mayor called. The sheriff is probably next."

She tilted her head. "What happened?"

"What did you do, Delia?"

"What do you mean?" she asked, smiling brightly.

I sighed. "Stop it. What did you put in the pie?"

Her smile faltered just enough to reveal the battle between wanting to sustain her charade and wanting to brag about what she'd done.

I waited.

Delia shrugged. "My secret ingredient, as always."

"Not *your* pie. Mine."

She shook her head.

"Admit it. You owe me that." I held my breath, craving an explanation but knowing where it would lead us.

Delia looked down for a long while, then lifted her chin defiantly. "Oh, Ellie. No need to be so dramatic. I thought yours could use a dash of secret ingredient, too." She laughed lightly. "Obviously not the same ingredient I use in mine."

The words hit hard, as if she had struck me, and I took a step back. "You *poisoned* them."

She returned to the items in her trunk. "Relax. It's not deadly. It'll just make them a bit nauseated. They'll be fine."

I stared at her, registering a distant rumble, like water crashing on sand. "Why would you do that?"

Delia spun around and approached me, a tire iron in hand. "You tell me."

The roar grew louder in my ears. I moved up the stairs, anxious to put space between us. "You wanted to win."

"One good sabotage deserves another," she snapped, her face distorted by rage. "Don't you think?"

My arms flew up in an attempt to prevent her from coming any closer. "I wasn't trying to sabotage you."

She made a frustrated sound, something akin to a howl. "Then what were you doing? Aren't we friends? How could you betray me?"

"No!" I cried, painfully aware that the next words wrung out of me would mean far more than she would ever acknowledge. "You betrayed *me*!"

"You don't deserve to win!" Delia screamed, raising the tire iron and rushing forward. My skin seemed to burn, reflecting the heat emanating from her.

I scrambled onto the top step as she climbed toward me.

The moment my hand closed on the doorknob, Delia slipped on the ice and went down, hitting her face on the stairs, the tire iron falling onto her head immediately afterwards.

I froze.

"Ellie—" she gurgled, then went limp.

I started to reach out to her but was shrouded by a hazy mist, with ghostly traces of all that she had taken from me.

I lowered my arm.

"Be well, Delia," I whispered to her back.

Like I always said, there's no point in holding a grudge.

I went inside, turned off the lights, and left through the front door.

As I slowly walked home, I tied a blue ribbon onto the end of my braid.

THE LAST WORD

By Shawn Reilly Simmons

A bad review isn't the only thing that's come between two old friends from culinary school.

James knew the exact table Simon would choose, the two-top in front of the picture window farthest from the door. He always sat there so the draft wouldn't cool down his meal before he could finish it, even though James had installed a heater at the entrance to keep out the cold that tried to weave its way across the floor into his restaurant. The thermostat was set at a perfect seventy-two, the ambient air providing comfort and the ideal environment for both entrees and desserts to maintain their integrity for up to seven minutes after they left the service window.

James knew how Simon thought. He knew he preferred Osetra caviar over Beluga, remarking more than once in their twenty-year friendship the nuttier flavor of Osetra was far superior to the more pedestrian version. He knew what Simon was going to say before the words ever left his mouth. At least he thought he did.

Friendship. Friends. He supposed that was how he'd describe his and Simon's decades-long trajectory in life. They'd been classmates first at culinary school, then colleagues working the line in a busy restaurant in the city. They had become competitors, then rivals, and now they'd entered their first phase of imbalance, where their paths were not mirroring each other and career comparisons could not be drawn.

James opened the smoker and removed the shucked oysters just as the pressure of the air inside the restaurant shifted as the front door swooshed open and closed.

Simon stood near the entrance, hesitantly looking around the empty dining room. James emerged from the kitchen, the smoked oysters wedged into a bed of rock salt, candied lemon peel and lavender sprigs garnishing the edges of the plate.

"Lock the door, would you?" James said.

Simon hesitated a moment then turned to twist the lock on the front door. James set the oysters down in the center of Simon's table, then motioned for him to take a seat.

“Where is everyone?” Simon asked, stepping lightly toward the table.

“Tonight is a special occasion, a private meal between old friends,” James said when Simon didn’t immediately take a seat.

“Jimmy, what is this?” Simon asked with a small laugh. He eyed the oysters with admiration and a touch of hunger and longing.

James pulled out one of the chairs and sat down. “I have questions. I thought we could have a private chat.”

Simon sighed and joined James at the table, clearing his throat. “Look, I know my review wasn’t—”

“Accurate?” James said.

“My reviews are always fair, Jimmy,” Simon said. James slid an oyster onto the plate in front of Simon and chose one for himself. “I’m sorry about the star. I didn’t think—”

“You didn’t think a pan in the *New York Review of Restaurants* would cost me my Michelin Star?”

“No, I didn’t,” Simon said quietly, dropping his eyes to the oyster.

“Eat,” James said. “Please.”

Simon hesitated a second, then gave in and picked up the shell, slurping down the oyster whole. His cheeks, reddened by either the wind outside or the liquor James could smell from across the table, shuddered with pleasure as he swallowed it down. He immediately reached for another.

“Maybe Gladys leaving you has colored your view of the world,” James said.

Simon snorted a laugh without taking his eyes from the platter on the table.

“I told you . . . nothing happened between me and Gladys,” James said.

Simon closed his eyes as he savored the second oyster. He began shaking his head before he opened them again. “No, Jimmy, the review had nothing to do with Gladys, or what might or might not have happened between the two of you,” he finally said. “Good riddance to that bitch.”

James sat back in his chair and crossed his arms. “I didn’t encourage her. When she showed up on my doorstep . . . she said some things. Things that reminded me of another time long ago.”

Simon waved a hand in the air. “Water under the bridge, Jimmy boy. Old shriveled up, useless water. And I didn’t tell her a thing.”

James stood up from the table and headed to the kitchen. “Do me a favor and open the 2010 Rothschild.”

“What’s the occasion?” Simon said, hurrying up from his seat.

"I told you. A celebration of our long friendship," James said, pushing through the doorway into the kitchen.

Simon found the bottle behind the bar and opened it, savoring the aroma of the wine that he felt was peaking on that very day, in the middle of New York City after its long journey from Bordeaux nine years earlier. Tasting what was inside would be a privilege, something unique only a select few in the world would experience.

James returned after a few minutes with two plates of perfectly seared duck breast topped with sage-infused blackberry glaze atop whipped potatoes that had been subtly kissed by caramelized onions.

"This is all very familiar," Simon said as he eyed the dish in front of him. He swirled his wine and watched the legs glide down the glass. "This is the same meal I reviewed."

"I thought I might convince you of its beauty the second time around," James said, retaking his seat.

"What is the goal?" Simon asked, squinting at him. "For me to retract my review? I'm sorry, old friend, but I'm afraid that's not how it's done. It's out there forever at this point."

"Do you have any idea of my monthly expenses here?" James asked. He picked up his knife and fork and began carving into the breast on his plate.

Simon took in his surroundings, the floor-to-ceiling window that looked out over Bleecker Street, the exposed brick walls, the modern tables and chairs, the sleek mahogany bar, fully stocked with top-shelf bottles of liquor and the finest bottles of wine from around the world.

"I have no idea," Simon said with a shrug.

"More than you can imagine, my friend," James said. He took another bite of duck and chewed thoughtfully. "I lost another investor today. The restaurant expansion won't be happening."

Simon dug into his plate as well, surprised at how sublime the duck tasted, how complex the flavors were on his palate, how the feeling of pleasure lingered there after he swallowed.

"Look, Jimmy," Simon said after a sigh and a sip of wine. "I regret now that what I wrote has had an impact on your career. It was meant as constructive criticism."

James set down his fork and laced his fingers. "Interesting. I hadn't thought of it quite that way. It took years for me to earn a Michelin Star. Years. Getting my second was just as important as my first. Now I'm back down to one. Bookings have fallen off."

Simon's cheeks reddened slightly, but he recovered and took another sip of wine. "Jimmy, it was my first cover review. I couldn't let our personal history color my critique of the place. You know that."

"Our personal history is the topic at hand," James said. "As you said, you're having the same meal you had that night. What is your review?"

"It's incredible," Simon said quietly. "It wasn't that night."

"I find that hard to believe," James said.

Simon faltered, then brought his eyes back into focus. "Let's have dessert then. I might be persuaded to pitch a follow-up piece. Maybe a feature story on your career."

James's lips twisted into a smile. "A puff piece?"

"A puff pastry piece, perhaps," Simon said with a chortle.

James considered him a moment before rising and heading to the kitchen once again.

A young couple stopped near the front window and peered inside at the nearly empty restaurant. The woman turned and gave the man a lingering kiss. He looped his arm around her waist and urged her to continue down the sidewalk.

James reappeared with two small chocolate domes, the dark chocolate ganache on top shining like a mirror.

"What did Gladys say?" Simon asked as he poured more wine into his glass. "When you saw her last."

"She said you were cruel," James said with a small shrug. "That you're a monster."

Simon seethed in silence, then sipped his wine testily. "She was the most insufferable woman. And why would she talk about it anyway? She left me. And came straight to you." He dangled a spoon over the chocolate dome, mesmerized by his reflection.

"After what happened with Sarah back in culinary school, I thought you'd have learned how to be a decent gentleman," James said, sitting back in his chair.

"What happened to Sarah was not my fault," Simon said evenly. "She misunderstood me."

James set his elbows on the table and leaned forward. "Sarah committed suicide after you went to the dean, telling the lies you carelessly let fall from your lips. You had a hand in what happened to her, might as well have fed her those pills yourself."

"It was her or me," Simon said. "I couldn't afford to get expelled."

"She didn't cheat on that test. She'd never plagiarize a recipe and turn it in as her own. You set her up," James said. "You forced yourself on her that night and when she said she was going to report you to the dean . . ."

"And you knew about everything, and did nothing about it," Simon countered, waving the spoon in front of his face. "Sarah was going to tell everyone that I'd raped her? No, I don't think so." Simon shook his head and scooped another bite of his dessert.

"Retract your review. Or I'll tell a story of my own. Highlights will be how you've abused and assaulted not one but two women in your lifetime, at least. I saw the bruises on both of them. Witnessed the devastation you've left behind."

"Why would you do that?" Simon scoffed. He looked around the restaurant and then back at his friend. "All of this would be gone. Believe me, old chum, I'll take you all the way down with me."

"I should've said something back then. You're right about that," James said. "But now it's time to set things right. For both of us."

Simon took a bite and closed his eyes once again. "Okay, I get it. I'll see what I can do at the magazine, okay? I promise."

James leaned back in his chair and considered his friend of twenty years.

Simon looked up at him, his eyes glassy. "You know what? You've convinced me to retract my review with this meal," he said, his words soft at the edges. "I'll sell it to my editor. We'll both be okay, old friend."

"I thought I might be able to convince you," James said with a quick flash of a grin. "But there's no need to talk to the editor. This morning, I mailed off a full accounting of what happened between you and Sarah all those years ago back in school. About how I covered for you and lied to the dean, backed up your story."

Simon's mouth fell open, then snapped closed, his eyes beginning to water.

"I sent some pictures of Gladys, too. One of the ring of bruises around her arm from where you grabbed her before she came here, and her bruised cheekbone. I'd finally gotten her to quit sobbing. She was traumatized by you, unsure where else to go. I think your bosses at the magazine will be very interested in all of that."

Simon looked at him with a flash of alarm. "Why? We had it all worked out . . ." Simon's voice faded as he lost his breath and his chin slumped onto his chest. He took a few more breaths then became still, a bluish tint to his cheeks. James reached over and took a spoonful of Simon's dessert, leaving the one in front of himself untouched. He wanted whoever found them to witness his final act of culinary perfection.

He picked up his wine glass and tasted the Bordeaux for the first, and the last, time, rolling the wine across his tongue, trying to imagine the fentanyl mixing with the wine, unable to taste it. The nine-year-old cork had allowed the syringe to slide in without resistance, and that was the final sign he'd needed to set things right. For both of them.

The long sleep was on the way, his final performance completed.

MURDER TAKES THE CUPCAKE

By Kate Willett

Two daughters, one with a gift for baking like their mother, the other making deliveries and basic chores around the shop. If only she didn't have that weird dream.

"Do you have it every night? The dream?"

My fingers twitch. The tea in the dainty cup I'm raising to my lips swishes with the sudden movement. Steaming liquid starts to spill over onto my t-shirt. I quickly put the cup back on the table and fold my hands over my knees. "How . . .?"

"You come to a psychic. Do you not expect the psychic should know things? Drink the tea. I will read your leaves."

I nod politely and pick the cup back up. The tea burns my tongue and throat as I sip it, but not because it's hot. I expect a smooth green or oolong taste, but this tea has a kick. I cough in surprise and move to put the cup down again. Miss Petroni catches my hand and lifts it and the cup back to my mouth.

"Is herbal recipe with special spices. Drink."

I take a breath and gulp the rest of the tea down.

"Turn the cup." Her left wrist rotates. "Three times."

I do as she says. "Some of the leaves are sticking to the sides. Should I do it again?"

"No. Flip the cup over. It must drain."

We sit for a moment in silence, then Miss Petroni says, "Turn the cup three times this way . . . good, good . . . turn it back over and point the handle this way . . ." She motions for me to tap the top of the cup three times, then takes it from my hands and peers into it. "A delicate situation is approaching. You must keep your wits and work wisely to resolve it." She studies the leaves more intensely. Her eyebrow arches.

I jerk forward. "Something bad?"

She smiles. "Your question, what was it?"

"Honestly?" I say, sheepishly. "I didn't have one."

She leans back in her chair. "Tell me the dream then."

"Are you sure? I mean, I only paid for a tea leaf reading, I don't really . . ."

"Is fine. Is freebie. My personal curiosity."

"Okay," I say, taking a deep breath. "I'm in my kitchen. It's Christmas. I mean, I assume it's Christmas. There are cookie sheets with gingerbread men all over the kitchen: on the counters, on the table, and in chairs. But they scare me. The gingerbread men, I mean." I hesitate, suddenly aware of how silly this sounds.

"Continue," Miss Petroni says.

And so, I tell her all.

Sometimes the gingerbread men chase me. Sometimes they point with their stubby little gingerbread arms and laugh. Sometimes they disappear and reappear in horribly deformed shapes. But always—always—they kill me.

The methods are different: a rope of twisted icing, a gumdrop gag, a candy cane dagger. Just before I die, I see a face. It's a person, someone I think I know. But I can't remember who when I wake up.

Miss Petroni nods. "Perhaps this is related to work, yes? You work with food?"

"In a way. My older sister owns a cupcakery downtown, in the historic district. It's called Cookies and Cupkakes. Cupcakes with two Ks. She thinks it's charming."

"Do you help your sister when she makes her cookies and cupcakes with two Ks?"

"No," I say, fidgeting in my chair. "Mom used to say I could turn sugar into salt just by looking at it. I do whatever odd jobs Kaitlyn needs done. Bussing tables, deliveries, that type thing." As I say this, I look at my watch and my stomach drops. I was supposed to be at the shop thirty minutes ago.

"Time to go?" Miss Petroni says, standing. "It was nice to meet with you, Polly. Perhaps you will come back again, for another visit?"

"Oh, sure, and thanks," I say, grabbing my purse and rushing out of her home.

Luckily, Miss Petroni's house is near a bus stop. The bus shows up right as I run out, but it's still another fifteen minutes before it pulls to a stop near the cupcakery.

Cookies and Cupkakes is in a two-story brick building located near the middle of the district, on a corner that juts out diagonally. Most of the square buildings in the historic district were built in the early 1900s. There's a yoga studio above us, but that's it. Across the street on one side are restaurants with fancy names like The Russian Teahouse and others more my style—like Pike's Deli. Off to the other side are clothing boutiques and a spa.

I pull out my key to the shop and unlock the door, locking it again once I'm inside. We don't officially open until ten-thirty.

Kaitlyn chose a retro vibe for Cookies and Cupkakes: Formica tables with padded chairs on a black-and-white tile floor, an old school soda machine, and starburst light fixtures. She has all of these tin signs on the walls, too, that say things like *Eat Here* or resemble those old labels they used to put on fruit crates.

The display case is the crown jewel of the shop. The cupcakes go inside, and the cookies go on top of it in old-fashioned glass containers. It really looks quite vintage.

The first thing I see each morning when I walk into the store, though, is a photo of my sister and my mother on the counter next to the cash register. Mom and Kaitlyn are at the stove, laughing and stirring spoons in a pot. As I walk by, I blow a little kiss toward the photo. "Morning, Mom."

Kaitlyn got all of our mother's cooking talent. I got all of Mom's Irish good looks. It would have been nice if the distribution had been more fifty-fifty. Kaitlyn has always had a clear career path; she was born to work with food. Me? I'm just the pretty one. I have a degree in English, but it took me seven years to get it and I still have no clue what I want to be when I grow up. At thirty-two, I thought I'd have figured this out by now.

"You're late." Kaitlyn doesn't look up when I push through the swinging door separating the storefront from the kitchen. She's bent over a row of cupcakes with a piping bag, carefully icing the tops. It's only nine forty-five but the ovens and smallness of the kitchen are already making the room hot. On another table, Magdalena, Kaitlyn's most senior employee, is using a scoop to fill cupcake cups.

There's a knock at the back door. I open it and let Rory in. He's still in school and normally works part-time, but has picked up more hours for the summer. Rory mans the cash register out front.

"Polly, go help Rory get ready to open," Kaitlyn says, still hunched over her cupcakes.

My first chore for the day. I grab a rag and some cleaning spray from the storage cabinet.

"So, Rory," I say, as I spritz and wipe down the tables and chairs. "What grade you gonna be in this fall?"

"Senior."

"Oh yeah? Go Werecats, Woowoowoo!"

He stops mid-air as he's stacking dollar bills into the cash register and stares at me, then smirks. "It's Wolverine. The Whilliby High School mascot is a wolverine."

"Really? Werecats are cooler than wolverines."

"And I'll be a senior in college."

That stops me dead in my tracks. Rory is really skinny and gangly, more like a sixteen-year-old than a guy in his twenties. He's surly like a teenager, too.

"Did you get straight As and stuff in high school?" he asks, taking a roll of quarters and whacking it against the side of the cash register until it cracks open. "Like your sister?"

"No way. I was a nightmare. I ditched class, hated homework, snuck out every night. My parents should've kicked—" Rory looks at me, amused. "Anyway, I was more of a C student. But I did graduate and finish college, so there's that." I shrug my shoulders and smile.

"Oh, sure. I guess." He closes the register.

Customers start filing into the shop as soon as we open. It's Friday, which is usually busy. We add special cupcakes to the menu every Friday, and people line up out the door to get them. Kaitlyn likes to come up with new flavors each week, but a few make it into heavy rotation. The most popular in the summer is the Iced Watermelon cupcake. Kaitlyn stirs real watermelon juice into the batter, along with mini chocolate chips for the seeds. Each cupcake is topped with a twirl of buttercream frosting and sprinkled with red and green sugar.

Not everything's a winner. Last week, Kaitlyn tried a blueberry thing with dark chocolate and nuts. No one liked it. To top it off, the food coloring she bought for the frosting made a horrible mess all over the kitchen. Today, Kaitlyn picked a Red Hot theme: red velvet cupcakes with cream cheese frosting and spicy red candies sprinkled on top.

Another reason Friday is crazy? Friday Night Live! Friday nights during the summer, the town green is filled with live music, food trucks, and people having a blast. The entertainment is free, the food is not. People come from all over the county, meaning more customers at Cookies and Cupkakes.

Usually I help Rory in the front, pulling products from the display and bagging them up for customers. Today, though, we have a ton of orders to be delivered. When I get back, it's almost five and Magdalena's running the register. Rory must be on a break. I head back to the kitchen and find Kaitlyn sifting flour into a bowl.

Beside her is a small bowl with freshly whisked eggs. "Hey, you crack eggs with one hand. How?" I ask. She starts to answer, but the back door opens and Rory returns, smelling faintly of cloves.

Kaitlyn scowls as he passes us. "Those things smell awful."

Rory grunts and heads for the front.

"Send Magdalena back! I need her help with cookie batter," Kaitlyn calls after him.

"I can help with the batter," I say, even though I know she won't let me.

Out front, voices are rising.

Kaitlyn rubs her hands against her apron. She's almost at the swinging door when Rory bursts into the kitchen.

"There's a guy out here mad about an order. He wants to talk to the manager." Rory's face is flushed.

We rush out and find Magdalena at the register, getting the full brunt of the customer's fury. "I'm sorry," she stammers. "We don't have any . . ." Magdalena looks like she's close to tears.

"D-I-C-K-E-R-S-O-N. Frank Dickerson. "

"Frank," a man next to him says, pulling on the sleeve of Dickerson's ugly plaid shirt.

"Get off me!" Dickerson screams. He turns back to Magdalena. "I placed this order six days ago! You stupid—" I wouldn't have believed it if I hadn't seen it. Dickerson stops yelling and spits in Magdalena's face.

Kaitlyn yanks a Cookies and Cupkakes box from the stack and pops it open, then shoves her way between Rory and Magdalena.

I run out, grab Magdalena, and pull her to the safety of the kitchen. Rory looks back at me helplessly as the swinging door shuts closed behind us.

"You said two dozen?" Kaitlyn says loudly. I crack the door open and see her hurriedly grab cookies from the display shelf. "Here, on the house! Next customer, please."

The man with Dickerson grabs his arm and drags him out. "C'mon now, Frank. You've got your cookies." Dickerson is still screaming obscenities at us as his friend pulls him down the sidewalk.

Kaitlyn brushes the hair out of her face. The next person in line, an older guy with bits of silver streaking through his black mustache, smiles at her timidly. "I apologize for your wait," she says. "Rory, please help this gentleman." Then she joins Magdalena and me in the kitchen.

Magdalena wipes her face with a towel. Kaitlyn paces and counts backwards from ten. I feel like I'm going to be sick. This, all of it, is my fault.

I clear my throat. "Um, I think I know what happened. Magdalena was busy with that large cupcake order last week and Rory was checking out a customer and the phone rang, so I wrote down the order and put it there on the desk."

I move to the desk and poke around it, getting on my hands and knees to look behind it. "It must have fallen off and, oh look! I just found it again!" I stand back up and hold the slip of paper in the air like it's a prize.

Kaitlyn doesn't say anything, which is bad. Very bad.

"Oh, Paulina, you gotta stick it on the pin . . ." Magdalena begins, pointing at the wire spindle sitting on the desk next to the phone. Kaitlyn holds her finger up in the air to cut her off.

"Rory!" she yells. He pokes his head in from the door. Kaitlyn glares at me. "Help Magdalena back here. I will handle the front."

"What can I do?" I ask.

"Go away, Polly. I don't care where, but go!"

The door swings wildly as Kaitlyn stomps back out to the front. I glance at Magdalena. She shakes her head and starts giving Rory instructions.

"Fine," I mumble and take off out the back door.

Outside, I lean against the building wall and bite my lip, trying to keep it together. Around me, the cool evening breeze begins to sway with echoing music and a buttered popcorn scent. I storm off to Friday Night Live!

When I make it to the green, a local cover band called Jeremiah's Bullfrog is starting their set. It's a rocking rearrangement of "Smoke on the Water." Some people are dancing in a spot near the stage, while others groove on blankets or in lawn chairs.

"Polly! Hey, Pol!" I turn around and see Bev, my best friend since kindergarten, running towards me. "You never called! Well, c'mon, what did she say?"

"What?" I say. "Oh, the psychic."

"Did she tell you anything cool? There was a swan in my tea leaves, which means good luck or health or something like that. Gah, I'm thirsty. Let's get a beer."

Bev drags me over to the food tents and buys beers for me and her. She guzzles half of hers down and then yells "Why aren't you at the store?" over the music.

I shrug my shoulders and take a sip of my beer, then head toward a tent with juicy looking BBQ chicken wings and sandwiches. The sweet smell of the sugary spicy glaze on the chicken is heavenly, but so is the savory meat scent of the burgers grilling one tent over.

"Let me buy you dinner," I say, holding up my beer. "To repay you."

We get homemade chips with our meal. For several minutes, we munch on crispy potato thins and thick burgers topped with grilled onions and crunchy lettuce.

"They've got sausages at that tent," Bev says, pointing.

I shake my head and wash the last bite of my burger down with my beer.

Near the stage, I notice a policeman arguing about the no-pets policy with a man holding a dog to his chest and shaking a leash in his fist.

Bev bumps my shoulder and grins. "There's always one, isn't there?"

I laugh, but feel like I'm playing hooky from school. Friday Night Live! doesn't end until eleven, so Kaitlyn keeps the shop open an extra two hours to pull in some late-night sales from stragglers. It doesn't feel right, me being here instead of there.

Bev and I sway to the music and drink another beer or two, then she's got to go. She waves goodbye as she stumbles away. I'm not worried; like me, Bev only lives a block or two from here. "G'night!" I yell as she disappears into the night.

I sigh. It's probably time to go back and face my own music. The party is winding down. I can go home, but Kaitlyn and I live together. Sneaking back and hiding in bed before she gets back seems cowardly. Best to woman up and see if Kaitlyn has cooled down.

On my way, I notice a commotion across the street from the shop. A crowd in front of the old Moose Lodge is being pushed back by a policeman, and bright lights are illuminating the area between the building and the tall fence surrounding it.

One of our regulars, Mrs. Tomlinson, is standing off to the side. She motions excitedly for me to come over.

"What happened?" I ask, straining to get a better view. The lodge is being renovated. I see planks of wood half-covered in tarp and paint buckets, but nothing out of the ordinary.

"A dead person!" Her eyes widen. She grabs my arm and points to a spot on the fence, just past a pallet of bricks. "Look, Polly. Isn't that your store's box?"

Now I can see the box, and the body. There's a nasty gash on the head. I also see a bloody brick and an ugly plaid shirt, just like the one the jerk from earlier was wearing.

Mrs. Tomlinson starts to say something else to me, but I'm already running toward the bakery. Kaitlyn is wiping down a table. She doesn't look happy to see me, but I don't care at the moment.

"That guy, the one that was so mad earlier—" I pause to catch my breath. "I think he's dead. Like, dead dead."

Usually, after the bands and vendors have packed up and gone, the historic district is still humming for a while. The news of Dickerson's death, though, has the place absolutely buzzing with excitement.

I'm outside sitting on a bench and talking to Bev on my cell phone, making sure she made it home okay, when I see a policeman leave the shop. I hang up with Bev and head back in.

Kaitlyn is standing behind the counter, closing out the register for Rory. He's sitting at one of the tables, scratching absentmindedly at a blue stain on his sleeve. He's a wreck. His hair is mussed, his foot is tapping crazily, and he's literally green.

"I sent Magdalena home," Kaitlyn says, looking over at him. "Why don't you go on, too, Rory?"

He nods, and goes to the back to get his bag.

Kaitlyn sighs. I start to say something, but she puts up her hand. "Don't. Not a word." She rubs her temples. "Let's just go home."

***

The next day, Kaitlyn is gone when I wake up. That's not odd, but she's also not at the shop when I get there at nine. No one is there, so I go a few stores down to the coffee shop to get caffeine.

Benny, the owner, is working the register when I come in. "Hey, Little Miss Polly! Heard there was some hullabaloo last night."

"You weren't here?"

"Nah, I don't hang around for that hubbub. When I was younger it was great, but now, not so much. I put Henry over there in charge and go home to sleep while the young party it up. What can I get for you?"

"I think a latte today."

He starts to froth the milk. "Heard y'all had a tiff with that dead guy before he got beaned in the head."

I glare at him. Benny's cool, but I'm not in the mood to discuss this. His hands fly up defensively. "Just making conversation, Polly. That's all."

When I get back to the store, Rory is at the front door. "Where's Kaitlyn?"

"Got me. Hold this," I hand him my drink so I can rummage through my purse for the shop key.

Inside, Rory puts his stuff in the back and starts getting the shop ready for business. I sit down at a table and sip my latte. There's not much I can do until Kaitlyn gets here and gives me orders.

"Do you know the code for the safe?" Rory asks. "I need to load the cash register."

I snort. "Like she'd trust me with something like that. Hey, Rory, did you notice anything weird last night?"

"Besides the murder?" Rory shakes his head. "But there is

something you should know. I didn't want to say anything when the cops were here. It's Magdalena. She . . . left last night. Around the time Mr. Dickerson was . . ." His voice trails off.

"Did she say where she was going?" It isn't like Magdalena to disappear.

He shakes his head.

Kaitlyn doesn't get to the store until almost ten.

"Good morning," I venture.

She ignores me. "Rory, you're in the back with me today. Magdalena's sick."

Rory and I exchange glances. "Looks like you've been promoted for the day," I say.

That night, after the store closes, I stick around waiting for Kaitlyn to finish. I watch as she scrutinizes the shop's ledger. I notice her hands as she writes. They're scarred from hot pans and cracked from constant washing. Mom's hands used to look like that.

Kaitlyn grumbles and scratches her head with her pen.

"What's wrong?"

"Last month's numbers weren't great. I barely paid the bills this month. We need a gimmick to get new customers."

"What about the thing you did for the Fourth of July last week? The firecracker cookies? People loved those."

She sighs and closes the ledger. "You know, this can wait. Let's go home and, I don't know, drink wine and watch a movie. I need to unwind or I'm going to go batty."

"Do you mind if we make a stop first?" I ask.

It isn't far to Magdalena's apartment. She is surprised to see us, and keeps us out in the apartment hallway. Five minutes later, I know why she disappeared from the shop on the night of the murder.

"My daughter, she and her husband have been having trouble. I am watching my grandson while they try to fix things. But I didn't have anyone to watch him. I've been leaving him alone so I could work."

"Oh, I didn't know you had a grandson."

She pulls out her phone. The chubby face of a little boy with dark eyes and hair fills the screen. "My Alejandro. He's ten, almost eleven, so he can stay by himself. But I worry."

"So last night when you disappeared . . ."

"I had to get home to my Alex. That horrible man was killed so close. My apartment is just around the corner."

"Rory said you left before that, too."

"Yes, to check on Alex and get him a sandwich and glass of

milk for his dinner. I was only gone fifteen minutes. I walked fast." A horrified look crosses her face. "I was right where the man was. What if . . . instead of him . . .?"

"That's why you called in sick today after the murder?" Kaitlyn says.

"I couldn't leave Alex alone after that. I worked something out with my friend's daughter, so I have someone to watch him now."

Kaitlyn puts her hand on Magdalena's shoulder. "Don't leave Alejandro alone anymore. Bring him to the store. We'll get colored pencils and paper he can draw with, or he can spread out on one of the tables and do homework."

For a moment, we all stare at each other reassuringly. But, when Kaitlyn speaks again, there is no warmth in her voice. "And the murder wasn't a random thing. Someone wanted that man dead. You don't need to worry."

***

Four days later, it's Thursday, and everyone is still on edge.

"Did you ever figure out what was odd?" Rory asks me, halfway through the day.

"No, but . . ."—I tap my forehead—". . .it'll come to me eventually."

That night, after we close, Kaitlyn tells me to go home without her. I make it to the drugstore on the corner before I turn around and let myself back into the shop.

Kaitlyn is in the kitchen with her sleeves pushed up and her apron on, rolling out dough.

"What are you doing?" I ask.

She stops rolling and wipes her face with the back of her arm. "Why are you back?"

"Because I've decided this is a family business and I want to be involved in it. When Magdalena was out the other day and you let Rory help, I didn't like it. I don't want to be the delivery girl anymore. I want to be involved, really."

Kaitlyn grins and goes back to her dough rolling. "Okay."

I move to the flour-coated table she's using and look down. "So, what are you doing?"

"You never listen, do you? Winter in July! The thing we're doing with the coffee shop and the ice cream parlor down the street? The gimmick I'm hoping will bring in some new customers?"

I stare at her blankly.

She holds up a cookie cutter shaped like a gingerbread man. "This weekend, Cookies and Cupkakes is handing out coupons to each customer for a free frozen hot chocolate from the coffee shop and a free ice cream scoop from the ice cream shop. They, in turn, are handing out coupons for a free gingerbread cookie at Cookies and Cupkakes. If you want to be more involved here, you'll need to pay more attention to what's going on."

"Isn't it supposed to be Christmas in July?" I ask.

"Yeah, but Benny thought that might alienate some customers."

"Oh."

"Listen, it's going to be a long night. I've got to get these baked so Magdalena and I can decorate them tomorrow. We're putting Bermuda shorts on half and flowery dresses on the rest."

"Well, that's corny."

"So what I'm saying is, you don't have to stay. It's okay if you go home and leave me here."

"No," I say. "What do you need me to do?"

"Roll this dough out. I'm running home to change into shorts. I'll melt if I keep these jeans on much longer."

Minutes after Kaitlyn slips out the back door, there's a knock against it. "That was fast," I say, swinging the door open. Only it's not Kaitlyn standing there. It's Rory.

"I forgot my bag," he says, walking to a cabinet near the door. He takes out a backpack and slings it over his shoulder.

"Oh, your bag—" It hits me then. The thing that was odd was the stain on Rory's shirt that night. It was blue.

Rory had started to leave, but now he stops and shuts the back door until the lock clicks. "Hey, you asked me a question the other day."

"Question . . .?" I say stiffly. As casually as possible, I make my way back to the table.

"If something was odd." He laughs, but he sounds dead inside. "You just figured it out, didn't you?" He lifts the backpack up with his shoulder. "I keep an extra set of clothes in my bag. In case I spill stuff on the ones I'm wearing. My old man used to say,"—Rory lowers his voice to a gruff growl—"'two is one and one is none.'"

My butt hits the edge of the table and I stumble.

"I forgot to wash the shirt last weekend, so it was still dirty from the week before. When Kaitlyn made those blueberry cupcakes, you remember. That food coloring got everywhere. She threw it all out that day because it caused such a mess."

I begin to edge around the table. He takes a few quick strides toward me and I stop. So does he.

"I was hoping no one would notice," he goes on. "The shirt I was wearing had blood on it, so what choice did I have? I had to change. You saw it, though. The stain on my shirt."

I look down at the dough. Gingerbread . . . the face . . . I can see it now. I can see Rory. I grab the rolling pin and glance at the swinging door. If I can make it to the door . . . Rory notices, and moves in closer.

"That night Magdalena left, I was out smoking when he walked by. I followed him," Rory sighs. "I wanted him to apologize, you know? For yelling at me and spitting in Magdalena's face. Like, no offense, but it was your mistake, not ours. He wouldn't, though." Rory clenches his fists. "People like that, I hate them. I thought just once I'm not gonna take it. So I picked up a brick."

"It's okay, Rory." My grip on the rolling pin tightens. "I won't tell anyone."

He looks at me sadly. "I didn't know how amazing it was going to feel. I mean, not at first. I really felt bad that night. But the next day, I felt awesome. Like I could do anything."

I have one chance. I lunge around the table and make a mad dash for the door.

Rory is faster, and grabs me around the waist. He whirls me around and puts his thick fingers around my neck, then starts to squeeze. I jab the rolling pin backwards at him frantically, but Rory won't stop.

Suddenly, there's a metallic clanging sound and he lets go. I drop to the floor and roll around, trying to breathe. Rory is on the floor, out cold. Kaitlyn is standing over us, a heavy cookie sheet in her hands. She lowers a hand down to help me up. And then she asks if I'm okay.

***

"So the dream, it came true?" Miss Petroni and I are sitting in her living room. It's been a few days since I almost died in my sister's shop and, while we're still dealing with police and trying to replace Rory, we are getting back to normal. Or some form of it.

"In a way, I suppose." I take a sip of Miss Petroni's herbal tea. Its warmth washes over me.

"The other day," she says, leaning forward and balancing her elbows on her knees, "I wasn't one hundred percent honest with you. I saw more than what I told you in your cup. Much more."

"Oh?" I say, taking another sip.

"It's possible that your mother had more than just one gift to pass along to her children. I think, maybe . . ." She pauses and smiles. "I can teach you to hone your skills. If you should want."

I'm taken aback by her statement. But I'm also totally onboard. "Yes. Yes, I want."

BULL DOG GRAVY

By Mark Thielman

A man from Appalachia who knows the difference between a scone and a biscuit also knows a thing or two about his boss's sudden death.

"Good morning, Bull Dog," Dr. Harris-Thanes said.

I took a slow drink of coffee from the delicate china cup. I preferred a mug for my morning joe, it held more. But the boss had rules. No mugs in the kitchen might have been one of the sillier ones.

I looked up from the newspaper and across the top of my cup at Harris-Thanes. "Mr. Smithson calls me Bull Dog because he pays for the privilege. If you wish to pay, you can as well. Otherwise, you'd best not."

His fingers made a small adjustment to the knot on his striped tie. "Apologies, Thomas. I meant no offense."

"None taken," I said. I had rules, too. I returned to the story I'd been reading. Sears, Roebuck had opened their first store here in Chicago; 1925 could be a good year for salesmen. I marked the article to clip for the boss. Among other things, he paid me to stay on top of the local news.

"Would it cost me more than a quid to find out why he calls you Bull Dog?"

I smiled. I had to admire the man's cheek. "How much is a quid?"

"About five dollars American."

"You can owe me the clams. Growing up in Appalachia, we'd eat bulldog gravy. Melt down some pork lard, mix in some flour and then thin it with water, or milk if you could afford it. Put a little cracked pepper in there if you had some. When it thickened back up to where you liked it, you had a meal."

"And you'd eat it like soup?" Harris-Thanes' lips pursed and his eyes narrowed.

"Nope, you slather bulldog gravy on a biscuit."

His face hardly seemed to show any relief. "Sounds like the ruination of a perfectly good biscuit," he said.

"Don't dismiss it until you've tried it." As I spoke, I reached toward the center of the table and picked up a biscuit from the table. "Don't tell Mrs. McCarthy I said so, but this batch of biscuits she prepared is stale, not up to snuff. Well, you pour a little bulldog on a biscuit that's been setting out for a day or so and it'll soften right up."

Harris-Thanes looked at the biscuit in my hand for a moment and then understanding flashed across his face. "You're talking about a scone, dear fellow. These language differences had me thoroughly flummoxed for a time."

"Come to this country, lose the high-falutin' language," I said. "Mr. Smithson will always call them biscuits."

A knock on the back-porch door interrupted us.

"Come," I said.

The door opened, and Buddy shuffled into the room. He lived at the farm down the road. The finery of the dining room contrasted with his hobnail boots and torn overalls. His eyes stayed rooted on the rug as he spoke. "Looking for Mr. Smithson. Owes me some money."

"He's not available, Buddy," I said.

"Owes me some money," he repeated.

"And what does he owe you?" I knew I should send him away until he could deal with Mr. Smithson. But the encroaching mansions had made life hard for working farmers like Buddy's family. The family likely needed the money.

His eyes came up to look at me. As they returned to the floor, I saw them linger over the remaining biscuits on the table. "Shot two squirrels for him. Said he pay me a nickel apiece."

I fished a dime from my pocket and laid it on the table. I put an extra nickel there as well.

His hand shot out and scooped up the dime, leaving the other coin behind.

"Momma said to not take charity from the man who aims to push us off our land," he said, answering the unasked question.

"Did you skin them for him as well?"

He nodded.

"I believe Mr. Smithson intended to pay for the cleaning, too. Before you ankle back yonder, sit down and have a biscuit while we decide."

Quickly taking a seat, he tucked a napkin into the neck of his shirt. He snapped off a crisp piece of biscuit, scattering bits across the table, and shoved it into his mouth.

Harris-Thanes tapped his index finger against his lips. "Tell me, Buddy, do you like to hunt?"

The boy nodded while chewing.

Harris-Thanes reached into his pocket and pulled out a revolver. “Hunt them with something like this?”

My reflexes pushed back when I saw the piece.

Buddy swallowed before speaking. “No, sir. I gots me a rifle.”

Harris-Thanes nodded and returned the gun to his pocket. I breathed easier once the rod was out of sight. He then shifted his focus to me. “So, Mr. Smithson has nicknamed you for a gravy?” The doctor’s face still looked pursed as if he had bitten into a lemon, but now his eyes were wide.

“Bulldogs are a tenacious breed. Bulldog gravy can keep a farmer full through a day of planting. As his jack-of-all-trades, I guess he thinks I’m able to go all day until I finish the task he assigns me. And we’re both from Kentucky.”

“Interesting,” Dr. Harris-Thanes said.

“Rounding out your psychological picture, Mind-Doctor?”

“I’ll tell you, but you’ll have to give me my quid back.” As he spoke, the corners of Harris-Thanes mouth were upturned in a small smile.

At that moment, I almost liked the man.

Dr. Harris-Thanes had arrived from London several months back with a steamer trunk full of degrees and letters of recommendation, attesting to his skill in treating disorders of the mind. Mr. Smithson had hired him to advise on matters psychological. The boss had come out of Kentucky many years before me with barely two nickels in his pocket. He had managed to amass a fortune by his natural ability to know what the public wanted to buy before they did. Perhaps he knew how to convince them that they needed what he had. He was a master at separating other people from their money. His talent had allowed him to buy this three-story house just outside of Chicago as well as the mahogany table around which I and Dr. Harris-Thanes presently passed a quid back and forth. It paid for the carriage house out back where Dr. Harris-Thanes performed his psychological experiments, training rats to ring bells and to run mazes. He and Mr. Smithson expected to have the research published soon in the *Gentleman’s Journal of Psychology*. It also paid Mrs. McCarthy’s wages to bake beaten biscuits for him every day, the labor-intensive kind that required the dough to be rolled again and again through her prized biscuit kneader until they were layered and satiny. The firm texture and subtle flavor made them delicious. Delicious that is, until today.

Mrs. McCarthy pushed through the kitchen door holding her favorite spatula in one hand and a pan of biscuits in the other. A solid woman with a bun of grey hair and a flour-spackled apron, she waved the spatula nervously. Mr. Smithson had hired her for cooking and housekeeping when he built this place a year ago. "I'm sorry to keep you waiting on breakfast, boys, but Mr. Smithson had a note on the door, barring me from the kitchen. I finally worked up the nerve to push through and found the kitchen a complete mess. He stayed up last night cooking, if you can believe that malarkey. I didn't get this morning's breakfast going until late. He left the place a fright. I even had to clean off this pan before I could make the breakfast." As she spoke, she worked her old spatula under a row of biscuits, dropping a pair of hot ones onto my plate. Behind on the pan she left a thin trail of crust where her spatula, bent with age, could no longer scrape the pan evenly.

"Mrs. McCarthy," I said, holding up my hot biscuit to show where the crust had been left behind, "that tool of yours is leaving the best parts stuck to the pan. When are you going to replace it?"

"You'll not speak ill about my Matilda." She raised the spatula as if to strike. "Matilda and I have been making biscuits together since before you were born. Someday, you'll understand about not discarding something valuable just because it gets some years on it."

"Mrs. McCarthy, Mr. Smithson wouldn't dream of replacing you," I said.

I looked to Harris-Thanes seeking an ally, but he wouldn't make eye contact. Perhaps his mind was off somewhere drawing another psychological picture.

He focused his attention on Mrs. McCarthy. "Was Smithson up late then, tying up the kitchen?"

"Mr. Smithson was banging pots until all hours. His right, since it is his kitchen." Her tone suggested that she didn't really believe her own last statement.

"Of course, it is," he said. "I merely wondered if he might be sleeping in and I had time to retire to the laboratory for some research."

She nodded. "I expect you have time to go to the carriage house and play with your pets."

His face returned to the pursed lip, offended look. "That is research in behaviorism, Mrs. McCarthy."

"Aye, and the boy down the street teaches his dog to fetch sticks. And that's a game."

I sat back in my chair, my big mitt swallowing my china cup. I took a dainty sip. I was in no hurry. If this battle turned to blows, I wanted to stick around to watch. Dr. Harris-Thanes and Mrs. McCarthy would fight in about the same weight class. She, of course, packed Matilda. He had brains aplenty. I wondered whether a student could study alley-brawling at Cambridge or Oxford or whatever school he had attended.

The bell had just sounded for the start of the second round when we heard the gunshot.

I took the stairs two at a time. At the landing, I headed straight for Smithson's bedroom. I grabbed the knob and prepared to force it with my shoulder. He usually kept the door locked. The door swung open and I nearly fell inside. I quick-stepped a couple of times to regain my balance. Although the bed remained unmade, nothing else looked out of the ordinary. I felt myself relax. I took a deep breath. The curtains fluttered in the morning breeze. The far window stood open. Calling for the boss, I moved to the foot of the bed. There I saw Mr. Smithson on the floor. I didn't need a degree from Oxford or Cambridge to tell me he was dead. It was as obvious as the hole in his face. He clutched a revolver in his hand.

I heard footsteps nearing the top of the stairs. I turned around. The others stood at the landing. I stepped out and closed the bedroom door. "Nobody needs to go in there. Mr. Smithson is dead."

Mrs. McCarthy started to wail. I sent Buddy down to call the police. Harris-Thanes wanted to see Mr. Smithson. "I'm a doctor," he said.

"And if he was a rat, you'd be the first one through the door. But he ain't, so you're not."

He gave me a stern look, like he was thinking about trying to force the issue. His fists clenched, and I could see his jaw muscles tighten.

"Think hard, Doctor," I said. "You might finish a crossword puzzle before I could write down the first word, but you take one more step toward this door and I'll put you down like I'm Jack Dempsey and you're some glass-jawed palooka."

His lip quivered a bit, but then he spun on his heels. "I'll be in the office." He stomped down the hall and went into the second-floor study, the room where he and Mr. Smithson met for their talks.

"Mrs. McCarthy, the police will be here soon. They'll be expecting coffee."

"I better make some sandwiches," she said. As she spoke, she sniffled and fanned herself with her hand. Mrs. McCarthy slowly started down the stairs, keeping a tight grip on the bannister.

When everyone had departed, I went back into the bedroom. The police might prove a problem. I read the papers. Chicago wanted this part of the county and claimed it. The county didn't want to share the tax money they made from all the rich people living out here. Deputies and flat-foots might soon be having a stand-off, getting in each other's way and doing their best to confound the other, more concerned with winning than in solving. I wanted to get a good look at things before they got here.

I tried to memorize everything. The window stood half-open, the curtains fluttering toward me. The boss, I knew, liked to sleep with fresh air. He said he learned it from reading Ben Franklin, another poor boy who made good. That was the boss, always reading, always thinking. "Bull Dog," he once told me, "I'll be the brains, you be the muscle. Between us, we know our onions." Looked like today, I was going to have to find other brains.

The boss lay on the floor in his robe, although he called it a dressing gown. He'd grown up poor like me, but while I was big and expected to work outside, he'd been small and skinny. He soaked up information like a sponge. That's why he'd invited Dr. Harris-Thanes to live here. Mr. Smithson had a thick, well-marked psychology textbook on his nightstand. Although he had a natural ability to know what people wanted, the boss wanted to learn about what the psychologists thought. "I'm marrying theory and practice, Bull Dog," he told me.

His sightless eyes stared up at the ceiling. The fatal wound appeared raised and red on the hairline side before collapsing into the bullet's hole. Blood-matted hair fell back over the wound, obscuring the injury. I didn't bend down to move the hair for a better view. I'd seen enough gunshot wounds in the trenches of France. Besides, I expected the police to arrive shortly, and I didn't want them to find me tampering with Mr. Smithson's body. In the battle between the city and county forces, I had no interest in becoming a prize.

On the bed sat a tray with a half-empty soup bowl, dirty napkin and a plate, littered with a few remaining shards of biscuit. I touched the plate, picking up a small piece and tasting it. I studied the tray, lifted a spoonful of soup and smelled it. It reminded me of home. I searched the bed, expecting to see a letter, some explanation for why he might have done this. The pillows showed a tortured final night's sleep, all askew and tossed. He had written nothing. I thumbed through the pages of the textbook, but again found no note.

I hustled down the hall to the study. Going inside, I found Harris-Thanes sitting in a chair, staring out the window. He glanced my way and then returned his gaze outside. Perhaps he was mourning Mr. Smithson or maybe trying to figure out what he would do now that his research benefactor and landlord had died. That was something we'd all have to set our minds to.

I bent over the desk. “I’m looking for anything before the coppers start grubbing around in here.” Beneath a lead paperweight lay Mr. Smithson’s check register. He’d often given me checks to deliver as part of my duties. I opened it. One check showed to have been written but the amount and payee had not been recorded. Although unusual for the meticulous Mr. Smithson, it told me nothing about why he might have shot himself. I closed the book.

I joined Harris-Thanes at the window.

“Suicide,” he said, his gaze not shifting from outside.

“How do you know?”

Harris-Thanes turned toward me. He had pulled off his tie. When he spoke, his voice seemed to come from deep in his throat. “All this talk about psychology. I don’t think he could square what we discussed with his own predetermined notions. He had begun to show signs of melancholy.”

“Don’t blame yourself,” I said. “I have to agree that recently the boss hadn’t seemed himself. After years of seeking to shed his roots, he had lately become fascinated with talking about my memories of Kentucky. Can’t pretend to be something you’re not, he’d tell me. A four-flusher will eventually be found out.”

Harris-Thanes nodded quietly. “We had some of the same conversations.”

“But wouldn’t you expect to find a note?”

“Not necessarily. The deviant mind does not operate like the rest of the world.” Harris-Thanes slipped now into the role of lecturer. “Although we might expect and hope for some explanation, Mr. Smithson had been hiding behind an illusory self for some time. While he might not be able to live with himself, I’m not at all surprised that he would be unable to come completely clean in the distress of his final hour.”

I chewed on what he said, although some of the words slipped past me.

“Let me ask you this, Thomas. Would you consider the men of Kentucky to be taciturn?”

I didn’t say anything, not being quite sure what that word meant either.

“Would you expect a man of your area to talk or to act?”

“Coal can’t be talked out of the ground.”

Harris-Thanes nodded. “I theorize that Mr. Smithson departed this world as a Kentucky man would.”

I left Harris-Thanes and his dictionary-mouth sitting in the chair. Back in the kitchen, Mrs. McCarthy moved aimlessly. She watched the coffee pot and then stepped to the crockery bowl where she mixed up more biscuit dough. Then, she stopped and, gathering up Matilda like an old friend, scraped a biscuit pan, leaving behind the familiar streaks of crust. On the stove sat the big cast iron pot where Mr. Smithson had crafted his last meal.

Mrs. McCarthy saw me looking at it. "He didn't even use the new pots. Pulled out that old thing."

"Everyone knows that burgoo has got to be made in a cast iron pot. It's a stew to sit over a campfire and cook until it's thick enough to hold a spoon upright. Cook the squirrel meat first and then add the potatoes, corn, tomatoes, and anything else a boy might've killed or dug up. My people always added a little cider vinegar."

She looked at me differently, surprised that I knew something about cooking.

"Maw raised me after Paw died," I said.

Mrs. McCarthy picked up the wooden spoon alongside the stove, turned the stew a couple of times, and then let go. The spoon remained upright for a moment and then began to list. She caught the handle before it fell inside the pot. "It does look ready."

"Of course, the best thing about a burgoo was that cooking up a batch became a community activity. With slow cooking, a group had time to do other things. Play games, swap stories, or set the table."

Mrs. McCarthy's shoulders began to quake. Turning her back to me, she skipped the biscuit brake and set to work, pounding the biscuit dough with a paddle, flattening and folding and then flattening some more.

Through the kitchen window, I saw the police cars beginning to arrive. The sheriff and the city boys jockeyed for position in the driveway. I feared we might have more gunshots outside the house than inside if calm heads didn't prevail.

I heard footsteps on the staircase. Dr. Harris-Thanes joined me at the window along with Mrs. McCarthy. Together, we watched a gauntlet form, city police along one line, sheriff deputies along the other. In the middle, a senior deputy and a police sergeant met. Everything began calmly enough, both men quietly discussing the situation. Soon, however, the gestures became more stabbing and the volume increased. The sergeant had his finger up in the face of the deputy, shaking it vigorously. Both men's faces grew red.

Through the window, I could feel the tension escalate. "So, Mind-Doctor, how would you handle this problem if these were your rats?"

"I'd toss a cat in the maze and start with fresh rats."

"Any volunteers to be the cat?" I asked.

Hearing nobody speak up, I opened the door and stepped

outside. As I walked toward the two men, I felt all eyes on me. Glancing back, I saw that Mrs. McCarthy and Dr. Harris-Thanes had followed me out onto the back porch.

"I'll tell you again, this is county jurisdiction . . ." the deputy said, unaware of my approach, his face now nearly purple with rage.

I coughed as I neared them. "Will you gentlemen excuse me for a moment?"

Both the deputy and the sergeant wheeled on me, their faces showing surprise.

Questions flew from both.

"Who the blazes are you?"

"What do you want?"

I kept my voice low and calm. I nodded to Wilson, the chief deputy, and introduced myself to the flat-foot sarge. "My name is Thomas. I am . . . was an assistant to Mr. Smithson. I'd like you to meet some people."

They followed me down the parallel lines of steely-eyed law enforcement officers. I walked them to the back porch and made the introductions. Buddy had reappeared and stood alongside the others.

"Hello, Buddy," the deputy said. Buddy, it seemed, was no stranger to the sheriff's boys.

"And this," I said, "is Dr. Harris-Thanes. He is a doctor of psychology."

The deputy and sergeant both took a step backwards. While I'd been jawing in the yard, Harris-Thanes had slipped on a tweed jacket paired with an ascot. He looked like the picture of English gentry. The men he stood among only wore a napkin like that at meal times.

"Gentlemen," he said, "I have been giving considerable thought to the psychological profile of Mr. Smithson, with special emphasis upon his last days. I believe the key is a Freudian complex rooted in the hardships of his youth. The vicissitudes of his meager childhood existence created a transference/counter-transference problem resulting in conflicted relationships. This was manifested in a host of odd rules around his household. The inner conflict eventually overwhelmed him and despite his strong outer appearance, his inner psyche was little more than a house of cards. He feared being revealed as a fraud. Smithson, I'm afraid, escaped the conflict through suicide, classic behaviorism."

"Biscuits."

The deputy, the sergeant, Harris-Thanes, everyone on the porch turned to look at me.

"Biscuits," I said again.

"Pardon, old man," Harris-Thanes said.

"No," I corrected, "I don't think a pardon is likely. I was trying hard to listen to what you were saying, trying to cut through the fog of some of them ten-dollar words, that's two quid by the way. I think you're right about Mr. Smithson having some ideas because he grew up poor. And I think that your talking to him about it might have made things worse, like scratching when you've been in poison ivy spreads the stuff, rather than gritting your teeth and ignoring the itch."

Buddy's hand began scratching at his forearm.

Deputy Wilson spoke. "Hush up, Bull Dog, we was larning."

I didn't threaten to charge him for the use of the nickname. The law gets certain privileges. To my mind, however, it bought me the right to continue.

"Mr. Smithson got to thinking about his poor days. He even got the notion to make himself up a batch of burgoo. Do you gentlemen know what burgoo is?" I didn't wait for the answer. "It's a thick stew made out of whatever you have around the house—just a whole bunch of mixed up ingredients."

I looked to the lawmen, who nodded understanding about the recipe although their eyes showed no clue how it related to the case.

"Dr. Harris-Thanes' psychology is a bit like that burgoo. I don't get all the words, but he mixes up his Dr. Freud and his rat training like he's out making a psychological burgoo. I could show you in the textbook Mr. Smithson had beside his bed. That's why he fired this quack."

Their eyes shifted to Harris-Thanes.

"Classic guilt transference," Harris-Thanes said, "entrusted to protect Smithson, he . . ."

"Like I was saying," I growled, drowning out the doctor before he could wind up again. "Mr. Smithson has a psychology book on his bedside, he smelled this four flusher out. Told me so in a roundabout way that I didn't pick up on until I listened to Harris-Thanes babble. I think he fired the man last night. If you look in his check register, you'll see Smithson wrote out a final check. He had the decency to give this man his final pay, but he didn't have time to record the amount in the registry before Harris-Thanes hit him over the head."

Harris-Thanes spoke slowly as if to an unruly child. "Classic transference, gentlemen. He overlooks the fact that Mr. Smithson was shot."

All eyes on the porch shifted back to me.

"When you look at the wound, you'll see swelling on the forehead. He got whacked first and then shot. You'll also find a pillow missing from the bed. Mrs. McCarthy makes his bed, she'll help you there. Harris-Thanes used the pillow to muffle the shot. My guess is he carried the pillow's remains outside to his laboratory in the carriage house, probably hidden inside a feed sack for them laboratory rats."

Harris-Thanes shook his head slowly from side to side. "But I was with you, old man, when we heard the shot."

The eyes darted back to me.

"He trains rats to pull levers. That is his research. Getting one of his white mice to pull a trigger is nothing more than a science experiment. I'll wager you'll find the apparatus in the lab along with the un-cashed check from Smithson. My bet is that he set it up in the office. Although Mr. Smithson was killed in his bedroom, I reckon the shot came from the office. We all heard a shot from upstairs. One of them trained, bar-pressing rats did fire that pistol while Harris-Thanes deposited himself down here, using me as his alibi. When I went into Mr. Smithson's bedroom, the body felt cool and there was no smell of gunpowder."

"He always kept the window open," Mrs. McCarthy said.

"But the breeze blew into the room. The smell should have hit me in the face when I entered the room. I smelled nothing. The doctor, meanwhile, scurried down to the study."

"Because you barred my entrance, Thomas."

"You played me like a cheap fiddle."

Mrs. McCarthy spoke up again. "You mentioned biscuits."

I nodded. "The biscuits are the key. Beaten biscuits are hard work."

Both the deputy and the sergeant muttered agreement. Biscuits were something that coppers understood.

"When Mr. Smithson made burgoo to remember his hard-scrabble youth, he wouldn't want beaten biscuits. They are eaten by people with money enough to hire others to do the beating and folding. He'd have made drop biscuits, the baking powder substitutes for all the effort. We can all tell the difference by the crumbs they leave behind."

"Yep," Buddy said.

I pointed to Harris-Thanes. "All of us except this man. He calls them scones and never thinks about biscuits. When he thought up this play to explain Mr. Smithson's death, he didn't know that the burgoo wasn't thick enough to serve or that the biscuits Mrs. McCarthy made yesterday weren't the right kind. Mr. Smithson's final meal doesn't prove suicide, it proves you murdered him."

"Absurd theory and hardly court evidence even if believed," Harris-Thanes said. "Now, if you gentlemen will excuse me, I'd rather not stand here and be slandered." He took a step off the porch.

"Oh, I think we can get courtroom proof," I said. "Don't let him get away, boys, and don't let him reach into his coat pocket."

The deputy and the sergeant both grabbed an arm and held him fast.

"Let's hear it," the sergeant said.

I faced Harris-Thanes. "You made a point to show us all the gun at the table this morning. Then I watched Mrs. McCarthy scrape the biscuit pan with Matilda, her favorite spatula. It left behind scrapes of biscuit crust. Got me to thinking about something I read a while back. The newspaper had a story of scientific thinkers over at the University of Chicago using a microscope to compare bullets. As a shot goes down the barrel, it picks up marks and scrapes just like Matilda makes on that pan. By comparing the killing bullet to a bullet from Mr. Smithson's gun, I'll wager that they don't match. Then, check them against the rod that Harris-Thanes keeps in his pocket."

The sergeant patted the outside of the coat, and then, reaching in, withdrew a revolver.

"Why don't you come down to the station with me, Doctor. Me and the boys would like to discuss psychology with you," the sergeant said.

"Nope, he's coming with us," the deputy said.

While a human tug-of-war broke out on the porch between the officers, Mrs. McCarthy, Buddy, and I went inside.

We sat around the dining room table.

"Poor Mr. Smithson," Mrs. McCarthy said.

"But I'm sure somehow he knows that your cooking helped to catch the killer," I told her.

She smiled at the thought. "Would you boys like a biscuit?"

And I didn't need a Mind-Doctor to know the answer to that one.

MORSELS OF THE GODS

By Victoria Thompson

On a warm summer's night on Long Island, what could be more delightful than a marshmallow roast, even if the host for the evening has some decidedly unpleasant habits.

Long Island, NY
Summer of 1900

"I can see why you chose this place for your cottage," Elizabeth Decker said, inhaling the deliciously clean air as she and her oldest friend, Anna Wilsey, strolled along the seaside path. The sight and sound of the waves breaking gently along the shore was a welcome change from the urgent din outside her home in New York City. Anna's invitation to visit her on Long Island had been most welcome.

"I didn't choose it," Anna said. "That was all Humphrey's doing. But let's not talk about him. Let's talk about something happy. Tell me about your grandchildren."

Elizabeth liked nothing better than talking about her grandchildren, so Elizabeth shared more than one story as they strolled. "And how are your children doing?" she asked at last.

Anna sighed. "The boys are doing well, but I don't see them as often as I would like. You know what they say, a son is yours till he takes a wife."

"But a daughter is yours all her life," Elizabeth finished for her. "So you must see Lily. She's finished school, hasn't she?"

"Yes, but she's still in Switzerland."

"Still? She must be very happy there, although I never could understand why you sent her so far away."

"It was, uh, for the school. Madame Baptiste's. A friend had told me about it, and Lily insisted."

"When is she coming home?"

"I . . . she always spends her holidays with friends. Come along. You must see this." They had reached the end of the seawall that protected the house from the ravages of the ocean, and Anna led the way up a small dune so that their return trip would take them along the other side of the wall. “Here,” she said with a flourish.

“What beautiful flowers,” Elizabeth said. Enormous flowering shrubs lined the entire length of the wall on this side. “I don’t think I’ve ever seen plants like this before.”

“They’re called oleander. I’m told they don’t usually grow this far north, but the wall shelters them from the worst of the storms, and Vincent, our gardener . . .” She gestured to the man at work a few yards ahead of them. “He covers them when it gets too cold. The previous owner of this property was from the South, and she brought them with her to hide this ugly wall. They are the only things left from the house that Humphrey tore down to build his mausoleum.”

“Mausoleum?” Elizabeth glanced up at the lovely Italianate villa. “Surely, that’s not how you think of it.”

“I try not to think of it at all. Elizabeth, you have no idea. But I promised myself I wouldn’t burden you with my problems.” She smiled determinedly. “You and Felix came to enjoy yourselves, and we intend to keep you entertained while you’re here.”

Anna’s forced smile didn’t fool Elizabeth, who had known her since childhood. Humphrey was Anna’s second husband. They hadn’t married for love, but Elizabeth had believed her old friend to be at least content. What could have changed? She would find out before their visit ended.

“These flowers are so fragrant,” she said as they walked along. “We should cut some for the house.”

“Have a care there, ma’am,” the gardener called when Elizabeth reached for the nearest cluster of blossoms.

Startled, Elizabeth dropped her hand. “What’s wrong?”

“Nothing at all, ma’am,” the gardener said, hurrying over and pulling off his cap. “I didn’t mean to scare you. It’s just that touching them can give some people a rash.”

“You mean like poison ivy?”

“Yes,” Anna said. “That’s why Vincent is wearing gloves. And why we don’t cut them for the house, even though they do smell wonderful.”

“Thank you for the warning,” Elizabeth told him.

Vincent bobbed his head and returned to his trimming.

“How odd that the previous owners chose such a dangerous plant,” Elizabeth said.

“Yes, it is odd,” Anna said, frowning thoughtfully at the lush growth.

Was she brooding again? Elizabeth couldn’t allow that. “So tell me what you have planned for us this weekend now that you’ve managed to lure us away from the city."

Anna looped her arm through Elizabeth's, like they were school girls. "Well, tonight we're going to have a marshmallow roast."

***

"A marshmallow roast?" Felix echoed when Elizabeth told him. She and her husband had retired to their lavishly furnished guest room to dress for dinner, but they were waiting for their servants to arrive to assist them. "What's a marshmallow?"

Elizabeth looked up from removing her sand-filled shoes. "Some kind of confection. They were invented in France."

"France. Of course." Her husband gave her an affectionate peck on the forehead on his way to hang his suit jacket in the wardrobe. His hair was now more silver than gold, and the years had carved lines in his face, but that only made him more appealing. Why did men grow more handsome with age while women just got old? "So explain to me how one roasts a piece of candy."

"It's not candy. I said it's a *confection*. Apparently, it's made of the root of some kind of plant. The mallow plant, that's it."

"Ah, yes, hence the name."

She glared at him with feigned disapproval. "Anyway, they mix it with other things and pour it into a mold so it comes out kind of rounded, like a dome."

"You still haven't explained the roasting part." He came back and sat down beside her on the sofa that their thoughtful hostess had placed in front of the fireplace, just in case the evenings got chilly.

"From what Anna said, we'll roast them on a fire, out on the beach."

"You mean *outside*?"

Elizabeth gave him a pitying look. "I don't think building a fire on the dining room table is at all practical, dear."

"Why can't we just roast them in the fireplace?"

"I have no idea, but after she explained it to me, I remembered reading about these marshmallow roasts in the society pages. Young people do it for fun when they visit the shore."

"Oh no, are we expected to have fun during this visit?" Felix asked with mock horror. "I suppose we'll be sitting around the fire singing 'Daisy Bell' or something."

Elizabeth gave him a playful swat. "No one will force you to sing, I'm sure. But I don't know how much fun we're going to have here. Anna seems very troubled. I'm worried about her."

"What does she have to be troubled about? She's married to one of the richest men in the country who just built her a beachfront villa."

"Rich people have problems, too. We've certainly had our share."

"But none at the moment, thank heaven, except possibly being immolated while roasting marshmallows."

"Anna says Humphrey is very fond of marshmallows."

Felix winced. "From the looks of him, Humphrey is fond of anything edible."

***

"They're morsels of the gods," Humphrey announced when Felix asked him about the marshmallows later at dinner. Elizabeth had been seated to Humphrey's right, although she would have preferred being seated elsewhere. Humphrey wasn't much for conversation unless the subject was himself. Or marshmallows, apparently.

"Morsels of the gods, eh? That's high praise indeed," Felix said from the other end of the table where he'd been seated at Anna's right. "And very poetic."

"Humphrey didn't make that up," Anna said. "He read it in the newspaper."

"It's still true," Humphrey insisted. "You're in for a treat."

"If Humphrey lets us have any," Mr. Rogers said. He and his wife were two of the four neighbors who had also been invited to dine with them and participate in the marshmallow roast. Mrs. Rogers was somewhat of a mouse, but her husband obviously wasn't cowed by Humphrey's wealth or bombast. "The last time, I tried to get seconds, but Humphrey had already eaten them all."

Humphrey patted his well-rounded stomach and laughed unrepentantly.

The maids were clearing the first course, which had been a delicious mock turtle soup accompanied by several kickshaws—or more correctly *quelque chose*, although Americans thought it an affectation to use the correct French pronunciation—of oysters, olives, celery, and pickles. Because there were eight of them at table, they also had a dish of minced meat and one of sole baked with tomato sauce, which were called sides because they lined the sides of the table. Removing all these dishes and setting the next course was a major undertaking. The contents of the plates not only had to be artfully arranged, but the platters themselves had to be carefully placed, along with bouquets of flowers and bowls of fruit, to provide balance, symmetry, and visual surprise to the table. Or so the etiquette books demanded.

Two young maids worked efficiently to remove all of the first course dishes and replace them with the second course, which consisted of a roast of beef and sides of roast chicken, spring peas, and a green salad. While the maids labored, Elizabeth tried to engage Humphrey in conversation, but he didn't even seem to notice. He was too interested in what the girls were bringing in.

But no, not the food. He was really just interested in the girls themselves. They were both lithe and fresh-faced. They most likely lived locally and had been hired for the summer, taking advantage of the opportunity to serve the wealthy residents who came out to Long Island to escape the city's unbearable heat each summer.

Humphrey's gimlet gaze followed their every move and studied every inch of them with an interest far too prurient to be proper. If he was inappropriately aware of them, they seemed more than cautiously aware of him. They moved unusually quickly when removing the dishes closest to him and watched him intently as they did so. Once he reached out and the maid darted away, leaving the dish she'd been reaching for behind. Her expression never changed, but her eyes blazed with fury.

Oh dear, no wonder Anna was unhappy. Elizabeth knew some men saw the help as fair game, but she'd never expected to find one was married to a friend. She looked down the table and saw Anna glaring at Humphrey, although her efforts were wasted. He didn't spare his wife so much as a glance.

What could a woman do when her husband thought he had a right to molest the servants? Short of leaving him, precious little, and leaving him would hardly solve the problem. Every young girl who passed through his life would still be at risk.

Poor Anna.

By the time they had finished the final course of their dinner—a lavish spread of sweetcakes, candies, and assorted berries which were in season on Long Island at the moment—darkness had settled securely over the island. After the guests had donned jackets and wraps as proof against the cool ocean breezes, Anna and Humphrey led them out through the French doors to the patio, then down the boardwalk that led almost to the ocean's edge.

The tide was out, leaving a nice expanse of smooth sand. The servants had built a fire, and someone had anchored torches in the sand so their blaze lit the area brightly. Wooden deck chairs were placed around the fire, and a table held the marshmallows. A domed silver tray sat in the center of the pristinely white tablecloth among arrangements of candies, fresh fruit, and flowers. Finally, and somewhat curiously, a pile of sticks also lay beside the silver dome.

"Are we supposed to eat the kindling, too?" Felix whispered, eying the pile of wood suspiciously.

But Humphrey was instructing the guests to take seats around the fire. When everyone had done so, he signaled to his manservant to lift the cover from the silver tray. Beneath it lay a mound of white globs as artfully arranged as anything they had seen at dinner.

"Behold," Humphrey said, gesturing grandly. "These delightful creations are delicious as you see them here, but when they are roasted—delicately roasted, I might caution you—their size nearly doubles and their flavor explodes into—"

"Morsels of the gods," Anna finished impatiently. "Just show them what to do and let's get on with it."

Humphrey scowled at her as he picked up one of the sticks. "One end has been sharpened for your convenience. Then you take a marshmallow like this . . ." He carefully chose one from the pile and, to everyone's amazement, stuck it onto the end of the stick.

"Well, I never," Mrs. Kilgallen said. She and her husband were the other neighbors who had been invited. "You can't expect us to eat something after you've driven a filthy stick through it."

"Suit yourself," Humphrey said. "More for the rest of us!"

"You won't mind a bit once you taste it," Mrs. Rogers assured her.

But the look on Mrs. Kilgallen's face said differently.

"Then you hold it over the fire," Humphrey continued, stepping forward to demonstrate. "Not in the flames. Don't want to char it. Just hold it over the coals and keep turning it while it gets brown."

They all watched, fascinated, as he carefully minded the roasting of the confection, turning it from pure white to golden brown. To their astonishment, it also swelled, nearly doubling in size.

"And now, it's ready to eat," Humphrey said, raising the marshmallow to his lips.

But Anna snatched the stick from him before he could take a bite. "Don't be rude, Humphrey. "The first one should go to a guest. Elizabeth, I believe this one is yours."

One of the maids helped Anna slide the gooey marshmallow onto a plate.

Humphrey grumbled, but Anna said, "Don't fuss. Look, here's Jenny with another one."

One of the maids handed Humphrey a stick with three marshmallows stuck on it, which seemed to placate their host. Meanwhile, the other maids had affixed marshmallows to the other sticks and were passing them to the remaining guests.

Felix took his gingerly. "Is this really as good as we've been told?" he asked the girl.

"I wouldn't know, sir. They're too dear for the likes of me," she replied with a shy smile.

"Here, taste mine," Elizabeth offered. Felix accepted the bite Elizabeth had gotten onto her fork. The look on his face as he savored it was rapturous, and when Elizabeth took a bite for herself, she almost moaned in delight as the delicate sweetness exploded on her tongue.

Everyone agreed that marshmallows were indeed morsels of the gods, even Mrs. Kilgallen.

Humphrey managed to eat at least half a dozen, but everyone else got as many as they wanted, too, so no one complained. When the last of the marshmallows was gone, the servants passed around the fruit and sweets, but no one was particularly interested. Instead they simply enjoyed relaxing by the fire. The servants added more wood to make it flare up again.

"Should we sing?" Felix asked.

"If you dare, I'll skewer you with my marshmallow stick," Mr. Kilgallen joked.

"Too late," Mrs. Rogers said. "The servants threw them into the fire."

"Ooooohhh, I shouldn't have had that last marshmallow," Humphrey said, clutching at his stomach.

"You always do eat too much," Anna said. "Jenny, run along to the house and prepare one of Mr. Wilsey's stomach powders."

The girl hurried off as Humphrey groaned again. He sounded as if he were in real distress. "I think I'd better get back to the house before I embarrass myself," he muttered. He pushed himself out of his deck chair and started toward the boardwalk.

He'd only gone a few steps when he staggered, and one of the male servants hurried to assist him.

"Maybe I should go with him," Felix said.

"He's fine," Anna said. "He always eats so much that he makes himself sick, but then he's fine by morning."

***

Except he wasn't fine by morning. They'd heard him being disgustingly sick all night, and Anna had finally summoned the doctor.

"I'm so sorry about this," Anna said to Elizabeth and Felix when they came down to breakfast and had gotten a full report on Humphrey's condition. "He's never been this sick before."

"It's probably just something he ate," Elizabeth said. "They don't call it Summer Complaint for nothing."

"I suppose so, but I hate for this to happen while you're here."

"Don't worry about us. Humphrey's welfare is the important thing," Felix said.

"Excuse me, Mrs. Wilsey," the maid, Jenny, said from the doorway. "The doctor would like to see you."

Anna made her apologies and hurried out, but the girl just stood there. Only then did Elizabeth notice how pale she was.

"Are you all right, Jenny?"

The girl raised a work-reddened hand to her forehead. "I . . . yes, ma'am." And then she fled.

***

"Humphrey is dead," Anna said when she returned a short time later, looking more stunned than grief-stricken. "The doctor said it was his heart."

"But he was so sick . . ." Elizabeth said.

"It was the strain of it, the doctor said. And his heart was already overburdened, with him being such a large man and everything."

"We're so very sorry, Anna," Elizabeth said, trying not to think about Humphrey leering at the maidservants.

Anna probably wasn't thinking about that either, because she suddenly burst into tears. "He's dead," she said between gulping sobs. "He's really dead."

Elizabeth wrapped an arm around her and led her to the chair Felix had pulled out for her. Felix went to fetch something from the liquor cabinet while Elizabeth instructed the cook to make a fresh pot of tea.

For her part, Anna laid her head on her arms on the tabletop and wept convulsively. When Felix returned with a bottle of very expensive brandy, Elizabeth poured it into a teacup and urged Anna to take at least a sip. She was still crying so hard she almost choked, but after a few sips, she calmed a bit.

"I know how difficult this must be," Elizabeth said. "Please tell us what we can do to help you."

"I couldn't possibly ask you to do anything. You're my guests," she said.

After ignoring some more of Anna's protests, Elizabeth finally managed to convince Anna to retire to her room. A while later, a black ambulance wagon pulled up to take Humphrey's body away, and Felix suggested they walk down to the beach while that grim task was done.

"Poor Humphrey," Felix remarked as they made their leisurely way down the boardwalk to the shore.

Elizabeth disagreed. "Did you notice how Humphrey looked at the maids?"

Felix blinked in surprise, but he said, "As if he'd like to eat them along with the roast, you mean?"

"So you did notice. I hoped I was imagining it. I think Anna noticed, too, and was very upset by it."

Felix frowned. "But she was still devastated by his death. You saw the way she was sobbing."

They had reached the seawall, and she saw the gardener trimming the oleanders a short distance away. "Let's go this way."

"These are very pretty," Felix observed. "They smell nice, too."

"Don't touch them. They can give you a rash."

"How do you know that?" Felix asked.

Elizabeth just smiled grimly.

The gardener stopped his work as they approached and doffed the battered straw hat he'd been wearing to shade his face. She noticed he was once again wearing heavy gloves. "Good morning."

"Good morning," Elizabeth said. "Mrs. Wilsey was telling me these plants usually don't grow this far north." She glanced into the wheelbarrow where the gardener had placed the trimmings.

"That's right, ma'am. We're close enough to the mainland here that we miss a lot of the storms, but it still gets cold sometimes and I have to cover them with burlap to protect them. That's why I keep 'em trimmed. They could be twenty feet tall if I didn't."

Elizabeth indicated the cuttings in the wheelbarrow. "Those look like the sticks we used for the marshmallow roast last night."

"Oh, not them, ma'am. We'd never use them to roast anything. Couldn't risk having people handle them."

"Do you suppose they could make someone sick if they did use them to roast something?"

The gardener frowned, obviously not liking her question. "I wouldn't know, ma'am."

Felix noticed his discomfort, too. "We'd better be getting back, dear." He took her arm. "What was all that about?" he asked when they were out of earshot. "You can't think he used those plants to make Humphrey sick."

"Of course not, darling." She didn't think the gardener had anything to do with it at all. "Do you think Frank and Sarah would be at all suspicious of Humphrey's death if they were here?"

Their daughter, Sarah, had married Frank Malloy, formerly a detective sergeant with the New York City Police Department. Together they had solved quite a few murders, and Elizabeth and Felix had helped them a time or two.

Felix gave her question only a moment's thought. "I certainly hope not."

***

To their surprise, Anna came down for lunch. She had apparently recovered from her fit of weeping, and she appeared clear-eyed and rested.

"Felix and I know you must be wishing us gone, and we've arranged to leave in the morning, but is there anything we can do for you in the meantime?" Elizabeth asked as they enjoyed their meal of bean soup, cold sliced beef, and an assortment of kickshaws from the previous night's dinner.

"I couldn't ask you to do anything at all, not after seeing your visit ruined."

"Maybe I could help you write some letters."

"I've sent Humphrey's valet around to the neighbors to give them the news, and I telephoned Humphrey's office. I've written to my children and told Lily to come home immediately. I don't expect she'll get here in time for the funeral, but I imagine she'll commemorate Humphrey's passing in her own way."

Elizabeth wasn't sure what to say to that, so she merely nodded and changed the subject. Jenny came in soon after to clear the table for dessert. As she took the plates, Elizabeth got a closer look at the girl's hands. What she had mistaken for simple redness was actually a rash.

***

Felix had been invited to go fishing with Mr. Kilgallen, so Elizabeth found herself alone on the veranda with Anna after lunch, sitting in lounge chairs where they could enjoy the view of the oleanders and the ocean beyond.

"I know you said you didn't want to burden me with your problems," Elizabeth began, her heart lodged firmly in her throat as she forced herself to continue. "But I think I have figured out what those problems are."

"Yes, you could hardly miss Humphrey leering at those poor girls last night. But now . . . Well, I don't have to worry about that anymore."

"So you did know about Humphrey's . . . proclivities?"

"Oh, yes. I caught him forcing himself on a maid a few months after our marriage," Anna said with remarkable composure. "He claimed the girl had seduced him, and I pretended to believe him, but I knew the truth. I was more careful after that. I kept an eye on the younger girls, and I didn't hire any of them to be live-in help. Even still, I couldn't stop him completely. Heaven knows how many girls he forced himself on, and I was powerless to stop him."

"Do you think Jenny was one of them?"

Anna looked up in surprise. "Jenny? What makes you think that?"

"Because . . . oh, Anna, I don't know how to say this, but I think Jenny may have caused Humphrey's illness."

The color drained from Anna's face. "Why?"

"Because . . . remember Vincent warning us about the oleander? I asked him if it could make someone sick."

"Sick? You mean like Humphrey was? What did he say?"

"He said he didn't know."

Anna frowned. "He probably just didn't want to alarm you. Oleander is poisonous, but only if you were to eat the flowers or leaves or even the berries. No one does that, though, and I can't imagine how Jenny could have induced Humphrey to do such a thing."

"Vincent was trimming the bushes this morning, and I happened to notice how similar the trimmings looked to the sticks we used to roast the marshmallows. If someone used an oleander branch to roast a marshmallow . . ."

Anna stared out at the sea, her expression grim as she considered the implications. "I see, you think perhaps the marshmallow might somehow be poisoned by the stick."

"Jenny was the one who prepared Humphrey's marshmallows last night."

"Oh, Elizabeth, that is very far-fetched. How on earth did you come to a conclusion like that?"

"Because Jenny has a rash on her hands today, just as your gardener warned could happen to someone who handled oleander."

Anna had no argument for that. She stared back at Elizabeth in stunned silence for a long moment. "I see," she said at last. "And what do you propose we do about this?"

Elizabeth had thought of little else for the past several hours. "I don't think there's anything we really can do. There's no proof at all, of course."

"Because the servants burned the sticks, as they usually do."

"Exactly, and Jenny's rash could have been caused by anything."

"Then why did you bother to tell me all this, if you have no proof and there's nothing to be done?"

"Because if you have a murderer in your home, I thought you should be warned. She might also blame you for Humphrey's behavior or think you condoned it somehow and want to take revenge on you, too."

Anna reached up and pinched the bridge of her nose, as if to ward off a headache. "Thank you for the warning, Elizabeth. You've given me much to consider. Now I think I need to lie down for a while."

***

Anna didn't join them for dinner that night or breakfast the next morning. When their luggage had been loaded into the carriage that was to take Elizabeth and Felix to the train, Elizabeth went to Anna's room to say good-bye.

Anna, still in her dressing gown, sat at a window overlooking the seawall and the lush blooms of the oleanders. "Thank you for telling me your concerns about Jenny," she said when Elizabeth had thanked her for her hospitality and expressed her condolences one last time.

"I'm sorry if I upset you."

"You didn't, and I've decided I'd better tell you everything so you don't later decide to do something that will harm poor Jenny."

"But I wouldn't—"

"Don't protest. I know all about Sarah and her husband and how they like to solve murders, but Jenny isn't a murderer."

"Can you be sure?"

Anna smiled sadly. "I didn't tell you the worst of Humphrey's sins. He preferred young girls, but they didn't have to be maids. One day I caught him with Lily."

"Oh, no!" Elizabeth wanted to weep. "Why didn't you leave him, Anna?"

She laughed mirthlessly. "Because I wouldn't have had a penny to my name. Some women might have managed somehow, but I knew I couldn't. And Humphrey would have demanded guardianship of Lily since I wouldn't have been able to provide for her. The mere thought horrified me, so I sent Lily to Switzerland, which was as far away as I could manage."

"I'm surprised he was willing to pay for that."

"He was furious, of course, but we reached an agreement. I wouldn't blacken his name with gossip and he would support Lily. But it's been almost three years now, Elizabeth. Three long years since I've seen my girl, and even though she's finished with school, I didn't dare bring her home, not while Humphrey was here."

"So you decided to kill him."

"But I didn't. At least not until yesterday, when we were out walking and I told you about the oleanders. I didn't know if it would kill him, but I thought it was worth a try."

"So you enlisted poor Jenny."

"No, she didn't know anything about it. I just told her I'd prepared a special stick for Mr. Wilsey's marshmallows, and she was to make sure he used it."

"And afterwards, they burned all the sticks."

"They always do. Besides, you know what the doctor said. It was his heart."

"Yes, his heart."

"Are you going to tell the police?"

"Tell them what?" Elizabeth asked, not bothering to hide her frustration. "That you poisoned your husband with a stick that no longer even exists?"

"He deserved it, Elizabeth. You have no idea how many girls he has assaulted."

And she didn't want to know. Just having seen the way he looked at the maids still made her shudder. "Don't worry, Anna. Your secret is safe with me."

***

"I don't understand why you want to leave," Felix said as they made their way outside to the carriage. "I thought you'd want to stay and help Anna plan the funeral at least."

"I just think our presence is more of a burden than a help," Elizabeth hedged. She couldn't share Anna's confession with him. He might insist on calling in the police after all, causing a scandal even if there was no way of proving what had killed Humphrey. She couldn't take that chance.

Jenny met them in the front hall to show them out.

"You should look after that rash," Elizabeth said, glancing at the girl's hands and wondering how dangerous the poison might be.

Jenny nodded, her fixed smile never wavering. "It's from the oleander stick. Vincent says not to worry, it'll fade in a few days."

MRS. BEETON'S SAUSAGE STUFFING

By Christine Trent

Would a publisher commit murder to avoid paying for a stolen recipe? A determined Mr. Latham entreats Violet Harper to prove that is what happened.

September 1870
London

Violet Harper hated Mrs. Beeton.

Well, perhaps it wasn't a murderous hate, one that causes a person to seek out knives, pistols, or ropes, but it was a seething animosity nonetheless.

Violet's years as an undertaker had disciplined her into demonstrating great patience for others. People in mourning were not typically at their best, and it required skill and empathy to deal serenely with some of her more . . . trying . . .customers.

But Mrs. Beeton was beyond the pale, Violet thought, as she opened the *London Times*, hoping her letter to the editor had been printed.

Isabella Beeton was a woman married to Samuel Orchart Beeton, the publisher of *The Englishwoman's Domestic Magazine*. Isabella had started a series of articles on domestic matters for the magazine. Her missives informed women on the precise ways to keep a home, manage servants, and prepare nourishing meals.

It was utterly impossible to follow her exacting instructions without losing one's mind.

However, British women had gone complete dotty for the woman's advice. Eventually, Mrs. Beeton's articles had been compiled into a thick doorstop of a book. It had quickly become a staple of many British homes and had gone through several reissues.

With each edition, the book grew in size—and advice—until this just-published edition, which could inflict serious damage upon someone if used as a weapon.

Violet sighed. Her letter protesting the reverence of Isabella Beeton and suggesting that women not take too much stock in the advice provided in its thousand pages had not made it into yesterday's paper.

Likely the editor did not want to anger the legion of fans of *Mrs. Beeton's Book of Household Management* by printing an angry screed from a woman who was in the minority opinion on Beeton—and who was an undertaker on top of that.

Such unseemly work, people frequently told Violet.

Her husband, Sam, was wholly unconcerned with his wife's lack of domestic skills, although he usually chided Violet gently when she became frustrated over an inability to live up to Isabella Beeton's rigid standards.

The shop's bell jangled as a customer entered, clearing Violet's mind of her irritation with the publication of a book full of unrealistic expectations for the average woman.

A tall, gaunt man had entered the shop with a newspaper under his arm. Violet stood and came out from behind her walnut and glass countertop full of mourning brooches, fans, gloves, and stationery.

"Good afternoon. I am Mrs. Harper. How may I be of service to you today, sir?"

"I . . ." The man's voice cracked. He stopped but quickly recovered himself. "My name is Elliot Latham and I need your assistance. For my wife, Winnie. She . . . She . . ." He stopped again.

"Please, Mr. Latham, won't you sit down?" Violet guided him to one of the overstuffed chairs located on the other side of the shop for consultation.

Once he seemed comfortable enough, with his long legs crossed and his hands working nervously in his lap, Violet asked gently, "How may I be of help to your dear wife?"

Latham pulled the paper out from under his arm and opened it to a particular page near the center of the issue, folding it to emphasize what he wanted Violet to read.

It was her letter to the editor. It had made it into today's paper.

Violet was nonplussed. "Why are you bringing this to me?" For a moment, she was fearful that Latham was about to accuse her of causing his wife's death by insulting the sainted Isabella Beeton. However, his actual intent was even more shocking.

"Mrs. Beeton murdered my wife and I want you to help me prove it," he said.

Violet had to keep herself from laughing. The statement was that of a madman. Completely ridiculous. Yet the man before Violet was in complete earnestness. She chose to tread carefully.

"Sir, I confess I am no fan of the esteemed Mrs. Beeton—which apparently you well know—but I do not understand why a busybody who writes advice to women would seek to murder your wife. Or anyone else, for that matter."

Mr. Latham bobbed his head up and down. "I knew that's what the police would think, too. That I was balmy. But I know what I'm about." The man tapped the side of his head with a finger. "I wasn't sure how to prove things on my own, but then I read your letter in the *Times* and I knew, that lady will understand and will help. 'All tripe and twaddle,' you said about *Mrs. Beeton's*. Plus, I remember you—didn't you get some kind of commendation from the Queen for saving one of the princesses from a murderer?"

Violet nodded as she contemplated Mr. Latham. He certainly seemed rational. Or did she think so simply because he approved of her ranting diatribe against Mrs. Beeton?

"Perhaps you can tell me how it is you believe Mrs. Beeton was responsible for your wife's death . . .?" Violet said, hesitant to hear the answer.

Latham nodded confidently. "Thank you, Mrs. Harper, for believing in me." Now the man leaned forward, clasping his hands together as he wove his tale for Violet.

"First of all, I must tell you—so few people know this—that Mrs. Beeton is actually dead herself. Probably gone five years now."

Now Violet was thoroughly confused. "I don't understand. There was just a new edition of her book published a couple of months ago. It was expanded from the previous edition. How could Mrs. Beeton possibly be long dead?"

"Humph," Latham growled. "Lies of the publisher to keep selling books."

"But her *husband* is the publisher. Surely he wouldn't besmirch her memory by—"

"No, he isn't anymore. Sold it off to Ward and Lock to pay off debts after Mrs. Beeton died of puerperal fever in the summer of 1865 giving birth to their fourth child. Poor woman was only twenty-eight. Since then, Ward and Lock has been quietly gathering up—*stealing*—recipes from women to include in the collection."

Violet had a glimmer of understanding. "And they stole a recipe from your wife?"

He nodded. "It was for a sausage stuffing that could be used with all different kinds of meats. She had a secret ingredient—an egg mixed into suet before blending it with the bread crumbs, which also got their own egg, to make the whole dish nice and moist. That hadn't ever been done before. She got the idea from that Miss Nightingale, what with her recommending eggs in most things as part of a healing diet."

Violet knew Florence Nightingale. What the man said was true—Miss Nightingale's nursing reforms included that of hospital food, and she was a proponent of mixing raw eggs into food and drink alike to get patients to more easily take nourishment.

Violet spoke gently again, keeping her tone neutral. "Are you suggesting that your wife died of a broken heart from having her recipe stolen?"

Latham made an impatient sound. "No, it's like I said. They murdered her. You see, my Winnie—Winnifred—she threatened to sue them after they had refused to buy the recipe, then published it anyway. Truly a fireball, Winnie was. Wouldn't take their thievin' lying down. I should have stopped her, but she was always able to handle herself proper."

Violet stopped him. "Mr. Latham, I'm not sure I'm following you. You're claiming that Winnie was murdered for threatening a lawsuit? That seems rather . . . far-fetched."

Latham grunted, still irritable. "It's not. You see, Winnie bought the latest edition of *Mrs. Beeton's*, and what did she find but her *Winnie's Secret Meat Stuffing*, renamed *Sausage-Meat Stuffing for Turkey*. It was too much for my wife to bear, and she marched right down to Ward and Lock's offices and demanded that they make payment to her. They laughed at her, of course, no doubt their practice for every woman who has dared challenge their thievery."

The man was working himself up into quite a froth, Violet thought. He paused and shook his head, as if in disgust at the memory.

"And then . . .?" Violet prompted him.

"Well, I'm afraid Winnie didn't take it too well. She had a harsh tongue when crossed, and just about everyone inside the offices felt it across their backs. And not just once. Winnie was determined to make them pay for what they had done to her and to others. She even threatened to hire a solicitor to haul them into court. Told them she was also headed to a journalist at the *Weekly Dispatch*, to expose them to the world." Latham sighed heavily.

"The following week, I came home to find Winnie at the bottom of the stairs. Her neck was . . . was . . ." He stopped and stared at the wall behind Violet.

Latham swallowed and finished his story. "I know what you're thinking, that Winnie must have just had a fall. But it wasn't natural at all. Besides, we've lived in our home near to twenty years. The woman wasn't daft, she knew the staircase like the back of her hand. She was pushed, I know it. Her dearest friend, Mrs.

Rickworth, was the first to suggest it and now I am convinced she is right. Besides her, you are the first person I've found who sees the evil in Mrs. Beeton's books."

As Latham had already noted, Violet was not wholly unused to solving crimes, as she had performed such services for Queen Victoria and as an odd part of her daily work.

But those had been clearly definable crimes. This was likely a grieving husband's flight of fancy, but there was no harm in inquiring casually about Mrs. Latham's recipe. Perhaps she could even reassure Mr. Latham that nothing untoward had happened to his wife—that she had simply had an accident.

***

Violet entered the Fleet Street offices of Ward and Lock with only a vague plan for questioning the staff, if she could even get as far as doing so. In the forefront of her mind was the knowledge that if they had seen her tripe-and-twaddle letter to the paper and realized she was the one who had sent it, she would most likely be escorted directly off the premises.

The humming of presses in the building's basement vibrated beneath her boots as she approached a bespectacled clerk sitting at a desk with his attention buried in a pile of papers. He was positioned almost like a moat keeper, preventing invaders from battering through any of the three doors positioned along the wall behind him.

The clerk looked up at Violet in irritation, as if a fly had buzzed nearby but was too far away to swat.

Violet swallowed. "Pardon me," she said. "My name is Violet Harper and I wish to speak to Mr. . . ."

She squinted at the three doors behind the clerk. They read:

Mr. Josiah Pleasant, Publisher
Mr. Charles Frith, Chief Editor
Mr. Peter Bryan, Proofreader

". . . Mr. Pleasant," she said. It was as good a start as any.

"Are you here with your own cookbook idea? Mr. Pleasant isn't taking any submissions at present." The clerk's tone was bored as he immediately returned to his work, a sign that he was dismissing Violet.

She should have been cowed, she supposed, but for some reason the clerk's attitude served to irritate her and all of Violet's trepidation fled.

"I am not. I am here to discuss the death of a woman who did submit an idea to Ward and Lock." She crossed her arms in front of her, trying to convey the seriousness of her visit.

The clerk made a couple of slash marks across a page he was examining and looked up again. "Name?" he said. "The dead woman's, I mean?"

"Winnifred Latham," Violet replied. "She submitted a recipe for sausage stuffing."

The clerk's expression was blank. "Why would my employer be concerned for her death?"

"That is what I am attempting to ascertain. She was found at the bottom of the stairs of her home with her neck broken after an altercation with several of Ward and Lock's employees."

The clerk frowned. "I recall no altercations as of late, and as you can see, little gets past me."

"I can see this, Mr. . . .?" Violet said.

"Norris. Hiram Norris, madam, at your service." The clerk stood and executed a small bow in Violet's direction.

"In that case, sir, the service I wish is an appointment with Mr. Pleasant, straight away."

Norris looked as though he had swallowed a poisonous toad, but he left his desk and tapped on the first door with Josiah Pleasant's engraved brass plate on it. Violet heard a bark from inside the room, and Norris opened the door, stuck his head inside and murmured to the room's occupant.

"Mrs. Harper, you may enter," Norris said as he retreated from the office and back to his desk.

Mr. Pleasant was anything other than what his name suggested. He was a bear of a man, looking as though he could single-handedly push a train off its track. He attempted a neutral expression but was unable to hide his annoyance at the interruption to his work.

"Yes?" he said, putting a lit cigar down into an ashtray as if her visit were the greatest inconvenience in the world to him.

"I am investigating the death of Mrs. Winnifred Latham." Violet paused, waiting to see if the man would react.

Pleasant merely shrugged and looked at her expectantly. "Who was she?" he finally said as a tendril of smoke slowly swirled up into the air next to him.

"A woman who submitted a recipe to you for her sausage stuffing. Apparently, you refused the recipe for the most current edition of *Mrs. Beeton's*, but then used it anyway without recompense to Mrs. Latham. She protested quite virulently, even threatening to both take you to court and go to a reporter for the *Weekly Dispatch*. A week later, her husband found her dead at the bottom of their staircase."

Mr. Pleasant shook his head as if perplexed. "The police were never here about this. If you are insinuating that I had anything to do with a woman tripping in her skirts and breaking her neck, you are sadly mistaken."

Violet had not stated that Mrs. Latham had fallen and broken her neck, but was that perhaps a reasonable assumption on Pleasant's part?

"I can hardly believe you would not remember a woman who entered the premises and made threats to you," she insisted. "How could you even—"

Pleasant waved a hand. "I have no recollection of this woman at all, Mrs. Harper. Of course, she wouldn't have been the first hysterical cook to barge in and demand all manner of placement and publication for a precious family recipe. I cope with daily outbursts in producing *Mrs. Beeton's*, plus I have dozens of other books at any given time that I am trying to get into bookstores and onto subscription lists. Sorry, I cannot be of any help to you."

Had Violet truly expected a different reaction? She expressed her thanks and turned to leave, then thought of another question.

"Mr. Pleasant," she said, facing him once more, "how long have you been the head of Ward and Lock?"

The publisher picked up his cigar and puffed on it, exhaling a cloud of smoke before answering. "Long enough to be wary of random strangers who barge into my office with unfounded accusations."

***

Mr. Frith—Ward and Lock's chief editor—was far more helpful, although Violet had to wait several minutes for him to return from attending to business elsewhere in the building.

Frith invited her into his office, which was layered in manuscripts over every available surface. The editor reddened upon realizing that he could not offer Violet a place to sit down. She politely disregarded the lack of seating and proceeded to question him as she had Josiah Pleasant.

"Yes, I do remember her repeated visits. Claimed she and her husband were poor as the mice living in the nooks and crannies of St. Margaret's Church and she wasn't sure how much longer she could manage. We hear that all the time from people. As though Mr. Pleasant's purchase decisions are based on the financial needs of the author, and not what we believe we can recoup in sales."

"Is it true that she threatened to take Ward and Lock to court?" Violet asked.

Frith, a slight man of nervous energy, nodded as he picked up a fountain pen from atop a manuscript bound with leather string and began fiddling with the button that retracted and extended the nib. "She was quite angry and had no ear for anything I told her. She stands out to me because she attempted to slap me when I refused to recognize her claim. Mr. Norris had to escort her from the building."

That was curious. Norris had claimed not to remember any sort of altercation.

"So you do admit that you stole the woman's recipe to include in the latest edition of *Mrs. Beeton's*?"

He continued to retract and extend the pen's nib. *Click-click. Click-click.* "Mrs. Harper, we do not steal anything. First of all, you must understand that Isabella Beeton died several years ago but we are keeping her memory alive here. Women practically worship her for her practical domestic advice. We are continuing—and expanding—that tradition of love and adoration." Frith finally stopped pressing the retraction button but continued to nervously rub it with his thumb.

"Second, we have women who compete with one another to have their recipes accepted into *Mrs. Beeton's*. I've seen sisters, best friends, even mothers and daughters, screech and flap over who has the best cucumber sauce or the most effective paste for polishing silver. They wish to see themselves in print, even without a byline, and will fight desperately with one another for the privilege. We would never have reason to offer payment for something so small as a family recipe, nor would we ever set such a precedent."

Violet tried a different approach. "It does seem . . . reasonable . . . that you would work very hard to protect the fable that Mrs. Beeton is still alive."

"Of course. We would be completely unable to continue expanding the book and selling updated editions to the same women over and over if they discovered that Isabella Beeton has been dead for half a decade. Exposure would be devastating to us. But surely you cannot suggest we would resort to *murder* in such a situation."

Violet didn't want to suggest such a thing, but was it really that far-fetched an idea?

She left Mr. Frith to visit Peter Bryan, Ward and Lock's proofreader.

Upon entering his office, Violet was struck by how decrepit the man looked as he sat hunched over a manuscript with a magnifying glass, his balding head dotted with liver spots pointed toward Violet.

He looked up and squinted through the magnifier at her. "Yes?"

he asked. “Are you the new assistant Mr. Pleasant promised me?”

“I’m afraid not.” Violet introduced herself and explained why she was there. Mr. Bryan blinked at her, his rheumy eyes enlarged as he continued to gaze at her through the round glass. How in heaven’s name was the man able to accurately proofread what were surely dozens of manuscripts each year?

“Oh. Mr. Pleasant said he’d get someone else for me. Last woman I interviewed was too tetchy. Couldn’t abide her peppery temper. You seem peaceable enough. Are you sure you aren’t seeking a position?”

“No, Mr. Bryan. But I should like to ask you about Mrs. Winnifred Latham. She claimed that Ward and Lock stole a sausage stuffing recipe from her, and she was prepared to hire a solicitor to sue the company.”

He frowned. “A solicitor!” His voice was raspy as it rose. “I’ve been here for nigh on thirty years and there’s not ever been a lawyer brought in.”

Bryan coughed. It was a combination of a wheeze and a choking sound. Violet wondered if the man was disguising a serious illness. Was his need of his position so great that he would work until he dropped on his desk?

“Mrs. Latham was very angry,” Violet said. “She even threatened to go to a newspaper about it.”

Mr. Bryan slowly put down his magnifying glass. “Yes, I remember that woman. A harridan. I nearly had to take a broom to her, to sweep her out of my office when she came to me. Seems she got no satisfaction from Mr. Pleasant or Mr. Frith, so she thought she might trample over me.”

“I see,” Violet said. “That’s very odd, given that Mr. Pleasant said he had no recollection of Mrs. Latham’s visit.”

Bryan’s watery eyes rolled their gaze around the room before nervously settling back on Violet. “I—well, perhaps I don’t remember events too well. I’m not as young as I once was, you know.”

As near as Violet could tell, nearly everyone at Ward and Lock had lied to her. Hiram Norris was not telling the truth when he said he recalled no altercation, given that Mr. Frith clearly remembered him escorting Winnie Latham out of the building. Josiah Pleasant was surely lying when he said he had no recollection of Mrs. Latham’s visit and accusations. And Mr. Bryan was almost certainly lying to protect Mr. Pleasant.

Violet contemplated the elderly man for several moments. Realizing he was unlikely to offer her anything valuable, she said, “Thank you, sir, for your time.”

The man's relief was palpable as Violet took her leave.

Hiram Norris was standing right outside of Bryan's door as Violet entered the center area containing Norris's desk. Had he been listening to her conversation?

He stepped back smoothly, although he still looked as though he hadn't quite digested that toad. "Mrs. Harper, I was just about to step away for my luncheon break and wished to know if there will be anything else you need . . .?"

Violet knew it was a dismissal. "I need answers, Mr. Norris. A woman died as a result of seeking payment for her work. There must be justice for it."

His response was unexpected. "Most people think love of money is the root of all evil. In my experience, madam, it is petty jealousies that inspire evil in man's breast," Norris said, blinking owlishly behind his spectacles.

Suddenly, everything clicked in Violet's mind, like Mr. Frith's dratted pen button. As she stared at the clerk, Violet realized what the plot involved and knew she had to get out of the building, quickly. It was time to return to Mr. Latham to tell him what she had discovered.

***

Latham responded to Violet's note the following morning, arriving at her shop not long after she had unlatched the front door.

As the door's bells jangled, Sam emerged from the rear of the shop, wiping his hands on a cloth. He spent most of his days immersed in photographic papers and solutions, as he handled the post-mortem photography services for the undertaking shop.

"Are you sure you don't want me to deliver the news?" Sam asked.

Violet shook her head. She escorted Mr. Latham to the seating area once again, while Sam busied himself behind the counter.

"You have news?" Latham asked hopefully.

"Yes, I do," Violet replied. "I wanted to let you know that I have discovered that your wife was indeed murdered—by you, Mr. Latham."

The room was so silent upon her accusation Violet could hear a child crying out in the street. But Latham quickly recovered. "Dear lady, what are you saying? I came to you and asked you to find my wife's killer. Why would I do so if I had done her in myself?"

Violet nodded. "I give you credit for being very clever, sir. Who would suspect a husband who was ostensibly seeking justice for his wife's death? I only realized the truth when the clerk at Ward and Lock commented to me that most people believe the love of money to be the root of all evil, when in fact it is petty jealousies that drive most men to commit crimes."

Latham's expression was incredulous. "Petty jealousy? Are you suggesting that I was jealous of my wife?"

"Not exactly. Mr. Norris made me realize that you are *not* like most men, and indeed the love of money is the root of your own evil. In fact, you loved it so much that you were willing to goad your wife into confronting the publisher for money, knowing exactly what would happen: they would dismiss her completely and do all they could to protect themselves. And so you sent your poor, unwitting wife back again and again with more threats against Ward and Lock. When she had delivered the final threat of exposing them to the *Weekly Dispatch*, you knew that her usefulness to you had to take another form.

"That was when you executed the second part of your plan, which was to do away with Winnie as quickly and easily as possible by pushing her down the stairs of your home. No doubt you told your friends and family how shocked you were by her 'accidental' fall. Whether Mrs. Rickworth even exists or was just a quick invention to bolster your story, I don't know."

"Mrs. Harper," Latham said, holding up his hands as if warding off blows. "I must protest this outrageous impugning of my name."

Violet ignored him, although she noted he did not insist that Mrs. Rickworth was real. "Once your wife was buried and no one could question the manner of her death, you were free to move into the final part of your plan, which was to harangue the publisher into paying you what was 'owed' to Winnie with an even greater threat of a murder accusation against them."

"This is madness," Latham said. "I made a grave mistake believing you could help me."

Violet nodded. "You did err in coming to me, but you initially thought it was your master stroke. You never went to the police because you knew they would see right through you. But if you could get some third party to support your claim, well then, the publisher would have no choice but to pay for your silence. How fortuitous that you discovered my letter in the *Times*. You knew—or thought you knew—that I would be the perfect dupe for finishing up your plan.

"I was fed varying degrees of lies at Ward and Lock, but I realized that that was because everyone there was primarily interested in preserving the company's reputation. So interested that they lie to cover up for one another even when no crime has been committed. When the company's clerk, Mr. Norris, made the comment about love of money, I realized that there was just one person for whom love of money was paramount. *You*, sir."

Mr. Latham eyed the door. Sam emerged from behind the counter to stand in front of it, his arms crossed over his chest.

Latham's gaze moved around the shop, but he seemed to quickly realize escape would not be simple. His shoulders sagged. "I should have let Winnie pursue the lawsuit first."

"Yes, that might have been wiser," Violet said drily as Sam moved to grab the murderer and escort him to the police station.

***

Violet still despised the busybody advice dispensed by *Mrs. Beeton's*, but somehow it seemed easier to tolerate, knowing that Isabella Beeton herself was no longer behind it. There would be no more letters to the editor coming from Violet Harper's pen.

Author's Note

The recipe for Sausage-Meat Stuffing for Turkey is on page 249 of Mrs. Beeton's Book of Household Management, *but assuredly this story is a work of fiction. Isabella Beeton did indeed die in 1865, and publisher Ward and Lock picked up the book from her husband. Subsequent editions included more advice and recipes, eventually turning it into the 1000+-page volume that exists today.*

BRING IT

By Terry Shames

Jenna has managed a fantastic makeover that she's unveiling at The Clarion Club, where her unusual offering for the annual Christmas potluck won't be the only surprise of the evening.

Jenna slid her shapely legs out of the Mercedes, admiring how elegant they looked in the five-inch Jimmy Choos. Her newly sleek body followed in an effortless, graceful movement. She smoothed the creamy silk, size-six skirt, not because there was a wrinkle in it, but to remind herself how it felt to be slender again. Forty pounds, lost in the course of a year, to gain back her darling little figure. To remind herself of what her husband had once adored.

Eliot handed the parking valet his keys and hurried around the car to join Jenna. Driving to the Christmas party tonight, he had not once looked at Jenna. He had scowled during the whole trip. Now that they were arriving at the Clarion Club, a smile sprang to his lips. She knew the smile wasn't meant for her; but just in case, she stood before him, striking a model's pose, and waited for his reaction. No response.

She tried again, tossing her head so that her perfectly coifed hair swirled and then settled at the line of her chin. Manuelo had assured her it was the perfect length. She remained invisible to Eliot.

Manuelo, her hairdresser; Suzie, her personal trainer; Gretchen, her eating coach; and Elsbeth, her wardrobe consultant, had been her best friends, her cheering squad, her trusted companions for one whole year. Yesterday she had assembled them at Cardoon's, the most prestigious restaurant in San Francisco, for a celebration of their mutual victory. While they pigged out, she confined herself to an asparagus salad and a shrimp appetizer. She didn't even flinch when they ordered dessert that was forbidden to her.

"I'll bet your husband is so proud of you!" Suzie wriggled her body like a wholesome puppy. Had Suzie gained a little weight?

"He is *so* grateful to all of you for your help," Jenna said, bestowing on each of them a beatific smile. Who knew what Eliot really thought? He had yet to mention the weight loss, the new hairdo, or all the money she had spent in the past year achieving her goals.

Now he gave her a cursory glance. “You look nice, darling,” he said automatically. She could have worn a nun’s habit and a potted plant on her head, and he would have said the same thing.

She had known it would be like that, and yet his comment was like a knife thrust into her. It was also the extra push she needed to remind herself why she had gone ahead with the final step of her plan.

He thought he was the smartest man in the room. But he was about to find out that he could be bested by the smartest woman in the room.

***

Their neighborhood had been holding the annual Christmas party at The Clarion Club in the leafy, upscale suburb of Moraga every year since long before Jenna and Eliot moved to the West Coast. The room was already half full, at least forty people chattering over the strains of Frank Sinatra singing “Santa Claus is coming to Town.” The room had never looked more festive. It was a venerable Mission-style clubhouse built of redwood with a massive fireplace, a beamed ceiling, and French doors that in warmer weather led out to a terrace. Tonight it was too cool for the doors to be open, and a fire blazed in the fireplace, lending a golden glow to the room. Each Christmas the members of the club spent hours decorating a massive Christmas tree that graced a corner of the room and hanging wreaths of fresh greenery wound with loops of tinsel.

The only drawback to the club was the miniscule kitchen, so everyone brought food to share. A few of the men cooked, but the kitchen was mostly the women’s domain—and the event had become a competition. At first it had been a relaxed, friendly affair, with the neighbors in playful rivalry. Over the years, though, the unacknowledged battle for who had brought the best dish had evolved from sporting to cutthroat. There were no prizes awarded, but there was always one dish that everyone knew in their heart of hearts was the winner.

Jenna was a great cook. Everyone said so, and she had reigned supreme for several years. But then, she had begun to lose her nerve. Each holiday season, as the party neared, she grew more and more anxious, and gradually Marcia Overton’s dishes took precedence. It had taken Jenna a while to realize that Marcia had systematically undermined her confidence.

Each year, as soon as the food was served, Marcia would scurry over to taste Jenna’s offering, smiling at Jenna with fake anticipation. She would sample the dish, and then pause with a little frown and come out with a tiny criticism. "This mousse is fantastic. If it had a touch less kirsch, it would be perfect." Or, "It's always so hard to get a custard to set properly without it being a little *too* firm, isn't it?" Little digs that got under Jenna's skin and made her feel less competent each time they happened.

Last year had been the ultimate straw. "Oh, Jenna! The pork tenderloin tidbits were divine. The sauce? Almost perfect. But . . ." A dramatic, excruciating pause. "You could have cooked the onions two minutes less."

What infuriated Jenna was that Marcia was right. Jenna had answered the telephone at a critical time and let the onions sauté the tiniest bit longer than necessary. At first Jenna didn't understand why she let it get to her, but then she got it: Eliot's eyes always seemed to be on Marcia, the charming divorcee, who had maintained her cute figure. A perky little blonde, Marcia dressed like a cheerleader in little short skirts and sweater sets. She had a tinkly laugh and enormous violet eyes that she trained on any man in her vicinity, but on Eliot in particular.

***

Tonight Marcia was at the front door to greet everyone, because, as always, she had organized the food displays, and knew exactly where she wanted each person to put their dish. She looked straight at Jenna and blinked. Then her mouth fell open. "Jenna? How . . .?"

Jenna had carefully planned for her appearance to be a shock. For the past six months, she had been making herself scarce while steadily losing weight. When she had to go out in public, she deliberately wore her baggiest clothes to conceal her emerging figure. In the past two months, when she realized there was really no way to get away with the ruse any longer, she had declined all invitations, pleading a sinus infection or another engagement.

"Hello, Marcia, you look very nice," Jenna said. "What a sweet sweater. Did you knit it yourself?"

A tiny squeak of distress escaped Marcia. "What? No. I don't know how to—"

"Oh, you have a loose thread. Let me tuck it in for you." Jenna ran her fingers under the hem of the sweater and patted it. "There, that's better."

Before Marcia could recover, Jenna fluttered her fingers at her and said, "See you later."

"Jenna, wait!" Marcia's voice was a screech. "Where's your potluck dish?"

"I'm having it brought!" Jenna sang out and plunged into the group of people hovering near the door, giggling as she imagined Marcia's astonishment at this transgression. Everyone was *required* to carry their creations to the buffet table themselves—so everyone could see what they brought. Not that these rules were written down anywhere; they had simply evolved into iron law by custom. Marcia must wonder what it could possibly mean that Jenna was having someone else bring her dish.

At the last moment Jenna couldn't keep herself from turning and looking back. Sure enough, Marcia and Eliot had locked eyes and were holding that pose. Not only had Marcia stolen Jenna's confidence, but she'd taken her husband as well.

Jenna didn't know how long their flirtation had been going on, but she did know it had gone way beyond the "just looking" stage.

It wasn't losing Eliot that galled her; she could live with that. It was the humiliation of the two of them making goo-goo eyes at each other in plain sight. And there was no one she could confide in or commiserate with, because everyone claimed to love Marcia. "She's just the sweetest, kindest, most selfless person." If Jenna heard that one more time, she'd scream. Marcia was a snake.

***

Eliot joined Jenna and put his hand at her back to steer her to the drinks table. "I'll have a white wine spritzer," Jenna said.

Ken Tarkenton got into line behind them and began to speak to Eliot. When his gaze fell on Jenna, his mouth stayed open in an unseemly way. "Jenna. Wow. I hardly recognized you. I mean, you've . . ."

"Thank you, Ken," Jenna said. "You look nice, too."

Eliot stared at Jenna, puzzled. His ice-blue eyes widened and then darted past her for a moment as if he were wondering what had become of his wife. His dumpy wife.

"Everything okay?" Jenna said to Eliot.

He frowned. "Yeah, it's just . . . you look different."

"*Vive la differénce*," Ken said, with a horrible French accent. "So, how's business?" He was speaking to Eliot, but his eyes were still on Jenna.

While the two men talked, Jenna turned her attention to the food table, where she could hear murmurs of appreciation as people surveyed the marvelous creations. Someone had gone all out on cooking a goose that lay bronzed and shiny on a silver platter, surrounded by tiny apples. There was a tumble of autumn vegetables from which wafted the scent of sage and rosemary. Jane Lucke had brought her usual gorgeous apple pie, and Mike Stronheim, who owned a bakery, had brought a lavish cake decorated with swirls of white and black buttercream. The partygoers could begin sampling at eight o'clock sharp, in ten minutes. Too bad most of it would be off limits to Jenna. Her eating coach, Gretchen, would be so proud of her for holding firm.

She noticed Ken's wife, Loni, heading toward them. Ken saw her, too. "Lucky you," Ken said, nudging Eliot's shoulder and winking at Jenna.

Loni grabbed Ken's arm and pulled him away, singing out, "Sorry, I need him for a minute."

"Did you say you wanted white wine?" Eliot spoke to Jenna as if he had run across an alien and needed to enunciate clearly and distinctly. His face had the dazed appearance of someone who was just emerging from a coma.

There was something unsettling about the way he was looking at her—as if he disapproved of the change she had wrought. He liked to be in control and he was probably mad that she had accomplished the makeover of her own volition, without him getting to tell her how she should do it.

"White wine *spritzer*," Jenna said. "I'll be at the food table." She walked away.

***

Standing next to the buffet, she glanced at her watch. She had insisted that the timing be perfect.

Sure enough, three minutes later Alain Perrault, a hunk her hairdresser, Manuelo, had introduced her to, prowled into the room. Dark haired, wide-shouldered, with a smile that could melt an iceberg, Alain had eyes only for Jenna, as the plan called for.

"*Chère Jenna, ma petite*, I've brought your lovely *fraises*." Balanced on his hand was a silver tray with Jenna's buffet contribution: luscious, plump strawberries (out of season, flown in from Turkey), surrounding a dish of pink cream. Alain looked from the strawberries to her and his look said it all. *I don't know whether I'd rather taste the strawberries, or you.* He set the tray down.

A hush had fallen over the room. Like a hunting dog on point, Marcia charged over to the table. "Strawberries?" she squawked. "That's it? You brought strawberries?"

Jenna savored the sense that Marcia was losing control of her cool. "Yes, Marcia, I've decided that too much emphasis has been placed on rich dishes that aren't really good for us. Don't you agree?"

Alain turned his liquid gaze to Marcia and smiled with the hint of a sneer. "*Les fraises à la crème. Parfait,*" he said, his voice smoky and inviting. He turned to Jenna, plucked a perfect red strawberry from the top of the heap, dipped it ever so lightly into the pink froth, and brought it to Jenna's lips. His eyes never left her mouth as she delicately nibbled it. He placed another strawberry onto his own tongue. Marcia whimpered and a couple of people sighed. "*Vraiment merveilleux*."

"Truly," Jenna said.

Alain kissed her hand and said, "*Au revoir, ma chère*," and strolled out.

Marcia stared after him.

"Oh, Marcia," Jenna cooed, "come and show me what wonderful dish you brought tonight."

She knew perfectly well that Marcia had prepared an artful display of salmon mousse containing three pounds of Scottish salmon at twenty-nine dollars a pound, organic cream churned by hand with organic herbs, hand snipped and measured out to perfection. She'd seen it in Marcia's refrigerator.

***

Before Marcia could say anything, Eliot suddenly appeared. "Darling," he said to Jenna, his smile tight, "may I have this dance?"

"Of course, sweetheart." Jenna couldn't resist a smile of triumph in Marcia's direction before she let Eliot guide her across the room toward the band. She reveled in the looks of keen interest that accompanied them, the handsome rich stockbroker and his slender wife. It was wonderful to have an audience.

Eliot pulled her close. "You look every inch yourself," he said, nuzzling her hair.

"Really?" She was trembling. "I wanted to surprise you."

"Yes, really . . . you bitch."

She gasped and tried to pull away, but he clutched her tighter. "I've watched every move you've made to try and destroy poor Marcia. Every year she attempts to be kind and tell you how to improve your cooking. And every year you get nastier."

"Tell me how to improve! I'm a great cook. I don't need her advice."

"She doesn't deserve to be treated so badly. You hurt her feelings."

"Oh, poor her. Have you started screwing her yet?"

"Don't be crude. Of course not. We're just friends. A harmless flirtation."

"You're lying. You've been sleeping with her for weeks." He was holding her so tightly that she was having trouble breathing.

"Don't squirm. It isn't sexy. You're going nowhere. You thought you were soooo clever, hiring all those high-priced makeover artists. Not to mention your phony French friend, Alain." Sweat had sprung out on his brow, and he pulled back and blinked at her as if he was having trouble focusing.

"Oh dear, and I thought you'd be so pleased at my new look." She batted her eyes at Eliot.

"Quite frankly, I don't care. I'm not putting up with you anymore. We're done."

"Oh, Eliot, no. Please. We can begin again. I promise I'll do better." She kept the smile plastered on her face so that people nearby would think they were having a pleasant conversation. "I hope you won't leave me penniless. Are you feeling okay, Eliot?"

"I'm fine. It's hot in here."

"The temperature seems perfectly comfortable. I wonder if you're okay. Could you have had trouble with something you ate? Something you had at someone else's house?"

"What do you mean?" He staggered slightly.

"Where were you this afternoon? Never mind, I know the answer. You were with *her*."

"How do you know?"

"That isn't important. But think about this afternoon. Remember the mushroom tarts? The ones that little *tart* Marcia served you *afterwards*?"

"What about them?" His face had grown white.

"Tasty, were they? I'm sure Marcia knows as well as I do that you're a sucker for mushroom tarts. How sweet of her to go to such trouble, especially since she doesn't care for them. And how strange that she didn't notice the mushrooms were not quite like the ones she bought."

Eliot groaned and leaned heavily on her. "Jenna, what did you do?"

"Poor Eliot. Who would have thought Marcia would be so careless to use bad mushrooms? What a shame. Oh, Eliot!"

He slipped to the floor, writhing. Several people swarmed over to help. "What's happened?" Ken Tarkenton asked.

Marcia shoved past Jenna and hurled herself onto Eliot. "Oh, El, honey. What's wrong?"

"Get away from him, Marcia," Jenna said. "He said he was terrified of you."

"What?" Marcia's face was stricken. "He would never say that."

Falling to her knees, Jenna moved herself between her husband and Marcia. Eliot was lying still. In her most distressed voice, Jenna wailed, "That's what he said, that he was afraid of you. I don't know what you've done, Marcia, but you'd better hope he's okay." She cradled Eliot's head in her lap. "Please, someone call 9-1-1."

***

Two weeks later, Jenna, dressed in elegant black mourning slacks and a sweater, met her eating coach, Gretchen, at Green's in Ft. Mason. Over a delicious, healthy meal, they discussed how Jenna would stay true to her diet on her European trip.

"I fully intend to be disciplined," Jenna said. "You've been such an inspiration to me."

Gretchen, a trim fifty-year-old, smiled. "I know how disciplined you can be."

The two women smiled at each other.

Jenna paid the bill. They rose and walked out of the restaurant. Jenna brought a fat envelope from her purse and handed it to Gretchen. "Have you decided which island you're going to settle on?"

"I'm thinking St. Lucia. So lush and green. It really inspires my art. It will be wonderful to get to pursue my creative spirit full time."

Jenna hugged her and stepped back. "Can I ask you one thing? How did you learn so much about mushrooms, anyway?"

"Research," Gretchen said. "Remind me sometime to tell you about my husband. May he rest in peace."

GUTBOMBS 'N' GUINNESS

By Lisa Preston

A horseshoer and a chef make life decisions at a crossroads diner—and so does an unknown third party.

The waitress gave me a gotcha look as I pulled apart the last third of my burger, covered the meat with a paper napkin, then scarfed down the greasy good remains of the bun and guts: red onion, iceberg, and 'maters. I bowed my head so my ponytail draped across my face while I licked my fingers, but that hovering waitress gawked.

"Honey, did you want a doggy bag?"

"This'll do." I unsnapped my blouse pocket to fish for the ten-dollar bill. Even in my physical job, I could manage on one meal a day if I picked hearty grub. And I could eat on way less than ten bucks, but for today's road trip—hunting for a place to sleep and hang a shingle—I splurged.

Guy said, "I still don't get the point of going to look at horses without bringing the trailer." He'd taken way too long asking after the ribeye lunch special, checked out the tea packets, then embarrassed me by ordering what most of his species would call girl-food. And he'd rolled his eyes when I'd ordered the gutbomb for seven ninety-nine, but I'd done the math, and drank water so I could leave a two-dollar tip, which seemed decent.

I want to be decent.

The waitress smirked at Guy. "Done with that salad, honey?"

He'd only eaten half the greens, but he pushed back from the roadhouse's table and nodded. She looked around, then looked annoyed as she bussed our dishes.

Guy frowned at the shakers on the table, sprinkled salt in his hand, and dabbed a finger to taste the white crystals.

At a booth across the almost empty restaurant, a grandpa-aged fellow called out, "Miss, we'll both have the ribeye. And she'd like more hot water." He was seated across from a gray-haired lady who evidently could not order for herself or pick a man who believed she had the capacity to choose her chow.

The mustachioed man alone at the other occupied table called that he'd change his order to pie. Guy scuffed his straight blond hair and crossed his ankles near my feet. His sneakers were half-again the size of my boots.

"Order up," the cook called.

Guy prefers they be called chefs, but I wasn't too sure anyone slinging lard on a highway grill halfway between Cowdry and Hermiston would agree. Maybe a little high-falutin', this Guy? He'd let me sleep in his garage for three straight nights and there'd been no naughty business, plus he'd slipped me a free burger—under the guise of trying out a new teriyaki version—a couple days earlier during his shift at the Cascade Kitchen. The Cascade is one of the few places to grab a bite back in the pokey town of Cowdry where Guy has a one-bedroom house on a few acres.

"Hello? Rainy?" Guy prodded.

I tried to remember what he wanted to know. It's weird to road-trip with a stranger, especially after sleeping in his garage a few days.

The waitress carried a distraction to the man at the window. The pie slice stood a proud three inches, crammed with blueberries, dolloped with whipped cream. I could have done justice to that fat wedge of purple pastry. Would have fueled a good several horseshoeings. I eyeballed the dessert while I answered.

"I borrowed that stock trailer just to get Red back." That part was true anyways.

Guy cocked an eyebrow. "So you're going to have to haul it empty a thousand miles back to California. But right now, we're looking at horses in Hermiston, yet you didn't tow it. Why look at horses for sale without bringing the trailer?"

The waitress asked, "Is this all together?"

"Sure," Guy said. "I've got it."

"Nope." I dropped my ten-spot, stood, and tightened my ponytail.

Guy sighed and twisted his lanky body to reach for his wallet. "Rainy, it's my turn. You brought that pizza home last night."

Yeah, yesterday I'd shod a little Arab for the daughter of some dude Guy knew, plus his neighbor's two Quarter Horses. I could have eaten that whole medium pepperoni. I studied the waitress while Guy handed over his credit card at the cash register. Her name tag read *Marla*. Tall, sassy, with auburn ringlets that clashed with her orange *Burke's Burgers 'n' Brew* apron. I wasn't sure if she really looked like a Marla.

Guy caved to my will and pocketed my tenner. I hoped he'd write a good tip on that credit card thingy. We're the same age, but my VISA is a prepaid debit card and I certainly can't buy a home.

Nor do I have to wait like a child while Guy squares up.

Outside the restaurant, I sucked in the pine-and-sage air that floats in this part of Oregon and enjoyed the clip-clop of an honest-to-goodness old cowboy riding up. He stepped off the bay mare and draped the reins over the hitching rail I hadn't noticed when I'd parked Ol' Blue. What a delight to see a horse parked near my rig. Too bad the immediate area didn't have enough population to support a shoer. I'd love to live where the local eatery offered a hitching post. An unmarked dirt road ran south from the highway. I figured the cowboy rode in over the open country on the north side. Oregon is interesting in the middle where it changes from high-desert empty to coastal conifers so dense that light can't hardly penetrate and the ground can only grow moss, fungus, and ferns. If Red's third-to-last owner hadn't sold him to the Butte County fellow I'd just bought him back from, I likely never would have set foot in the Pacific Northwest.

The cowboy's mare cocked a well-shod hind hoof. He tipped his straw Stetson and raised his grizzled chin as I stepped off the swept boardwalk.

"Psst. Hey, wait up."

It wasn't Guy's voice hailing me; it was high and feminine. I turned. The restaurant's girl Friday was hauling big bags of garbage through the side door. She looked to be, like me, young twenties with average height and weight, but without the shoulders and back needed to shoe horses. Pixie haircut, cute little waist, stick arms maxed out on trash bags.

The cowboy removed his hat. "Tilly. Last day?"

"Yep. Can't wait to leave this place behind."

I knew the feeling of not blooming where you're planted, needing to make a mark in the world.

"We'll miss you," the cowboy told her.

Tilly gave a girly snort. "You'll be wanting a beer?"

"Or two. Yes, ma'am."

"Head on in. Marla or I will fetch it." Tilly heaved the bags into the dumpster then called out to me. "I saw your dog. You want scraps?"

Charley's head was visible in the driver's open window, like he'd stared at the building the whole time I was inside. Shepherds are like that.

"Sure," I said. "That'd be great."

"Let me grab a to-go box."

Good to her word, she bounced in the side door and was back in barely enough time for me to unload the burger scrap into my mouth while my back was turned to Charley and Guy. Maybe Guy was being nice, pretending not to notice as he walked under a parked-out giant cedar and kicked the ground.

Tilly handed over a paperboard box and shot a guilty look at the roadhouse. "They'd kill me if they saw. Not supposed to hand scraps out but why throw them away?"

I opened the to-go box. Strips of steak fat coiled inside, scraped of the gravy, but with plenty of meat on the rind. Good thing Guy had brought a little cooler along for the road trip.

"Thanks heaps," I told her.

***

Wasn't a quarter-mile down the highway that Guy started up.

"The server lied about the ginger on the salad. It was from a jar, not fresh."

"Is that a fact?" I'd known him a matter of days, but already knew well that Guy's debriefing of a meal is a thing to be endured.

"And they had the wrong kind of salt in the shaker. What's that about?"

I kept myself from challenging him. I'd salted my fries—a horseshoer needs her electrolytes—and lived.

Guy counted the food crimes on his fingers. "And she said they used local criminis on the ribeye."

I shifted Ol' Blue and stomped the diesel up to sixty-five. Charley rested his head on my thigh.

Guy eased his left forearm onto my dog like he thought little gold Aussies were born to be armrests. "Rainy?"

"Mmm." It was going to be a long day. Good thing I hadn't towed the trailer—not hauling let me drive faster. B'sides, one oughtn't look at sale horses while towing an empty trailer. I needed a second horse like I needed to drop my anvil on my foot, but I wished Red wasn't living alone this week in Guy's little pasture. Horses need company.

"Can I hold your hand?"

Were I still a potty mouth, Guy's question would have caused me to curse. Four days I've known the man; this morning I say I'm road tripping, he asks to come along, and now he's putting the moves on? And holding hands is his big move?

"Knock yourself out." My agreement allowed all the romance of his notion. "Actually, you mind reaching Charley more steak fat?"

He'd watched when I gave Charley several chunks of scrap before stuffing the to-go box in the cooler next to his iced tea. Ol' Blue is a stick shift, so the cooler was on the floor in Guy's foot room.

Guy cracked the cooler open and hand-fed steak fat into

Charley's sweet furry face. "Native criminis? Come on. *Pholiotina*, sure, but crimini, no way."

I ached for mercy. Couldn't we talk about the fine Quarter Horses we'd see at the sale? There was a gangly sorrel colt in the Hermiston catalog that I was kind of dying to eyeball. But Guy's been good to me. Maybe it wouldn't kill me to engage his interests a smidgen while I figured out my next move. I spoke with all the enthusiasm I had to offer.

"Mm hmm."

***

Hermiston turns out to be a fine western town on a serious river. Looked to be as good a place to live as any, with its own kind of pretty, though a good deal drier than Butte County. This land crunched, a brittle feeling through my boot soles. Cowdry's on the west, wetter side of Butte, so we get greener pastures.

Not we, he. Guy and me aren't together or anything.

I followed signs to the sale, parked Ol' Blue, and grabbed a copy of the *Thrifty Nickel* paper, piled up free for the taking right next to the *Hermiston Herald* and local real estate pamphlets. Ads under the ranch services section offered three listings for barefoot trimmers, one calling herself an equine podiatrist. A trainer-slash-shoer. Four more ads for reasonable, professional horseshoeing. Mercy. I eyed the rental section. No rooms for rent. A few apartments listed, the cheapest a one-bedroom at nine hundred a month. Maybe I could camp in Ol' Blue a while longer? I'd slept in the cab all winter. Sure felt good to stretch out on that cot in Guy's garage Wednesday night.

Guy had let me use his computer and I'd plunked through enough ads west of Cowdry to know I couldn't afford the Portland outskirts any more than I could swing the expense of Bend. I needed a small town that wasn't too spendy, with enough horse folk to give a start-up shoer living money.

The back page of the real estate pamphlet showed an area map, with little dots pinning property locations as far as Umatilla and Pendleton.

"This trip isn't about looking at horses, is it?" Guy frowned at my finger, still trained on the last rental ad.

"Sure it is. I've always wanted to see the Hermiston livestock sale."

Guy hooked his thumbs in his front pockets. "You're moving up here?"

My shoulders crept up in a shrug under Guy's wounded look. "I've got to get myself established. No clients equals no food and diesel money."

"Well, fine," Guy said, "but why not give Cowdry a try? You shod for people I mentioned. You said working the rodeo might get you some customers. And I'd like to get to know you."

Nope. There's parts of my past I can't have him or anyone else knowing. I studied low brown hills on the horizon. "At the Butte County fairgrounds? That's a horse show, not a rodeo."

I'd been excited to see the flier at the Cowdry Co-op. A horse show could bring jumpers and dressage people in addition to western riders, maybe customers wanting clips or tap-and-die shoes that can take screw-in studs. Cowdry does have rodeo and, yeah, I got a couple jobs, but I'd need regular clients to survive.

A headache pestered my temples. I released my ponytail.

Guy smiled. "I like your hair loose."

I finger-raked my hair and retied the ponytail. Should I drive to Pendleton? Would it be any better than Hermiston or any other place? This finding a place to live and work was like throwing a dart at the planet. "Let's go."

"You don't want to look at the sale horses? You want to head home right away?"

"I just want to go." I let Charley out for a pee, gave him water and a bunch more steak fat, then headed us back for Cowdry like I had someplace to be, which I didn't.

Miles on, it was dusky as I slowed through the reduced speed area by the roadhouse. We hadn't eaten since lunch, but I had no more eating money for the day and hoped Guy wouldn't ask to stop. A cop stood by his cruiser, talking to a man who pointed at Ol' Blue as I drove past.

In another half-mile, I got pulled over, lights and siren.

"Miss, you were at Burke's earlier today?" In this county, they dress their deputies in green and give 'em crew cuts.

"That burger place?" I asked.

Deputy Crew Cut gave me a look like I wasn't the smart one in the conversation.

I said, "We ate there for lunch."

"I'm going to ask you real direct, did you tamper with anyone's food?"

"What? No sir." But as I replied, the cop studied Guy, waiting for another answer to the same question.

Guy shook his head. "Not a chance."

"Mind pulling into the parking lot at Burke's to chat?" Deputy Crew Cut headed back to his car as though I'd agreed.

I drummed my fingers on Ol' Blue's steering wheel with one hand, ruffled Charley's yellow fur with the other.

"Well, fine," Guy said. "Guess we ought to go back."

"What's going on?"
"No idea."

***

An ambulance and another deputy's patrol car occupied the spaces where a good horse and Ol' Blue had parked at lunchtime. Tilly sat on the steps, crying. Marla stood some distance away, arms folded over her chest. A deputy with a big enough gut to hang over the spare magazines on his gun belt faced off against a young man in a smeared apron. The mustached man who'd had pie for lunch paced the boardwalk. He'd been the one who'd pointed Ol' Blue out to the cops when I'd driven past.

The young fellow spoke like he'd been repeating himself. "I didn't do nothing."

Deputy Beer Belly said, "I heard you, Skeeter, but you see how it looks. The hospital sent us to—"

"Hey, that's them!" Skeeter-the-Snitch pointed at Guy and me as we followed Deputy Crew Cut to the boardwalk.

Pie Man raised a hand to hush Skeeter then patted Tilly's shaking shoulders. Deputy Beer Belly asked that we all go inside for a chat.

The boardwalk was covered in gravel and dust like a hurricane had blown through the parking lot. Guy scraped a sneaker along the planks and asked, "What happened?"

Deputy Crew Cut ushered us inside as he explained. "Helicopter had to land in the parking lot for a medevac."

"I don't want to clean that room," Tilly cried. "I can't go in there."

I hadn't noticed earlier that Burke's had rooms for rent. Who would make this nameless crossroads an overnight stop?

"It's not pretty," Marla said. "But it's your job."

"Not anymore." Tilly wiped her eyes.

Deputy Beer Belly motioned everyone into the dining area and asked us to sit where we'd been for lunch, which left Guy and me in the middle, and Pie Man over at the window. Skeeter the cook, Marla the waitress, and Tilly, the sad girl Friday, stood near the register by Deputy Crew Cut who pointed at Guy and me, then asked the roadhouse people, "So, Verlon Epps was the only other person here at lunch or since, except for these two?"

Pie Man raised a hand and nodded. "Real slow for a Saturday."

The deputies exchanged a look, then Crew Cut sighed and told Beer Belly, "Guess I'm drawing the short straw and going to drive all the way to the Bar X to chat with Epps."

Deputy Beer Belly nodded.

"Verlon only had beer," Tilly said. "He didn't touch anyone's food."

"Two Guinnesses," Marla said, then pointed at Guy and me. "He had the ginger salad. She had fries and a burger, no cheese."

I'd have loved cheese on my burger, but the extra dollar would have meant less tip for her. I shifted on my wooden chair. Hadn't noticed this seat being so uncomfortable when I'd been stuffing the gutbomb in my face.

"That right?" Deputy Crew Cut asked Guy and me.

We nodded.

Deputy Beer Belly checked his notebook. "Everyone belong to the Clean Plate Club?"

"No!" Marla pointed at me and Guy in turns. "She put a big piece of her burger in her napkin, and he didn't finish his salad."

Deputy Beer Belly looked at us hard and turned on a tape recorder. Pie Man jumped to his feet and crossed the floor, making both deputies tell everybody to sit tight. But Pie Man stepped out the restaurant's side door and held it open. One deputy muttered to the other about helping the medics manage the stairs. That's when I saw paramedics down the far hallway, wrestling a gurney toward the open side door.

The woman aboard was still as death, eyes half-closed, gray-skinned. An oxygen mask and a heart monitor hissed and beeped. She crooked a finger to make Crew Cut lean an ear by her mouth. Muffled words blurred through the oxygen mask, then the deputy helped the medics load the gurney in the ambulance. They peeled out like they meant business.

Back at the side door, the deputies started to confer but Pie Man interrupted to ask Deputy Crew Cut, "What'd she say to you?"

"Said she's going to sue you. Sit down where you were for lunch again."

Pie Man winced and obeyed. Guy looked thoughtful and I could see his conclusion about why Pie Man was still here. He owned Burke's Burgers 'n' Brew. He was Burke. And Burke had a hard-edged question for Guy and me. "Neither of you finished your meals?"

Deputy Beer Belly waved him down, indicating he wanted to be the one asking the questions and he'd tear into Guy and me in due course.

"There was a fellow with that lady at lunchtime." I meant to offer information, but everybody looked at me like I was the Reaper, sickle in hand.

"That was the husband who got evacuated by helicopter,"

Deputy Beer Belly explained like he was talking to the terminally stupid. "Hospital said his kidneys are gone and it looks like poisoning. They asked us to check the situation here. By the time we arrived, an ambulance had been called for the woman."

Marla said, "At least her room isn't like his."

Pie Man nodded. "She wasn't sick enough to need a helicopter. Look, they're ill from something medical, not from my restaurant. No way would anyone here tamper with food."

"Yeah, I didn't do nothing," Skeeter said. "Everybody blames the cook, but I didn't do nothing."

"Chef," Guy corrected. He gave a sympathetic nod to Pie Man, like food tampering was any restaurant's worst day.

"I'd never try to make a customer sick," Tilly sobbed. "Never."

I believed her. No one's voice cracks that bad when lying. If an employee messed with the dying man's last meal, it was the waitress. Or the cook. Or the cowboy. Or Burke himself. Or . . .

Or maybe it was the dying man's wife. Why hadn't the couple been sharing a room?

The deputies gave everyone a good looking-at.

I leaned toward Guy with a sideways glance at the waitress. "You said she lied."

Before Guy could respond, the deputies asked if maybe we'd detoured to the kitchen, maybe on our way to or from the restrooms, and what else we saw or heard. Articulate, Guy was, as he lives for parlay on an eating experience. We gathered that the grandma in the ambulance had become so woozy she couldn't stand, but the scene up in the grandpa's room was a vile sight, with the kind of vomiting that can kill, and ruin the housekeeper's day as well.

I a-hemmed. "They're a couple, but they got separate rooms?" I know well that the po-lice should look twice at the man of any killed woman. No reason why it wouldn't work both ways.

"They said he snores so bad they always get two rooms," said Marla. Her boss nodded like he'd heard the same.

"Okay," one deputy said to the other, "the couple got sick hours and hours after eating—"

"Food poisoning affects people a lot faster," Burke said. "So it wasn't—"

Deputy Beer Belly raised a hand. "And the only thing in common in the two sick people's food was the ribeye."

Guy rubbed his jaw. "Which had a basic brown sauce with—"

I cut Guy off with a roll of my eyes, which says awesome things about the power of my scowl. "It's called gravy in these parts." Then my distracted brain caught up to the fact that the meat was suspect and it took hours for the deadly effects to work their horror.

"Charley!" I jumped out of my seat, ignoring the deputies who ordered me to stop as I ran for the door.

***

No head popped up from Ol' Blue's bench seat as I hollered across the parking lot.

"No, no, no!" I yanked the passenger door open.

Charley yawned. I pulled the to-go box out of the cooler and bumped into Deputy Crew Cut as I turned.

"What you got there?" he asked. The whole rest of the line-up was outside on the boardwalk: Guy, Marla, Tilly, Skeeter, and Burke, all standing beside Deputy Beer Belly.

"She gave this to me." I pointed at Tilly with the box, which the deputy snatched away. "Charley, boy, you okay?"

"She did?" Burke shook his head. "I don't know how many times I've told her not to do that."

I coaxed Charley out of Ol' Blue. He hopped down wagging, but I pictured how many meat scraps I'd fed him over the hours to and from Hermiston.

Guy squatted down to eye Charley from his distance. "He looks fine."

"On a lot of ribeye scraps?" Deputy Crew Cut asked.

"Yessir." I obeyed his wave that indicated I should rejoin the group.

Guy turned to Marla. "You said the ribeye had local criminis on it. And you said the ginger on the salad was fresh, but it was from a jar."

"She did?" Burke asked.

Marla waved her hands in self-defense. "So I talk up the food. A little silly maybe, but I'm just being friendly and selling it. We have good food here."

Skeeter folded his arms across his chest, lips sealed.

Guy looked at Burke. "The salt shaker on our table held potassium chloride, not sodium chloride."

I stared at the man who owned the little house where I'd be sleeping tonight. Pretty sure he was wearing an invisible Sherlock Holmes-skin suit. The deputies stared at him, too, so maybe they could see the Sherlock suit. Then we all looked at Burke for an answer.

Burke looked a mix of confused and fussy: *confussed*. "I guess Tilly or Marla or Skeeter put the wrong salt in a shaker. Even I could have done it. But light salt won't hurt anyone."

"Excess potassium can bother some people with sensitive

medical conditions," Guy said. "And there was ginger on the salad and ginger tea in those packets. The woman was drinking tea. Did she have salad?"

Marla nodded. Burke looked more than irritated.

Guy suffered stares from both deputies and all four roadhouse people as he explained. "Ginger might make some people more susceptible to chemical interactions. So, perhaps the lady in the ambulance has underlying health issues. She's understandably upset about her husband, then the excess potassium and ginger tilt her condition. Maybe she's not poisoned at all."

"Well, her husband sure is," Deputy Crew Cut said. "Hospital has him on life support. That's why we got sent out here. And he and his wife had the ribeye."

Deputy Beer Belly squared off against Burke. "And everybody but Tilly, who was outside, remembers you were going to have the ribeye but you changed your order."

A huff of exasperation burst from the owner. "I changed my order because I knew there were only two steaks left. That's why we had it on special. It was left over from Friday night. When I heard two patrons wanting the ribeye, of course I let them have it."

The deputies exchanged another look, but Guy nodded and said, "That's what I'd do at my restaurant."

The Cascade is not Guy's restaurant, though he practically runs the place and does most of the cooking.

Burke folded his arms. "If this was a food tampering situation—and I don't think it was—the safest thing for the offender is to not eat. You'd better find Verlon Epps."

Deputy Beer Belly nodded. "He was here an hour and a half, but only had beer?"

"Guinness," Marla said. "He does that liquid lunch every Saturday."

I thought about the cowboy they called Verlon, remembered the mare's nice shoeing job. He was about the age of the poisoned man. Maybe they had an old beef. Then I looked at Tilly. "That cowboy said it was your last day."

She'd managed to quit crying. "Well, I want out of this town. It's not even a town."

No, it was a crossroads. And the turn picked at an intersection makes all the difference. Charley leaned against my leg, ready to go, like me.

Wouldn't my dog be sick if the ribeye was bad? I rubbed his soft yellow head.

"The gravy," I whispered to Guy as he slipped to my side.

"The mushrooms in the sauce." Guy pointed to the big cedar

and called out to the deputies. "I took a mushrooming class. Those little tan toadstools under that tree are *pholiotina rugosa*. I kicked them over when we were here earlier. They're one of the deadliest mushrooms in the Pacific Northwest. Ingestion causes extreme vomiting, though not until hours after consumption. And they kill the kidneys."

Deputy Beer Belly asked, "How much would a person have to eat?"

"Half a mushroom could kill you," Guy said. "It'd be easy to slip one in the mushroom sauce or onto a prepared meal."

Tilly gasped.

I looked at Burke. "She didn't quit, did she? You fired her."

He made a wry face. "She's a good kid but her ex-boyfriend was here and she sugared his gas tank. He probably had it coming, but I can't have an employee messing with a patron's . . ."

We looked at Tilly, who said, "I thought they just make a person sick."

I spoke to her, loud enough for everyone to hear. "You meant that meal to go to your boss, didn't you?"

Marla and Skeeter gasped with Burke. "Tilly!"

"I didn't think it'd be this bad. I only meant . . ." Tilly had put the poisonous mushroom on the ribeye she expected would be served to her soon-to-be-ex boss. But she'd been outside when he'd allowed a patron to have his steak.

Deputy Beer Belly told her he was going to read her her rights and ask for a formal statement. As she got searched and put in the cruiser's back seat, Tilly's cries became howls.

Takes guts to try revenge-poisoning your boss. It also takes guts to stay where few folks scratch out a living in a dusty crossroads or in a scrubby town like Cowdry. Take Guy, buying a foreclosed little house and cooking at the Cascade. Sometimes he takes a trail to town, running through the forest and farmland. I'd been tempted to try it on Red, but my priority had been figuring out where to establish myself.

"Can we go?" I asked.

With Deputy Crew Cut's nod, I headed for Ol' Blue.

Guy fell in step beside me, opened the driver's door for me, too. Our fingertips brushed, and I sort of hoped he'd ask again to hold my hand. I considered him, how he made a pretty good burger, and seemed more than a decent fellow. Maybe my way forward could be in Cowdry, Oregon. Bloom where I'm planted.

When Guy slid into Ol' Blue on the other side of Charley, I posed a pretty good question. "You know that dirt area behind the Cascade?"

He leaned toward me over Charley, who licked his face. “What about it?”

“You reckon the owner’d mind if I was to put a hitching rail there?”

DEADLY IN-FLIGHT DINING

By Sara Rosett

Airplane meals in coach class are usually nothing to look forward to. But you don't expect one to be deadly.

I stepped from the Jetway into the airplane aisle, which was crowded with people, luggage, and flight attendants moving against the tide. The line bottlenecked to a halt, and Alex, who was behind me, said, "Not quite the Orient Express."

"No, but they do seem to have good coffee." I drew in a breath of the aroma of dark roast drifting out of the first-class cabin.

"Always a good thing on an early morning flight." Alex's eyelids were heavy. He'd been up late last night coordinating an upcoming meeting for our location-scouting business, and then the three a.m. alarm had cut short our sleep.

The line straggled forward and I inched along, lugging my carry-on bag and trying to avoid bumping passengers' elbows. The return journey of our honeymoon was quite a contrast from the first leg of our trip. Alex had surprised me with tickets on the Orient Express. Agatha Christie fan that I am, I loved every minute of it, even though the journey from Paris to Venice didn't follow the same route as the train in *Murder on the Orient Express*. Once we reached Venice, we'd made our way leisurely through the rolling hills of Tuscany, down to the busyness of Rome, and then on to the chaos of Naples. Along the way, we'd indulged in delicious cappuccino, antipasto, prosciutto, spaghetti alla carbonara, buffalo mozzarella, margherita pizza, gelato, and tiramisu. I also never passed a display of *pains au chocolat* without sampling one.

"I have a feeling that the food will be quite a comedown after what we've experienced for the last few weeks," Alex said. "Airline food is always terrible."

I patted the insulated bag perched on top of my suitcase, which contained a *mezzo* kilo of creamy buffalo mozzarella packed in a water and whey mixture and sealed like a goldfish in an airtight bag. "That's why we're bringing some Italy home with us." Buffalo mozzarella, a specialty of the Campania region around Naples, was unlike any mozzarella I'd ever had. Not dry and crumbly, it had a smooth texture and a rich flavor that complemented the acidic bite of tomatoes in a Caprese salad. Topped with a drizzle of olive oil, fresh basil, and a sprinkle of pepper, the dish was a perfect combination of Italian flavors—and the colors of the Italian flag, to boot. I couldn't wait to make my own version. We'd also picked up biscotti, not having much faith in the airline-provided "light breakfast."

We reached our seats, and Alex stowed our carry-on bags in the overhead bin. The flight was packed, and we weren't sitting side by side. The economy cabin was designed with two seats on each side of the plane and a row of four seats between them. I took the aisle seat in the middle of the cabin with three other empty seats stretching out to the right of me. On my left, Alex took the other aisle seat. "Sleep well," I said.

"I'm looking forward to a few extra hours."

I'd barely sat down when a man in his early twenties with dark curls poking out from under a droopy knit beanie paused beside me. He removed one earbud and pointed to the seat down the row. "Sorry, I'm over there."

"No problem." I slithered into the aisle as he pulled his canvas messenger bag close to his body and moved down the row. He settled in, removing a tablet, phone, and two external battery packs, then stowed his messenger bag under the seat, the flannel of his shirt straining against his skinny back. He arranged his tablet and phone on his lap and hunched over the screens.

"Ugh. I'm on the wrong aisle."

A compact woman with short blond hair in a pixie cut had halted beside me. She wore a pale blue shirt made of high-performance wicking fabric along with khaki capris. The small gold studs in her earlobes were her only jewelry, and she wore no makeup. Her shoes were sturdy walking sandals I'd seen many tourists wearing. I wished I'd had a pair when we were crisscrossing the cobblestone streets.

"Are you on this row?"

I shifted to slip out of the seat again, but before I could move, she said, "Yes," and stepped over me, her tanned calves bulging. Her huge backpack came within millimeters of my nose as she shifted by. She muttered, "It'll be a miracle if we land at the right airport. These bozos can't even tell me which aisle is closest to my seat." She stowed her backpack and threw herself back against her seat, her hands gripped together in her lap and her eyes closed.

I took out my book, *Death in the Clouds,* as the flight attendants closed the overhead bins. A well-padded woman dashed down the aisle. Her bobbed brown hair had a single swath of neon blue on one side. She hurried forward, a cardboard cup of gourmet coffee extended ahead of her like a rapier. Her huge purse bumped from shoulder to shoulder as she dragged her suitcase, banging it against seats and passengers.

She flew past, and her suitcase smacked Alex's leg. He opened an eye and rolled his head toward me.

"Late passenger," I explained.

"Oh, I thought it was turbulence."

"No. We're not off the ground yet."

The woman reversed, banged against Alex again, then jerked to a stop and pointed to the empty seat beside me. "I think I'm right there." After a flight attendant found a place for the woman's suitcase, she shuffled by me, her huge hoop earrings swinging. She plopped into her seat and immediately turned to me, tossing the blue section of hair off her face. "Whew. That was a close one, but I *had* to have my coffee. Airline food—and coffee—can be horrendous. I'm Beatrice Cannon."

"Kate Sha—I mean, Norcutt." Alex slit one eye and sent me a grin. I still wasn't used to my married name.

Beatrice noticed my stumble and the look Alex and I exchanged. "Newlyweds! You must be. Am I right?"

I didn't want a fuss, but I couldn't keep it quiet now. Heedless of the promptings to put away everything and prepare for takeoff, Beatrice dropped down her tray table and set her coffee on it while she rooted around in her enormous purse. "That is just the sweetest thing, honeymooning in Italy. Not at all what Russell and I did. It was Florida for us." She wrinkled her nose. "I was lucky to get Russell that far—such a homebody. Doesn't want to leave the US of A. He didn't want to come with me on this art trip either." She reached into the side pocket on the purse, took out a packet of artificial sweetener, and dumped it in her coffee. "It's a good thing Nell is willing to travel." Beatrice pointed with the empty pink sachet to the compact blond woman down the row who sat with her eyes closed and appeared to be doing deep breathing.

Beatrice shook her head. "Nell hates to fly, but sometimes you must do things for work." Beatrice stuffed the pink sachet in the seatback pocket in front of her, shoved her purse under the seat, then whirred the stir stick around her coffee. "Nell Halloway, my business partner. Although only partially. I own sixty percent of the company stock. I got the business off the ground. Nell popped in later to give me support with the day-to-day, but she understands how important it is for two of us to be on this trip."

Beatrice noticed my finger in my book. "Sorry, I'm running on and on. I'm a nervous flyer. It tends to make me a chatterbox. Instead of doing yoga breathing like Nell, I talk. I'm an absolute mess before a flight." She nudged her purse with her toe. "It's a good thing Russell takes care of me. I couldn't concentrate on picking out clothes. He packed absolutely everything for me before I left, even my purse."

I couldn't imagine letting Alex pack my suitcase. I was too Type A for that.

"Of course, when I put everything back it doesn't look nearly as good." Beatrice sipped her coffee and sent me a strained smile.

I'd never had anxiety when I flew—I'd done so much of it I barely thought about it—but I could sympathize. I closed my book. "So this is an art trip?"

She waived the coffee in a circle, indicating the rows around us. "Most of these people are students." She tilted her head at the young man on her right-hand side. "This is Tanner Trevino."

He didn't look up from his tablet, and she bumped his shoulder. "Tanner is the son of one of my oldest friends. He's into anime."

When Tanner finally looked up, Beatrice pointed to me. "This is Kate. She's on her honeymoon. That's her husband over there, sleeping."

Tanner gave a quick nod, then returned his gaze to his screen. Beatrice hitched around so her shoulders were angled toward me. She lowered her voice again. "Diane—his mother—hoped this trip would break him out of his online world. We weren't successful. It's sad—some of the most beautiful art in the world, and he's fixated on those tiny screens."

She sighed, then pointed to a woman on Tanner's other side. "Nell's a sculptor. Her pieces are powerful. Very powerful."

"Is that a bad thing?" Beatrice's tone indicated it was.

"Well . . . it can be. Nell doesn't realize when people buy art for their home, they usually want something beautiful. For instance,"—she took a sip of her coffee then lifted it in the direction of the couple in the row in front of Alex—"take Mr. and Mrs. Ruiz. Although I should say Dr. and Dr. Ruiz. She's an orthodontist. He's a cardiologist. They want art in their home, but they don't want to look at something disturbing and grim every day. They want something attractive." She shook her head. "I suppose Nell will learn eventually. And then we have the water colorists on this row . . ." Beatrice went on, describing each person, which carried us through takeoff and well into the flight. I couldn't keep up with the names or art styles, but Beatrice didn't seem to mind, and the longer she talked, the more relaxed she seemed.

The fasten seatbelt light went off, and the flight attendants trundled down the aisle with the drink and food carts. The flight attendant plucked down cocktail napkins for Beatrice and me. I asked for black coffee, but Beatrice lifted her cardboard coffee and shook her head. I wrapped my hands around the Styrofoam cup and inhaled the scent of dark roast.

Beatrice studied the cocktail napkin with the airline logo and made a tsking sound. “So boring.” She traced her finger along the edge of the design. “If they’d only added a shadow here, they could have used it as contrast to highlight the lettering. It would’ve made it so much more interesting.” She looked up and grimaced. “Sorry. I’m a graphic designer. Sometimes I can’t help myself.”

“I thought you ran an art school.”

She was about to take a sip of coffee but burst out laughing. “Art school? Far from it. The art classes and trips are a side hustle. We had to do something to bring in revenue. We’re a graphic design firm, but there are logo generators online now. A few clicks, fifty dollars later—and *presto*—you’ve got a logo. We can’t compete with that. But we can share our artistic and design expertise. We have painting and wine evenings, art classes, and trips. This is our first international one.”

“Interesting.” Alex and I were branching out into the online world, creating a website to connect location scouts and owners of stately homes. Before I could mention our venture, Beatrice blew out a long breath. “Of course, now that things are finally picking up, Russell wants me to sell my stock and then . . .” She shrugged. “I don’t know. He has some sort of idea we’ll join the country club and golf every day.” She touched the streak of royal blue in her hair. “I’m not exactly country club material, and I hate sports—all of them. He spends hours at the gym, and I’m not going there either.”

She squared her shoulders and gave a sharp shake of her head. “No matter what Russell thinks, I know I’m better off working.” She lifted the cup in a salute. “Here’s to *not* retiring.”

The flight attendant on the other aisle parked her cart and handed a tray of food to Nell, who passed it down the row. I reached for the biscotti, but before I could wave off a tray, I had one settled in front of me with anemic slices of ham, a cherry tomato that resembled a pink gumball, a crumbly roll, and prepackaged yogurt, juice, and jam.

Beatrice’s mouth pressed into a flat line as she contemplated her food. “Well, there’s a reason you never hear anyone say ‘I love airline food.’” She peeled back the lid of the yogurt.

I settled my book in front of the tray and opened the bag. The murmur of conversation faded as everyone hunched over their meal. I was several pages into the first chapter when Beatrice made a gasping sound. Her skin was flushed bright red, and she had one hand pressed to her forehead. "The turbulence—" She swallowed hard. "It makes me ill."

"But there's no turbulence." She didn't seem to take in what I'd said. "Are you okay?" I asked.

She gasped and a spasm ran through her body. The contortions of her legs knocked her breakfast tray sideways, and food cascaded to the floor. Then she collapsed onto the empty tray table.

Stunned, I stared at her. "Beatrice? Are you okay?"

I couldn't rouse her. Tanner had looked away from his screens, and his wide-eyed gaze locked on me as I pushed the call button.

Carts and trays were pushed away. The other passengers and I scrambled out of the row to let the two doctors in.

I was close enough to see the husband and wife exchange a glance of dismay. Dr. Ruiz—the cardiologist—motioned for the flight attendant. "There's nothing we can do," he said. "Looks like she was poisoned. Cyanide, I believe."

***

Several hours later I paced around a featureless room in the Frankfurt airport with a single long table and several uncomfortable plastic chairs. Our flight had been diverted, and as soon as we landed, everyone had been escorted off the plane. We had to leave all our belongings in place, and Alex and I had been separated. Those of us on the row with Beatrice, along with the flight attendant who'd handed out the food trays, an Italian woman in her twenties with dark hair, gorgeous brown eyes, and a lithe figure, were escorted to the gray room. Each of us had been questioned separately by the team of investigators who all spoke impeccable English, then we were escorted back to our gray room. The lead investigator appeared to be a Detective Weber, a man with a penetrating stare and the habit of twirling his pencil when it wasn't tucked behind his ear.

Alex had managed to talk his way into the room a few hours ago. He and the other passengers had been cleared to continue with their travel as soon as their luggage was released from the airplane—the crime scene. I'd told Alex he should go on. "We have that meeting about Archly Manor. It could be a big boost for us."

He shook his head. "I may be a new husband, but I know it's bad form to leave your wife when the woman next to her has been murdered." He squeezed my hand. I squeezed back.

The Italian flight attendant paced back and forth. "This is unacceptable. I must leave. My sister's wedding is in two days. Two days! I have to be in Milan." She switched to staccato Italian, her torrent of angry words edged with fear.

Nell, who had been silent the whole time but had kept wiping the back of her hand across her eyes, slapped the table. "A woman is dead. That's more important than a wedding. Stop blubbering. You're not even the bride."

"I need to get back, too," Tanner said and mumbled something about an exam. Without his tablet and phone, he slumped in one of the chairs, looking confused like an underground creature suddenly finding himself in blinding light. Nell transferred her glare from the flight attendant to Tanner. He fell silent.

The flight attendant said, "Yes, it is a terrible thing. Awful. Tragic." She pressed her hand to her chest. "But *I* had nothing to do with it."

Nell surged forward. "You handled the food, and Beatrice was poisoned. Dr. Ruiz said it was cyanide."

I stepped between the two women. "Perhaps. He wasn't sure. There will have to be tests."

"Tests take time," the flight attendant said. "I don't have that."

"And I want to know who killed Beatrice." Nell fisted her hand. She had the vibrating energy of a small angry dog.

"I'm sure we all want to know that," I said. Tensions on location sets could run high, and it was always best to diffuse the situation. Out of habit, I grabbed a chair and sat opposite Nell. "Let's see if we can figure out what happened."

Alex pulled another chair forward. "Good idea. Maybe we can expedite things."

Nell stared at Alex, then at me for a moment, and gave a sharp nod. "All right. How?"

Alex looked toward the flight attendant. "What can you tell us about the food?"

She whirled around from where she'd been pacing at the other end of the room. "I did not put anything in the food. Like I told all of those *polizia*."

"We're not saying you did." I ignored Nell's muttered comment. "All we want to know is how the food is handled. Right, Alex?"

"Yes. How does the food arrive on the plane?"

"Oh." She deflated. "I don't know much about that. I'm Lucia, by the way." She came to the table and sat as far from Nell as she could. "Food service loads the meals. We have nothing to do with the preparation."

"Do you warm it?" I asked.

"No. It was a cold breakfast. We simply take the cart and hand out the food."

"And how do you distribute the food?" Alex asked.

Her forehead wrinkled. "What do you mean?"

"Are the trays matched up with the seats? Does a certain tray go to a certain seat?"

She waved a hand. "No. Too confusing. We just hand them out. No set pattern."

"And you didn't see anyone messing with the trays?" I asked.

"No passengers were in the galley. That comes later, at the end of the flight when everyone wants to use the restroom."

"Did you know Beatrice?" I asked.

"They asked me that, too. No! She was one of over a hundred passengers."

Alex used his most soothing tone as he said, "Of course. It was a full flight."

I switched my attention to Nell. "So Lucia handed a food tray to you, and you passed it on?"

"Yes."

We all turned to Tanner. He raised his hands. "I didn't do anything to it. I passed it to Beatrice."

Nell leaned forward, "But your mom thinks she got a raw deal and blames Beatrice."

"What?" Tanner said.

"The logo thing."

Tanner's face relaxed. "From art school? My mom didn't hold a grudge over that."

Nell crossed her arms and scowled at Tanner. "That's hard to believe."

Tanner shook his head so hard that his knit beanie slipped. He dragged it back into place. "*Now* she wishes she'd taken the job, but she says you can't change the past. She's moved on. And if you think I'd hurt Beatrice because of something that happened twenty years ago to my mom—you're crazy."

I leaned forward. "What logo are we talking about?"

Nell swiveled toward me. "Back when Beatrice and her best friend Diane were in art school, a company needed a logo. Diane was going to do the freelance job until she found out she was going to be paid in company stock." Nell cut her gaze towards Tanner. "She walked away. Beatrice took the job and came up with a completely new design, which they loved."

Alex asked, "What was the company?"

Nell said, "Genius Technologies."

"Oh." I fell back in the chair. Genius Technologies was one of the biggest tech companies in the world. Even I—someone who didn't keep up with stocks—knew it had to be priced in the thousands of dollars per share. If Beatrice owned their stock, it would be worth a huge sum of money.

Tanner said, "It's true, my mom missed out on a lot of money, but she doesn't hold a grudge. She'll be devastated when she finds out what happened to Beatrice. If anyone had a motive for wanting Beatrice out of the way, it was you." Tanner pointed at Nell. "You were her business partner, and everyone in the art classes knows you argued all the time."

Nell looked as if someone had slapped her. "Yes, Beatrice and I disagreed—I don't know any business partners who don't—but that's not something I'd kill her over. Besides, her share of the company goes to Russell." Nell's face changed as she said the last words. A wrinkle appeared between her brows.

"What is it?" I asked. "You look as if a thought popped into your head, and you don't like it."

"It's nothing, I'm sure."

"I think you should tell us," Tanner said. "You're throwing around accusations about my mom. What are *you* trying to hide?"

"Not trying to hide anything. I just don't . . . know . . ."

Lucia said, "I agree with Tanner. If you know something—or suspect something—you should tell us."

"All right. Beatrice thought Russell might be having an affair."

"But he sounded as if he was very caring towards Beatrice," I said. "She talked about him, how she was so nervous about flying that he helped her get ready for the trip."

Nell lifted her shoulder. "All I know is Beatrice said he was secretive about his phone lately. He wouldn't let her use it. Then," —Nell looked away as she said,—"I saw him at the gym a few weeks ago talking with another woman. It looked like . . . well, like it was more than friendly chitchat. That's all I can say. I don't *know* he was having an affair. And I don't see how it matters because he's not here."

"Are you sure he's still in the States?" Alex asked.

Nell's shoulders, which had hunched as she spoke, relaxed. "Yes, Beatrice FaceTimed with him last night. He was in their backyard. He's not here. And even if he were here, Beatrice was poisoned with cyanide. Where would he get that?"

"It's not that hard to get cyanide," Tanner said.

We all turned toward him, and he shifted back in his chair at the force of our glances. "Hey, it's a common fact," he said. "Cyanide is in all sorts of foods—apple seeds, cherry and apricot pits, almonds, all kinds of things like that."

Nell narrowed her eyes. "How do you know this?"

"I'm a chemistry major. I wrote a paper on it. And even if I wasn't, there's the internet. Anybody could find out."

"But how would someone get cyanide into the food Beatrice ate on the airplane?"

The door opened and startled us. Detective Weber came in, his pencil tucked behind his ear. He carried a paper bag in one hand and a cardboard container of coffee and sodas in the other. "Help yourself. Sandwiches in the bag."

I stared at the food and drinks he'd placed on the table, my thoughts whirling.

"Kate."

I turned to Alex. "Hmm?"

He tilted his head at Tanner, who'd removed a sandwich from the bag and now held the open bag out to me.

"Oh, sorry." I passed the bag to Alex.

Weber had taken out his notebook and twirled his pencil as he addressed Lucia. "These things take time. I'm afraid I can't tell you how much longer it will be. We should have some answers soon. Now, a few more questions—"

Lucia groaned and waved away the food.

I shifted toward the detective. "I think you might be able to clear this up quickly."

"Oh, you do, do you?"

"Yes." I waved my hand around the table, indicating our group. "We've had a little chat, and I think we figured out what happened."

"We did?" Nell said.

"Yes, I think so." I turned to Weber. "Lucia told us the food wasn't handed out in any particular order, and that she didn't have any connection to Beatrice. It would be difficult to put cyanide on a tray without someone—a flight attendant or another passenger—noticing in such close quarters. And none of us saw Nell or Tanner add anything to Beatrice's food as the tray was passed down the row, right?" I looked from Lucia to Nell to Tanner. They all shook their heads. "So," I continued, "Beatrice's food wasn't poisoned, but her coffee was."

Weber rotated the pencil slowly. "My expert tells me it can take anywhere from a few minutes to fifteen minutes for cyanide to have an effect. It's not always instantaneous." The pencil turned faster. "And if she'd eaten earlier, food could delay the symptoms." He didn't look happy at this news. He tucked the pencil behind his ear and flipped back through the notebook pages. "You said she brought her coffee onto the plane, Mrs. Norcutt." His hand dropped to his side. "That means we've got to go all the way back to the Rome airport."

"I don't think you will," I said. "If you check the seatback pocket in front of Beatrice's seat, you'll find a small packet of artificial sweetener. It's empty—but I bet you'll find traces of cyanide in it."

Weber squinted at me. "And why would you think that?"

"Because Beatrice's very helpful husband packed her suitcase *and* her purse—she told me about it. Beatrice mentioned her husband wanted her to sell her stock and retire. I thought she was talking about stock in her graphic design company, but Beatrice owned stock in Genius Technologies. She'd owned it since the company was a startup. It's apparently worth quite a bit of money, right?" I looked towards Nell with raised eyebrows.

"Oh, yes. At least a million by now."

Weber dropped his pencil.

"Her husband definitely wanted her to sell her stock, but she told me she wasn't going to do it. And it sounds as if her husband might be having an affair."

The detective gazed around our little group for a moment. "It couldn't hurt to check."

***

A month later Alex and I were in the kitchen of our Derbyshire cottage in our village, Nether Woodsmoor, with rain racing down the window panes. Italy seemed a million miles away, but we'd found a shop that imported buffalo mozzarella, and I was drizzling olive oil over chunks of creamy cheese and cherry tomatoes. Our greyhound, Slink, was stationed by my knee, sitting at attention. She'd never had buffalo mozzarella, but her dark-eyed gaze conveyed she was sure she'd adore it.

Alex came in with the mail. "We have a package. It's from Nell."

I put down the olive oil. "I didn't think we'd ever hear from her again."

The package contained a note along with a framed sketch of an Italian feast of pasta, bread, and wine spread on a table by a balcony overlooking the Italian countryside. "It's gorgeous," I said.

Alex opened the note and read it aloud.

> *Dear Kate and Alex,*
>
> *I'd like you to have this sketch Beatrice did while we were in Italy. I appreciate what you did for Beatrice and thought you might like an update on what happened. Russell is awaiting trial, and I have no doubt the outcome will be 'guilty.' His fingerprints were on the packet of artificial sweetener—the inside of it—which describes him to a tee. He's always been*

slipshod. He set it up so that Beatrice's death would happen when she was across the ocean from him, but he didn't wear gloves when he opened the packet and added the poison. He even resealed it so that it looked like a normal sweetener. I suppose he thought the packet would be thrown away or overlooked.

He had another surprise, too. Russell didn't think to check Beatrice's will. She must've suspected something because she made a new will recently, and Russell isn't listed as a beneficiary. The Genius Technology stock was in her name alone, and she specified it be divided among her favorite charities, family members, and friends. I'm using my portion to set up a scholarship fund for art students. I think Beatrice would like that. I hope you enjoy her sketch.

I studied the drawing. "How thoughtful—and unexpected—of Nell to send this."

Alex folded the note. "Yes, she didn't seem to be a very . . . um . . . considerate kind of person."

"She was under a lot of stress. Where should we put it?" I asked, looking around our tiny cottage. We didn't have much wall space.

"What about the nook by the breakfast table?"

"Good idea." None of our pictures were the right size for that sliver of wall. I inched around the table and held up the sketch. "It's perfect."

CARNE DIEM

By Sharon Lynn

Hawaiian barbecue ribs at a marina party sounds fantastic until the first guest in line finds out what "at your own peril" means.

Attend the marina party at . . .

Lucy Davidovich's blue eyes crinkled in delight as she picked up the piece of paper placed between the coils of her dock line. Today's resort-hosted marina party was the highlight of every summer, and this would be her first one. She couldn't wait.

Tucking a brunette curl behind her ear, she unfolded the note and read *Attend the marina party at your own peril.* She turned it over, head cocked.

"What?" The threat looked so normal, like something Lucy could print at home. She checked coils next to the forty-seven-foot trawler across the dock finger from her thirty-two-foot express cruiser for a similar message but found nothing.

Clutching the note, she walked along E Dock, took the extension to F, and went to the end. Her new boat friends, Adam and Amanda Harper, sat on the top deck of their sixty-footer.

Adam's surfer-blonde head poked over the side. "Hi, Lucy! Come on up!"

Lucy's mood lightened as she climbed the portable stairs on the finger, stepped onto the gunnel, and then scampered to the top level. Even though she'd known them only a month, her neighbors had welcomed her to the marina like family.

"Coffee?" Adam offered. "It's Kona."

"In anticipation of Yamaguchi's Hawaiian barbecue ribs they'll serve at the party over at the hotel," Amanda explained, tying her long raven hair into a ponytail.

Accepting a cup of the aromatic brew, Lucy took a sip. Delicate, silky mouthfeel, sweet, with a smooth, clean, finish. "Mmmmm. It's almost like milk chocolate."

"Perfection," Amanda agreed, pouring herself another cup.

As Lucy sipped, Bill Swift's tall, sinewy form came from below decks and tumbled next to Amanda. He owned a sailboat one gate over, yet he seemed like a permanent installation on the

Harpers' boat, almost a part of the furniture.

"Hey, Lucy." Bill gestured to Adam for coffee.

Lucy held the note out to them. "Did you get one of these?"

Adam read it and shrugged. "No, but don't worry about it."

Lucy's eyes went wide.

"There's always someone unhappy with management. Some of the folks who've been here forever think if they cause a fuss their rates will get lowered. Ignore it."

Lucy shook her head. "I mean this, and the warning to not go near the Coast of Mexico. It's a lot to take in."

"Oh, that's just silly," Amanda asserted. "We've been here a decade, and every time we've run into someone off the Baja, it's a fisherman, not some crazed yacht thief."

Adam pointed at her. "Except that one time it was a guy selling hash." He turned to Lucy. "Again, not a big deal."

"You sure?"

He nodded, patting the bench next to him. "Yep. Sit."

"Every year someone threatens the marina office." A crease formed between Amanda's deep brown eyes, marring her perfect complexion. "Although no one has ever said 'peril' before."

Adam shrugged. "The dock master's only six months on the job. The old timers think they can bully him. I'm sure it's fine. Besides, Hawaiian ribs."

His nonchalance comforted Lucy and excitement about the event bubbled up. "You've mentioned the ribs twice now. What's the deal?"

"You've never had them?" Amanda's expression bordered on flabbergasted.

Lucy grinned, shaking her head. "And apparently my life is incomplete."

"You have no idea. Meat perfection. Subtle, not smoky. Almost a subdued sweetness."

Practically salivating, Adam picked up the description. "They're like self-contained kebabs. The bone is perfectly weighted. And you know how I feel about bo—"

"Don't even go there," Amanda warned.

Without a pause, Adam continued, "A hint of spice. Tender, but not like, you know—"

"Just falling apart. It comes off in bite-sized chunks of . . ."

"Heaven," they concluded in unison.

Holding her hands in a stop motion, Lucy laughed. "Okay, okay, I get it! The ribs are worth risking peril."

***

As the four of them piled into the elevator of the hotel next to the marina, a large hand shot through the closing doors, causing Lucy to jump. The hand belonged to Herbert, who forced his bulk into the center of the group, followed by his French bulldog, Boola.

"Hey, Herbert." Amanda's greeting received only a grunt in reply.

An old-timer who would make a threat, Lucy thought. She shrank back until the elevator doors opened onto the rooftop terrace, sparkling in the late afternoon sunshine. They bolted to the table nearest the buffet.

When the bamboo lid was lifted from the chafing dish, the whispered scent of ribs drifted through the crowd, and like seagulls the guests descended on the feast. Adam and Amanda pushed Lucy near the front of the line.

"You won't be disappointed," Amanda assured her.

Lucy looked over her shoulder. "I feel like I'm being initiated into a cult."

"Oh, you are," Adam said in mock seriousness. "You are."

Amanda peered around Lucy. "Adam? Who's that?"

The man at the front of the line wore a torn t-shirt, cut-off jeans, and flip-flops. Typical for the docks, but for this event everyone else had dressed up.

Adam craned his neck and watched the man pile ribs onto his plate. "Peter. You know, he owns Pepe's. The poop guy."

Pepe's pump out service emptied out holding tanks at the moorings.

"Why is he here, though?"

Lucy was curious, too. She rarely used the bathroom on her boat, preferring the nicely furnished restrooms the marina provided, but she had booked Pepe's service for today. It wasn't appetizing to think about.

Adam raised one shoulder. "Don't know. Why is he taking so many ribs?"

Plate overflowing, one rib in hand, Pepe munched as he walked off, clearing the way for Lucy. Not wanting to seem greedy, she selected two ribs.

"Take more," Adam advised.

A rumble in Lucy's stomach served as further encouragement. The scent of chilies, ginger, and garlic wafted to her nose. She grabbed two more.

They looked beautiful. Uniform in size, crispy caramelization on the edges and a dusting of white sesame seeds created a picture-perfect dish.

Carrying the plate back to her table, Lucy ignored the growling hunger and waited for her friends. Her mouth watered.

As Amanda, Adam, and Bill approached the table, all three waved her on.

"Don't wait for us! Dig in!"

Lucy picked up the top rib, feeling the weight. A slight tremor in her hand let her know she'd waited too long to get fuel, but she'd wanted to be hungry so she hadn't eaten.

Just as she opened her mouth, an ear-splitting scream echoed through the courtyard.

Lucy's view was blocked. Reluctantly setting aside her food, she made her way to the commotion.

"Somebody do something! Who knows CPR?"

Amanda looked around, wild-eyed. "Adam! Help him!"

He pushed forward. "I'm a doctor," Adam proclaimed.

"You're a dentist," someone called derisively. But no one laughed.

The crowd parted.

Pepe with the pump-out service, who shouldn't have been at the party, writhed in pain on the ground, foaming at the mouth. Then he went stiff.

Adam turned him over and put fingers inside his mouth to clear the airway for CPR.

"Stop!" a voice filled with years of whiskey and cigarettes commanded. Herbert stomped his way to the victim. "See the foam? It could be poison."

"Poison." The word spread through the party like fire. Everyone's plates dropped.

"But?" Adam looked hopeless.

Herbert shook his head. "It could spread to you, then we'd have twice the trouble." He raised his head, eyes searching. "Where's the dock master?"

The man in charge stood paralyzed. Lucy understood how he felt. She didn't know how to help either.

Herbert pointed. "Pull it together, man. Call hotel security." He pointed to someone else. "Call 9-1-1."

Adam checked for a pulse then shook his head.

A rib fell from Pepe's hand.

Pepe Le Poo was dead.

Bill stumbled to Amanda and Lucy, holding out his arms. "Come on, ladies." He steered them underneath the tent where a cool breeze whipped the tablecloths.

A shiver ran through Lucy.

"Did you know him well?" Lucy asked as Adam joined them.

Amanda bobbed her head. "I guess. Adam worked on his teeth at our office."

He nodded. "Yeah, a couple of times."

Lucy looked at Bill who appeared befuddled. Without eating he'd still managed to get a stain on his shirt.

"Did you know Pepe?" she prompted.

Bill smiled. "Whenever he finished with the boat, he'd text two emojis. A thumbs up, and a smiling pile of poop."

***

Hotel security and the police arrived in force, covered the body, and corralled everyone under the tent.

Cold and hungry, Lucy forced the image of Pepe's lifeless body from her mind. But she couldn't stop her mind from going back to the note.

She drew Amanda aside. "Do you think the threat I found this morning was meant for Pepe? He was going to service my boat today."

"What I don't understand is how he got an invite. If we can find out who invited him, that'll tell us something."

"Maybe tainting the food was the message to management that Adam mentioned."

Amanda shook her head. "I don't see how poisoning the party's food would convince management to lower our slip fees."

Lucy shrugged. "Neither do I. And how did Herbert recognize the poison so fast?" She rubbed her arms, looking for a warmer area, her hunt derailed when a man in a suit arrived.

"I'm Detective Tony Nardovino. Each of you will be questioned then released back to the marina."

The tall, muscular detective's face remained serene amidst the onslaught of complaints that followed from the hungry crowd.

Lucy turned and discovered Bill and Adam each draped across two chairs to keep anyone else from sitting. Adam stood, indicating that Lucy should sit while Amanda sank next to Bill.

Looking at the bar, Bill tipped his chair back until he lost balance. Reaching a lanky arm to catch himself, he stumbled upright, muttering something about a drink.

"Bill," Lucy called. "I don't think that's a good idea."

He waved, heading to the abandoned bar.

A hotel staffer made to intercept.

Chuckling at his friend, Adam said, "It won't matter. They won't give him any."

His gesticulations provided a welcome distraction.

Lightheaded, Lucy regretted not having breakfast. Or lunch. Even though her stomach churned, the lack of food poked at her nerves.

As Bill came back empty-handed, the detective called out a request.

"What?"

"He said your name," Amanda told her, eyes bulging. "What did you do?"

"Nothing!"

"Lucy Davidovich?" Nardovino repeated.

She stood so quickly she had to steady herself before walking.

Quiet fell over the crowd, all eyes on her.

"Ms. Davidovich?"

Lucy nodded, not trusting her voice.

Nardovino tapped on a tablet, then made eye contact, shooting electricity into Lucy's fuzzy brain. Bright hazel eyes bore into hers.

"How well did you know the deceased?"

"Me?" she squeaked. "Not at all. I mean, I texted him about servicing my boat, but that's it."

He frowned, consulting the tablet again, then tapped and turned the device to her.

"Is this your signature?"

Lucy wanted so badly to say no, but she couldn't.

Nardovino must have seen the admission on her face. "He attended the party as your guest."

Relief flooded into her. "Nope. I didn't invite anyone." She lifted three fingers. "Scouts honor."

A smile flashed across his face. He indicated they should walk and talk.

"But this is your name?" His conversational tone put Lucy at ease.

She recalled all of the transactions she'd had at the marina office. Almost everything required a signature. "I sign for stuff all the time. Parking passes, ice, access cards. They have a computer, but the office keeps everything in duplicate."

He blinked a few times, processing the information. "You're saying they use carbon copies?"

"Yep. Old school," Lucy confirmed.

He came to a table and held out a folding chair for her.

She'd been so distracted by the conversation she hadn't noticed they'd gone through an employee-only corridor and were now in a square, white-walled area, like an interrogation room. Did she need a lawyer? Hunger robbed her of the ability to think.

"Do you have any food on you?"

He checked his watch. "When did you last sign for something?"

She thought back to mid-week and pictured Bill hoisting a

twenty-pound bag of ice for her. "Wednesday." Her fingertips tingled, indicating an impending sugar crash. "So, no food? A mint would help."

Sighing, he told her, "I'm going to send you to your boat. You are to stay there until an officer clears you. The Coast Guard is blocking the mouth of the marina. No one gets out."

Lucy bolted up from her chair, but black spots formed in her eyes and she dropped back. "One sec," she said. Standing more slowly, she weaved her way out of the hotel to the marina. As she pulled out her access key, she noticed a burly policeman following her.

"You're a quiet one," she told him.

Once on board, she crammed a handful of graham crackers into her mouth while searching her tiny pantry for more food. They tasted gummy, but she had another one since there wasn't anything else.

"Okay," she said, formulating a plan. "Cooking it is."

The kitchen consisted of a dorm-sized fridge, two burners, and a microwave. Lucy pulled out her rice maker in the hopes that it would act as an oven.

Flour, Dutch-process cocoa, sugar, and baking powder went into the bowl of the cooker, milk, eggs, oil, and vanilla in another dish. She combined them using a wooden spoon. The brown rice setting had the longest runtime, so she chose that.

Then she waited.

With the lack of activity, panic nibbled around the edges of thought. How did her signature get on Pepe Le Poo's invitation? Was Pepe the intended victim or was the poison a general threat?

"Or . . ." Lucy popped up and paced the five feet of the boat's interior. "Or what if the dock master was supposed to be"—she hesitated, not wanting to say the word—"murdered?" *Was he supposed to eat first?*

A knock echoed through the hull.

Lucy shrieked, then poked her head out to the aft deck.

"Ahoy!" Nardovino called out.

Lucy ducked her head, fluffed her hair, then took the three steps to the back of the boat. "Come aboard! How's it going? Do you have a suspect?"

He glanced at his watch and shook his head. "It's a bit early."

She sat on the aft couch and invited him to join her, relieved to have someone to talk to. "Here's the thing. Was Pepe supposed to be the one to die? What if someone else was supposed to eat the ribs?"

In the blandest voice imaginable he replied, "We're looking

into all areas."

Lucy ignored this brush-off. "Yeah, yeah. But I got a threatening note this morning—"

"What?" His hazel eyes brightened, turning almost green with interest. "Why didn't you mention this before?"

Lucy held up her hand. "First off, you didn't ask. Second, I forgot."

A small laugh escaped his lips before he threw on a mask of formality. "Where is the note?"

"I . . ." Lucy didn't know. "I found it between my ropes," she recalled. "I took it out, thinking it was another invitation. Then I took it over to Adam and Amanda's to see if they had gotten one."

"Had they?" Nardovino took out his tablet.

Shaking her head, Lucy continued, "No. Anyway, it could have been meant for Pepe because I'd scheduled him for a pump-out today."

"What did it s—"

"But Adam said that it was a general threat because the new dock master just started and some of the long-time owners don't like his policies. So the threat could have been real and meant for him," Lucy suggested.

Nardovino blinked a few times, then checked his watch.

She waited for his response but got nothing.

Lucy slumped. "Look, I don't want this to be about me. Why did I get the threat? Why did Pepe's invitation come in my name?"

Instead of answering, Nardovino sniffed the air. "Chocolate?"

Inhaling the sweet scent, Lucy nodded. "I'm starving. I had to bake since my lunch and dinner was, well, you know, poisoned."

She caught the tiniest head bob from her guest, telegraphing denial.

"Wasn't the food poisoned?"

Nardovino stood and stepped toward the saloon door. "It smells like brownies. You have an oven?"

Grinning, Lucy danced around him and descended the steps to the galley. "Come on."

The rice maker finished its cycle. She opened the top to find a perfectly cooked bowl-shaped muffin. It slid easily onto a cutting board. Lucy took a slice and placed in on a plate, handing it to Nardovino, then did the same for herself.

"Chocolate muffins." Pride showed in her twinkling eyes.

"Mmmmm," he nodded his approval.

"So, how did Pepe die then? If not from cyanide in the food?"

Instead of answering, he eyed the chocolate goody and helped himself to another slice.

“Nothing?” Lucy prompted. “No exchange of information for food?”

His lips twitched in a trace of a smile, but he shook his head.

“Speculation it is, then. Not natural causes.” A shudder tore through her as a flash of Pepe writhing on the ground came to her mind.

“Why cyanide?” Nardovino asked.

Lucy stared for a second then tilted her head in thought. “I guess it’s the only poison I know about. Spies always have the capsules in case they get caught. Do you think Pepe was a secret agent?”

Nardovino smirked at the absurdity.

“Okay, not a spy. But he is awfully close to international waters, and he had a boat. Maybe he’s a pirate. There may be a stash of rum in a nearby cave.”

“Ah.”

Lucy knew non-committal when she heard it. “So, not a rum-runner. And you’re sure he was the intended victim?”

Nardovino put his elbows on the table and rested his chin in his hands.

“So how did he get the poison? I mean, if he had a capsule you’d find the residue. Right?”

She glanced at her guest who stood to leave, giving nothing away. “Thank you for the muffins. *Grazie*.”

Scrambling after him she called, “Why did you stop by?”

Hazel eyes met hers. “Please stay on the boat.”

Lucy’s heart sank. With nothing else to cook, she needed a distraction. “Can I go see my friends? They’re one over on F. I don’t even have to go through the gate.”

Each locked entrance accessed three docks. To go to a slip farther away, she’d need to use her key to get out and proceed down the boardwalk to another gate. “Please?”

Nardovino gave a nod then paused. “Your phone?” He held out his hand. She gave it to him.

He typed his number. “Call me if you think of anything,” he told her. “Anything at all.” He hopped lightly onto the finger.

Ducking into the salon, Lucy snatched a hoodie and then hurried over to Amanda’s.

As she rounded a corner, sinister growling caused her to freeze. A terrifying row of teeth poked from behind a dock box.

“Nice doggie,” Lucy squeaked, backing away.

The snarling advanced from the shadows and Lucy recognized the animal. “Boola?”

Its ears went up, and Lucy let out a long sigh. “Come here, girl.

Where's Herbert?"

"Boola." The bark of Herbert's voice commanded the dog to his side.

"Hi, Herbert," Lucy called.

He swayed off his boat, stalking toward her in his rolling gait. "Any news?" he demanded.

Lucy shrugged. "The food wasn't poisoned."

"Stupid way to kill someone. If I wanted you dead, they'd never find the body." Boola rubbed against his leg. Herbert's gruff tone disappeared as he hoisted his dog in one arm. "Isn't that right, Boola?" Without another word, he slipped away.

Wide-eyed, Lucy half-ran to see her friends, the three of them sitting on the upper deck.

"We saw that hot cop with you," Amanda shouted down. "What did he say?"

"Gorgeous, isn't he? Those eyes?" Lucy scrambled aboard.

"Totally!"

"Easy, girls," Adam warned.

"And can I just say, what is up with Herbert? Have you ever heard him threaten anyone?"

Bill started as if the conversation awoke him. "Herbert? Ex-Navy. I wouldn't cross him."

"Well, if I disappear you'll know who to blame."

Adam poured her a margarita. Lucy took a taste then flinched. "How much tequila did you put in this?"

He waved a hand and asked, "What did you find out? Nardovino hardly spoke when we saw him."

"The food wasn't poisoned."

"What?" Adam practically shouted. "Can we have the ribs?"

Lucy shook her head, ignoring him. "I asked about a capsule. You know, like in the movies. But he didn't respond. How else could a person get poisoned?"

"Through the skin," Bill offered, brushing the salt off his arm that had spilled from his drink.

Contemplating, Lucy sipped her cocktail. The strong alcohol worked its way into her muscles, relaxing her. "Snakebite? Injection? Was anyone near him when he collapsed?"

Adam shrugged, Amanda shook her head, and Bill stared out at the water. Lucy followed his gaze. The sunset illuminated the clouds in a deep, vibrant red with orange flaring across the sky. It was breathtaking, but tonight the colors reminded her of blood and flame.

Lucy took a stiff gulp.

A chunk of ice, not blended with the rest, shot into her mouth.

Rolling it around on her tongue sparked an idea. "What if the poison was in a time-release pill? It floats around in digestive fluids, then once the gelatin dissolves the poison goes into the system."

"Clever!" Amanda chimed.

Adam guffawed. "You're a little too good at this. What gives?"

Lucy didn't want to confess to her new companions, but she needed to explain her interest. "Pepe's party invitation came from me."

"Why?" Amanda demanded, holding her glass across Bill for Adam to refill. Bill's head lolled as he nodded off.

"I don't know. Nardovino showed me my signature."

"Weird," Bill mumbled, eyes closed.

"I want to be helpful so that I don't get blamed for anything."

Adam returned to the blender. "You're overthinking this. It was a simple mistake. Relax that brain of yours."

Relieved, Lucy sipped more of her margarita. "How would you do it?"

Adam shook his head and grinned. "Laughing gas, of course."

Lucy smiled, but the incoming fog chilled her, sobering her thoughts. "Could you hide toxin in a tooth?"

Adam cocked his head to the side, considering. "I don't see how."

Lucy's mind wouldn't let it go. Nardovino should hear her ideas.

Besides, Lucy wanted to see him again, so she got up.

Amanda protested, voice slurring. "No, don't go! We can put on music and dance." She stood, did the twist, then collapsed onto the bench by Bill.

Adam went to his wife and propped her feet up. "No dancing for you, disco queen," he said, kissing her forehead.

"I'll sit." Amanda's head bopped, affirming her decision.

"Have another," Adam tempted, but Lucy shook her head.

"One more conversation with the dashing detective before bed."

She grinned at the thought, then hugged Amanda and Adam, waved to Bill's sleeping form, and left to text Nardovino.

Lucy's legs wobbled as she descended the ladder to the first landing. She held on tight as she stepped from the aft to the temporary stairs. On her boat she could hop from the swim deck, so she wasn't used to the slippery transition.

Once both feet connected with chilly cement, relief swept over Lucy. Her hand reached out to the smooth, cool hull next to her to combat the tequila in her addled brain. She lost her footing and splashed into the water.

Cursing her inattention, she gasped, saltwater flooding into her mouth. Panic robbed her of coordination as her hands flailed at the dock, and she went under.

Forcing her eyes open to stinging water, she reached out for a bumper and pulled herself up. Face to the sky she took a deep breath.

A shadow crossed over, and she knew she would be crushed by the boat looming over her if she didn't move. Dreading submerging her head again, she pushed herself down and swam under the finger, hoping she was aimed to the open channel and not trapping herself underneath another yacht.

Using the wooden pilings as a guide, she kicked. The sea life invaded her touch with slimy tentacles. Barnacles caught strands of her hair, sea anemones wriggled, and sea moss tangled around her.

After an eternity, she cleared the dock, pushed to the surface, and took a grateful breath.

As she turned, an oar bashed onto her shoulder, missing her head by inches. She was under attack.

"Help!" she called as the paddle smashed at her again.

Plunging under the surface, she swam away from her assailant to a slip across the way.

He followed, dry and secure, keeping the paddle aimed at her as he ran.

The cold harbor, strong tequila, and wounded shoulder sapped Lucy's strength. She wouldn't last if she had to tread water much longer.

With shaking fingers, she unzipped her hoodie and dumped it on the finger. She wanted to follow it, but the man with the oar came closer.

Squeezing her eyes shut for courage, she dove under water, willing herself to swim silently.

She got to the far side of the original dock before having to come up for air. Taking only a quick breath, Lucy shot to G Dock and paused. Her pursuer would have to go out a gate and along the boardwalk before he could get to her.

Pulling out her phone, she hoped it was waterproof. It came on, but wouldn't unlock. Tears stung her eyes as her hope of rescue slipped away.

A gate slammed shut, and a yelp of alarm escaped her.

Go! a fierce determination whispered inside. "Go!" She set her sights on the end of the marina and swam.

She made it to J Dock, where the enormous yachts were moored. A couple sat on their aft deck sipping Chardonnay.

Relief at the thought of help made her limbs heavy and she sank, her eyes unfocused.

A two-foot-long fish swished its tail into her face, slapping sense into her. She swam toward the couple, pulled herself out of the water, and collapsed onto their swim deck.

***

The owners gave Lucy a robe as she perched at the end of a stateroom bed.

Nardovino wrapped a wool blanket around her, infusing her with warmth. “I thought I told you to stay put.”

Lucy’s head shot up. “I was attacked!”

“Your friends didn’t see anyone,” he pointed out.

She glared at him. “I didn’t go swimming in the harbor for my health, you know.”

“You tell me why.”

“Maybe someone overheard me when we were talking. Sound carries from the top deck. Maybe one of my ideas was right.”

He raised his eyebrows, questioning.

Shivering, she gave him her thoughts. “The poison could have been in a time-release pill.”

His thoughtful expression encouraged Lucy. “Can you describe your attacker?” he asked.

She shook her head. “Probably male, because of the way he moved, but I couldn’t swear to it.”

Nardovino stowed his notes. “If I had a pill, how would I get my victim to take it?”

“Good question.” Lucy returned to her tooth idea, recalling the dental work she had earlier that year. “What if the poison filled a temporary crown, and it took a healthy bite of food to dislodge the tooth and release the poison?”

“Did anyone do mouth to mouth at the party?”

Lucy pictured the scene. “My friend Adam was going to but Herbert stopped him. Adam’s a dentist, but he said he’d use laughing gas to . . .” She trailed off, remembering something. “Pepe was his patient!”

The detective’s face brightened and he left the room, speaking rapidly into his phone.

He returned much later, pulling Lucy to her feet and hugging her. “Brilliant,” he said before regaining his composure and releasing her.

“What?”

“The victim had a tooth prepped for a crown, but they didn’t find the temporary. The medical examiner found traces of poison on the tooth. Just like you said.”

Lucy's eyes got big. "Wow." Elation at solving the crime crumbled at the betrayal. Legs giving way, Lucy plopped onto the bed. "Adam tried to kill me?"

"Perhaps. We haven't found the paddle. But you figured out his perfect murder in less than a day."

"But why?"

Nardovino's grin went from ear to ear. "Pirates."

Lucy couldn't help but return the smile. "I did suggest that, you know."

He nodded. "A group of armed assailants have been stealing pleasure boats and selling them in the Baja. The last heist got violent, and a man died. Peter, *aka* Pepe Le Poo, was identified as one of the attackers. A bank account ties him to Adam's practice. He was the ringleader."

Excited, Lucy interrupted. "Did Pepe want out?"

"That's my guess."

"Poor Amanda." Lucy couldn't imagine what she must be going through. Amanda functioned as Adam's hygienist, so she was out a husband and a job.

Nardovino shrugged. "Adam is vehemently protesting his innocence, so I doubt we'll get much out of him."

***

After the arrest, the police and Coast Guard cleared the area and Lucy went to check on her friend. She saw Amanda return through the far gate, a box from the Hawaiian restaurant in hand. "Aman—"

Her voice faltered at the appearance of Bill, striding confidently toward Amanda. He slipped his arm around her waist, kissed her, and together they walked to his sailboat.

"Amanda!" Lucy shouted.

They waved in unison. After releasing the lines, Bill's boat coasted quietly out of the slip.

"Stop!" Lucy needed to tell someone they were getting away, but her phone was dead.

With a sly smile, Amanda lifted a rib in Lucy's direction in a silent toast as they cruised out of the marina to open waters.

The name of the sailboat filled Lucy's vision as it turned. *Carne Diem*.

TURN THE SAGE

By Stephen D. Rogers

Combine Thanksgiving dinner with a New England winter, icy roads, and a medical situation and you need some sage advice about keeping safe.

Siobhan was on the road for three hundred and sixty-one days last year. She played over three hundred and fifty shows in almost that many towns ranging from Cape Cod to Omaha and back. Three hours after arriving at her mother's house for Thanksgiving dinner, Siobhan was dead.

She almost took me with her.

The day started innocently enough. I woke to a cat sleeping on my face, and after I nudged Pudding aside, the chill that quickly drained the warmth from my face made me wish I'd been more agreeable to swallowing fur.

I pulled the covers around me as I spun to sit on the edge of the bed, bare feet held up off the cold wooden floor. The effort of maintaining that pose had to be working some muscle group or other. This might even be yoga.

Wait until I told Jennifer I'd done yoga. She would not believe me.

Shivering, I forced a smile for Pudding's sake. "Come on back to bed. All is forgiven."

Pudding apparently wasn't concerned on that front because she turned away and strode into the open closet.

I wrapped the covers tighter.

Even though the annual deep freeze was still three months down the road, that hadn't stopped my heating system from failing early. Or the temperature from dropping a hundred degrees overnight.

Welcome to New England and the puritan experience of living in a house built just this side of Independence.

"Pudding," I coaxed. "Wouldn't the closet be more comfortable if you brought me my padded winter boots? Just think how much more room you'd have."

Or not.

Perhaps I should adopt a dog. My luck, it wouldn't understand 'fetch.'

Gritting my teeth, I leapt off the bed and ran on my toes as fast as I dared to the bathroom, covers still gripped around me. The tile was colder than the bare floors, and the tub colder still, but I told myself as I shucked my cocoon that the shower would eventually heat past lukewarm.

After closing the curtain, I turned the handles.

Screamed as the frigid spray sliced through me. I bounced in place to keep from jumping over the side. I could stay here, I could. Just had to tough it out until the water warmed. Or I lost all sensation.

Spring was coming. Summer days so scorching I stuck my head in the freezer.

Hardy New Englander. I could do this.

The pressure dropped as the pipes gurgled, and then after a moment I felt the water turn tepid. Tepid grew to warm, and then warm to hot.

Hot! I dove for the handles, frantically making adjustments, gross and fine, until the water pounding my back reached a temperature that was just about right.

I straightened with a contented sigh.

Slowly I shuffled in careful circles under the nozzle, warming the patches of frostbite, cooling the burns.

Raising my face, I washed the last of the sleep from my eyes.

Who needed coffee to wake up?

***

The phone rang as I sat hunched over my bowl of hot oatmeal.

Pulling my face out of the steam, I answered, "Jennifer's best friend speaking. How can I help you?"

"Happy Thanksgiving! So tell me you're joining us."

"Sorry, but I decided to stay in and teach Pudding how to fetch. Here's something that's really interesting though. I did yoga this morning!"

Jennifer snorted. "You went to a yoga class? I don't believe that for a second."

Ha. "Jennifer, I don't need no stinking class. You can learn anything on the internet."

"Seriously? You work at a college. Isn't what you just said sacrilegious?"

"Jennifer, achieving 'Cat reaching for yarn' isn't exactly comparable to earning a degree."

"Neither is it a yoga pose. Listen, you have to come today. I bought way more food than we can eat, and my mother is always saying how much she misses you."

When Jennifer and I were growing up, we split our time between each other's houses, first because the toys were better, and then because the other house wasn't so lame, and finally to get away from our own parents.

To be honest, I kind of missed Jennifer's mother. She was the one who taught me there were herbs beyond salt, pepper, and ketchup.

"I'll see if Pudding is willing to cut the lessons short."

"Just plunk her down in front of the internet. I hear you can learn anything there."

I had to give Jennifer that one. "Pudding doesn't like the computer. She finds the whole 'mouse' thing offensive."

"I have a great idea. Bring Pudding with you. The kids will love her!"

"She hates to travel."

"It's Thanksgiving. The only people not traveling are cooking for those who are."

Lowering my voice in case Pudding had snuck into the kitchen while I'd been engaged, I confessed, "I hate to break it to you, Jennifer, but Pudding isn't actually a people."

"I'm relieved to hear you say that. Sometimes I wonder." Jennifer laughed. "Dinner's at three. Leave early because it's ugly out there, and the roads aren't going to improve."

I glanced at the kitchen window, squinting to see through the condensation. "What do you mean?"

"While you were dreaming up yoga moves, a freak ice storm came down out of Canada. The roads are wicked slippery."

I covered my eyes. "Jennifer. You studied in London and Paris, and still that's how you talk?"

"Three o'clock. If only because I promised my mother you'd be here. Crossed my heart and hoped to die."

"That's not fair." I stuck the spoon in the middle of my oatmeal. Shouldn't it, like, move? Maybe I didn't add enough milk. Maybe I didn't add any. "Assuming I can come—and I'm not saying I can—what do you want me to bring?"

"You know that cranberry mold you're so proud of?"

I nodded, smiling at memories of Thanksgivings stretching back to my youth. "My grandmother's recipe."

"Don't even think about it."

***

I was coming down Old Orchard when I hit the patch of black ice. Feeling the tires lose their grip, I turned into the skid and waited for the car to respond, which it finally did, straightening out just in time for me to return to my lane before I reached the curve.

My heart pounding.

I tapped the brakes.

The road ahead dry.

I exhaled.

Back roads mercifully empty.

A story to tell while scooping candied yams with marshmallow onto my plate.

I imagined Jennifer gasping, her mother patting my arm if we were sitting close enough.

A story we'd be laughing about by the end of the day.

A white van came out of a side street, knocked down a stop sign, and swerved into my lane. I yanked the wheel left. The driver of the van corrected. I yanked the wheel right. The van missed my car by inches, and in the rearview mirror I watched it cut across the road and drop into a ditch. I heard it hit the tree.

But the road here was dry.

I stopped and pulled the phone from my purse with shaking hands.

The face behind the windshield. Why did it make me think of Siobhan?

***

Jennifer picked me up at the hospital.

While I may have been okay to drive—the nurse had frowned as she reluctantly nodded—I didn't really want to.

What I wanted was to see my best friend. To disappear in her hug while she agreed that what happened had been horrible and then reassured me everything would be okay.

I wanted to complain about the effects of tryptophan, vacillate between pumpkin and apple, and laugh at something silly.

Jennifer took me home, bundled me into my bed, and held my hand as I reached for the abyss.

***

Jennifer placed a cup of tea on my nightstand. "So what's with your heat?"

"When I woke up this morning . . ." This morning? Was it still today? "The furnace is older than the house." I pushed myself into a sitting position. "Where's Pudding?"

"I think she resents my being here."

"Only when you're here. After you leave, she always mentions how much she enjoyed the visit."

Jennifer pointed at the tea. "Can I get you anything else?"

"Just stay with me for a while."

She sat on the edge of the bed. "I'm not going anywhere."

"I'm sorry I missed dinner."

"You made me miss dessert."

"I'm so sorry, Jennifer. If you go into the refrigerator, there's a cranberry mold—"

"Don't you dare." Her smile allowed me to laugh.

Laugh? How could I laugh?

"I don't understand what happened. The road was dry."

Jennifer dipped her head. "According to the news, they think she went into convulsions while she was driving."

"She?" The face at the windshield had reminded me of Siobhan. "Who was it? The detective who interviewed me at the hospital, a Detective Wells, he wouldn't tell me anything. He just kept asking me the same questions in different ways."

"You don't want to hear this right now."

"And later the news is going to be better?"

Jennifer stood and walked the perimeter of the room. "Siobhan cancelled tour dates to come home for Thanksgiving. Her family said she ate as though she hadn't seen food in months." Jennifer stopped pacing. "She left to go get something, medication for her mother, and then . . ."

I closed my eyes. "She lost control and went off the road."

"I've seen interviews. Her family said she arrived exhausted, so tired she was slurring her speech. She never should have volunteered to go back out."

Opening my eyes, I pulled back the covers. "I need to go see them, assuming they're up to having a visitor."

"No." Jennifer marched to my side. "You need to rest."

"Resting can wait. This can't."

"You know who else thought resting could wait? Siobhan. And look where it got her."

"Jennifer, I was the last person to see her alive."

***

Bringing Jennifer along for moral support, and allowing her to drive because I wasn't quite ready to get behind the wheel, I stared out the window at branches coated with ice.

My friend liked to say there were two kinds of people: people like Siobhan who went out into world, and people like me who tread the same patch of ground cursed by ten generations of ancestors. Somehow, when Jennifer said that, I never felt at the receiving end of a compliment.

"It doesn't make sense."

"What?"

"Why Siobhan? We were both on that stretch of road. It could have just as easily been me."

“I told you. They think she experienced a seizure.”

“How many miles does she drive every year? The one time she crosses my path, she goes off the road.”

“Don’t blame yourself. It’s not your fault.”

“It just doesn’t seem fair, that’s all I’m saying. Siobhan represented something to people in this town. Her death is a loss on so many levels.”

“And, what, yours wouldn’t be?” Jennifer shook her head. “You should rest. That’s what the nurse said. Are you sure you want to go out?”

“I’m sure I don’t. Unfortunately, I’m just as sure that I must.”

Trees sheathed in ice. Rock walls reinforced with ice. Tears frozen on my face.

***

Siobhan’s cousin, Gail, brought us into the den. “The rest of the family isn’t up to seeing anyone right now.”

“We’re so sorry about Siobhan.”

“Thank you. It shouldn’t have come as a surprise, but still, it did.”

Jennifer studied a painting that depicted a fishing vessel fighting high seas. “Why wouldn’t it be a surprise?”

“Siobhan lived a gypsy life. No cares, no responsibilities. While I stop in every day to check on her mother, Siobhan’s off gallivanting. Then when the prodigal daughter returns to celebrate Thanksgiving, she barely finishes eating before she rushes off to pick up her mother’s medication. That’s when the universe finally said, ‘No more.’” Gail slumped as though sharing her true feelings had drained her.

I helped her to a couch. “This is a very difficult time for everyone involved.”

“I’m not like Siobhan. I can’t just pick up my guitar and go. I’m needed here, especially now.”

I patted her arm. “I’m sure the family appreciates all your efforts.”

Jennifer turned away from the painting. “What medication did her mother need on Thanksgiving?”

“Anti-seizure. I never would have allowed her pills to get so low, but the bottle was spilled over the bathroom sink.”

“I didn’t know her mother had seizures.”

“That’s not the kind of thing Siobhan would have shared with her friends. It doesn’t scream ‘free spirit.’ A chronic medical condition is an obligation, and Siobhan would have none of that.” Gail covered her mouth. “I must sound awful.”

I gave her leg a squeeze. “No, not at all. When something

horrible like this happens, all sorts of feelings find their way to the surface. It's only natural."

Gail nodded. "I can't help thinking, I worked so hard putting together that Thanksgiving dinner, and then she went and ruined the day. But of course I can't say that to anyone."

"We understand." I wished Jennifer would stop examining what hung on the walls and help me with Gail. "What did you make?"

"I started the day with scrambled eggs, pancakes, and sage sausages. It was a late breakfast, just to tide people over. Then we had turkey with sage stuffing, sage pasta with parmesan sauce, and sage butternut squash. We also had fresh peas, corn on the cob, and turnips."

"You had a real sage theme going there for a while."

"It's one of her mother's favorite herbs. Sage and cinnamon."

"Jennifer's mother taught me about spices . . ." Mentioning my friend's name didn't succeed in drawing her into the conversation. My idea to come here. My responsibility.

Gail leaned forward. "I have leftovers if you're hungry. Just a quick reheat."

Eat before going to Jennifer's mother's? "No, thank you."

Awkward silence. I knew enough about Siobhan to ask leading questions, but Gail was a blank to me. She was Siobhan's cousin.

"Did Siobhan also have a history of seizures? The police say it might have been convulsions that caused her to go off the road."

"Siobhan lived the life she wanted to live. I don't think she would allow herself to be swayed by cold, hard facts."

"So she did . . . or she didn't?"

Gail covered her face. "I can't believe she's gone." Gail's entire body shook as she sobbed into her hands.

I frantically waved at Jennifer until she noticed me, and motioned her to take my place on the couch so I could find the bathroom.

What I wanted was a little privacy.

I didn't like how Gail wouldn't answer my question. I didn't like the heavy emphasis on sage in the day's menu. No matter how much someone might enjoy the herb, one thing Jennifer's mother had taught me about cooking was that over-emphasizing a single flavor dulled the palette to its pleasure.

And, to be completely honest, I didn't like witnessing Gail's grief, if that's what it was.

After locking the bathroom door behind me, I pulled out my phone and started an internet search for 'food allergy sage'.

While sage was one of the herbs that could cause allergic

reactions, the reactions were generally mild.

Another search: 'sage side affects'. Yes, I meant 'sage side *effects*'.

Apparently some species of sage contained a chemical called thujone, which could be poisonous if ingested in a large enough quantity. While I couldn't find definite body-weight ratios, I assumed a second or fortieth serving of sage butternut squash wouldn't be fatal.

I froze. Thujone was considered a convulsant.

What's the difference between a convulsion and a seizure?

Oh, convulsions were seizures.

I was an instant sage. Just add internet.

Outside of epilepsy, seizure triggers included lack of sleep, stress, and hormonal changes associated with the menstrual cycle.

Siobhan had driven overnight to reach her mother's house, where she had to deal with at least one hostile family member, and Gail may have been the rule rather than the exception.

Gail, who prepared a meal heavy with an herb that could cause seizures. Who might have emptied that pill bottle, knowing that Siobhan would volunteer to drive for more, Siobhan who easily overshadowed the cousin who did all the work.

Gail the martyr.

Gail the murderer.

I called the police station and asked to speak to Detective Wells, the officer who had questioned me at the hospital.

I finally had information worth repeating.

BAD JU-JU

By M. A. Monnin

Fire ants and family have bride-to-be Chelsea willing to do anything for a good cup of coffee.

I went for the gumbo. But if there's one thing Louisiana is known for after food and Mardi Gras, it's our cemeteries. Elsewhere, the deceased are buried with ever-decreasing visibility. In Louisiana, burial crypts rise stately and silent, like something out of a Poe story, architectural curiosities in a city of the dead. And the Labranche family mausoleum was a sight to behold. Standing twelve feet high and eight feet wide, with Ionic columns and a gabled roof topped by a sturdy cross, it ranked among the best. Marie Laveau's crypt in Saint Louis Cemetery No. 1 might get more visitors, but my family's was an architect's delight.

My fiancé, Troy, and I had recently graduated from Alabama, both newly-minted architects, so the weekend we visited my Aunt Jackie to get the family gumbo recipe, that was the first place I took him.

Jackie met us at the cemetery gates, then walked us to the tomb.

"What do you think?" I asked Troy as the three of us stood in the grass in front of the granite crypt.

"Great proportions." He pushed his glasses further up his nose. "Interesting cross between Gothic and Greek Revival."

He took photos while I got reacquainted with Jackie.

"I never knew them," I said, reading the familiar, yet distant, names chiseled on the mausoleum door. The most recent were my grandparents. My own parents were buried in Atlanta. *George Labranche, Vietnam War. Bronze Star. 1938-1988. Judy Labranche 1940-1989.*

"How'd he earn the Bronze Star?" Troy asked, focusing on a close-up of the angel carved in the pediment.

Jackie put her e-cig to her lips, then removed it. "I don't know. Dad didn't have real conversations with us kids. Went to Vietnam a second lieutenant and came back a heroin addict. Between the flashbacks and the drugs, we were happy to stay out of the way."

Families are funny. Troy comes from a close family, all Alabama fans. We met at a Florida Georgia Line concert and it was love at first sight. I'd grown up in Atlanta, but my mother was from a small town twenty-five miles outside of New Orleans. Dad was a northerner, having moved from Chicago after meeting Mom at Mardi Gras in 1990, so I guess you could say history repeated itself.

Mom's home life hadn't been the easiest, and after she graduated from LSU, she and Dad had settled in Atlanta. Both passed away my sophomore year in college when their car was T-boned by a furniture delivery truck on a mission. The emptiness that overwhelmed me after their deaths had been devastating, but Troy's family welcomed me right from the start. For the most part, I couldn't complain. My parents' life insurance covered my college expenses, and Mom's parents, while unsupportive in life, had left a trickle of income from two poorly-producing oil wells that provided a meager allowance that I supplemented with a job at the campus pizza joint to support my shoe habit.

I'd never missed the ties of an extended family, but as our wedding approached, without Mom to help me pick out the dress or Dad to walk me down the aisle, I found myself holding Mom's picture to my chest, remembering little things she'd said, the food she used to make. I hadn't cared when Mom tried to teach me to make gumbo in high school, but now it was terribly important. *I'm sorry, Mom*, I thought. *I'll make it up to you.*

The only family I had left was Aunt Jackie, mom's sister. Strong and resilient, she'd stayed in their home town and hadn't let their father's drug habit hinder a successful career as an event planner. There had been a large family home at one time, but it burned to the ground during one of my grandfather's bad binges, taking him with it. The town library now stands on that plot of land, a severe contemporary space without much character.

"Didn't your mother ever tell you how he got the Bronze Star?" I asked Jackie, more for Troy's sake than mine. Mom had never told me. The only reminder she'd wanted from her parents was a necklace her mother used to wear, one my grandmother had promised to pass on to her, an old-fashioned cameo. But it had been lost the night the house caught fire. I swatted the back of my leg while I waited for Jackie's answer.

"Mosquitoes?" she asked. "They leave me alone, but I've got something at home that will help."

Did I mention the mosquitoes in Louisiana? You can't get away from them. That's four things we're known for.

"They don't usually bite me, either," I said, scratching my leg where it now itched like crazy.

Jackie contemplated the Bronze Star emblem on the crypt door.

"Mom didn't talk much when Dad was indulging in his drugs, and that was most of the time." There was a hard edge to her voice, which softened when she turned to me and shrugged. "*C'est la vie*."

Since I'd never known my grandparents, the quirks and struggles that made life difficult for my mother and Jackie didn't affect me personally, and I had a more sympathetic view. War is ugly, no matter how just the cause, and those that participate must cope with the horrors of what they've seen and what they've done. Soldiers and airmen who've come back from Iraq and Afghanistan know. Troy's brother was treated as a hero when he returned from Fallujah, given counseling and antidepressants to bring balance back to his life. History class taught me that my grandfather and his compatriots weren't treated as heroes, and for them, asking for help was a sign of weakness. Men strong enough to face war expected to be able to pull themselves up by their bootstraps, and though most Vietnam Vets did, some fell into a black hole they couldn't crawl out of.

My grandfather was one of the latter, self-medicating with heroin to banish the nightmares. When he refused to quit, my grandmother simply couldn't cope and shut down emotionally. Or so my mother always said. Mom was leery of drugs in any form, even tobacco, which I knew was the reason I was so ashamed of the smoking habit I picked up after my parents' death. With the wedding coming up, I'd quit, but it was a struggle.

"Chelsea, let Jackie take our picture," Troy said.

After handing Jackie my cell phone, I tossed my leather bag on the ground at her feet. My brush and a mini hairspray fell out, along with the two weeks' worth of mail that I'd grabbed before leaving on our road trip. Finals didn't leave time for the mundane.

As Jackie bent forward to pick up the items, a necklace swung out from the open neckline of her shirt, and I caught my breath. An old-fashioned cameo. It couldn't have been the one my grandmother promised to Mom—that had been destroyed in the fire. It surprised me, that was all. Mom once told me she would've liked to have given the cameo to me on my wedding day. Instead, I wore her wedding ring on a gold chain.

I nestled under Troy's arm and we posed in front of the mausoleum while Jackie carefully replaced the things in my purse, then stood up and took our picture. Returning to her side to inspect the photo, I glanced at Jackie's throat, but she'd tucked the necklace back inside her shirt.

Troy took the phone and grinned at our picture. "This would have looked great on our wedding invitations. 'Till death do us part.'"

"Oh, you are tempting fate, my friend," Jackie said with a laugh. She turned to me. "Ready to make some gumbo?"

"You bet," I said. "Ow." I smacked my leg again and looked down. A fire ant, not a mosquito, had bitten me. More of them crawled up my legs.

Jackie slapped at her calves, too. "Geez."

I couldn't see an ant pile, but the angry insects were swarming all around. I leapt off the grass, swatting at my ankles and calves as I made it onto the paved path. Jackie followed, doing the same.

"What's going on?" Of course, Troy hadn't been bothered by the fire ants.

"Bad Ju-Ju," I said, my good humor restored now that I was no longer under attack. "My grandparents don't want to be disturbed. Did I mention voodoo comes with a Cajun heritage?"

Troy rolled his eyes.

Jackie turned her back on the vault, slapping a rogue ant that had made it to the back of her thigh. "Who's ready for some air conditioning?"

***

Jackie lived in a newly built, energy-efficient country French house with all the amenities. Troy carried our overnight bags into her living room.

"Whoa." He stopped short at his first sight of the shrine to Louisiana State University's football team on the wall. Purple and gold fleurs-de-lis and expensively framed LSU posters dominated the décor.

In turn, Jackie smirked at his bag with the Crimson Tide bumper sticker.

"Geaux Tigers," she said.

"Roll Tide," Troy replied.

They were bosom buddies from that moment on, and I was content that the two sides of my family had clicked. For myself, the LSU regalia reminded me of Mom.

Later, Jackie and I sat on two bar stools pulled up in front of the stove, taking turns whisking flour and oil into a roux.

"There are two clues that tell you when it's ready," Jackie said. "Color is one, fragrance is the other."

The rich, earthy, almost nutty scent of roux had often filled my childhood kitchen. A twinge of guilt at my rejection of Mom's tutoring pierced me, and I frowned down at my legs and the pus-filled blisters left by the fire ants.

"The wedding's in two weeks," I said "Do you think the bites will have healed by then? My gown is tea length, so these ankles are going to show."

Being raised on sweet tea and dirty rice, curves are part of who I am, but I'd downed ten glasses of water each and every day for a month and sacrificed French fries and potato chips to slim my ankles down for the big day. It would be a travesty to have them marred by red-scabbed bites.

Jackie, slim as a willow, didn't have to worry about unsightly ankles. She got up to chop the holy trinity of Cajun cooking—onions, green pepper, and celery.

"You're going to be a beautiful bride no matter what," she said, waving her unlit e-cig in the air before setting it on the window sill.

Either my precarious emotional state showed on my face, or Jackie read the craving I felt at the sight of her cigarette, unlit and artificial though it was. She placed a large onion and a butcher knife on the cutting board, then wiped her hands on a dish towel.

"I'll get the calamine lotion. Those old remedies work wonders."

"After that, you can take over roux duty," I said, familiar enough with Cajun cooking to know if the roux sat idle for the minute or so it would take to apply the calamine, it would burn. We'd already been working on the roux for fifteen minutes, and I wasn't going to risk ruining it and disappointing Troy.

Jackie returned with the bottle and a couple of cotton balls, then peeked into the stainless-steel gumbo pot.

"Look at that beautiful color," she said, "it's almost perfect. You keep stirring. I'll just dab this on."

When she knelt on the tile floor behind me, I jumped at a series of quick, sharp jabs.

"Yikes!" Not expecting the lotion to sting, I turned and stared at the glittering green fleur-de-lis stickpin in her hand.

"I lanced the bites," Jackie said, sitting back on her heels. "They'll heal quicker. Be honest—would you have let me if I told you?"

Not likely, I thought. "Anything to get them to disappear by the wedding." I watched her apply an exorbitant amount of pink cakey liquid on my ankles. "What about yours?"

Jackie stood up and grimaced as she examined the back of her legs. "I've got so many, I'd look like I was dipped in cotton candy. I took a couple of Benadryl when we got home." She washed her hands, then started on the onion. "I saw the way you glanced at my cigarette. Are you a smoker, too?" She pointed the knife at a brown glass bottle on the windowsill. "E-cigs are the way to cut down. I mix my own juice, so they're pretty weak. Half the time I don't refill them."

That explained why she never seemed to inhale. Determined to quit cold turkey, I didn't want to be tempted by her crutch, so I lied.

"No," I said. "Come look at the roux." It was a lovely mahogany color, rich and fragrant. I was quite proud of my first attempt.

Jackie finished chopping the onion, then brought the cutting board to my side, wiping the corners of her eyes with the back of her hand as she looked into the pot. "Perfect. You're on your way to being a real Cajun cook."

"I'm glad I left the onions to you," I said as her watering eyes threatened to overflow. "My eyeliner would be a mess. I'll take care of the rest."

She stirred the onions into the roux while I chopped celery, green pepper, green onions, and garlic. When I finished my *sous*-chef duties, I got a good look at the back of Jackie's legs. All of a sudden my six little bites didn't seem like such a tragedy. She must have had ten times as many bites up and down her legs as I did.

"They got you bad, Jackie," I said as I brought the vegetables to the stove. "Are you sure you don't want any calamine? Mine don't itch anymore at all." It was true—I felt much better. But maybe the heavenly aroma of toasted flour heightened by the sharpness of the freshly diced holy trinity contributed to my well-being.

Jackie picked up her e-cig again and gestured at her legs. "I wasn't as quick as you. They're like poison ivy. Once you get bit, the ants smell it on you, and attack all the stronger."

"That's not how poison ivy works," Troy said, taking a break from the TV to join us and be literal. "You become more sensitive to it with each exposure."

"That's what I said, Bama Boy," Jackie told him. "Grab an Abita from the fridge. And bring us each one, too."

Troy and I shared a smile. I leaned back against the counter, more relaxed than I had been since we started making wedding plans. Connecting with family was exactly what I needed. Troy brought our beers, then took his and left us with the gumbo.

"Nice house," I said while Jackie put on the rice. "If Lucky One and Lucky Two hadn't petered out, you could have bought a house like this in the Garden District, in New Orleans proper."

Lucky One and Two were the nicknames we'd given to the oil wells owned by the Labranche family. Unlucky was more accurate: the quarterly dividends were down to two figures, the last check I received being exactly $11.32. Before long, the leasing company would start charging us postage to mail the checks.

"No, thank you." Jackie hit the cook button on the rice maker for emphasis, then gazed out the window at a newly planted oak. "I sometimes think if Dad hadn't had the oil dividends, he would have had to go to work, and he'd have learned to cope with his demons. He was funny and smart, when he was clean. It just didn't happen often enough."

"We won't have that burden," I said cheerfully. I certainly wasn't counting on any extra income. Troy and I had jobs waiting for us after the honeymoon, both accepted as junior architects in the same Atlanta firm.

"My parents were lost souls, doing the best they could." Jackie turned back to me, her eyes alight. "I'm happy in my modern little house. I don't look back."

***

Later that night, I ran a bath, hoping a soak in Epsom salts would reduce the swelling of the bites. Wrapped in my robe, I'd just stuck a toe in to test the water when hands grabbed me from behind.

I yelped, then hit Troy on the shoulder. "Don't scare me like that."

He laughed, wrapping his arms around me. "Don't get me wrong, LSU has a good football team and all, but you aren't planning to change our wedding colors to purple and gold, are you?"

"As if they could be anything but crimson and white." I searched his face. "So, you like Jackie?"

"I like her, and your gumbo, too." He let me go, then looked over his shoulder as he left the bathroom. "I expect it every month once we're married."

"Fat chance," I called, dropping my robe and stepping into the tub. "You'll be cooking for me."

Troy wasn't my only visitor. Jackie surprised me when she leaned against the bathroom doorjamb. Feeling exposed, I leaned forward in the water and massaged my ankles while I waited for her to speak. Although she was my aunt, I'd only seen her a few times growing up, and just once since Mom died. I didn't think we'd reached a nude-conversation comfort level yet.

She looked at me with concern. "How are you feeling?"

The vicious red bites were magnified by the water. "I'd be better if I knew these would be gone tomorrow."

"That's a whirlpool tub. The jets don't always work, but you can try." Jackie reached to turn them on. "The builder keeps telling me he'll fix it."

I lifted a hand from the water and stopped her. Safety had been drilled into me during electrical engineering class.

"That's okay. If something's wrong with the wiring, I'll pass."

Jackie looked doubtful, as if swirling water would make all the difference. "Just put more lotion on when you get out, then."

After setting the bottle of calamine on the counter, she left me in peace. I laid my head back on a folded towel and closed my eyes. Between bringing Troy to Louisiana, the ant bites, and the upcoming wedding, I was longing for one of Jackie's e-cigs. Her comment about the tub worried me a little, too. Attractive exteriors sometimes hid shoddy construction. Tomorrow, Troy and I could take a look at the rest of the house, just to be sure it was up to code, as a thank you for the gumbo lesson.

***

The next morning Jackie greeted us with another family favorite that Mom had failed to pass on: coffee with chicory. Troy and I took our cups out front to the raised veranda where Jackie sat in the morning sun.

"Since the house is new, I don't smoke inside," Jackie said. "Even the vapes. You're lucky you don't smoke, Chelsea."

With a glance, I dared Troy to mention my smoking, and like a good fiancé, he kept his mouth shut about how happy *he* was that I'd quit. Right now I could hardly look at Jackie's crutch without craving one of my own, but I was determined to be strong. That falsehood, so necessary for my willpower, led me to make another one when I saw how much Jackie enjoyed the chicory. I owed it to my mother's memory to make an effort.

"Coffee's great," I said. Nothing that I couldn't force down in the name of family bonding. "A little bitter."

"It's an acquired taste." Jackie scratched a bite on her shin.

"How'd the Benadryl work?" Troy asked.

"It helped. I'll take a couple more later. They put me to sleep, and you're only here for one more day."

A second sip of the chicory told me I just couldn't drink it. Without nicotine, I needed coffee. Real coffee, and lots of it. I set the cup on the floor near the edge of the veranda.

"Why don't you take them now, then this afternoon we can all go into New Orleans? I want to show Troy around town. Aren't there a couple of historic houses nearby?" I asked, shifting my foot. The cup dropped into the mulch below, spilling its bitter brew.

Jackie scratched her legs again as she stood up. "All right, but let's have another cup of coffee before you go."

"Great," I said.

When Jackie went inside, Troy gave me a sidelong look. "Be honest. Tell her you don't like chicory."

"Would you tell your mother you'd rather have gone to Georgia Tech?"

He was quiet after that.

Jackie brought the coffee out in a fresh cup, this one advertising Tabasco. “Last of the pot,” she said “You can have it. I took a couple of antihistamines when I went in, so I’m going to lie down and watch TV until they knock me out. We’ll go to New Orleans when you get back.”

I accepted the cup with a forced smile and went to the guest bedroom. After dressing, I popped my head into Jackie’s room. She did look miserable, staring at the television with such a melancholy expression that I wondered if meeting at the mausoleum yesterday had been a bad idea.

“I’ll put my makeup on in your bathroom,” I said, seeing the master bath door was open. “That way we can talk while I finish getting ready.”

“Bring your coffee,” she said, brightening.

She needed some, too, I decided, to perk her up. I went to the kitchen and, rummaging through the gorgeous no-slam maple cabinets, I found the chicory mix, with just enough left for one last pot. After setting the coffee maker to brew, I threw away the empty bag and noticed two medicinal bottles in the trash. Liquid nicotine, like the bottle on the windowsill. My glance lingered on them long enough to convince me I needed a strong espresso, and fast. How many shots would fit in a venti-ultra-grande?

Not willing to wait until the fresh pot brewed, I poured my untouched coffee into Jackie’s LSU cup and while it reheated in the microwave, rinsed and filled mine with cold water. I returned to Jackie’s room with the two cups in hand.

“So you found the coffee.” She wrapped both hands around the mug I’d given her and drank deeply, watching me over the brim as I went to the guest room for my purse and straightening iron.

“Are you sure you don’t want to try the calamine lotion as well?” I asked when I came back. She looked uncomfortable, with a bead of sweat forming on her upper lip, blinking to stay awake from the antihistamine.

Jackie shook her head. “Tell me all about the wedding.”

“It’s going to be small,” I said, walking into her bathroom. Not just a bathroom, it was an entire suite, consisting of an outer room with sinks and a jetted tub, a separate shower, and a walk-in closet.

I plugged the straightening iron in, then while it heated, peeked into the closet, just to see if the architect had designed it for maximum efficiency. What struck me most wasn’t the array of sleek drawers and hanging rods, but the absence of any cigarette odor. The smell clings to everything: clothes, shoes, purses. How had Jackie managed to keep the odor from her clothes? I invested heavily in Febreze, myself. Poor Troy. No wonder he was happy I'd quit. I walked farther into the closet, curious if she'd bought an entirely new wardrobe when she quit smoking. Some items were newer, but many had the tired look of well-worn favorites. Jackie hadn't lied about smoking, had she? Reaching up to touch Mom's wedding ring on the chain around my neck, I flashed back to the necklace I'd seen Jackie wearing. Maybe it wasn't the first time Jackie had lied.

I shook off the suspicion. With no caffeine, no cigarettes, and my wedding only two weeks away, I was a mess. Why would Jackie lie? She'd probably bought a necklace similar to her mother's, and sent all of her clothes to the cleaners. Something I could afford once I got that first paycheck.

Leaving the closet, I started on my makeup.

"Friends of ours opened a brewery," I said, loud enough for Jackie to hear. "We're going to have the ceremony there." I dug in my purse for my eyeliner, then rimmed my eyes. "But don't worry, it'll be beautiful. And we won't run out of alcohol," I joked.

Jackie called out, but I didn't catch what she said. In talking, I'd messed up my eyeliner, and looked around for Q-tips. I found them in a medicine cabinet artfully situated in a slim column of maple cabinets that ran floor to ceiling—a storage trick I'd be sure to suggest to prospective clients once I started working. Next to the cotton swabs were another bottle of nicotine and the calamine lotion that I'd returned to Jackie. With my ankles itching again, I picked up the calamine, but my willpower weakened and I put it back, going for the nicotine instead. Strong stuff. One hundred mgs and the bottle was nearly empty. Maybe vaping wouldn't be so bad. I opened it, feeling like a kid sniffing glue. A speck of pink tinted the rim.

Crap. *That's what I get for snooping in someone else's bathroom*, I thought guiltily. I must have gotten calamine on my hands. Wiping off the nicotine bottle with a tissue, I wondered if a whiff would satisfy my craving for a smoke. Then I caught a glimpse of myself in the mirror—I *looked* like a kid sniffing glue. I put the cap back on. It was time to come clean and confess my smoking habit to Jackie and get her advice on persevering.

I checked my hands for a calamine smear, but didn't find one. When I dropped the tissue into the wastebasket, I froze. Two more nicotine bottles sat in the bottom of the chrome trashcan. This was serious. Jackie was going through nicotine like crazy. Four and a half bottles in what—a few days at most since she'd probably taken out the trash? Only a heavy smoker could safely go through that much nicotine in such a short time. And yet, I hadn't seen her inhale deeply at all.

A chill ran through me. Jackie didn't act like she'd been a heavy smoker, and her closet didn't smell like it either. That left a question I didn't want to ask.

I opened the cabinet door again and looked hard at the bottle of calamine. I'd felt relaxed yesterday after Jackie so generously applied it to my ant bites. More relaxed than I'd been since Troy and I started making wedding plans. More relaxed than I'd been since I quit smoking.

Why? I wondered, looking around the bathroom. My eyes fell on my purse, open, with the mail still sticking out. Jackie called out again, but I ignored her and reached for the letters. One was from the lawyer who'd transferred Mom's property to my name after the accident. The one who sent the last dividend check. I hadn't opened it, not so desperate for eleven dollars that I couldn't wait until we got back to Alabama.

With shaking hands, I slit the envelope with my nail file. No check enclosed, just notification that Lucky Two had started producing again, and that Jackie and I, as co-owners, could now expect yearly dividends approaching six figures.

I swallowed. Jackie had seemed surprised that, like her, mosquitoes didn't bother me. But the fire ants had bitten us both, yet she refused to use the calamine lotion. I picked up the bottle of calamine, comparing it to the nicotine bottle. The calamine might hold one and a half bottles of liquid nicotine, yet there were four empties in the trash.

With slow steps, clenching the letter in my hand, I walked to the doorway to face her.

Jackie's mouth twisted in a grimace as she stared at me from the bed. Her legs jerked spasmodically, then the empty LSU cup flew from her stiff fingers and shattered on the hardwood floor. By the time I reached her, she was dead.

***

Two weeks later, Troy and I once again stood in front of the family crypt. I was careful to stay on the paved path this time. After rolling Jackie's casket inside, the cemetery staff closed the tomb and left us alone.

With my grandmother's cameo around my neck and the family gumbo recipe etched on my heart, I laid a simple bouquet of white lilies on the top step.

Troy's expression was grim. "Flowers? After she tried to poison you?"

"They're not for Jackie," I said, contemplating my grandparents' names chiseled into the granite. I no longer felt so detached. Bad Ju-Ju? Or had they tried to warn me? I didn't believe in the supernatural, in ghosts or spirits. Not really. But I did believe in redemption.

AUTHOR BIOGRAPHIES

AUTHORS

MARCIA ADAIR spent her childhood reading mysteries by flashlight under the covers. By the time adulthood rolled around, she had earned a master's degree in journalism and launched her career as a professional writer and editor. Her first published short story, "Mum's the Word," appears in *Dark Side of the Loon*, the latest anthology from the Twin Cities Chapter of Sisters in Crime (May 2018). She received the 2018 Dorothy Cannell Scholarship and is a member of Sisters in Crime.
www.facebook.com/MarciaAdairAuthor/.

LAURA BRENNAN's eclectic career includes television, film, theater, fiction, and news. Her podcast, *Destination Mystery*, features interviews with mystery writers of every subgenre. Her short stories have appeared in numerous anthologies, including *Mystery Most Edible*, *Last Exit to Murder*, and *Hell Comes to Hollywood*, while her historical mystery, *The End of All Things*, won the 2018 Freddie Award for Writing Excellence at SleuthFest. Her first children's book, *Nana Speaks Nanese*, helps families talk to young children about changes in behavior brought on by dementia. It will be published in the spring of 2019. Find out more at LauraBrennanWrites.com.

LESLIE BUDEWITZ is the best-selling author of the Seattle Spice Shop and Food Lovers' Village mysteries. The fourth Spice Shop mystery, *Chai Another Day*, will be published by Seventh St. Books in June 2019. "All God's Sparrows" (*Alfred Hitchcock's Mystery Magazine*), her first historical fiction, was nominated for the 2018 Agatha Award for Best Short Story. Her stories have appeared in *Ellery Queen, Thuglit*, and other journals and anthologies. *Death al Dente*, the first Food Lovers' Village mystery, won the 2013 Agatha Award for Best First Novel; her guide for writers, *Books, Crooks & Counselors*, won the 2011 Agatha Award for Best Nonfiction. A past president of Sisters in Crime, Leslie currently serves on the Mystery Writers of America board. She lives in NW Montana.

RICHARD CASS is the author of the Elder Darrow jazz mystery series: *Solo Act* was a finalist for the 2017 Maine Literary Awards in Crime Fiction. Its prequel, *In Solo Time*, won the 2018 Maine

Literary Award in Crime Fiction. The third book in the series, *Burton's Solo*, was released November 1. Cass serves on the board of Mystery Writers of America's New England Chapter. Cass holds a graduate degree in writing from the University of New Hampshire, where he studied with Thomas Williams, Jr. and Joseph Monninger. He has also studied with Ernest Hebert, Ursula K. LeGuin, and Molly Gloss. He has been an Individual Artist's Fellow for the state of New Hampshire and a Fellow at the Fishtrap Writers' Conference in Oregon. His fiction and nonfiction have appeared in *Playboy, Gray's Sporting Journal, ZZYZVA*, and *Best Short Stories of the American West*. Visit: rjcassbooks.com.

LYNNE EWING is the author of *Drive-by*, an ALA Quick Pick for Reluctant Young Adult Readers and a New York Public Library Book for the Teen Age; and *Party Girl*, an ALA Quick Pick for Reluctant Young Adult Readers, an Amazon Editor's Choice, and a Teen People recommended read. She also wrote all thirteen books in the bestselling Daughters of the Moon Series. Her last book, *The Lure,* was an ALA In The Margins 2015 top ten titles for Youths in Custody. She is a member of Sisters in Crime and Mystery Writers of America.

Judge **DEBRA H. GOLDSTEIN** is the author of *One Taste Too Many*, the first of Kensington's new Sarah Blair cozy mystery series. She also wrote *Should Have Played Poker* and 2012 IPPY Award-winning *Maze in Blue*. Her short stories, including Anthony - and Agatha-nominated "The Night They Burned Ms. Dixie's Place," have appeared in numerous periodicals and anthologies including *Alfred Hitchcock's Mystery Magazine, Black Cat Mystery Magazine,* and *Mystery Weekly.* Debra serves on the national boards of Sisters in Crime and Mystery Writers of America, and is president of SinC's Guppy Chapter and the Southeast Chapter of MWA. Find out more about Debra at www.DebraHGoldstein.com.

Award-winning author **MARNI GRAFF** writes The Nora Tierney English Mysteries (*The Blue Virgin*, *The Green Remains*, *The Scarlet Wench*, *The Golden Hour*), featuring an American writer living in the U.K.; and The Trudy Genova Manhattan Mysteries (*Death Unscripted*, *Death at the Dakota*), based on Graff's work during her nursing career as a medical consultant for a NY movie studio. The Managing Editor of Bridle Path Press, Graff also writes a crime review blog: www.auntiemwrites.com. She's a member of Sisters in Crime, the NC Writer's Network, and the International

Association of Crime Writers. All books are in PB, Kindle, and Audible at Bridle Path Press and Amazon. Graff and her husband live in rural eastern NC with two Aussie Doodles, Seamus and Fiona.

PARNELL HALL is the author of the Puzzle Lady crossword puzzle mysteries, the Stanley Hastings private eye novels, and the Steve Winslow courtroom dramas. He co-writes the Teddy Fay thrillers with Stuart Woods. Parnell has won the Shamus Award, and been nominated for the Edgar® and the Lefty. He is an actor, screenwriter, singer/songwriter, and past president of the Private Eye Writers of America. His music videos about mystery writing can be seen on YouTube.

KRISTIN KISSKA used to be a finance geek, complete with MBA and Wall Street pedigree, but now she is a self-proclaimed *fictionista*. Kristin contributed short stories of mystery and suspense to the Anthony Award-winning anthology, *Murder Under the Oaks* (2015), *Virginia Is For Mysteries—Volume II* (2016), *Fifty Shades of Cabernet* (2017), *Day of the Dark* (2017), *Mystery Most Geographical* (2018), *Mystery Most Edible* (2019), and *Deadly Southern Charm* (2019). She is a member of International Thriller Writers, Sisters in Crime, and James River Writers. When not writing suspense, she can be found blogging on her website~ *KristinKisska.com,* posting on Facebook at *KristinKisskaAuthor,* and Tweeting *@KKMHOO*. Kristin lives in Virginia with her husband and three children.

CYNTHIA KUHN is an English professor and author of the Lila Maclean Academic Mysteries: *The Semester of Our Discontent, The Art of Vanishing*, *The Spirit in Question,* and *The Subject of Malice*. Her work has also appeared in *McSweeney's Quarterly Concern, Literary Mama, Copper Nickel, Prick of the Spindle, Mama PhD,* and other publications. Honors include an Agatha Award (Best First Novel), William F. Deeck-Malice Domestic Grant, and Lefty Award nominations (Best Humorous Mystery). Originally from upstate New York, she lives in Colorado with her family. For more information, please visit cynthiakuhn.net.

ELLEN LARSON writes mystery fiction, science fiction, and mainstream fiction. Her short stories have appeared in *Yankee Magazine*, *Alfred Hitchcock's Mystery Magazine* (2010 Barry Award finalist), *Big Pulp*, *Bloodroot*, and *Stoneslide Corrective*. She is the author of the NJ Mysteries (Poisoned Pen Press 2013,

2014; "Sturdy prose and diverting sub-plots"–*Library Journal*), *The Measure of the Universe* (Savvy Press 2000; "Engaging weekend read for language lovers"–*Booklist*) and *In Retrospect* (Five Star 2013; "Carefully crafted"–starred *PW*, "A cleverly structured mix of science fiction and mystery"–*Booklist,* "Twisty plot"–*Kirkus*). A New Jersey native, Larson lived for seventeen years in Egypt, where she discovered a love of cultures not her own. These days she inhabits an off-grid cabin in upstate New York, enjoying the solitude.

JOAN LONG is a third-generation Floridian who writes mysteries and suspense set in Florida and on tropical islands. She has been a finalist for a St. Martin's Minotaur/Malice Domestic Award for Best First Traditional Mystery, MWA-Florida's Freddie Award for Writing Excellence, and a William Faulkner-William Wisdom novel-in-progress award. Joan has also written for universities, public television, healthcare corporations, a magazine, and more. She is a member of Sisters in Crime, SinC's Guppy chapter, Mystery Writers of America, and The Authors Guild.

SHARON LYNN's mystery short story, "Death on Tap," is published in the award-winning SoWest anthology series in the *Killer Nights* volume. She has edited projects that include prize-winning short films and published novels. A college professor and yoga teacher, she is always on the hunt for new stories. The vibrant cultures and scandalous crimes of the Southwest are her inspirations. Her husband, daughter, and a Maine coon cat keep her on track.

LD MASTERSON lived on both coasts before becoming landlocked in Ohio. After twenty years managing computers for the American Red Cross, she now divides her time between writing and enjoying her grandchildren. Her short stories have been published in numerous anthologies and magazines and she's currently working on her second novel. LD is a member of Mystery Writers of America, Sisters in Crime, and the Western Ohio Writers' Association. You can catch her at:
ldmasterson-author.blogspot.com.

EDITH MAXWELL learned to make sushi more than four decades ago while living in Japan and teaching English for two years. She writes the Quaker Midwife Mysteries, the Local Foods Mysteries, and award-winning short crime fiction. As Maddie Day she pens the Country Store Mysteries and the Cozy Capers Book

Group Mysteries. Maxwell, with seventeen novels in print and four more completed, has been nominated for an Agatha Award six times. She lives north of Boston with her beau and two elderly cats, and gardens and cooks when she isn't killing people on the page or wasting time on Facebook. Please find her at edithmaxwell.com, on Instagram, and at the Wicked Authors blog.

RUTH M. McCARTY's short mysteries have appeared in Level Best Books anthologies, *Flash Bang Mysteries*, *Kings River Life Magazine,* and *Over My Dead Body! The Mystery Magazine Online.* She won the 2009 Derringer Award given by the Short Mystery Fiction Society for her story "No Flowers for Stacey," published in *Deadfall: Crime Stories by New England Writers.* She is former editor at Level Best Books, a member of Sisters in Crime and MWA, and a founding member of the New England Crime Bake.

ROSEMARY McCRACKEN has worked on newspapers across Canada as a reporter, editor, and restaurant reviewer. Her first novel in the Pat Tierney mystery series, *Safe Harbor*, was a finalist for Britain's Debut Dagger in 2010. It was published in 2012, followed by *Black Water* in 2013 and *Raven Lake* in 2016. Jack Batten, the *Toronto Star*'s crime fiction reviewer, calls Pat Tierney "a hugely attractive sleuth figure." Rosemary's short stories have appeared in numerous collections and magazines. "The Sweetheart Scamster" in *Thirteen* was a finalist for a 2014 Derringer Award. Rosemary lives in Toronto and teaches novel writing at George Brown College.

M. A. MONNIN is an avocational archaeologist and Air Force veteran. She loves to travel, and has lived in Germany, The Netherlands, Spain, and England for a total of 22 years, as Army brat, airman, and Air Force wife. Her short mysteries have appeared in anthologies, and her article, "Embracing the Sphinx," about Victorian reception of ancient Egypt, is included in the journal *Nineteenth-Century Contexts.* When she isn't writing mysteries or histories, she travels the world for fun and research. She lives in Kansas City, Missouri, with her husband and Siberian husky, and is currently working on a mystery that takes place in the Greek isles. A Cajun by marriage, she is still working to perfect her roux. Find her at mamonnin.com.

JOSH PACHTER is a writer, editor, and translator. Almost a hundred of his short crime stories have appeared in *EQMM,*

AHMM, Black Cat Mystery Magazine, and many other periodicals, anthologies, and year's-best collections. *The Tree of Life* (Wildside Press) collected all ten of his Mahboob Chaudri stories, and he collaborated with Belgian author Bavo Dhooge on *Styx* (Simon & Schuster). He co-edited *Amsterdam Noir* (Akashic Books) and *The Misadventures of Ellery Queen* (Wildside Press), and edited *The Man Who Read Mysteries: The Short Fiction of William Brittain* (Crippen & Landru). His translations of stories by Dutch and Belgian authors appear regularly in *EQMM*'s "Passport to Crime" department. You can find him online at www.joshpachter.com.

ELIZABETH PERONA is the father/daughter writing team of Tony Perona and Liz Dombrosky. Tony is the author of the Nick Bertetto mystery series; the standalone thriller, *The Final Mayan Prophecy*; and co-editor of the anthologies, *Racing Can Be Murder* and *Hoosier Hoops & Hijinks*. Tony is a member of Mystery Writers of America and Sisters in Crime. Liz Dombrosky graduated from Ball State University in the Honors College with a degree in teaching. She is currently a stay-at-home mom and preschool teacher. She also is a member of Mystery Writers of America and Sisters in Crime.

ADELE POLOMSKI has an MA in Creative Writing from Rutgers University. She is published in several anthologies including *Busted!* and *Noir at the Salad Bar.* She lives and writes from her home at the New Jersey shore.

ANG POMPANO has been writing mystery for more than twenty years. His stories have been published in several anthologies. His novel, *When It's Time for Leaving,* will be released in October 2019. In addition to his fiction writing, he has written many academic pieces including one on teaching detective fiction. He is a member of Mystery Writers of America and a past recipient of the Helen McCloy/Mystery Writers of America Scholarship for a novel in progress. A brother member of Sisters in Crime, he is a long-time board member of the New England chapter. He has been on the New England Crime Bake Planning Committee for fourteen years. He lives in Connecticut with his wife, Annette, an artist, and his two rescue dogs, Quincy and Dexter.

LISA PRESTON is a former police sergeant and paramedic who now writes full time. Previous titles include the standalone psychological thriller, *Orchids and Stone*, and the standalone psychological suspense, *The Measure of the Moon. The Clincher*

(Skyhorse Publishing, 2018) launched her horseshoer mystery series featuring young Rainy Dale of "Gutbombs 'n' Guinness," with the second in the series, *Dead Blow*, coming in late 2019.

STEPHEN D. ROGERS is the author of *Three-Minute Mysteries* and more than 800 shorter works. Please visit his website, www.StephenDRogers.com, for a list of new and upcoming titles as well as other timely information.

VERENA ROSE's story, *Death at the Willard Hotel,* is the third story featuring Constable Hezekiah Wallace set during the year 1860 in Washington City. Tensions are high regarding the issue of slavery and the Civil War is on the horizon. An avid reader of history, Verena loves researching the pre-Civil War period. She continues to work on an idea for a novel featuring her characters "Zeke" Wallace, Horace Kingsley, and Noah Hackett. Verena also works full-time as a tax accountant and is the long-time Chair of Malice Domestic, an Editor of the Malice Anthologies, and an Editor and Co-publisher at Level Best Books. She lives in the Maryland suburbs with her four cats and loves, whenever possible, spending time with her two grandchildren.

USA Today and Audible best-selling author **SARA ROSETT** writes lighthearted mysteries for readers who enjoy interesting settings, quirky characters, and puzzling whodunits. Sara is the author of the Murder on Location series, which follows Kate's adventures as a location scout for a Jane Austen documentary. Sara also writes the Ellie Avery series and the On the Run series. Most recently, Sara combined her love of history and her Anglophile tendencies in a historical mystery series, the High Society Lady Detective series, which is set in 1920s England. *Publishers Weekly* called Sara's books, "satisfying," "well-executed," and "sparkling." Sara loves to get new stamps in her passport and considers dark chocolate a daily requirement. Find out more at SaraRosett.com.

HARRIETTE SACKLER has served as Grants Chair of the Malice Domestic Board of Directors as long as she can remember. Assisting unpublished writers along the road to success brings her a great deal of satisfaction. Harriette is a multi-published, Agatha Award-nominated short story writer. As a principal of Dames of Detection, she is a co-owner and editor at Level Best Books which publishes mystery, thriller, and crime fiction short story anthologies and novels. Harriette lives with her husband and their three rescue Yorkies in Maryland. She is the proud mother of two daughters and grandmother of four grandkids. Her work with animal rescue organizations is close to her heart. "Honor Thy Father" is loosely based on her father's memories of growing up on the Lower East Side. Website: www.harriettesackler.com

TERRY SHAMES writes the Samuel Craddock series, set in small town Texas. The books have been finalists for numerous awards and won the Macavity Award for Best First Novel and the *RT* Reviews award for Best Contemporary Mystery of 2016. The eighth in the series, *A Risky Undertaking for Loretta Singletary,* comes out April 23, 2019, and was named a Top Pick for Cozies in *BookPage*. Terry lives in Northern California and is a member of Sisters in Crime and MWA.

NANCY COLE SILVERMAN credits her twenty-five years in news and talk radio for helping her to develop an ear for storytelling. In the last ten years, Silverman has written numerous short stories and novelettes. In 2014, Silverman signed with Henery Press and writes The Carol Childs' Mysteries, and, debuting this fall (2019), The Misty Dawn Mysteries.

SHAWN REILLY SIMMONS is the author of the Red Carpet Catering Mysteries, which are published by Henery Press and inspired by her experiences as an on-set movie caterer. She serves on the Board of Malice Domestic, and is co-editor at Level Best Books. Her short stories have appeared in various anthology series including Malice Domestic, Bouchercon, Best New England Crime Stories, and the Crime Writers' Association. The next book in the Red Carpet Catering series, *Murder on the Chopping Block*, will be published in September 2019.

MARK THIELMAN is a criminal magistrate working in Tarrant County, Texas (Fort Worth). Formerly, he spent 27 years as a prosecutor for the Tarrant and Dallas County District Attorney's Offices. Mark has a law degree from the University of Texas in Austin as well as Bachelor of Arts and Master of Liberal Arts degrees from Texas Christian University. A two-time Black Orchid Award-winning novella author, Mark's short fiction has been published in the *Alfred Hitchcock's Mystery Magazine*, *Malice Domestic 12: Mystery Most Historical,* and the recently released anthology from Mystery Writers of America, *Odd Partners*. Mark lives in Fort Worth with his wife, two sons, and an oversized dog. Markthielman.com.

VICTORIA THOMPSON is a former Malice Guest of Honor. She writes the Edgar®- and Agatha-nominated Gaslight Mystery Series, set in turn-of-the-century New York City and featuring midwife Sarah Brandt and detective Frank Malloy; and the Sue Grafton Memorial Award-nominated Counterfeit Lady Series, set in 1917 New York City and featuring con artist Elizabeth Miles. *Murder on Trinity Place*, the 22nd Gaslight Mystery, was published April 30, and *City of Scoundrels,* the 3rd Counterfeit Lady book, will be published in November 2019. She also contributed to the award-winning writing textbook, *Many Genres/One Craft*. Victoria currently teaches in the Seton Hill University master's program in creative writing. She lives in the Chicago area with her husband and a very spoiled little dog. www.victoriathompson.com.

CHRISTINE TRENT is the author of the Florence Nightingale Mysteries, as well as the Lady of Ashes historical mystery series and three other historical novels. Christine is also a first-person interpreter of Florence Nightingale, visiting book stores, conferences, and other locations to tell the riveting story of the great nurse's life from Florence's own point of view. Learn more at www.christinetrent.com and follow Christine on Facebook at www.facebook.com/ChristineTrentBooks.

GABRIEL VALJAN is the author of two series, The Roma Series and The Company Files, available from Winter Goose Publishing. His short stories have appeared in Level Best anthologies and other publications. Twice shortlisted for the Fish Prize in Ireland, once for the Bridport Prize in England, and an Honorable Mention for the Nero Wolfe Black Orchid Novella Contest, he is a lifetime member of Sisters in Crime National, a local member of Sisters in Crime New England, and an attendee of Bouchercon, Crime Bake, and Malice Domestic conferences.

KATE WILLETT lives in Northern Virginia with her husband and two cats. She is a member of the Mystery Writers of America, the Historical Novel Society, and Sisters in Crime. Kate loves vintage things, old-time radio, Korean dramas, roller-skating, notebooks, pens/pencils, and cookie dough ice cream. She gained her love of mystery novels from her mother, a former librarian who always had copies of Agatha Christie and Sue Grafton novels stashed around the house. "Murder Takes the Cupcake" is her first published mystery story.

STACY WOODSON is a U.S. Army veteran and her time in the military is a source of inspiration for her stories. A California native who lives in the DC area, she misses good Mexican food. She made her crime fiction debut in *Ellery Queen's Mystery Magazine's* Department of First Stories and won *EQMM's* 2018 Readers Award. Her short fiction will also appear in *EQMM* this year and in these future anthologies: *Chesapeake Crimes: Invitation to Murder*, *Mickey Finn: 21st Century Noir*, and *The Beat of Black Wings: Crime Fiction Inspired by the Songs of Joni Mitchell*. In 2017, she won RWA's Daphne du Maurier Award for best romantic suspense in the single-title, unpublished category, and was a finalist for the 2016 Killer Nashville Claymore Award for the same novel. When Stacy is not writing fiction, she contributes to diyMFA and *Publishers Weekly*. You can visit her at www.stacywoodson.com.

www.ingramcontent.com/pod-product-compliance
Lightning Source LLC
Chambersburg PA
CBHW030824310726
48980CB00006B/623/J